Elif Shafak was born in Strasbourg, France, in 1971 and spent her adolescent years in Spain before returning to Turkey. Her first novel, *Pinhan*, was awarded the Mevlana Prize for literature. Her second novel, *The Mirrors of the City*, is about the expulsion of the Sephardic Jews from Spain and their subsequent flight to the Ottoman Empire. Her third novel, *Mahrem*, received the Turkish Novel Award. *The Flea Palace* is her fourth novel.

Shafak holds an MSc in Gender and Women's Studies and a PhD in Political Sciences. Her academic background has been nurtured by a critical, interdisciplinary and gender-conscious rereading of the literature of the Middle East and of the West. She is currently a Visiting Scholar in Women's Studies at the University of Michigan and writes for a number of Turkish newspapers.

Müge Göçek is an associate professor in the Department of Sociology at the University of Michigan. She studied at Bosphorus University in Istanbul before gaining an MA and a PhD at Princeton University.

THE Flea Palace

By

Elif Shafak

Translated by Müge Göçek

MARION BOYARS
LONDON • NEW YORK

First published in Great Britain and in the USA in 2004 by
MARION BOYARS PUBLISHERS LTD
24 Lacy Road, London SW15 1NL

www.marionboyars.co.uk

Distributed in Australia and New Zealand by Peribo Pty Ltd
58 Beaumont Road, Kuring-gai, NSW 2080

Printed in 2004
10 9 8 7 6 5 4 3 2 1

A CIP catalogue record for this book is available from the British Library.
A CIP catalog record for this book is available from the Library of Congress.

ISBN 0-7145-3101-4

The publishers would like to thank the Arts Council of England for
assistance with the translation of this book.

Set in Bembo 11.5/14pt
Printed in Great Britain by Bookmarque Ltd, London.

Residents of Bonbon Palace

Flat 1	Musa, Meryem and Muhammet
Flat 2	Sidar and Gaba
Flat 3	Hairdressers Cemal and Celal
Flat 4	The Firenaturedsons
Flat 5	Hadj Hadj, His Son, Daughter-in-Law and Grandchildren
Flat 6	Metin Chetinceviz and HisWifeNadia
Flat 7	Me
Flat 8	The Blue Mistress
Flat 9	Hygiene Tijen and Su
Flat 10	Madam Auntie

PEOPLE SAY I HAVE A FANCIFUL MIND – probably the most tactful way ever invented of saying 'You're talking nonsense!' They might be right. Whenever I get anxious and mess up what I have to say, am scared of people's stares and pretend not to be so, introduce myself to strangers and feign ignorance about how estranged I am from myself, feel hurt by the past and find it hard to admit the future won't be any better, or fail to come to terms with either where or who I am; at any one of these all too frequently recurring moments, I know I don't make much sense. But nonsense is just as far removed from deception as truth. Deception turns truth inside out. As for nonsense, it solders deception and truth to each other so much so as to make them indistinguishable. Though this might seem complicated, it's actually very simple. So simple that it can be expressed by a single line.

Let's presume truth is a horizontal line.

_____

Then, what we call deception becomes a vertical one.

As for nonsense, here's what it looks like:

With neither an end nor a beginning to its trajectory, the circle recognizes no horizontal or vertical axis.

You can plunge into the circle from anywhere you want, as long as you do not confuse that point with a beginning. No start points, no thresholds, no endings. No matter at which instant or with what particular incident I make the first move, there will always be a time preceding that start of mine – always a past ahead of every past and hence never a veritable outset.

I never saw it myself but heard from someone wise enough, that back in the old days, when the garbage cans on the streets of Istanbul had round lids of greyish aluminum, there was a game that local boys and girls played together. A certain number of people had to join in; few enough not to crowd, large enough to entertain, just the right amount and always an even number.

First in the 'Garbage Game' came the question 'When?' For an answer, four different segments would be chalked on the round lid with a separate word corresponding to each direction: 'Right Now–Tomorrow–Soon–Never.' The lid would then be spun from its handle in the middle as swiftly as possible and before it found a chance to slow down, the person in line would stop it with the touch of a finger. The same would then be repeated one by one for all the participants of the game, so that each one could fathom which time frame he or she stood closest to. In the second round, four separate responses would be written down as possible answers to the question 'To Whom?': 'To Me–To The One I Love–To My

Best Friend–To All of Us.' Once again the lid would be given a spin and once again the players would reach out to stop its delirious circumvolution. The third round was intended to find an answer to the question 'What?' Four auspicious and four ominous words were marked on the remaining eight spaces, always equal in number, to add a dash of fairness to the whims of fate: 'Love–Marriage–Happiness–Wealth–Sickness–Separation–Accident–Death.' The lid would turn once again with the answers now building up so the players could finally reach the long awaited response to the question, 'What will happen to whom and when?': 'To Me–Wealth–Soon,' 'To The One I Love–Happiness–Tomorrow,' 'To My Best Friend–Marriage–Right Away,' or 'To All of Us–Separation–Never'...

Starting the ball of narration rolling is not hard. I too can employ the logic of the Garbage Game with some minor adjustments here and there. First of all, one needs to find the time frame of the narration: 'Yesterday–Today–Tomorrow–Infinity.' Then, the places should be designated: 'Where I Came From–Where I Stand Now–Where I Am Headed–Nowhere'. Next, it would be the player's turn to assign the subject of the act: 'I–One Among Us–All of Us–None of Us.' Finally, without upsetting the four-to-four balance, one needs to line up the possible outcomes. In this manner, if I spin an imaginary garbage lid four times in a row, I should be able to construct a decent sentence. What more than a sentence does one need to start off a story that has no start to it anyway?

'In the spring of 2002, in Istanbul, one among us died before the time was up and the line closed into a complete circle.'

★★★

On Wednesday May 1st 2002, at 12:20 p.m., a white van – in need of a wash and decorated with the picture of a huge rat with needle-sharp teeth on one side, a hairy humongous spider on the other – failing to take notice of the barriers ahead found itself in the middle of a crowd of two thousand two hundred people. Among these, about five hundred were there to commemorate Workers' May Day, one thousand three hundred were policemen ordered to prevent the latter from doing so, a number of others were state officials there to celebrate the day as a Spring Holiday by wreathing Ataturk's statue, and all the rest were elementary school children made to fill up the empty spaces, waving the Turkish flags handed out. By now, these children had almost broken into hives from standing under the sun for hours on end listening to the humming of dreary speeches. Incidentally, a good number of them had only recently learnt how to read and write, and with that impetus kept shouting out the syllables of every single written word they spotted around. When the ratty, spidery van ploughed into the crowd, these kids were the ones who yelled out in unison: 'RAIN-BOW PEST RE-MOV-AL SER-VICE: Call-Us-And-We-Will-Re-move-Them-For-You'.

The driver of the van, a ginger-haired, flap-eared, funny-looking, baby-faced man with features so exaggerated that he hardly looked real, lost his cool when faced with this onslaught. On steering the van in the opposite direction to escape the wrath of the children, he found himself in the middle of a highly agitated circle of demonstrators surrounded by an outer circle of even more agitated policemen. During the few minutes when the driver was paralyzed into inaction, he was alternately either 'booed' with glee or stoned in anger by demonstrators sharing the same ideology yet apparently interpreting it differently. Steering his van toward the other half of the circle in a desperate move only helped the driver get held up once again, this time by the police. He would most probably have been arrested at once — and things would have conceivably taken a worse turn for the others as well — had the police not darted, at exactly the same moment, toward a tiny, impetuous group determined to start the march right away. The van driver was drenched in sweat when he finally succeeded in getting out of the tumultuous square. His name was Injustice Pureturk. He had been in the pest removal business for almost thirty-three years and had never hated his job as fervently as he did that day.

In order not to get himself into trouble once again, he shunned the shortcuts and made his way through the winding roads, only to arrive a full hour and forty-five minutes late for his appointment at the apartment building he had been searching for. Shaking off his trauma bit by bit, he parked along the sidewalk while staring suspiciously at the cluster of people blocking the entrance of the building. Having no idea why they had gathered there, but nevertheless convinced they would do him no harm, he managed to calm down and again checked the address his chatty secretary had handed to him that very morning: 'Cabal Street, Number 88 (Bonbon Palace).' His chatterbox of a secretary had also included a note: 'The apartment building with the rose acacia tree in the garden.' Wiping away the large beads of sweat on his forehead, Injustice Pureturk stared at the tree in the garden that was in bloom with reddish-pink flowers. This, he thought, must be what they called 'rose acacia'.

Still, since he did not at all trust his secretary whom he intended to replace at the next possible instance, he personally wanted to see the building's signpost with his own short-sighted eyes. Parking the van askew, he jumped down. No sooner had he taken a step, however, than a small girl among a group of three children standing in the crowd screamed in horror: 'The genie is here! Grandpaaa, grandpa, look, the genie is here!' The round, greying, bearded elderly man the girl was tugging turned around and inspected first the van and then the van's driver, each time with an equally disappointed look. Evidently dissatisfied with what he saw, he screwed up his face so that it looked even more sour and drew the three children closer to him.

Injustice was done to Injustice Pureturk. He was not a genie or anything, but just an ordinary man who possessed a disproportionate face with mammoth ears and unfortunately coloured hair. He also happened to be short. Indeed very short: one metre and forty-three centimetres in all. Even though he had been previously taken for a dwarf, this was the first time he was accused of being a genie. Trying not to mind, he doggedly pushed his way through the group toward the ashen apartment building. He donned the thin-framed thick-lensed glasses he habitually carried, not on his nose as the doctor had recommended but inside the pocket of his work overalls. Despite the help of the glasses he still could not make out what the messy protrusion at the front of the building was until it was an inch away: a relief of a peacock with the feathers darkened with dirt. Had it been cleaned up, it might have been appealing to the eye. Underneath the relief it read: 'Bonbon Palace Number 88.' He was at the right place.

A business card squeezed in-between the lined-up buzzers next to the door drew his attention. It belonged to a rival firm that had two months previously started to work in the same neighbourhood. Since the people around no longer seemed to be paying any attention to him, he took the opportunity to remove the business card and put one of his own in its stead.

RAINBOW PEST REMOVAL SERVICE

Do not do injustice to yourself

Call Us and Let Us Clean on Your Behalf
Experienced and specialized staff with electrical and
mechanical pumps against

Lice • Roaches • Fleas • Bedbugs • Ants • Spiders • Scorpions • Flies

Spraying done with or without odour, manually or
mechanically employing an
electrical pulverizer/atomizer and/or misting devices
appropriate to both open and enclosed spaces

Phone: (0212)25824242

Upon having these business cards printed, he had hired a university student to distribute them all around the neighbourhood, but it had not taken him long to fire the young man without pay, for doing a lousy job. That was typical of Injustice Pureturk: he never trusted anyone.

To unload the pesticide sprays he walked back to his van. Yet, the moment he had shut his door, a blond woman with a hairdresser's smock tied around her neck reached in through the half-open window and gawked at him cross-eyed:

'Is this van all you've got? Won't be enough, I tell you,' she hooted knitting her well-plucked eyebrows. 'They'd promised at least two trucks. There's so much trash, even two trucks would have a hard time.'

'I'm not here to pick up your garbage,' Injustice Pureturk frowned. 'I'm here for the insects... the cockroaches...'

'Oh,' the woman flinched, 'Even then, I tell you, what you've got won't be enough.'

Before Injustice Pureturk could fathom what she was talking about and what exactly these people had been waiting for, two red trucks ploughed onto Cabal Street as if they had heard the call. The crowd stirred upon noticing a van from a television channel right behind the trucks. Injustice Pureturk, utterly unaware of the excitement around him, was trying at that moment to find a better spot to park. However, finding himself amidst chaos upon chaos against his will must have somewhat tattered his nerves by now, for the vein on the right side of his forehead started to thump at a crazy pace. The single movement he made to press down on the vein was more than enough to make him lose control of the steering wheel. Trying to back up in a panic, he rammed into the piles of bags slung next to the garden wall separating the apartment building from the street. All the garbage inside the bags was scattered onto the sidewalk.

★★★

If truth be told, Bonbon Palace was used to garbage, having

struggled with it for quite some time now. From early February to mid April – the period following the bankruptcy of the private company collecting the garbage in the area and preceding the resumption of service by a new one – a considerable garbage hill had collected here, bringing along with it an increasingly putrid smell. Things had not improved much with the new company either. In spite of the regular nightly collection, both the Cabal Street residents and passers-by kept throwing garbage next to the garden wall, thereby managing collectively to raise up a new garbage hill every day.

If interested you can go there even today to see with your own eyes how, along the wall separating the apartment's garden from the street, the garbage hill levelled by dusk rises anew the following day with no ultimate loss to its mass. Garbage bags are thrown away, garbage bags are then picked up, but despite the continual rise and fall the garbage hill perpetuates its presence. The hill comes with its own hill people – seekers who show up daily to collect pieces of tin, cardboard, leftover food and the like, as well as an army of cats and crows and seagulls. Then, of course, there are bugs; for wherever there is garbage, there are also bugs. Lice, too, have taken over in Bonbon Palace...and trust me on this, lice are the very worst...

In order to observe this one needs to spend some time there. If you have no time, however, you'll have to make do with my version of the story. Yet I can only speak for myself. Not that I'll foist my own views onto what transpires but I might, here and there, solder the horizontal line of truth to the vertical line of deception in order to escape the wearisome humdrum reality of where I am anchored right now. After all, I am bored stiff here. If someone brought me the good news that my life would be less dreary tomorrow, I might feel less bored today. Yet, I know too well that tomorrow will be just the same and so will all the days to follow. Nevertheless, with my fondness for circles I should not give you the impression that it is only my life that persistently repeats itself. In the final instance, the vertical is just as faithful to its recurrence as the horizontal. Contrary to what many presume, that which is called 'Eternal Recurrence' is germane not only to circles but also to lines and linear arrangements.

From the monotony of lines there deviates only one path: drawing circles within circles, spiralling in and in. Such deviation resembles, in a way, being a spoilsport in the Garbage Game: not abiding by what comes up when you spin the round lid of greyish aluminum, spoiling the game by not waiting for your turn, craving to spin again and again; messing around with subjects, objects, verbs and coincidences while comforting yourself throughout: 'In Istanbul in the spring of 2002, the death of one among us was caused by Herself–Me–Us All–None of Us.'

On Wednesday May 1st 2002, Injustice Pureturk applied pesticide dust to one of the flats of Bonbon Palace. Fifteen days later, upon returning for the baby cockroaches born from their dead mothers' eggs, he found the door of that particular flat deadlocked. However, it is too soon to talk about these things right now. For there had been another time preceding this moment and, of course, one before that as well.

BEFORE...

THERE WERE ONCE TWO ANCIENT CEMETERIES in this neighbourhood, one small, almost rectangular and well-kept, the other huge, semi-lunar and visibly neglected. Surrounded by ivy-covered fences and shadowy hills, leaning onto the same dishevelled wall, they had spread out over a wide terrain, jointly and continuously. Both were crowded to the brim yet deserted to the extreme. The small one belonged to the Armenians and the large one to the Muslims. On the six foot wall separating the two cemeteries, rusty nails, jagged fragments of glass and, in spite of the fear of bad luck, broken mirror pieces had been scattered upright to prevent people trespassing from one to the other. As for the two-panelled, iron-grilled, gargantuan doors of each cemetery, they were located exactly on opposite ends, one facing north and the other south so that if a visitor perchance harboured any inclination to cross from one to the other, he would be discouraged by the length of the road he would have to walk. Just the same, no one actually had to put up with such an inconvenience since there had never been a visitor with a relative buried in one cemetery who wished, once there, to pay a visit to the other cemetery as well. Be that as it may, there was many a being that hopped and jumped from one cemetery to the other as they pleased, be it night or day: the wind and thieves, for instance, or the cats and lizards. They had all mastered the many ways of going through, over and under the barrier separating the two cemeteries.

That would not last long. An incessant wave of migrations

cluttered up the city with buildings marshalled in tandem like the soldiers of a sinister army, each and every one looking much alike from a distance. Amidst the muddled waters of 'citification' surrounding them in all directions, the cemeteries remained intact like two uninhabited islands. As new high-rises and rows of houses were built continuously, around them up popped small, sporadic, circumscribed streets resembling from far above the veins of a brain. Streets cut in front of houses and houses blocked streets; the whole neighbourhood swelled, bloating like a foolhardy fish unable to feel satiated even when beyond being full. Finally when just about to burst, it became inevitable that an incision must be made and an opening created on the stretched tight node so as to relieve the pressure mounting from within. That incision in turn meant a new road had to be built before too long.

Due to this unforeseen, unstoppable growth, all the streets in the vicinity had become wedged at the edges like water with nowhere to go. An avenue, by linking them all into a single channel, could make them re-flow.

Yet, when the time came for the authorities to take a birds' eye view to decide where and how to build this avenue, they realized an onerous quandary awaited them. At all the possible sites where such an avenue could be constructed, there was, as if by design, either a government building or the property of the local gentry and if not those, the jam-packed low-income shanty-houses that could be effortlessly taken down one by one but were not that easy to erase when there were so many. In order to be able to build the road that would open the way, they would first have to open the way for a road.

Istanbul being a city where houses were not built in accordance with road plans but road plans made so as not to upset the location of the houses, the construction of the new road required tearing down as few houses as possible. Given this precondition there remained only one option: making the road pass through the hilly terrain of the two cemeteries.

Once the reports detailing this plan had been approved by

the authorities, it was decided that within two and a half months the two cemeteries should be removed and the hilly terrain flattened out. Those who had loved ones in these cemeteries need not worry, they said. After all, the tombs could be moved in their entirety to various spots around the city. Muslim tombs could be transported to the slopes overlooking the Golden Horn, for instance, and the non-Muslims to their own graveyards in various other quarters.

Most of the tombs were so ancient that along with their occupants, their descendants had also changed worlds by now. There were also those that, despite having descendants still above the ground, might yet go unclaimed. In spite of all this, the number of people snooping into the fate of the tombs turned out to be far more than the authorities had initially expected. Among them, some relatives simply wanted their dead to be left alone while others discovered the proposed alternate graveyards were already crammed full. Both of these groups had instantly started to search for ways to reverse the decision. Still, the majority of the relatives acquiesced to do whatever was deemed necessary and to this end set off to shoulder the burden.

In the following days the Muslim cemetery played host at all hours of the day to all kinds of visitors, each singing a different tune. The task of hiding the traces of the nocturnal visitors from those paying homage in the daytime fell upon the cemetery guards who at dawn gathered the spilled bones and closed over the tombs dug up during the night. Then, towards noon, the authorities showed up to inspect the guards, and in the afternoon, families worried about their dead getting mixed up with other people's dropped-by in large crowds, all the while talking and complaining, if not to the tombstones, to one another.

Until the cemetery was officially forbidden to accept visitors, the old and middle-aged women of these families were there almost every single day. When tired of standing up, they would line up with their blankets spread right there around their relatives' tombs. Once seated, they would either weep alone or pray together, clutching their children tightly to force them into reverential silence. Then time would drift by, the air getting heavier, some children would fall asleep while others escaped to play; and a cloud of languor would daintily follow, forming a canopy over the women on the ground. 'The descent of the spiritual,' this can be called. After all, even the most otherworldly cannot remain oblivious to the forces of gravity pulling them down to earth. In this state the women would make it through to the night. Rooting about in their long tattered bags, bought who knows when and mutated over time into the same grimy tone of brown, they would fish out aniseed crackers, pour tea from thermoses while at the same time circulating lemon cologne to wipe both their sweaty faces and the reddish skin marks around their knees left by knee-high nylon socks that, no matter which size you chose, were always too tight. Next they would peruse the pages of the notebooks of the past, recalling one by one the names of all those who had made life living-hell for the dearly departed. Once they started to hammer out past controversies, it would not take them long to abandon the mourning of the dead and switch instead to gossiping about the living. All tea gone and only a handful of aniseeds left from the crackers, one among them would remind the others of how the dearly departed, as if not having suffered enough on earth, were now denied peace even deep down under the ground. With that reminder, the gloom of the setting would engulf the cloud of languor. 'The ascent of the material,' this can be called. After all, even the most worldly cannot remain indifferent to the celestial. Thus, these old and middle-aged women would step by step wander off from prayers to curses, from curses to gossip, only to retread to the beginning to wrap up this undulating conversation in a final prayer.

As they retread, they would start searching for the children spread among the tombstones recklessly roaming the cemetery. The children would be sought, collared and dragged back to the gravestone of their relative for a last supplication. By then, the men would also have returned to the same spot, dog-tired from struggling all day long in vain to speak up to the deaf ears of bureaucracy, having acquired all in all a few fragments of documents and the map to the new burial ground but still not a wee bit of clarification about where their dead would be buried within it. Pretending everything to be under control and within their purview, the aforesaid males would austerely confront each and every galling question and gloomy interpretation that their mothers, younger sisters, wives, mothers-in-law, older sisters, aunts, sisters-in-law and daughters put to them. While blankets were gathered and tombstones bid farewell to, several women would notice the many inconsistencies in the men's responses and ask either new questions or re-formulate the old ones, only more persistently this time. With that final touch, the men's nerves, which were stretched tight as bow strings by the gears of bureaucracy, would snap. With them yelling at their wives and their wives yelling back at them, families would leave the Muslim cemetery in utter chaos and without having resolved anything. Then night would descend, the two-panelled, iron-grilled, gargantuan door would close down, and thus the hours of the cats and tomb thieves would commence.

As for the Armenian Orthodox cemetery, it too had plenty of visitors around the same time. With one difference: the majority of these visitors were there not to transport their tombs but rather to say their final goodbyes. Even if able to procure the necessary permit to transport, in what burial ground among the orthodox cemeteries of Istanbul, long diminished with loss and shrunk through constriction, could they have buried their dead? Some prominent families and church members managed to move a number of graves but that was all. Among the dead left behind there were cherished ancestors of eminent families, as well as those long unclaimed or recently abandoned; those whose grandchildren had scattered to four corners of the world and those whose families still lived in Istanbul; those who had remained all their lives utterly faithful to their religion and loyal to their state, as well as those who refused to recognize either God or a state...

For that is how things are. It is not their *quantative* scarcity vis-à-vis the majority that makes minorities hapless but rather their *qualitative* similarity. As a member of a minority group, you can be as industrious as an ant, even hit the jackpot and acquire a considerable fortune, but someday, just because you presently and will always belong to the same community, you could in an instant find yourself on a par with those of your community who have idled their lives away since birth. That is why the affluent among the minorities are never affluent enough; neither are their exceptional members ever sufficiently so. In the Turkey of the 1950s in particular, the moment a rich Muslim bumped into a poor one, what he would see on the latter's face would be 'someone so very unlike him,' whereas a rich minority member running into a poor one would encounter on the latter's face 'someone so very unlike him and yet treated alike.' Accordingly, the same misery might awaken compassion in the rich Muslim who has the comfort of knowing that he will never sink to that position, whereas for a member of the rich minority it might easily trigger angst, with the unease of foreseeing that he too might unexpectedly end up there. Once a person starts to fear injustice, however, he can end up missing the real target and mix the results up with the causes. Hence, while the gentry of the Muslim majority may demonstrate a tender mercy toward the miserable in particular and to misery in general, the cream of the minority will approach the materially and spiritually downtrodden of their own community with chilled unease.

All these nominal distinctions go no further however. At the end of the two and a half month period, only a sprinkle of tombs were transported from the Orthodox Armenian cemetery; the majority of the minority had thus remained behind. As for the Muslim cemetery, far more tombs had been transported: the minority of the majority was left behind.

These two clusters of dead, with not an iota in common regarding family trees, upbringing or profiles, nevertheless concluded the very last stage of their presence in Istanbul alike. One could bestow upon them a common rank: 'Those Unable to Depart'. The worst part of being one of those incapable of leaving a territory is less their inability to *depart* than their inability to *reside*.

It was at precisely this stage that a twist of fate occurred. Way ahead of the bulldozers, thieves looted the tombstones, dogs embezzled the bones of a number of Those Unable to Depart. Among some couples long buried together, due to name similarities or the negligence of cemetery officials incapable of deciphering the Ottoman script on the old tombstones, one ended up in one corner and the other at another. Some of the dead got mixed up and landed in different tombs, while a large majority were done away with silently, stealthily, systematically. Yet ultimately, it was simply fate that would determine the destiny of many of Those Unable to Depart.

Once these procedures came to an end, all that was left of that vast land was a field replete with holes, as if fallen prey to a horde of moles. When the time arrived to level the ground in its entirety, however, the authorities would be startled to discover two tombs had fortuitously remained intact. Their stone sarcophagi were made of crimson-veined white marble, decorated with *cintemani* and plant motifs germinating into three wheels of fate, their turbans almost as big as cart wheels, the distance from the base of their tombstones to the headstones measuring approximately one hundred and forty-six centimetres in height, surrounded with railings as sharp as arrows and painted a green the colour of raw leaves. While both were in the Muslim cemetery, one of the tombs was located at the southern slope and the other at the northern edge, at the bottom of the wall separating the orthodox Armenian cemetery. This detail aside, they were exactly alike. On the outside surface of the accompanying stone, both had hyacinth and tulip motifs. Exactly the same turban on their heads, the same sharply pointed arch around their seats, the same heading, '*Allah bas baqiya hawas,*' in Ottoman cel sulus★ script on their tomb inscriptions. Odd as it was, next to each one rested a rusted sign, probably posted at the same time by the same people:'Here lies Saint 'Hewhopackedupandleft' who performed countless heroic deeds for the conquest of Islam while serving in the army of Ebu Hafs-i Haddad and who reached God's mercy before witnessing the fall of the infidel city. A prayer to his soul.'

When ordered to remove these two sarcophagi, the worker on the bulldozer had to leave work early with a awful pain in his groin. Though the pain had abated by the following day, he refused to drive the bulldozer all the same. On the third day, instead of the worker, his grandfather, who had no teeth in his mouth and no might in his muscles but ample 'oomph' when it came to words, turned up instead. He narrated to whomever he came across spine-tingling stories about the dire fate of those hapless souls who had attempted to plunder the tombs of saints. By the morning of the fourth night, not a single worker was willing to drive the bulldozer. If truth be told, no one except them seemed much interested in Saint 'Hewhopackedupandleft,' and things would have remained so had the authorities not taken a sudden interest in the topic, upon being warned that their political opponents might use the current state of affairs against them. The year was 1949 and the political balance extremely fragile. Both the newly burgeoning opposition as well as the government itself constantly tainted one another with the brush of alleged 'insolence toward religion'. It was at this point that 'The Three Consultant Buddies' showed up.

The First of the Three Consultant Buddies came up with the idea that in order not to disturb the saints' tombs, the avenue should take two separate twists at two points. His suggestion might have been considered had it not been the

★ '*Allah bas, baqiya hawas*' means 'God is strength, the rest is folly' and Ottoman cel sulus script is a historical Turkish script of the Ottoman Empire

case that no one took him seriously; not since that ominous day when he had been given a ruthless tongue-lashing at his workplace by his wife, upon her discovery that he'd spent their entire month's rent at a nightclub. The Second of the Three Consultant buddies, in turn, proposed the avenue continue in a straight line, right up to the two tombs, where it would bifurcate like a piece of string cheese. Though everyone knew he managed, albeit with difficulty, to gain the upper hand over his wife, even dared raise his voice at home and smash unsavory food against the wall, his idea was not accepted as no one wanted to take responsibility for possible future traffic accidents. It was then that the Third of the Three Consultant Buddies asserted in a meandering speech, that they were committing a grave error by rushing to a solution. First they had to grasp what exactly the problem was and, had they done so, would indeed detect more than one peculiarity in this particular case. Thus he paraphrased his oration: 'First diagnosis, then treatment!'

The points of emphasis the Third of the Three Consultant Buddies wanted clarified for diagnosis were as follows:

1. What exactly was this army of Ebu Hafs-i Haddad? What was it doing in Istanbul?
2. If this army was one of those Arab forces that had long ago come as far as Istanbul with the intent of conquest, what was someone like Saint 'Hewhopackedupandleft' – whose name did not at all sound Arabic – doing among them?
3. If Saint 'Hewhopackedupandleft' had indeed been martyred while fighting for the conquest of Istanbul on the side of the Arabs, why on earth did he have two tombs?
4. Last but not least, which of the tombs was genuine?

Meticulously elaborating each point on his agenda, the Third of the Three Consultant Buddies arrived at the conclusion that though there was no harm in skipping some of these points so as to save time, it was absolutely essential to clarify the last detail to ascertain which of the two tombs was the real one. Indeed he was a better orator than the others and a bachelor to boot.

Be that as it may, digging a saint's tomb at a time like this was analogous to accepting a gift package with unknown content from an anonymous sender: it probably did not contain anything harmful but what if it did? Just to make matters worse, right at this time, a foul-mouthed journalist notorious for stirring bread into his *rakı* for breakfast but nonetheless alert enough to have his ear to the ground, had already picked up the scent and written a piece in the leading opposition newspaper entitled, 'Government's Gravediggers in Business Suits.' Though the editorial itself was not as accusatory as its title hinted and the claim behind it rather hazy, these could be due more to the journalist's having passed out before finishing the piece than to his concern not to further poke his nose into this business. There was no way to tell that once he sobered up he would not write another editorial, this time even more aggressive.

Still, the tombs were dug up all at once and without any prior notice. Set to accomplish this unpleasant duty in the fastest way possible and without any onlookers present, two officials, three guards and five workers gathered with their briefcases, flashlights, pickaxes and shovels before dawn. They dug up the tombs of the saints under the stunned looks of a few vagabonds who had settled in the vacated cemetery once the thieves and street dogs had stopped coming. Nothing came out of the first tomb; neither a coffin, nor a shroud, nor bones or a skull, nor the personal belongings of the saint. At least there were tree roots, cracked rocks and worms – even these were missing in the second tomb. It was at this point that the authorities committed the fatal mistake of supposing the problem had thus been solved. With too much sanguinity, they removed the stone sarcophagi and took down the surrounding railing.

The following day, an unsigned editorial appeared in the leading opposition newspaper with the title, 'Government's Three-Piece-Suited Assassins of Saints' – only this time the beginning and the end of the piece had been connected into a meaningful whole. It contended that the government, which had hitherto demonstrated at every opportunity what little respect it had for the Ottoman cultural heritage, had now taken upon itself to one by one raise to the ground all the saints' tombs in Istanbul; that some politicians who feigned in public to uphold customs and tradition secretly belittled everything about the populace; that the faith bursting from within the nation was sacrificed for the sake of an abstract Western model; and that in the name of cleansing religion of superstition Islam was altogether opposed. Towards the end, an open call was placed to all Muslims to safeguard their saints.

Despite the fact that the piece did not lead, as feared, to an upsurge of emotions, still like a signal rocket it triggered into action all sorts of individuals and organizations all around the country. It was as if all these people had suddenly assumed the discovery of what had happened to the two saints' tombs in the vacated cemetery as their sole purpose in life, demanding an explanation from the authorities. The issue was not only extremely sensitive but also remarkably exploitable. The discussants started with 'the negligence of modernization' and concluded with a suggestion that instead 'modernization itself be neglected'. Like a diving beetle that skids on water, they hopped and skipped on ostentatious notions, such as 'the oblivion of the nation,' 'contemporary *Bihruzes,*' 'enforced Westernization,' 'sinister secularization' and so forth, thereby traversing a whole lake of antagonisms, splashing water around all but themselves.

A local newspaper that came out in the provinces but happened to be particularly interested in what was going on in Istanbul even though it had no distribution there, thus declared: 'What is termed 'Westernization' is nothing but a loving marriage between the East and the West. Yet, one should never forget that in this matrimony the West is the woman and East the man. The latter is therefore naturally the head of the household. For that reason it should be those swanky streets built for a few overindulged ladies to gallivant on and for dressed up dandies to show off their cars that show respect to the saints, not the other way around.'

With the detection of a crime necessitating the disclosure of the criminal, the time was ripe to get some people into trouble. After a brief consideration of possible options, trouble flew around to finally perch on the heads of the old and loyal cemetery guards. Having managed to hide all traces of nightly disturbances at the cemetery from people who visited in the morning, they were not able to hide themselves from the notice of their chief, and after being found guilty of trampling the tombs of saints, were laid off temporarily. Of the three guards, two were elderly men who believed there was a silver lining to every disaster. Of these two, one returned to his village and the other retired to his house to dedicate the rest of his life to his grandchildren. Yet the third one, relatively younger and not easily content with little, could not accept the injustice that had been committed. In the months to follow he penned reproachful letters to the directory of the cemeteries, the mayor, ministers, prime minister and high ranking members of the military, all the while complaining to each and every person he encountered. During this time, there was a change of government and the opposition assumed power, but all the same, his letters remained unanswered and the authorities indifferent. As they became increasingly deaf to his pleas, he became muter, drifting inward. Everyone expected him to eventually get over the past, but just when they thought he had, he did something utterly unexpected.

Now this man had a wife whom he had not touched in years and whom he had banished from his bed for snoring till daylight like an elephant. One day out of the blue, it was this woman that he started to chase around the house utterly unconcerned about the blame neighbours would place on him for such lust at this age. He finally caught his wife after a long, scream-filled chase and, paying no attention to her excuses, objections, entreaties and curses, with total doggedness and the help of fortune impregnated her at the age of fifty.

He did not waste a second to rush to the registrar's office as soon as the baby was born. In order to make sure neither he himself, nor anyone else would ever forget the wrong done to him, in spite of all the protests of his wife and after giving fistfuls of bribe to the civil servant on duty, he officially named the son God had given him after all this time: 'Injustice'.

★★★

Long before Injustice had become implanted in his mother's womb, however, the scandal of the saints started to fade away. Within two weeks after the removal of the tombs of Saint 'Hewhopackedupandleft', the political agenda had entirely altered and both the government and the opposition focused their full attention on the forthcoming elections. The municipal authorities who had meanwhile speeded-up the road construction project could thus assume the case closed and easily finish up the project without further trouble. What was done was done since the stone sarcophagi were removed during the excavation of the cemetery. Even so, during those prickly days when every event clustering more than ten people was bound to be crowned with a propaganda speech, the Third of the Three Consultant Buddies would have no difficulty in convincing his business partners not only that the saint's file should not be closed, but also that it should be fully utilized for a public ceremony.

A few weeks before the elections, a brief ceremony attended by a large number of spectators occurred on the southern slope of the old Muslim cemetery. Since the uneven ground next to the wall that once separated the orthodox Armenian cemetery was not suitable for the occasion, the question as to which tomb would be treated as genuine was automatically answered. Some among the spectators were people hired specifically for this purpose. As for the rest, they were either totally unaware but curious passers-by, or, on the contrary, conscientious citizens who wanted to see with their own eyes how the scandalous event they had followed from the newspapers would come to an end.

The ceremony comprised of three main parts. In the first part, two men, one young with an aged voice and the other old with a youthful voice, recited verses from the Qur'an which they had committed to memory in its entirety. During the second part, an official dressed up to the nines delivered a rather indicting but essentially passionless speech in response to all the accusations so far voiced. The third part was the most complicated. Pieces of the saint's stone sarcophagus and an empty coffin – brought along at the last minute so as not to confuse those with barely any knowledge of the situation – were carried on shoulders and loaded onto the hearse. Then everyone got on buses heading to an empty, rusty-soiled lot surrounded by dilapidated buildings. There, immersed in mud, orations and applause, the empty coffin of Saint 'Hewhopackedupandleft' was first buried, then the pieces of the stone sarcophagus joined and erected, appearing far more magnificent now surrounded by a tall ornate wood railing. The Third of the Three Consultant Buddies had prepared the text of the speech he was to deliver days in advance. Yet that morning, having finally mustered the courage to propose marriage to the daughter of his maternal aunt with whom he had been in love for years, he had been so badly rejected that he took to the streets wandering aimlessly, thus failing to get both himself and his speech to the ceremony on time.

Upon arriving at the site of the ceremony with a delay of almost an hour, the Third of the Three Consultant Buddies could not find anyone around. Only scattered cigarette stubs and tangled footprints remained of that boisterous crowd. He sat down by the tomb in grief and, wiping his sweaty forehead, started to read the text that had consumed so much of his time aloud to himself. There was actually no need for the paper since he knew every single line by heart. In a voice that quivered at first but got stronger eventually, he declared how the person lying in the tomb was a most distinguished saint who had kept his appetite for worldly pleasures captive in the turquoise-covered ring on his finger. He declared also that the saint had, in accordance with his convictions, refused to sleep under the same roof for more than one night or eat from the same bowl more than once; used a brick for a pillow in perpetual pain; never gotten married to leave behind any descendants, or any property or goods; wandered all year round deeming the earth his house and the skies his roof; in short, the name Saint 'Hewhopackedupandleft' had been bestowed upon him for spending his whole life with no roots nowhere. Hence it would not at all be contrary to tradition to move the tomb from one place to another and whomever argued otherwise should be mistrusted not only as to their intentions but also the depth of their religious knowledge. At the conclusion of his speech, turning pensive he distractedly caressed the words '*baqiya hawas*' on the inscriptions of the stone sarcophagus. Then, as if responding to a distant call, he sprung up and hurried in the direction he had come from.

It wasn't until this point that the graveyard of Saint 'Hewhopackedupandleft' achieved the unspoiled calm and composure it had yearned for so long. Leaving aside the visitors occasionally praying by his grave who rubbed their bus, train, ferry or plane tickets on his tombstone, not a single event would occur for about thirty-six years to upset its turbulence-free peace. Probably because of the ad infinitum movement of the saint's tomb from one location to another, it became a custom among travellers setting on a long journey to stop by this place a day before their departure to seek his blessing and to thumbprint a corner of their tickets, as if getting the approval of an imaginary customs officer, with the rust-coloured soil of the tomb. After the second half of the 1960s, these travellers were gradually replaced by 'guest-workers' off to Germany and their relatives. During those years, the most faithful visitors of the saint were the women left behind by the guest-workers going abroad. Since in their case there were no tickets to be had, they ended up rubbing the rust-coloured soil on their fingertips or palms, which resembled henna when dry. In time, most of these women went to join their husbands so the number of visitors gradually diminished. At the end of thirty-six years, first the wood railing, then the crimson-veined white marble and finally the rust-coloured soil of this imposing tomb were secretly swallowed-up by the stores, workshops and restaurants engulfing it in the ever-shrinking circle of a chase or hunt. Thus the tombs of Saint 'Hewhopackedupandleft' that once numbered two and then reduced to one, finally reached nil.

***

As for the hilly land of the two old cemeteries, it was there that the fastest transformation occurred upon the completion of the avenue. Along the slope on the northwest side of the orthodox Armenian cemetery sprung up graceful apartment buildings, tailed by, like kites with multi-hued ribbons, stores with glittery windows, sidewalks to promenade with flair, new locales throbbing with rhythm. When the value of the buildings skyrocketed, those who had a house or land in this area pocketed large amounts of money in no time. Many of the flats facing the avenue were rented out to businesses; mostly to doctors or lawyers. Such offices mushroomed so far and wide that before long there would be at least one doctor or one lawyer in any shared taxi operating in the neighbourhood. So much so, that in each of these shared taxis, one frequently encountered people with plenty of health complaints or legal problems but no money, only there for a free consultation with the doctor sitting next to them or the lawyer behind. Some of the minibus drivers themselves, thanks to their eavesdropping on such conversations from dusk till dawn, accumulated an impressive amount of knowledge on both medical and legal matters. If truth be told, one highly fashionable general neurologist, whose constant use of a particular route meant he became the best of friends with one of the most astute of the drivers, had actually got into the habit of referring some of the queries he received to this driver. Though the elderly mischievous doctor had originally proceeded with this game out of boredom, he eventually got great enjoyment from it. The young driver was one of the few with a mind sharp as a razor and a tolerance unique to bohemians. Besides, having little regard for the physician's rules of etiquette or for weighing each word, he blurted what he thought right out, utterly oblivious to the hopes he might shatter in doing so. As he drove the shared taxi, he would mimic the obsessions of neurotic ladies and angst-ridden gentlemen, even managing to get them to laugh at themselves. His performance so impressed the elderly doctor that after a while he offered him a job. In spite of their good intentions, however, the witty friendship of the two could not survive the rigorous formalities of the office environment, and the young driver ultimately returned to his minibus.

In no more than fifteen years, the appearance of the vicinity was entirely transformed. Not a single person remembered that there had once been, and still were, hundreds of graves under these grandiose offices, stylish stores and fancy apartments shining along the avenue with the perfection of porcelain teeth. Most of the flats had narrow, double-door, carpeted elevators. Had these elevators operated not only between the ground and upper floors but also further down into the ground, one would have seen, like slices cut from a colossal cake, all the segments of life's inner workings. At the very bottom, there would be layer upon layer of the earth's crust, then rough, knobby soil; upon that a stratum of decimated graves, followed by a very thin line of tarmac road, a couple of flats piled up on one another, a layer of red-brick roof and, on top of it all, a sky of endless cerulean plastered and diffused all over. Occasionally, some people were heard to mutter softly as if to themselves, 'Once upon a time there were graves all over this place…' Yet these words had a somewhat surreal sound to them though the time referred to dated no further than fifteen or twenty years ago. It was reminiscent of saying, 'Once upon a time, girls more beautiful than fairies took baths of light in the thousand room crystal palace of the sultan of the moon.' That is how real it sounded, a past that had never been experienced or an ethereal silver setting somewhere outside the mundane flow of time.

Bonbon Palace, its garbage cans knocked over by Injustice Pureturk on Wednesday 1st May 2002 while parking his van, was built in 1966 in this neighbourhood which had by then little left of its former splendor. As for the husband and wife who built the apartment house, though they were foreigners here, they had been to Istanbul previously.

EVEN BEFORE...

WHEN AGRIPPINA FYODOROVNA ANTIPOVA saw Istanbul for the first time in the fall of 1920 from the deck of a freight ship, she did so with one small swelling in her womb and a larger one on her back. With the help of her husband, she ploughed her way through the crowd of passengers, who had all stood up for the entire three days since they left the Crimea. She clung to the rails to see what the city that awaited them looked like. Ever since she was a little girl, she relished playing games with colours more than anything else. Wherever she went, she needed to discover the colour of the place first in order to feel at home there. The mansion in Grosny where she was born and had spent her childhood, for instance, was rhubarb, and the church they attended every Sunday parchment yellow. In her mind's eye, the villa they lodged in during religious festivals was a sparkly emerald awash in dew; the house she lived in with her husband after their wedding was the orange of a winter sun. Not only places but also people, animals, even moments had colours each of which, she had no doubt she could see if focused fully. She did so once again. At first with curiosity, then with frustration, she stared and stared without a blink at the silhouette of the city in front of her until her eyes watered and the image became blurred.

Istanbul was under a heavy fog that morning, and as all Istanbulites knew too well, during foggy days even the city herself could not tell what her colour was. However, Agripina Fyodorvna Antipova had always been pampered with great care since birth and had been subsequently led to presume that others were to blame whenever she could not obtain anything she desired. Hence she interpreted the persistance of Istanbul in withdrawing herself behind the veil of fog as a sign of intentional hostility and personal insult. She still, however, wanted to give the city a chance, as she firmly believed in the virtue of forgiveness. Lifting her small silver Virgin Mary icon toward the city she smiled benevolently: 'What you just did to me was not right, but I can still show tolerance and forgive you. For that would be the right thing to do.'

'And I will give you water and bread in return,' replied a voice.

When she bent down the rails, Agripina Fyodorovna Antipova saw there in a boat at the side of the ship a wiry man gesturing at her with bread in one hand and water in the other. Before she could even fathom what was going on, a chubby, rosy-cheeked, blond woman with shorn hair pushed her aside, tied the gold ring she took off her finger onto the belt she released from her daughter's waist and lowered it from the ship. The swarthy man in the boat grabbed the ring, lifted it in the air giving it a quick inspection with disgruntlement and relayed the belt back with a round, black loaf of bread tied in its stead. As the blonde, who had sheared her hair when a lice epidemic broke on the deck, and the scrawny daughter standing by her started devouring the bread, Agripina Fyodorovna Antipova looked at the sea with her eyes wide open in bewilderment and noticed that not only the ship they were in, but all the ships anchored in the harbour were surrounded with such boats. Cunning Turks, Greeks and Armenians waved foodstuff from these boats haggling with the White Russians who had been without food or water for days. Figuring out what was going on, Agripina Fyodorovna Antipova fretfully withdrew her silver Virgin Mary as if it too would be snatched away from her. Over the boats and sellers and waves she stared fretfully at the city in the background to grasp what sort of a place she had arrived at.

Istanbul was in dire straits at that time and also under

occupation. She therefore paid little attention to the half-baffled, half-haughty gaze of this nineteen year old woman on the deck of yet another newly anchored ship. Her tolerance for putting up with such selfish children having long run out, Istanbul returned to her own hubbub with a shrug of her shoulders. Agripina Fyodorovna Antipova was left standing there frozen in her smile. Though she had seen people behave coarsely, witnessing the insolence of a city was an utterly novel experience for her. Once she had managed to overcome her confusion, she closed down all the curtains, windows and shutters of her heart and instead got cross with the city. Such was her state of mind when she landed from the boat. Even after two months, when the swelling in her womb had grown in contrast to the one on her back which had shrunk in next to no time, she was still cross at Istanbul and Istanbul was still of an unknown colour and just as indifferent to boot.

Unlike his wife, General Pavel Pavlovich Antipov did not pay any particular attention to Istanbul, either that day or at any later point. He happened to be a man whose survival depended on his assuming responsibility for others — one of those who either loved weak women or ended up weakening the women they love. Hence that day as they alighted, he embraced Agripina with the warmest consideration. His grip held not only her but also their soon-to-be-born baby and the entire wealth they had been able to smuggle out of Russia.

The pieces of jewellery Agripina had hidden at the back of her body corset would, however, soon be sold one by one and for much less than their true worth. Thousands of white Russians fleeing from their homeland after the Bolshevik Revolution had so far crammed into Istanbul and it was rumoured that thousands more were on their way. When the jewellery was being auctioned off, there were hardly enough buyers even for medals of honor, family heirlooms and decorations of nobility. And after two months, nothing remained from the wealth that the couple had initially hoped would enable them to live comfortably for at least two years.

One morning at the dormitory converted from a decrepit detention centre provided by the French Red Cross wherein they slept with fifty people on stained, shallow mattresses, Agripina Fyodorovna Antipova vindictively pulled the silvery head of her husband who was thirty years her senior toward her and forced him to listen to the baby in her swollen belly. Pavel Pavlovich Antipov knew too well what this gesture meant. He had two options: to find a job as soon as possible or to write a letter to his disgraceful brother in France asking for help. Since even the thought of the second option was more than enough to wreck his nerves, he chose the first.

Yet just as the military fails to provide one with a profession, neither does the rank of general constitute a job experience you can rely on when seeking employment. Pavel Pavlovich Antipov then realized two things about himself: he did not know what to do and he could not do what he did know. While everything that had ever happened to him up till now had fallen into place as arranged, the revolution had caught up with him just as he had been promoted to the rank of general, shattering the authority he had acquired and the life he had erected year by year. Yet even back in those days of pestilence, he had not had to face, as he did today, the malady termed 'ambiguity'. In order to defeat ambiguity, he first had to know where to find it. Neither taking up a defensive position anywhere, nor acting in accordance with a particular strategy, it could attack from anywhere at any time, changing weapons all the while as it pleased. If this were an ongoing war, it had no battleground, no rules, no morals. If not a war, the situation would have been even worse as Pavel Pavlovich Antipov did not possess the knowledge to earn a living any other way. Until now, he had lost many things one after another, his property as well as goods, influence, privileges, esteem, friends, relatives, orderlies, the army he belonged to, the cities where his past was, the country where he had presumed his future would be... However, deep inside he assumed he was still what he had always been: a loyal soldier.

Conversely, thousands of soldiers of all ranks from the Czar's army had long been scattered into the least expected and most excruciating jobs at hotels, concert halls, cabarets, gambling houses, restaurants, bars, café chantants, movie theatres, beaches, nightclubs and streets. They washed dishes and carried trays in restaurants, worked as croupiers in gambling houses jam-packed with lies, peddled dolls at street corners, provided piano accompaniment to cabaret dancers in boisterous entertainment halls. Every corner was appropriated and each job filled. Amidst this chaos, Count General Pavel Pavlovich Antipov tried to find his way with steps as shaky as those of a new born foal learning to walk on its trembling legs. After looking around for weeks on end, the only job he could finally find was that of a checkroom attendant in a café chantant – a place frequented by arrogant French and English officers out with their delicate, sable-coated, cherry-lipsticked lovers; by sybarite Italian painters carving Eastern gravures with women always portrayed as being pasty and plump and streets as shady and snaky; by glum Jewish bankers in need of pumping loans to the palace so that they could get back the ones previously provided; by profligate Turkish young men satiated with the wealth inherited but insatiable in spending it; by spies not letting anything slip away even when blind drunk; by bohemians, dandies and all those lost souls in search of lust or adventure.

The bald, flabby-cheeked, multiple-chinned, constantly gesticulating Levantine owner of the café chantant had been looking to hire someone ever since the previous checkroom attendant – whose sort he had not approved of from the start – got involved in a fight ending with his face smashed up. Observing the imposing appearance and majestic posture of Pavel Pavlovich Antipov, he did not hesitate even for a moment before offering him the job. Yet when the new checkroom attendant put on the red coat with shiny tasseled epaulets on the shoulders and diagonal yellow cords hanging in front, his admiration was replaced by disparagement:

'Life is so strange, isn't it Monsieur Antipov? We're both

witnesses to the demise of two glorious empires. You've started
to Westernize at least a century before us. Peter the Great! It's
rumoured he would have those who didn't learn Western
etiquette whipped – is that true? He inspected women's
underwear and men's beards, is that so? Peter's city must be
really pretty: a palace rising from the swamps. Take a look at
Istanbul in comparison: open on all four sides, exposed to
every breeze blowing from each direction. A rudderless, out of
joint city! Did you know that until a decade ago, young and
courageous intellectuals escaping from your mighty empire sat
side by side at the same Parisian cafés with young and
courageous intellectuals escaping from our mighty empire:
plunging into zealous discussions to draw godknowswhat sort
of short-sighted conclusions. The French waiters serving them
would eavesdrop first at one table then the other. Imagine the
contradictory things they must have heard! Those who fled
from your empire would rave about destroying their state at all
costs. Those who fled from ours would instead rave about
saving their state from destruction at all costs. Within a decade,
yours succeeded and ours failed. I don't know which one to
lament more? Life is so strange, isn't it Monsieur Antipov? You
escaped from a collapsed empire to seek refuge in one about
to collapse. Could it be that your running away from the
uniformed Reds to find yourself in a red uniform here is yet
another one of Fortuna's tricks?'

That night, as Pavel Pavlovich Antipov held up the
customers' coats, he heard nothing other than the daunting
echo of the things his boss had said. Only for three more
accursed days could he stand that terribly ridiculous uniform.
After that, he stopped working, stopped doing everything he
would normally do, to instead just stand still as if rooted to the
spot, as if there was no job to be sought, no life to build and
no purpose to wear oneself out for. At the end of that week,
Agripina Fyodorovna Antipova carefully inspected her
husband as if trying to determine his true colour. Only then
was she forced to accept that he was too rigidly fixed in his

ways to ever change. He was so because of his age (too old; having always advanced a couple of steps ahead of his age, he had now stopped and was waiting for his age to catch up with him); because of his title (too elevated; having always focused on rising even further up, he had suddenly become aware there was not much space left to rise to and froze in his tracks); and lastly, because of his frame (too imposing; he had a frame that was so unbendable and inflexible that he chose not to go through the doors that required his bending down). Pavel Pavlovich Antipov was a man who in essence was weak and fully aware of it, who clung to his power with all his might less to avoid being like others than to avoid being himself. A man who knew too well what he craved and worked all his life to achieve it, struggling bit by bit, climbing step by step, to reach success in the end. The last type of person to accommodate drastic changes!

Being so young and inexperienced, having never had to work or even accomplish anything, and in utter harmony with her advancing pregnancy, Agripina Fyodorovna Antipova was one immense, round zero. As such she could remain forever anchored in whatever inertia she was entangled. Yet just as easily, she could be sent rolling ahead with a strong gust. She possessed that sheer boldness peculiar to the ignorant and that virginal expectation that things would turn out well, an expectation nurtured by the very fact that she had never acquired anything in life by herself alone. Everything she did attain had been bestowed upon her and all she had lost would one day just as easily be somehow returned to her. She still spent most of her life preparing long lists about what she would do once she returned to Russia. However, just as easily she could spend this time working until that day arrived. Hence she gave up expecting help from her husband and decided to do something she had never done before: to look for a job herself.

Fortune was on her side because fortune loves to test those emerging with such a challenge, so she found a job as a waitress in one of the most stylish pastry shops in Beyoglu. In that mirrored pastry shop decorated with elegantly stained glass, all day long she went back and forth between customers dressed to the nines and the kitchen that smelt of cinnamon and whipped cream. From all the cacophonous languages spoken there, each sounding to her just as unmelodious as the other, she acquired fragments of words sufficient to understand the orders that were more or less the same and never tried to learn more than that. Actually, she never opened her mouth unless she had to. In spite of the high workload and low pay, no one had ever seen her frown or complain. Though the boss had ordered every employee to smile continuously when serving the customers, others grimaced the moment they left the field of vision of either the boss or the customer, but Agripina's smile stayed on her face throughout the day as if it had been nailed on. While all the other women tried to avoid work whenever they could or kept searching for a rich middle-aged man to rescue them from this torment, she alone did nothing but work continually. It was more a dedication to suffering than an effort to leave behind these insufferable days that kept her going. It was almost as if she was secretly proud of her suffering, as if embitterment purified her and giving herself up to God's mortals brought her closer to Him. The more insurmountable the difficulties she encountered, the more insufferable the dangers she had to overcome, and the more vulgar the people she served, the more she felt God became indebted to her. She would sooner or later receive what was her due. 'This is a test,' she assured herself with a smile. 'The more arduous it is, the more exalted the outcome will be.'

'Why is there that grin on your face! How dare you laugh at our faces?'

Agripina Fyodorovna Antipova looked in surprise at the Muslim woman yelling at her but her bewilderment only made the latter even more furious. The woman was a member of the Contemporary Women's Association which advocated the deportation of all White Russian women; whom they believed were ripping out Muslim men's reason from their minds and money from their pockets. Prioritized among the agenda items of the association were the following:

1) To determine and record one by one incidents of immoral behavior performed by white Russians with soft and silky blond hair, fair complexion, shameless looks and aristocratic pretensions

2) To wear out the gates of the upper echelons of state administration in order to gather support for their cause

3) To ensure the closing down of all the dens of thieves and nightclubs capable of drawing the wrath of Sodom and Gomorrah onto Istanbul

4) To 'shoo' away all the prostitutes who had descended from Kiev and Odessa to bed down on the quarters of Galata

5) To constantly and ceaselessly warn the innocent, inexperienced Muslim youth about the danger awaiting them

6) Until the authorities took the necessary precautions, to pursue by their own means a policy of intimidation by mistreating all white Russian women they encountered.

Overcoming her initial confusion, Agripina Fyodorovna Antipova reached her neck and squeezed the silver pendant bearing the picture of Saint Seraphim. The strength she thus drew enabled her to smile at the woman whom she regarded as a recent incarnation of the torment-filled 'divine test' she had for such a long time been going through. 'What you just did was not right but I can still be tolerant and even forgive you. For that would be the right thing to do.'

That night, only cursorily did she mention this event to her husband. He never asked her anything anyhow. Not only did he not want to learn a single thing about the world outside, but he also envied her for managing to survive in that insane world which had roughly shaken him up and tossed him aside. Rarely did he leave the dump they considered home ever since their departure from the dormitory provided by the French Red Cross, passing his days in front of the window as he penned never-to-be-posted letters to his brother in France, got lost in thoughts, looked outside at the Muslims passing by and watched the streets as if waiting for someone. Almost as if arriving to put an end to this monotonous wait, their baby was born in seven months.

Yet Agripina Fyodorovna Antipova could not welcome her daughter with the same excitement as her husband. Her early and painstakingly onerous childbirth may have contributed another life to this world, but that life had been stolen from her. She had felt far more important and so very different during her pregnancy compared to how she felt now. She had convinced herself all along that God had chosen her from among many and had subsequently considered every calamity yet another crucial phase in the strenuous test that was being put to her. Never having lost her faith in God or herself, she had wholeheartedly believed herself to be the heroine of a cautionary tale of damnation the people around her could never understand. In order to save from the claws of this idle world both her husband and herself, she had struggled for them both but always on her own, awaiting, like a pearl rolled into mud, that day when she would be cleansed to shine once again. Yet now she started to imagine she had been mistaken all along, that God did not look after her but the baby in her womb and, for that reason, abandoned her to her fate as soon as the baby was born. However hard she tried, she could not get rid of this feeling of diminution and abandonment. Not one fleck of glitter remained on her face from that arrogant luminescence; her body had shrunk and withered as if pails of water had been drained from it. Only her breasts, they alone were still large and full. Now and then they leaked milk like blood oozing away from a bleeding lip. She ran home in the afternoons to breastfeed the baby only to encounter time and time again a cruelly poignant scene. She found her husband and the baby on top of the sofa by the window, either in play or fast asleep in each other's embrace with infinite happiness and unmatched innocence under the daylight that sprayed golden glitter upon them, as if it was emanating not from the sun but from seventh heaven. Every time a pang of sadness seized her as she realized how the spirit she had once carried within and believed to be a part of had now excluded her.

So, she thought, a roily river of muddy waters this city was. The very reason for her thrashing about all this time amidst the water was simply because she had been entrusted with delivering her baby from the bank of the river it was on to her husband on the other. That was precisely what pregnancy had been to her: sailing to the other shore within the body of a boat you were swollen into, to get the baby wrapped in an angelic bliss, and to then carry her safe and sound across to the other bank. Upon the occurrence of the birth and the deliverance of the baby to the other shore, she had all of a sudden become worthless, as if pushed back into the water and abandoned to the tide. It was useless to struggle. Far away from the bank she was kept by the waters she belonged to and the current she was caught in. It seemed as if even the baby was aware of this situation. The moment she was picked up from her father's arms, she would turn bright red in a fit of fury; while being breastfed, she would crumple her face as if to prove she was doing this solely out of need and, as soon as she was full, would let go of the nipple and cry to be released also. The general would then take the baby in his arms and tenderly calm her down while Agripina Fyodorovna Antipova escaped from the house so as not to witness this scene that hurt her more every passing day.

Back at work, she would have to endure, along with the emptiness swelling within, this other feeling of suffering a terrible injustice. Every day she hated her body even more. Her body lived for one cause only; every bite she took, every drop she drank, every ray of sunlight she received, every particle of air she breathed; all were moulded and converted into milk for the baby. The more robust the baby grew, the more strength Agripina Fyodorovna Antipova lost, with every passing moment swaying further and further from the vim and vigour of life.

Impossible as it might sound to those who believe that every woman is by nature maternal and that motherhood is as sacred and pure as the rivers in heaven, Agripina Fyodorovna Antipova did not love 'the thing' she had given birth to. Upon coming face to face with the child she had carried within her for so long, the child she had considered a part of her without knowing what it would look like or bring about, she became scared of this being that was so tiny in size but enormous in need. She became scared of the impossibility of reversing time to go back to being a young woman again, of being given no other choice than to love unconditionally. One thing she knew for sure, she wanted to get rid of the baby. Inconceivable as this might seem to those who believe every woman by nature maternal and motherhood as sacred and pure as the rivers in heaven, Agripina Fyodorovna Antipova was no exception. It is not only nationhoods that coin official histories of their own, so do motherhoods. Mothers often create a maternal historiography written retrospectively and gracefully, dating back to the very first day, picking out the weeds and furnishing the stepping stones along the way. For love does not always come without effort but sometimes flourishes belatedly and grows gradually, drop by drop, under the tutelage of time. The care of those around them, a poignant instance, a fleeting moment of affection and myriad sediments of tenderness, these may coalesce in the mind of a new mother to chase away, like an industrious fan with a harsh yet invigorating breeze, all inappropriate thoughts and unpleasant feelings. As long as the fan is kept on, a young mother might manage to increasingly love her baby, the maternal halo embracing them both. In fact, she might in time come to love the baby so much that she would succeed in believing she had loved her with the same intensity right from the very first day. That she might not have done so, is so unspeakably appalling that it could not be confessed to anyone. Not to the husband, for instance, saying: 'I at first felt miserable for having given birth to your baby but then recovered.' Not to the child: 'I really did not love you at first but gradually developed warmer feelings.' Not to herself: 'How could I fail to love my own child?' So the official history of motherhood necessitates a meticulous cleansing of the secluded corners of memory. Agripina Fyodorovna Antipova's misfortune was that before she had a chance to start loving the baby, that is, to love her year by year, degree by degree, to eventually arrive at such a depth in love so as to have no difficulty in convincing herself she had always loved her so, she lost her.

That afternoon, back home at the usual time to breastfeed, she encountered her husband and the baby on top of the sofa by the window fast asleep in each other's embrace under the daylight that sprayed upon them golden glitter as if it was emanating not from the sun but seventh heaven. Everything was cloaked in shades of yellow. The beams curving through the curtains were a hue of amber, the general's face alabaster, the fabric of the sofa apricot, the baby's swaddling layette vivid saffron and the tiny ball on top of it an aureate vermiculated with purple. Blinking her eyes dazzled by the sun, Agripina Fyodorovna Antipova walked towards this peculiar ball with an uneasy curiosity. She stood there, though she unconsciously knew only too well what she was looking at.

She was right about colours. Just as cities and places came in colours and hues so did moments and situations; including deaths. Death too acquired a new hue in every person and each ending. In a newborn baby, it must be an aureate vermiculated with purple.

After a while Pavel Pavlovich Antipov woke up. Standing up carefully so as not to disturb the baby in his lap, he stretched a bit, yawned indolently and looked out the window, still unaware of his wife's presence. Down in the street, a ragged street-seller, with a small screened kitchen cupboard filled with livers mounted on a horse on the brink of death, was haggling ferociously with two old Muslim women each more quarrelsome than the other. While talking back to the women on the one side, the liver-seller also tried to chase the clingy flies drawing circles-within-circles around the cupboards while his horse, looking like it might give up living any moment, accompanied him with a swing of his tail. The weariness was scattered around by the wind that had been continuously blowing warm air since the early hours of the morning, penetrating everyone and everything so deeply that even the commotion of the liver-seller and his customers could not disturb the lethargic silence that prevailed on the streets. Pavel Pavlovich Antipov absentmindedly closed the windows, leant back and looked at the baby. He looked and at first did not comprehend a thing. The baby's mouth was slightly ajar, her eyes open and her eyebrows crossed as if she were trapped inside a dream, dejected. Hair-thin, striped, purplish veins had covered her entire face. She resembled a porcelain bowl that managed not to break even after a rough fall to the ground, but had instead acquired multiple cracks across its entire width and length. Pavel Pavlovich Antipov cupped this round, cold and purplish yellow head in his hands like a crystal ball within which he hoped to see his future. And like all people who having not cried for years have totally forgotten how, in order to cry he too had to first howl.

The liver-seller, putting the livers he could not sell to the cranky old women back into the screened cupboard, instantly sensed the ill-omen behind the scream and sauntered away, tugging at the halter of the drowsy horse, dragging behind him regiments of flies and divisions of cats.

★★★

After the funeral, Pavel Pavlovich Antipov wrote a letter to his youngest brother whom he had not seen for a long time as the latter had settled in Europe long before the revolution: a brother whom he had secretly looked down upon for choosing trade over the family profession of the military thereby serving money rather than the Czar, and whose offers of help he had constantly turned down because of the pride that prevented him from taking shelter with him. In a letter to him Pavel asked whether they might be able to join him in France and, unlike the previous letters, he did send it this time.

During the long years they spent in France not once did the general and his wife talk about that inauspicious Istanbul morning; they became more and more estranged-from one another, as well as from any spiritual rapport they once had. However fast and easy arrival in this new country might have been, they were only too ready to risk everything just to escape Istanbul's wickedness. After the baby's death, Pavel Pavlovich Antipov had fully realized one thing right: they had to leave this city of mourning as soon as possible. Either Istanbul had not been good to them or they not good enough for Istanbul. To them the city's gates of good fortune were shut, or perhaps had never been open. The same end awaited those whose family trees did not take root to branch out in this city, but whose paths led here at one stage of their lives: Istanbul, initially a port of escape enabling people to run away from everything, would herself become a reason for escape.

***

When Agripina Fyodorovna Antipova reached Paris in the spring of 1922, she carried a pregnant worry in her soul. As she looked at the war worn city with indifferent eyes, discovering its colour did not even cross her mind. She had contracted a strange eye disease on her last day in Istanbul and had thereby lost all contact with the world of colours. Now everything she saw, the streets and buildings, the people and the reflections in the mirrors...all were in black and white. It was as if the world was cross at her and had closed down all its curtains, windows and shutters. She cared not. Not only did she not care, she found the world's behaviour ridiculously childish. She simply did not want to struggle with the world and all of its endless burdens. Her only true desire was to see God, to see what colour God was, if any. Until she saw that straight out – and along with it, God's intention in taking her baby away – she did not care at all to see the colours of this world of illusions. To her husband's continuous insinuations about having a second baby so as to start life anew and to his consolation about time healing all wounds she reacted with revulsion. Agripina Fyodorovna Antipova had realized that babies who died before their first birthdays and cities abandoned before their first year of settlement ominously resembled one another. No baby arriving after a dead one could fully detach its existence from the absence of the dead sibling, just like no new city reached would fully welcome those exiled by the previous one.

Pavel Pavlovich Antipov did not pay any attention to Paris either that day or later. The helping hand his disgraced younger brother extended with a pleasure he did not feel the need to contain, Antipov accepted with a displeasure he felt he had to suppress – and did not let go until he had taken and learnt everything he could from him. He gradually started to think that trade was no different than the military, and once he had believed in that, he fully dedicated himself to it. He had the unprincipled resolve of all those who, at a certain stage of their lives, suddenly plunge full force into an option they had once turned their nose up at. He was reckless and impatient, as if to make up for the time he had lost.

However, it was only much later, with the start of another World War that his luck fully took a turn for the better. From black-marketeering during the war, he acquired a considerable fortune and an abscessed standing in society. Like a rubber ball he succeeded in bouncing his way through the ruins of war, at times even conducting business with the Germans. It did not matter to him at all. The war that raged on was not his. He no longer believed in the victory of states or of causes but only in the victory of individuals. And the face of victory, however attained, was always turned to the past. Triumph in life did not mean reaching step by step a future too good to pine for, but rather restoring an unfulfilled past to its former freshness.

That is what he did. He acquired a new woman instead of the one who no longer fulfilled her wifely functions, a new baby for the one he had lost and a new authority to replace the one wrested away from him. All, yet none of them were new. When he held in his arms the baby the young Frenchwoman he lived with had born him, he was exactly fifty-nine years old. Like his first baby, this too was a girl with ash-coloured eyes. He hid this from Agripina for years. Had he not done so, however, it was unlikely that she would have minded, let alone have been jealous. If one went by what was written by the chief physician who treated her, she was utterly indifferent to everything around her. Exhibiting no sign of recovery she passed her entire time painting black and white watercolours of the peasants whom she watched at work in the vineyards on the northern slope of the clinic's grounds. Pavel Pavlovich Antipov read these letters with great care, concern and sorrow to then forget about them once they were stored in his drawer. Content with his new relationship he seemed determined to bestow upon his second baby all the love he could not give the first one. Still, never did he attempt to get divorced from his wife. Though long ago having given up visiting her, he was always careful to keep Agripina within easy reach. His wife had at first been his little lover, most steadfast admirer, then the victim of his weaknesses and infirmities, and eventually the only mirror that reflected all that he had lost on route to where he had arrived; she had been the closest witness of his personal history. Neither a partner, nor a friend, but perhaps a logbook... And just as a logbook would not know what was written inside, Agripina too was unaware of what it was exactly that she had been a witness of. Pavel Pavlovich Antipov decided to keep this precious memento in a safe place until it was time to go and pick it up.

Yet when that time came, Pavel Pavlovich Antipov had lived so long and had become so old that he had started to carry his age like a dilapidated outfit worn over and over throughout the years, so comfortable that it could still be worn again and again were it not for the embarrassment of being seen in it by other people. All his goals he had actualized one by one, he had recovered all he had lost and lived as long as he had hoped. Yet still, even though life was done with him, it did not come to an end. There was not a single person around him who had lived that long. As all those people so much younger than him that he had loved, protected, fought or hated, departed one by one, his torment at the death of each was deposited on his chest layer upon layer, throbbing at night with a sharp, piercing pain. He could not help suspecting that the relatives of the deceased, even his own woman and daughter, blamed him deep down, that everyone hated him for living so long in such a damned age when not only life but even death had lost its enchantment. Though ninety-four years old, not only had he not aged, let alone become senile, he had barely even grown old. There was nothing he could do about it. The only way he could make up for his fault was through death but one did not die on demand and he did not demand to die either.

At times, he blamed himself through the persona of the flabby-chinned Levantine who had been his boss for a total of three days, but whose castrated voice he still, after all these years, could not forget: 'How old are you Monsieur Antipov? So almost a century! Within this century, states fell like a house of cards, people were wiped out like flies, the Trumpet of Israfil* grated on our ears not only once, but at least a dozen times. But what about you, did you erroneously go through the gates opening up to a time beyond time or did you knowingly make a pact with the devil? How much longer do you intend to live Monsieur Antipov? Could it be that you leaving your country to escape death's clutches, to now wait

* It is believed that the Trumpet of Israfil will be heard on the Day of Judgement.

here in this country of others for death to come and take you, is another one of Fortuna's tricks?'

★★★

Just when the agony brought by his incurable fault had started to make Pavel Pavlovich Antipov grow more and more distant from people, he received a letter from the chief physician: Agripina had suddenly taken a turn for the worse. One morning, under the startled looks of the patients, nurses and physicians, she had suddenly ran screaming outside and tried to talk one by one to the peasants at the vineyard but, upon realizing that none of them understood a word she said, had suffered a nervous breakdown. When brought back inside and having been somewhat calmed down with the help of tranquilizers, she had spilled out her unintelligible words to those at the clinic. Noticing how scared the other patients were, she had become scared herself and had withdrawn. The head physician wanted Monsieur Antipov to come at once to see his wife because as far as he could tell, the foreign language that his most silent and most easygoing patient had started to speak after all these years — without the presence of a single event that would have triggered such a transformation — was Russian.

When Agripina Fyodorovna Antipov saw Pavel Pavlovich Antipov, she embraced him with a contentment brought on less by seeing her husband after all these years, than by finding someone who could understand her. Then she started to talk. Her words had neither meaning nor coherence. She blubbered about the songs the peasants at the vineyards sang at sunset. Then she complained about the childish jealousies of the elderly patients at the clinic and also about God's callousness. She did not stop. That day in a monotonous voice, neither raised nor lowered but eventually hoarse, without the slightest indication of happiness or sorrow, she kept switching topics all the while mentioning a kitchen with smells of cinnamon and whipped cream. As the night drew closer and her exceedingly patient audience-of-one got ready to leave, she asked him with a hurt smile when he would come again, but sunk without awaiting his response into the sticky, obligatory slumber of medication.

The taciturn visitor returned the following day; this time with a single rose in his hand and a box under his arm. Agripina did not pay any attention to the rose, but upon taking the fancy wrapping off the box, she greeted with exuberant happiness the bonbons glittering on the round varnished tray. This lovely tray that Pavel Pavlovich Antipov had bought from a canny antique dealer included a study by Vishniakov. It depicted the scene of a boyar abducting the woman he loved from her father's house. The boyar had stopped just before going down the last few steps of the wooden ladder, using one arm to hold with superhuman strength his loved one on his lap, and grabbing onto the ladder with the other, while gazing at the half-shady half-green forest they were about to disappear into. Pavel Pavlovich Antipov withdrew to the side to watch the reaction this tray would create on his wife. One of the physicians he had consulted on his way over had stated that memory occasionally played vindictive tricks; the brain rewound when the body was nearing the end. Many patients, upon reaching a particular, often the very last stage of their lives, returned to their childhoods and to their mother tongue. Even a single object or a dream was sufficient to trigger such a transformation. Watching his wife Pavel Pavlovich Antipov wondered if the logbook was now turning the pages backwards to erase line by line all that was written within.

Yet Agripina Fyodorovna Antipova looked much more interested in the bonbons than the Vishniakov tray. Unaware of her husband's worries, she randomly picked one, held it out with a grateful smile and asked what flavour it was. 'Since it is pink, it must be strawberry,' was the response she got. Pink! It had been so long since she had last seen pink. She took the wrapper off and threw the candy into her mouth. The colour pink had a nice smell and a syrupy flavour.

As the bonbon melted in her mouth, first the anxiety-stricken lips of the beautiful lover in the boyar's lap, then everything around that was coloured in pink started to come to life. Agripina immediately reached for the other bonbons asking her husband the flavour each time. The yellow ones were lemon, reds cinnamon; greens were mint, oranges tangerine; browns caramel and the beige ones vanilla. Then she tasted them. Yellow was a sour colour, red sharp; green scorched, orange tangy; brown was astringent and beige puckered. With each new bonbon she tasted, the colours Agripina Fyodorovna Antipova had left in Istanbul returned to her. She watched as her bed against the wall, the chair and desk in front of the window, the cherry tree side table with all sorts of medicine on top, the Virgin Mary icon and the august face of Saint Seraphim swinging from her necklace revealed themselves. She ran to the windows in bewilderment only to be taken aback by the scenery that greeted her. All the colours were in place. Burnt was the colour of the vineyards extending from the slope of the hill into the horizon, tar the dresses of the peasant women singing as they filled their large baskets with thick skinned grapes, sharp the trees that sheltered shrill swallows and sour the sun in the sky. Colours were everywhere, but not as many were inside as outside. An idea occurred to her just then. She went back and collected the myriad of wrappers of the bonbons she had eaten. Through these spectacles she looked at the clinic where so many years of her life had been spent. As she put down one wrapper and picked up another, the dreary whiteness of the cold stone building's halls, the walls of the rooms, physicians' uniforms, the pale faces of the nurses adorned with reserved smiles, the pills she had to swallow twice a day, the bed sheets changed by the maids every other day and those tasteless soups placed in front of her; all of these things were suddenly dyed in their own colours – as was the man standing across from her. The only thing that did not change was the fretful look on his face.

Agripina did not stop. Not only did she not stop, she placed the wrappers on top of one another creating new hues. After a few attempts she placed red on top of blue and witnessed the whole world turn purple. A wheezing cry escaped her lips: 'Istan-bul!' She had found it. She had found the colour that had escaped her on the deck of that rotten, reeking boat where she had stood at the age of nineteen with a small swelling in her womb and a larger one on her back. In the spectrum of colours and hues, Istanbul was purple; a greyish-bluish purple the eye-dazzling sun reflecting from the lead-plated domes blotted drop-by-drop and scorched strike-by-strike. She remembered that accursed mixture of yellow and purple. Over and over, again and again, she heaved in gasps: 'Istanbul!' It was as if she were not repeating the same name hundreds of times, but pronouncing one single, lengthy name of unchanging syllables. Pavel Pavlovich Antipov could not bear it any longer; taking his wife's hands into his, 'Agripina,' he muttered, 'Did you remember Istanbul?'

In the following days, Agripina fantasized two things about herself: first, that she was young, and second, that she was in Istanbul. Occasionally Turkish words spilled from her lips. Her palms were sweaty all the time; her reason came and left. Every time it left her, she found herself in Istanbul, and when it returned she would have left yet another piece of her mind back there. There was no noticeable improvement in her condition. Every passing day not only steadfastly replicated the previous day but also hinted that there would soon be no more repetitions.

She should not die like this, with such an untimely departure leaving behind the unbearable burden of her absence. On the morning of a troubled night, Pavel Pavlovich Antipov came to the clinic. 'Agripina,' he asked, 'Would you like us to go to Istanbul once again?' When he saw her blushing smile, as if she had heard something obscene, he ruled it to be a hidden 'yes'. He felt that he should do such a thing so that his wife's death, even if it were to occur before its time and much before his own, would at least be more dignified than the life she had so far led. To this end, in spite of all the delay, he had to provide her with the opportunity to avenge the pain of those earlier days, by returning years later to the city where at such a young age she had been so scorned, trampled, belittled and defeated. He wanted to make sure this incomplete and stumpy tale would be completed in peace; while he spread out in front of her the pleasures she had once been deprived of, the luxuries she had not tasted, and the bliss she had not felt. He had made up his mind. Agripina should spend the rest of her life not at this clinic but in Istanbul, only this time not as a refugee or deportee or stranger or guest or tenant. She should not be in the others' Istanbul but her own. To make her a home there, he would first make her a homeowner.

***

Thus they arrived. They arrived but at first glance neither the city could recognize them nor they the city. Having no desire to spend a day more than necessary in hotel rooms, Pavel Pavlovich Antipov started immediately to search for a suitable house. He did not yet know if the local laws permitted foreigners to acquire property or not. However, given that there were so many people in the world willing to tamper with the gage of their nature for personal benefit or illicit gain, he did not have the slightest doubt that he would somehow find a way. Nonetheless, the opportunity that presented itself within ten days was more than he could wish for. By chance a usurer they sat next to during a dinner reception, hosted by the owners of their hotel, mentioned how the construction of an apartment building in an exclusive neighbourhood of the city had recently been halted midway due to the unexpected bankruptcy of the owner. Pavel Pavlovich Antipov did not miss this opportunity that had come his way.

The following morning, the first thing he did was to go visit the construction site. The construction was not, as the usurer had recounted, halfway through. As a matter of fact, there was nothing there except a pit, but this was better, much better. He then started to track down the White Russians who had shared the same fate with them in the 1920s but had stayed to become Turkish citizens. Realizing the advantage of having the name of a Turkish citizen on paper to ease the legal procedures, but unable to trust anyone not from the same origin as him, after some research, he finally reached an agreement with a reticent couple who had become Turkish citizens and made a living selling delicate lampshades at a dingy shop in Asmalımescit. A company in which the couple had no shares provided a front to cover the ownership of the apartment building. Without a single false move Pavel Pavlovich Antipov calculated everything precisely and paid abundantly. His chequebook speeded up transactions that would have otherwise taken a long time and cause ample trouble. For an architect he hired an Armenian Istanbulite whose family he had conducted business with in France. He had also left a large chunk of money to his mistress there, to make the lies he told her more convincing. Hardly did he complain. For the first time in years, he was content spending money freely without any reservation. Whilst he did not withhold any expense, he did want control over all the expended materials. Even though he did at times consult his wife about the trimmings such as the gates, the garden walls, the iron grills of the balcony, the frontal decorations, the curl of the stairs or the marble used in the entrance, all in all he did what he wanted.

Agripina did not seem interested in such details anyhow. Ever since her arrival in Istanbul, she spent her time either watching the sea from the window of the hotel room or listening to the squabbles of her Alsatian companion and her Algerian maid who did not even for a moment leave her side. The expression on her face while looking at the waters of the Bosphorus was no different from that which she had worn whilst gazing at the vineyards from the window of the clinic in France. Not only did she seem unmoved at being back at the place where they had buried their baby but she occasionally confused which city she currently was in. And yet, she did not look unhappy either. Like a timid, tremulous raincloud she floated above Istanbul, ready to shed tears but impossible to touch.

For Pavel Pavlovich Antipov, his wife's insulation from the world was an indication not of her illness but her innocence. Many a time at the front, he had witnessed how soldiers of different nationalities retained a common belief that if there was even one innocent person among them, this would spare them all from a portentous end. He too sought refuge in his wife with a similar conviction.

When the outside walls were painted in ashen tones, the window frames and iron grills of the balcony in two shades of grey and the fine decorations on the double-panelled entrance door completed, the apartment building emerged in all its dazzling beauty. The most striking characteristic of the building was that no two storeys were alike, having been constructed upon Pavel Pavlovich Antipov's insistence in Art Nouveau style, even though no longer in fashion. As if to compensate for their lack of balconies on the facade, the flats at the entrance had much larger windows than the rest. The balconies too changed from one floor to the next. Those of the second floor extended outward in a semi-circle, while the balconies on the third floor were buried so far inside the building one could easily sit in the apartments without worrying about being seen from the outside. Instead of an iron-railing, the sides of the balconies on the fourth floor had been surrounded by a stone wall adorned with floral reliefs and two large marble flowerpots on either end. So striking were the differences that one could not help but think the residents of the building shared the same space without living in the same place.

In front, the relief between the windows of the first and second floors was particularly eye-catching. Here placed within a circle was a small-headed, large-bodied peacock. The five feathers of the peacock, one on top, two to the left and two to the right, pointed in five different directions. Suitably large eyes were drawn at the tips of the feathers and the eyes in turn were adorned with thin, puny lines resembling eyelashes. Contrary to the feathers, one heading to the sky and the other four in four separate directions, the head of the peacock was bent down. At the spot on the tip of its feet, which it looked towards, embroidered within an oval frame and barely visible from the street were the first letters of the names of the husband and wife.

'What will you name it?' he asked when he showed her the apartment building with pride. A jasmine-scented offshore breeze sweetly blew in between them and gave voice to things Pavel Pavlovich Antipov could not express: 'Agripina, here is your baby with eyes the colour of ashes. She'll always love you very much but will not expect in return more love than you are capable of giving. She'll solely and completely be yours but will not demand dedication from you. Never will she fuss, cry, get sick or die. Nor will she ever grow up. She'll not abandon you as long as you do not leave her. She'll be referred to as whatever you say. What name will you give your baby?'

Agripina Fyodorovna Antipova listened with excitement to what the offshore breeze murmured. She remained pensive for a moment and then, with a spark in her eyes exclaimed: 'Bonbon!'

Pavel Pavlovich Antipov stared at his wife puzzled. Then he must have concluded that she had not understood what they were talking about for he repeated the question, this time adding in a few suggestions himself. She could choose names that alluded to their motherland; or a word that would remind them of the Istanbul of the 1920s, as a tribute to those days. Or, even better, she could select names that could demonstrate how very different their second arrival in the city had been from the first. 'Triumph' would be highly befitting, for instance, as would 'Pride', 'Blessed', 'Zenith', 'Memory', 'Escapade', or 'Saga'. It could just as well be the 'Forget Me Not' apartment. 'The Reuniting', 'The Placatory' or 'The Appeasing.' There were hundreds of meaningful names with which they could crown their success, and should indeed do so, since there was so much effort, suffering and also money behind it. Agripina Fyodorovna Antipova listened to her husband's soliloquy with a docile smile. But each time her response remained the same.

★★★

When Pavel Pavlovich Antipov and Agripina Fyodorovna Antipova moved into Flat Number 10 of Bonbon Palace on September 1st 1966, the entire sky was filled with plump, lead-coloured clouds. The whole world had assumed the same insipid tone as if God had run out of bonbons with coloured wrappers. After giving the flat a cursory look over, Agripina, trailed by her Algerian maid and the sullen Alsatian companion, headed directly to the balcony. She opened the double-panelled door and stepped out. The city was spread out right in front of her. It had changed...and how... She looked at Istanbul with the malicious pleasure of a woman who years later encounters the rival whose beauty she once secretly envied, now aged, decrepit and shrivelled. Then a strong northeast wind blew, her own image confusedly crossed her mind and her eyes became misty but she still continued to smile. At that moment, Pavel Pavlovich Antipov watched from afar with pleasure the smile that had settled on his wife's face. She looked so content! There, it had been worth it, worth returning to this city after all this time. Men, especially those like Pavel Pavlovich Antipov who expect life's uncertainties to confirm their truths, relish in the satisfaction of their women as proof of their own success. Looking at his wife that Istanbul night, as a strong northeast wind replaced the jasmine-scented offshore breeze of the past few days, Pavel Pavlovich Antipov too felt proud of himself.

★★★

Time proved Pavel Pavlovich Antipov right. His wife died

before him. The Alsatian companion and the Algerian maid returned to France soon thereafter. Yet Pavel Pavlovich Antipov did not go anywhere. After losing Agripina, he lived alone in Flat Number 10 of Bonbon Palace for another two years. When he died, he was neither a year more nor less than one hundred years old.

In 1972 Bonbon Palace was inherited by Pavel Pavlovich Antipov's daughter, born out of wedlock. Valerie Germain, who lived in a large house in the Paris countryside with her husband and four children, the last of which she had given birth to when forty, did not attend the funeral of her father whose presence had been nothing but an echoless void for her. Not only did she not visit the grave where he was laid next to Agripina, she also remained equally indifferent to this unexpected inheritance. Neither then nor later did she feel the need to come and see the building. Renting out all the flats with the aid of a rather greedy but just as competent Turkish real estate agent and managing the business from afar, she did not interfere with anything as long as money was regularly deposited into her bank account.

Less than three weeks after she had rented out Flat Number 10, however, she received a letter gracefully penned in proper French. It was from the tenant. She was informing her that the personal belongings of Pavel Pavlovich Antipov and his wife were still there. Since the furniture was rather large in quantity and value, she indicated, it would be worthwhile for the owner to come and see things for herself. However, if this was not possible, she could find a shipping company to transport it all to France and help with the arrangements.

In her response, Valerie Germain thanked the tenant for concern she had shown and expressed her sorrow for having inadvertently caused such trouble, but then indicated in no uncertain terms that she was not interested in receiving any of the mentioned items. Her tenant could choose among these any she wanted to keep for herself, to use them as she saw fit, or dispense them to others; she could then throw the rest in the garbage. The decision was hers. Of course, if any expense would be incurred in moving the furniture out of the house, she was ready to deduct it from the rent.

Another letter arrived soon after. The woman in Flat Number 10 stated that she could not bring herself to throw the belongings into the garbage, and that she believed her landowner would agree with her if and when she saw the furniture herself. Volunteering to safe keep them for her until then, she had attached to the end of her letter a list of one hundred and eighty items describing each and every one in detail. Also included in the letter was a black-and-white photograph. It was a picture of Bonbon Palace, probably taken by Pavel Pavlovich Antipov right after the construction was completed but before anyone had moved in.

The apartment building appeared colourless and soulless in the picture. There was not a single person in it, neither on its windows or balconies, nor on the sidewalks or the streets. It resembled a child of war with no living relatives and no eyes to watch her lonely growth. It looked equally placeless. One could not get a clue about what the city surrounding it, if there was one, looked like. It could be anywhere in the world and of any time other than the present...

Valerie Germain liked this picture. For a long time she kept it posted on her refrigerator along with shopping lists, invoices to be paid, calorie counts, food recipes, vacation postcards and the pictures her children had drawn. Then, the children grew up, her age advanced and she lost the picture of Bonbon Palace sometime, somewhere.

AND TODAY...

Flat Number 3: Hairdressers Cemal and Celal

'Oh God, what wrong have we done to deserve this smell? We literally live in garbage. It won't be long before we start scrabbling around like roosters.'

It was none other than Cemal uttering these words and whenever Cemal said anything at the beauty parlour, female laughter, some genuine, others out of politeness, would immediately follow. That, however, was not the case this time. On the contrary, as soon as he stopped, a heavy silence descended upon the place.

Here such pure silences were rare as rubies. For silence to occur, the cessation of many street-sounds had to miraculously coincide. These included the ear-splitting horns of the cars turning down Cabal Street to avoid the traffic jam of the avenue, only to clog the road here too, and the yelling of both the watermelon vendor at his stand on the corner and his competitor circling the neighbourhood in the run-down pickup truck (whose loudspeaker could be heard from the same place every twenty minutes)... Not forgetting the shrieks of the children filling up the hole-in-the-wall playground squeezed in between the apartment buildings, comprising of two swings, one seesaw and a rickety sheet-iron slide that when heated up in the sun burnt the bottoms of those sliding on it... All of these parties had to agree among themselves to concurrently hush.

Since the sources of noise inside the beauty parlour were just as plentiful as those in the world outside, for a true silence to rule even for a short period of time, here too, a number of highly extraordinary events had to happen. The television in the corner which was constantly on and always showing the same music channel, had to fall silent even if only for a moment – a chance event that could only happen during the few minutes when either the lights went out, kicking in the generator, or one of the customers sat on the remote-control by mistake. The bellowing air from the small hairdryers, the monotonous hum of the large dryers placed on each customer's head like the transparent turban of a grand vizier, the constantly bubbling *samovar* in the kitchen, the mechanical hum of the ceiling fan, the crackle of the aluminum folios wrapped on one by one to colour and highlight streaks of hair, the splashing water when it was time to wash the hair, the nagging of the customer who found the water put on her hair suddenly either too hot or too cold, the itchy feeling buzz of the manicure file upon the nails, the sizzling of the wax emanating from the body hair removal room, the rustling of the broom and duster brought out continually to sweep the shorn hair, and the chats ebbing or flowing with the inclusion of new participants, often never to be concluded or completed…for there to be a genuine silence in the beauty parlour, all these had to simultaneously stop and stay this way. Of course, on top of it all, Cemal would have to stop talking.

However, the world is full of miracles. At least Bonbon Palace is. All of a sudden lumpy clouds of silence of unknown origin crowded into the room through the wide open windows and, like a muffler, softly spread onto all the sources of noise. In that flawless silence Celal, the second hairdresser in the salon, sighed gratefully. He had never liked the uproar and commotion or the noisy chatter that went on day and night but there was nothing he could do about it. After all, the one who triggered this wearisome *katzenjammer* he had to suffer all day long, was none other than his twin, born of the very same egg as he had been. Cemal talked so much. He always had a desire to talk and also a topic to talk about. He chatted with the customers all day long (not minding his broken accent in Turkish which he still had not been able to get rid of), kept an eye on the television to vilify every single music clip, incessantly scolded the apprentices, eavesdropped on others' conversations to put in his two cents' worth…and he did all these things, not in any particular order but all at once…

Still Celal could not get angry at him. Like many who believe their younger sibling's childhood to have been more difficult than theirs, Celal nurtured a tender love toward his three and a half minutes younger brother. The twins had been separated when they were children. Celal had stayed in the village with his mother; in a suffocating yet affectionate, limited yet protected womb, always where he belonged, with and within his own roots. Cemal, on the other had, had gone to Australia with his father; uninhibited yet unshielded, in a boundless but entirely solitary universe, communicating with an estranged language, always half-settled, half-nomadic. Upon Cemal's unexpected return to Turkey, their harshly parted paths had crossed once again after a youth spent apart. Their relatives had all presumed that the reason behind this sudden return could be nothing but 'homesickness' and had therefore forgiven Cemal for not coming back years ago to attend his mother's funeral. The truth is, the state of affairs in a country always tinkers with the perceptions of its citizens. The natives of less developed countries love to love those who, after spending years in a developed country and despite having the option to remain there, come instead to live with them. As soon as he had returned to Istanbul, Cemal too had benefited from that distinctive love reserved for those such as Christians who convert to Islam, foreigners who settle in Turkey, tourists who spend their vacations here every year and above all, Western brides married to Turks who are willing to bestow Turkish names to their children.

Be that as it may, Cemal actually considered Australia his country and did not much like either Turkey or the Turks, especially Turkish women! With their narrow shoulders, generous hips and frames they let carelessly widen from top to toe, each one was a small, unkempt pear. Besides which, they were so conservative about their hair! Always the same colours, the same cuts. He had not yet met a Turkish woman who would ask for her hair to be cut as short as a man's. It was so strange for those who could not tolerate the presence of even a single hair on their bodies to not be able to come in to have their hair cut short. Oh, no, Cemal was not happy to be here. The only reason he did not pack up and leave this very moment was because he knew too well that his twin was effectively nailed down in Turkey. Indeed, Cemal was in Turkey for the sake of his remaining half, the person whose name he had been separated from by a single letter of the alphabet, the resolute breach in his highly irresolute soul. If only he could tear him away from this country, Cemal thought he would surely take his twin to Australia. However, as he could sense deep down that Celal would not come with him, and even if he did, could not survive anywhere other than his own country, Cemal had no other alternative than to gather all his belongings and savings and after all these years come to settle in Istanbul.

As for Celal, though he would never be able to confess this to anyone, a deep distress had enveloped him the moment he had been re-united with his twin. Standing at the international airport terminal, he had stared, first with astonishment and then embarrassment, at the curly-haired, large-nosed, big-bellied man running to him with open arms and cries of ecstasy. His outfit was completely bizarre – a T-shirt adorned with kangaroos, a *legume*-green pair of shorts and those leather sandals that thrust his pink, hairy, ugly feet into plain sight – and his movements hugely vivacious. He made dozens of gestures just to say a single word, forever running into people and knocking things over. That he was so garrulous himself was hardly surprising. He made whopping promises that they would never again be parted, squealing with tears in his eyes about ridiculous plans and, damn it, never shutting up. If one took the things he said seriously, it seemed as if he wanted to use the money he had brought along as capital in a joint endeavor. Amidst the bear hugs and gluey kisses, he had waved his arms left and right like an inexperienced tightrope acrobat trying to regain his balance to stay on the rope, yelling in the middle of the airport, 'Here are the magnificent twins! It doesn't really matter what we do. So long as we don't part again. If we make it, we'll do so together, if we perish, we perish together!'

Speaking of perishing, Celal in his embarrassment had felt like he had already started the process and silently wished that, if disappearing from the airport was not a feasible option, he could disappear from the face of the earth. Instead, all he could do was to watch with deep astonishment and even deeper distress this utterly unfamiliar and stranger-than-a-stranger, exact replica of his.

Though Celal was far from being the type to plunge into risky businesses, his twin's excitement must have softened his heart for he could not put up much resistance. When it was time to figure out what common job they could find, a startling fact awaited them: during the time they had been apart and entirely unaware of what the other was doing, they had, albeit for different reasons and through separate venues, undertaken the same profession. Celal was a hairdresser and Cemal had also spent years in a unisex haircutting salon. The coincidence had instantly doubled Cemal's unrestrained exuberance. 'Twin hairdressers!' he had shouted with pride, and then, as if stating something different, had echoed himself with even bigger excitement: 'Hairdresser twins!' Looking at the contentment on his face one imagined that each and every item on his wish list had been granted. While his sluggish brother kept calculating the 'pluses' and 'minuses' of opening a beauty parlour, Cemal had already taken the plunge and started to look for a place. That he did not have a clue what sort of a city Istanbul was did not seem to trouble him at all as he rushed to find a place by himself, and before the week was over he had already rented a flat, paying one year's rent in advance. It was an apartment in one of the many illegally constructed buildings on the steep plains overlooking the Bosphorus, with a wonderful view of the river. However, the moment Celal saw the flat, he struggled in vain to explain to his twin that the panoramic view, which he could tell was the main reason his twin had rented the place, would mean nothing to their future customers.

Still they moved in and had no customers for months. Then heavy downpours started and the main room got flooded, four times with water and once by creatures which they guessed, from the traces left behind, were street cats. At the end of the fifth month, they finally scavenged, along with the money left over from Cemal's hasty investment, whatever soaked and cat-hair-covered furniture they could salvage and decided to try once again – only this time Celal was to choose the place. After searching for a long time and carefully weighing all the choices under the present conditions, his choice was the flat on the garden floor of an ashen, fairly old and unkempt but obviously once grandiose apartment building, located in a rather lively neighbourhood on a well-trodden street that opened up to a busy avenue.

'It's so odd, isn't it?' said Cemal on their first work day here. 'I'm an incessant chatterer but I went and found a place in a lifeless neighbourhood. You're always quiet, yet you chose such a noisy place. So we're opposites not only of each other but of ourselves as well!'

Just the same, their opposing characters were not reflected in the fifty by sixty centimetre photograph, enlarged and framed right across the entrance upon Cemal's insistence, taken at the Marmara Region 19th Annual Hairdressers' Competition that they had entered three years ago. On that day, despite the fact that Cemal had worn a T-shirt with carroty-parrots on it and Celal a matte olive-green shirt, both had ended up competing with the same hair model and getting eliminated before the finals. The hairstyle they both liked the most involved a strand of copper red hair from the nape of the neck being curled, thickly braided and loosely fastened into a bun. The similarity between the photographs of the two of them creating the same bun on different models at different times was startling. The customers loved to keep looking at the two photographs to try to locate the differences between them, one by one and over and over. Repetition is, after all, an intrinsic part of beauty parlours, there everything and everyone relentlessly keeps repeating themselves. Time, hurriedly chasing its own tail outside, gets chubby in here as it slows down; like dirty gum stuck to the bottom of your shoe, time here lengthens when pulled, lengthens when pulled, lengthens... The best thing about repetition is familiarity. When surrounded by repetition, one feels safe and secure as if in a well-known place amidst old buddies. Women's hairdressers owe their languor, a quality not usually welcome in any other workplace, to the constant turn of their wheel of repetition. Everything the customers do in here, not only have they certainly done many times before, but are also able to repeat infinite times in the future. Though all the beauty parlour catalogues are identical, each and every one still gets looked through again and again. The women's journals being passed around are never read until the end, they are just desolately thumbed instead. No one feels there is any harm in going back to the same sections again and again. The women in front of the mirror keep scrutinizing each other; keeping at it even though there is barely a change in the other person's appearance from one glance to the next. Newspapers are read not page by page but instead endlessly scanned; the tea they serve always remains half drunk, gets cold, is replenished, stays in the half-full cup, gets cold once again; the continuing chats get cut here and there, topics keep changing, the same things are talked about repeatedly, the same music videos appearing on television are watched in bits and pieces; the same singers and songs are subjected to scrutiny over and over again, to the same comments...nothing has to be completed. Life is a series of perpetual repetitions with no beginning or ending. Though the world may have a bottom to reach and the Judgement Day a cut-off date, you can be sure that Israfil will not blow his sur while you are sitting in the beauty parlour. An earthquake can happen in Istanbul at any moment, any second, but definitely not while you are at the beauty parlour. Not in there.

Distinguishing the differences between the two photographs on the wall was a recurring delight for the women customers. The female gaze has, after all, a predilection to identify differences before similarities. For three seconds show a man the picture of five beautiful, young models in blue bathing suits and ponytails lined up by a pool. What he sees would probably be this: a ponytailed, young and highly good-looking model in a bathing suit x5. Then show the same picture to a woman. What she in turn sees would probably be: x5 models by the pool, some with good postures, some not; some carrying the ponytail well, others not; the blue bathing suit fitting the figures of some well, others not; some are more good-looking than others.

Be that as it may, when it came to the photographs of Celal and Cemal taken at the Marmara Region's 19th Traditional Hairdresser's Contest, even the female gaze would have a hard time detecting the nuances. Leaving aside their clothes and Cemal's silver accessories, they were identical, right up to their facial expressions. From the way they leaned their heads sideways to the angle with which they bent over the models whose hair they fixed, from the way they crossed their eyebrows to emphasize how seriously they took what they were doing to how they bent their fingers... Still, there was a small difference that did not escape the eye: Cemal lightly bit his lower lip – perhaps because he knew he was not as good a hairdresser as his brother, or he was not as enamoured with the thickly braided buns with the curled strand of copper red hair from the nape of the neck as he had thought. Alternatively, perhaps all he could think of at that moment was finishing up what he was doing so he could go and get something to eat. How Cemal, with his infatuation with food and his non-stop consumption of all sorts of pastries since returning to Turkey, managed to maintain exactly the same figure as Celal, who ate as little as a bird and basically survived on soup, was a mystery even the regular customers of the beauty parlour did not think they could ever solve.

Yet the similarities between the twins came to an end when you considered the style with which each executed the many tasks that their jobs involved. It was due to this that Cemal's customers differed from those of Celal. Of course, it did happen that on certain days, a particular customer preferred one twin to their usual choice of the other. Even those who loved to shoot the breeze with Cemal made sure at certain times that Celal fixed their hair. When it came to significant days like engagements, weddings, celebrations and other important appointments, the preference of all customers was for Celal. In addition to the special occasions, he was also the unerring choice for emergency situations. Those who had messed around with their hair at home and ended up with it scruffily cut, looking lightning-struck due to a cheap perm, turned into a bird's nest, dyed the colour of corn tassel when attempting to lighten with bleach or dried out for following word-of-mouth folk remedies...hair done in the morning, hated at night, sacrificed to the careless experiments of novice hairdressers...all of these disasters were delegated to Celal's adroit hands. In such difficult situations his even temperament that was not at all like his brother's went into effect, enabling him to calm down even the most distressed of customers. It was unanimously agreed that there couldn't be any hair in so calamitous condition that he could not save it. There was never a problem between the brothers concerning which of them should look after which customers. An unspoken agreement reigned here as well; no one took offense as long as the accepted distribution of roles remained intact. Most of the time they would understand what a woman's concern was within the first two minutes after she had entered through the door and they would greet her accordingly. If the arriving customer blundered in roughly enough to make the chimes on the door jangle and with a hopeless look on her face, Celal would greet her, gauging the size of the problem awaiting him all the while. Whereas it would be Cemal's turn to welcome in customers whose situations were less of an emergency. He would stop the conversation he would most probably be having and bend down to greet the customer with levels of politeness which he could never get right; never forgetting, if the person was an acquaintance, to throw in a few reproachful words about how long it had been since they last saw her. If it were up to Cemal, he would require every woman to spend at least an hour every day at the beauty parlour.

Yet there was one person who had from the very beginning had her hair done exclusively by Celal – someone who relished the silence that had just descended in the salon as much as he did: Madame Auntie. This tiny, elderly woman living alone on the top floor of Bonbon Palace at Flat Number 10 came once every two weeks without fail to have her thin, sparse hair trimmed and, once a month, coloured platinum yellow. That specific colour, however, had become a source of worry to the hearts and a balm to the tongues of the regular customers of the beauty parlour. They thought she was too old for platinum yellow or else platinum yellow was too much for her age. She was seventy-eight years old, certainly an inappropriate age to be a blonde. Given that she still chose to be blonde, it was considered that she should at least wipe off that serious look, not be so grave or such a model of dignity. If she was instead a witty, at least a little goofy, garrulous and cheerful old woman with eyes twinkling the traces of the bohemian life she had once led, paying no heed to moral prohibitions or to what anyone said, then her hair would have been appropriate. Yet here she was, as far removed from being 'a slacker' as a proper granny, as straight as if she had been drawn by a ruler, as heavy as cast metal, and, to top it all, platinum blonde. That was simply too much for the regular customers of the beauty parlour.

It was too much because, in the coded world of colours and hair colours, the rules are clear-cut. Yellow has little to do with respectability. A blonde woman can pierce through this rule on only one condition: if she is a genuine blonde! Originality is a problem peculiar to blondes. The brunettes, red heads and albinos can have their hair coloured as often as they like and in as many different shades as they please and yet never have to encounter fifty times a day the question as to whether this is indeed their natural colour. The desire to be blonde makes women predisposed to be sly and forces them to lie. Yet their attempts at fraud are foiled very quickly. While they are busy convincing people, truth insidiously grins from their roots. Blondness makes the enthusiast dishonest and the genuine anti-social.

Yet neither her hair colour nor her wearing make-up at this age weakened the respect Madame Auntie awakened in those around her. It was evident from the first day that she, with her solemnity and taciturn nature, would be Celal's customer and always remain so. If judged by the gleam in their eyes upon seeing each other, they got along fabulously yet, given they rarely opened their mouths to utter a few words, it was hard to figure out how they had bonded. If it were up to them, words should have been rationed to people every month. Everyone should have known that words uttered are like drinking water and tilled soil, a scarce resource, and whenever one spoke, they depleted their limited share.

However, this afternoon the tranquility of this silence-loving pair could only last four minutes. Suddenly, the door was pushed, the bell jolted. In accompaniment to the watermelon vendor's mechanical voice, which made him sound as if he was firing orders, a young woman entered the beauty parlour with quick yet unhurried steps. Three indolent women, all Cemal's customers, all with leopard-patterned plastic smocks tied to their necks and lined up next to one another on the swivelling chairs in front of the wall-length mirror, turned their heads with all the rollers, hairpins, hair caps and aluminum folios to give the newcomer a once over, looking from top to bottom. Upon realizing who she was, with a deeper curiosity, they eyed her up again, this time looking from bottom to top. This was a historic moment, for up until now the Blue Mistress had never set foot in the beauty parlour.

Celal stole a look at the door and went back to work. At that moment, he was interested in no hair other than the platinum yellow strands of his friend; whoever this young woman might be, she did not look like his type of customer anyhow. Cemal, however, was neither as indifferent nor as ignorant as his twin. On the contrary, from the gossip lavishly dispensed at the beauty parlour from morning until dark, he had distilled ample information about the Blue Mistress. He knew, for instance, that she was only twenty-two years old. He had also heard how a couple of weeks ago, upon being harassed by a man at the entrance to their street, she had poured all the contents of the garbage bag she had taken out to dump over the head of her assailant. Furthermore, he was also informed that she had picked a fight with the exceedingly religious apartment manager, Hadji Hadji, who, when dividing the apartment's joint water bill among all the flats according to the number of people residing in each unit, had prepared her invoice for not one but two persons, It was scarcely news to anyone that although the Blue Mistress had leased Flat Number 8 by herself stating she would live alone, a sour-faced, olive oil merchant old enough to be her father lived with her at least four days a week. Cemal knew all this and was dying to find out more.

Turning over his highlighting brush to the pimpled apprentice, as he veered toward the door with a stuck-up smile on his face, he took a full-length shot of the unexpected visitor. You could hardly say that her body was great; though not quite a pear, it was still pear-like. She was wearing a long gauzy dress with straps that covered up too much for a mistress. However, under the sunlight trickling through the glass door, her legs were entirely visible as she had not worn an underskirt. It looked as if she simultaneously wanted to hide and expose her body; or perhaps she was just confused...and her face... her face was the most interesting part. Some people's faces are like magnets covered with skin. All the ins and outs, ups and downs, core and gist of their personality reside there. They think with their faces; converse, promenade, quarrel, get hungry, feel happy, love or make love with their faces. Their bodies are necessary, albeit unimpressive pedestals, merely added on to carry their faces. Such people are essentially walking faces. Accordingly, they can never hide their feelings away. Whatever they feel gets reflected, totally and immediately, upon their faces. The petite, pale face of the Blue Mistress, adorned with an azure *hizma*, screamed out that, right at that moment, she was trying hard not to show her distress. Cemal took a step toward her and though this was not at all his habit, shook hands with the Blue Mistress, flagrantly violating women's hairdressers' custom of greeting customers. Like all repressed homosexuals who generally got along well with the delicate sex but also somewhat sneered at them, he too was particularly interested in those women who are partly envied, partly hated by other women.

Trying to ignore the inquisitive, impish stares directed at her from different angles of the beauty parlour, the Blue Mistress moved with brisk, uncertain steps toward the swivel chair Cemal pointed out to her. As she took her place in front of the long, wide mirror with other women, the looks directed at her folded into one another and multiplied. The blonde with a slight cast in her eye, the jittery chain-smoking brunette who kept shaking her pedicured toes with cotton pieces stuck in between each one, the short and plump gingerhead sitting with two thick carroty lines on top of her eyes having her eyebrows coloured along with her hair, and finally the elf-like elderly lady at the very corner; all stared at her as if waiting to be introduced.

The pimpled apprentice tied the leopard-patterned, plastic smock with dubious stains onto the neck of the Blue Mistress, careful to touch her as little as possible. It was an agonizing misfortune for the apprentice to have to work at a beauty parlour at this sensitive stage of his life, hearing all sorts of obscene jokes from women about the way his face divulged the sins his hand must be committing at nights. As the teenage boy backed off with unsteady steps, he did not notice the cat that had without a sound snuck in through the open window. All eyes were turned toward the animal when it let out a mighty 'meow' upon having its tail trampled.

It was a thick-coated, grim-faced, strapping cat as black as tar: one of those that looked upon every human they saw with narrowed eyes as if there had been a bloody fight between cats and humans from time immemorial. Still, as the round strand of hair starting from the sides of its nose down under its chin looked as if someone had dipped it in a bowl of yogurt, it had a cute side in spite of everything.

'Come, Garbage! Come here, you nuisance!' Cemal called out when he realized that the Blue Mistress was fond of the cat.

'Why do you call the cat "Garbage"?' asked the Blue Mistress. The animal had immediately sensed who to get attention from and started rubbing against her feet. The Blue Mistress grabbed it with her two hands and lifted it up, directing the same question this time to the cat in the sugary syrupy voice women use when admiring babies: 'Why do they call you Garbage? Tell me why, my beauty? How could one call such a beautiful cat Garbage?'

'Perhaps because this Mister Garbage never leaves the garbage dump,' Cemal remarked with joy. Now that Garbage provided a means for him to communicate with the Blue Mistress, it seemed cuter to Cemal than ever. 'There is probably no other street cat in all of Istanbul as fortunate as this one. Not that he has an outstanding beauty, look at his face for God's sake. Have you ever seen a cat with such dirty looks? It is as if he was going to be a snake but could not find the appropriate skin. But he still finds a way to get people to like him. Does he have an irresistible charm or what? How does he manage to wrangle food out of whomever he visits? But do you think he'll be satisfied? Never! He eats his fill and then ends up in his kingdom: the garbage dump. I swear I would not have believed it if I hadn't seen it with my own eyes. We had just rented this place, were in the middle of the final preparations, dog-tired from working all day long and hungry like wolves. We decided to order food from the chicken place. You know how huge their portions are, don't you? Rice, salad, fried potatoes, all come heaped high. Well, let me cut to the chase. There was some mix-up and they had sent an extra chicken. We didn't return it as we thought we could eat that one as well. Of course, we couldn't. Everyone could barely finish what they had in front of them. Especially Celal, he pecked at it like a bird. As we were eating, guess who picked up the scent and showed up? I didn't know then that they called him "Garbage", but along he comes, begging food so desperately you'd think the poor thing had been starving for days. So we put the extra chicken in front of him and may the curse of God befall me if I'm lying, he gobbled that chicken down so ferociously you'd think a pack of Dobermans were chasing him. Not a single bone was left behind. Can you imagine, he devoured a plate of chicken heaped full right in front of our eyes. Back then the "Cat Prophet" lived in Flat Number 2. Had you heard of him? Another nut! He had some twenty, thirty cats. The whole place smelt of cat piss. Still, even that was better than the stink of this garbage. We were talking about that before you arrived. I was just saying to Celal, we live in so much garbage, we'll soon start to peck·like roosters. Right, Celal?'

Celal shook his head in agreement.

'After all that he had wolfed down, this Mister Garbage here went after the cat food of the Cat Prophet, but her tribe must have given him a sound beating for he returned with his tail between his legs for our leftovers. We put out the fried potatoes which he pretended not to like much but he finished them off all the same. At that point we all stopped working to watch the animal; we placed bets on when he was going to explode.'

Not only the women lined-up by the mirror but also the manicurist and the apprentices who had heard this story at least forty times were all ears listening to Cemal. He may not have been as fine a hairdresser as his brother, but when it came to garrulousness, he beat everyone hands down. His linguistic aptitude was amazing. If he were picked up from here and dropped off in a country he could not even place on a map, he would learn their language in a flash just to be able to understand what was being spoken around him and then put in his two cents worth. Likewise, in just five years he had been able to repair his Turkish, which had lost its lustre during the long years he spent in Australia and had polished it brand new. The only problem was his telltale accent. However, Celal was not certain as to whether his three and a half minutes younger brother actually failed to get rid of his accent or deliberately kept it intact thinking the customers liked it more this way.

'He ate and ate, then got up stretching. The animal had turned into a giant stomach! He couldn't even walk, dragging along that tummy. We dashed after him, following him outside where he jumped on the wall of this side garden…and what a jump! He had become so heavy that his belly got caught and he almost fell down. We thought he would curl up somewhere and sleep for at least two days. No way! Instead he leaped to the other side of the wall. You know those garbage bags they leave there? Alas, we live in a garbage dump! Anyway this one had found a bunch of fish heads. I honestly have no idea what else he could have eaten that day. We felt sick as we watched him, you know. I swear I have been frightened of this cat ever since that day. We've heard a lot about cats who eat their owners when hungry but this Garbage here, he could gobble all of us down even when full. What's more, I bet he would polish it all off with what he finds in the garbage!'

'I swear he's understood all we've been saying about him,' exclaimed the plump gingerhead with a frozen face, afraid of getting wrinkles on her forehead if she laughed.

'Let him understand. Is it all lies? He has a trash can instead of a stomach! Hence the name: Garbage!' grumbled Cemal as he shook the hairdryer in his hand towards the cat carefully watching him behind narrowed eyes.

The hairdryer! Knowing that being subjected to the breath of this howling monster was worse than falling into a bucket full of water, the cat took off in a blink from the lap of the Blue Mistress and leapt onto the open window. After staying there for an instant to give those in the beauty parlour a final and unhappy once-over, he jumped towards the nearest empty space like a stuffed toy filled with swagger instead of stuffing. However, before his paws reached the garden, something weird landed on his head: a cerulean child's dress, adorned with many tiny mermaid figures ruffled all around and a starched collar, which descended like a dry leaf or a piece of paper with an almost surreal slowness from the top floor of Bonbon Palace, for approximately five seconds, landing just moments away from the soil right on top of the cat who had cut across its path. Both landed on the ground at the same time.

'Oh, look, look! It's raining clothes from above!' shouted the manicurist in excitement, having been rummaging through the shelf in front of the window to find the Number 113 burgundy nail polish.

Cemal, the plump ginger-head, the blonde with a slight cast in her eye and the apprentices all dashed over to the window in an instant. A little later, upon their insistence the Blue Mistress came also with reluctant steps and the jittery brunette limped over trying not to step on her pedicured feet. Clothes were indeed raining from above; children's clothes in all types and colours. Judging by the crowd of eight to ten people gathered on the sidewalk, there were other spectators of this unexpected show. All had turned their heads up and were fixated on a single point trying to see the person throwing the clothes. Yet the perpetrator of the incident refused to reveal themself. Just a naked, unadorned, snow white woman's arm appeared at regular intervals from the window on the flat at the top floor of Bonbon Palace, on each appearance dropping yet another piece of clothing.

As the clothes rained down one after another, the manicurist stretched out of the window to catch the falling clothes with the happiness of someone trying to touch the first snow of the season. From among the dresses, socks, sweaters, shirts, pullovers, she managed to catch a resin yellow ribbon.

'Don't do that, it's not proper,' said Madame Auntie who had maintained her composure through it all. Her lifeless voice raised and lowered like a knobby wall or a jagged piece of paper.

The manicurist grumbled with the deep disappointment of being forced to be virtuous just as she had started to savour being witness to another person's insanity. With a long face, she threw the ribbon on top of the mound of clothes in the garden. It did not last long. After a minute or two the rain of clothes stopped by itself. The concluding act of the show was a royal-blue school uniform. Like some sort of coy parachute it opened up to land quietly on top of its predecessors. The windows of the top floor were noisily shut and the snow white arm retreated inside. As the spectators on the sidewalk dispersed one by one, the ones inside returned to their places as well.

'Sonny, make all of us coffee,' said Cemal to the apprentice without pimples. 'God knows, our nerves are on edge.' He collapsed onto the large couch, suddenly feeling exhausted. 'We're sick of it. Ever since we moved in here, things have been raining on our heads. The cracked woman has not left a thing in the house, she opens the windows whenever she loses her temper and "whoosh!" whatever there is comes down. One of these days she's going to throw down a TV set or something like that and whichever one of us gets it in the head will die for nothing.'

Though he remained pensive for a moment, it would not take Cemal long to collect himself together. He was always somewhat scared of sadness settling in with no palpable reason.

'So inventive! Never have I seen her throwing the same

thing twice. Celal, do you remember, she once threw down her husband's ties and they remained stuck on the rose acacia tree for days.'

A hearty response from his brother being one of the last things he expected to get at this moment, Cemal turned not to him but the customers instead: 'Celal got out and brought the ties down. He didn't let the young ones out fearing they'd break the branches of the rose acacia. He climbed himself. Had it not been for him, the stupid man's ties would have been hanging out for days.'

Celal smiled with a visible distress. 'I hope someone will gather the clothes up. It's getting dark, god knows someone could steal them,' he mumbled to escape being the focus of the conversation.

'She's gathering them up. The new cleaning lady is down there gathering all of them up. What a shame, the poor woman is red with embarrassment as if she'd thrown them down herself,' blurted out the manicurist.

'It won't be long. This one will soon quit as well,' mumbled the jittery brunette as she puffed away, examining the permanently waved strands of hair that had started to appear from under the thin rollers that the apprentice with the pimples had started to undo.

'Oh, can any cleaning lady survive Tijen? Whoever comes runs away,' remarked Cemal.

'Hygiene Tijen! Hygiene Tijen!' giggled the blonde with a cast in her eye. 'The woman hasn't stepped out of her house for exactly four months. Can you imagine? She hasn't been able to go outside for fear of catching a disease. She's utterly mad these days.'

'Come on, what do you mean by these days, for God's sake? Those who are in-the-know will tell it straight, she's always been nuts. Madam Auntie's known them since day one. Isn't it so, Madam Auntie?' shouted the manicurist. Like many of her peers, she too felt the need to raise her voice when talking to an elderly person.

All heads turned to the old woman. Actually no one knew why she was called, 'Madam Auntie'. Neither had they hitherto wondered whether she was Muslim or not, though if asked, chances are they would affirm that she was a Muslim and a Turk just like everyone else. The reason they could not help but call her 'Madam', was not because they had any doubts about her religion or citizenship, they just felt deep down that she was different, though they were unable to explain why. It was not because she was so advanced in years (though she certainly was) or because her manners were unusual (though they certainly were) that she differed from others; her oddness was less visible and yet was easily detectable. Since her nature little resembled that of the others, 'Madam' she remained. Besides, having been here for so many years she had much older roots than anyone else, she was the only one among them who was born and raised in Istanbul. While most of the neighbours were immigrants, her entire life had been spent in this neighbourhood. Unlike the others, she had not popped up out of nowhere, turning her back to a future that never came and a past that was never left behind. Here she was, neither dragged along by others nor having dragged others behind her. Her name was 'Auntie' because her very being was a residue of a past none of them had lived.

Madam Auntie lowered her head with a withered smile. She looked at her blue, purple and burgundy hands with brown spots drizzled over them. The same spots, only smaller and more faded, had been randomly sprinkled from her temples to her cheeks. If these had been the loudest colours on her skin, she would have looked, like many women her age, too old to age further. Yet the orange of her lipstick that seemed less spread on than glued on, the sunny yellowness of her leaf-shaped gold earrings, the rouge on her cheeks that made the concentric wrinkles stand out line by line, the purple tones of eye shadow that collected on her eyelids layer upon layer, the navy, blue and grey twinkle of her turquoise eyes, and then of course, the platinum yellow of her hair, had opened up wayward passageways to the unknown, behind her far from sombre appearance. Her putting on so much make-up regardless of her age had bestowed upon her a grand ridiculousness. Like all grandly ridiculous people, she too had a scary side.

As such, she was a live-wire that added extra spark to all chats. When she was around, it was hard to talk behind people's backs or get any pleasure from the art of slander or exaggeration, but the opposite was also true. The air of sobriety of Madam Auntie made the women in the beauty parlour recall the mixed pleasure they had last tasted during their high school years when they took a common stand against a very righteous teacher, while craving to impress her at the same time. Their convoluted chats were tidied up so that they reached the right consistency as they trod around and penetrated from many directions the principles she voiced and the values she defended. In addition, the pleasure they received multiplied when they were at times able to include her in their aspirations. For great is the pleasure of drawing the pure to slovenly ways, to then see how they are like everyone else, worth only as much.

The plump brunette must have felt the same for she could not resist; she backed the manicurist in a collective attempt to convince the old woman: 'They say Hygiene Tijen was no different as a young girl but definitely got worse after getting married. She's a hygiene-freak.'

'Come on, is that so bad. She's just a fastidious woman,' objected Madam Auntie making an effort to put the matter behind them.

'Auntie, this isn't fastidiousness, it's an illness,' shouted the manicurist with the courage pumped into her from the reinforcements. 'Maybe even worse. When you're ill, you know it. You go to the physician and get treated, right? There's no cure for hygiene-freaks! If there was one, Misses Tijen wouldn't put it in her mouth, she'd find it too filthy!'

'What a shame! Her child suffers the most,' said the blond with the one eye cast.

'Don't say that,' muttered Madam Auntie. 'Tijen dotes on her daughter. How can a mother possibly want any harm to come to her child?'

'Fine, Madam Auntie, but what kind of a love can we understand from it. Look, she threw down all of the poor kid's clothes,' yelled the manicurist.

'Really?' uttered Madam Auntie in astonishment.

The manicurist exclaimed with the thrill of having finally said something the old woman could not object to: 'Of course, all those clothes raining upon our heads belong to that poor kid. See that she doesn't throw out her own clothes. The woman is nutty but not insane. She's perfectly sane when it suits her interests!'

The old woman puckered her thin lips with suspicion. 'Really, so she threw out the child's clothes. Why, I wonder?'

'Why do you think, because she's nutty...'

Madam Auntie's face darkened. Realizing she had gone too far the manicurist hushed, nonetheless pleased that she had said all she wanted to say.

'Oh, what's it to us? If she's nutty, so be it!' roared Cemal. Though enjoying the gossip, he was worried the manicurist's idle talk would bother the old woman and so anger Celal. 'Are we to bother with the troubles of every nutter? Is there anything more in Istanbul other than nutters? Here we see lots of them, as many as *bulgur*. If we talk about each one of them, we'll do so until the end of our lives. Sonny, what happened to the coffees? Bring them here, we're parched.'

In an attempt to change the topic, Celal intervened. 'This garbage smell has increased again. We complained to the municipality so many times. It didn't help at all.'

'What did they say? They said they've turned the garbage collection business over to a private company,' added Cemal instantly, always fond of completing the half-uttered sentences of his twin. 'Then we found the company's phone number. They too are boors. They send the truck out right in the middle of rush hour when people are on their way back from work, as if out of spite.'

'They do come and collect the garbage regularly, though at the wrong hour. Alas however, we still haven't been able to get rid of this smell,' summed up Celal.

'Of course we can't get rid of it. With so much *bulgur* around, we can be rid of neither garbage nor cultural backwardness.' Cemal said heatedly. 'Now can you believe it, Madam Auntie. We spend our days scolding the people who leave their garbage by this wall. All the ignorant illiterate women in this neighbourhood leave their garbage by our garden wall and always the same types – so pig headed. I'm tired of repeating it! There's one in particular you especially don't want to know about. The woman's house is right at the end of the street. She doesn't mind, she walks three hundred metres every day to dump her garbage here. I long pondered why on earth someone would do such a thing. I finally came up with an explanation: there was probably a field here long before this apartment building was constructed. Back then, this woman's grandmother would dump her garbage here. Eventually, that woman had a daughter and when that one was grown up, she too would always dump her garbage at the same place. Then she too had a daughter. That's the *bulgur* I have a row with every one of God's days. Their interest in garbage is hereditary, passes from mother to daughter. A type of family tradition! Mind you, what could she do, she's just continuing whatever she has seen. But unlike her ancestors, she doesn't pour it out of a pail, she puts it in a plastic bag first. A modern *bulgur*!'

While the others laughed and Cemal grumbled, Madam Auntie shook her head deep in thought. 'But Cemal,' she said, 'this place wasn't a field in the past. Underneath this entire neighbourhood are graveyards...'

Not at all prepared for such an objection, Cemal swallowed back all the words that were getting ready to leave his tongue. As he looked around him in distress as if for help, he was waylaid by a teeny-tiny, constantly moving shadow at the bottom of the counter in front of the mirror. It was a cockroach. It had climbed the basket of rollers, moving his antenna as if listening to the chat. Good thing it had not yet attracted anyone's attention. However, if it decided to get out of the basket and walk along the counter, it would shortly be parading in front of each and every customer. Cemal grabbed the large bristle hairbrush and approached sideways in a crab-walk, at the same time talking even more excitedly so as not to let on.

'"Look here, woman!" I say, "Do I come and dump my garbage on your carpet? With what right can you leave your garbage on someone else's wall? Wait for the garbage truck to come at night, then you can take it outside your own door and the garbage men would pick it up." No, she doesn't understand at all – because of that *bulgur* I tell you!'

'What *bulgur*?' asked the Blue Mistress, popping her head up from the third page news where she was hiding from the constant looks of the apprentice with the pimples.

'Oh, don't you know my *bulgur* theory? Let me tell you right away,' said Cemal without taking his eyes off the cockroach. 'It's actually very simple. Now, is there population planning in Turkey? No! Oh God gives them to you, so keep giving birth and let them loose onto the streets. Okay, let's say you let them loose, but how are you going to feed so many kids? One person you feed with meat, five people with meat and *bulgur*, ten with only *bulgur*. OK, is this *bulgur* beneficial to human intelligence? No! You can then keep on telling the woman as many times as you want. "Come on sister, don't dump your garbage in my garden!" I keep on hollering. She stupidly stares at my face. Then the following day at the same time she comes again and dumps again as if wound up like a watch. She doesn't understand, how could she, with the brains of *bulgur*?'

Celal coughed clumsily. Cemal had received the message, but preferring the interest of the Blue Mistress over the political correctness of his twin, he did not back down.

'Just this past month I personally confronted this woman. It was an afternoon like this one; late, we were fixing a bride's hair. The bride was on one side, the relatives of the bride on the other; the bun of one was finished and the other one had just been started. We'd been up all day long, totally beat. I looked outside and saw this woman coming again wobbling with garbage bags in her hand. I opened the windows, stuck my head out, waiting. "Maybe she'll be embarrassed when she sees me and go back," I thought. No way! This creature of God came looking right into my eyes and still threw down her garbage. Oh, if I could only understand! Who declared our garden wall a dump? Who told these people, "Come throw your garbage in front of your neighbour's house?" The apprentices could barely hold me back. I was going to tear the woman to pieces. I lost it, I was hollering, hurling insults. You'd think a person would be a little embarrassed and at least feel reluctant in front of all the people, right? Guess again! She stares at my face with a stupid naivety. I swear to God she didn't even understand why I was angry. She must've thought I'd escaped from a mental institution. "Even if she doesn't understand, she'd probably be afraid to come again," I said to myself. Yet didn't she come again at the same time with the garbage in her hand? There she was, eyes wide open, fixed in an idiotic stare to see what I was going to do. She'll make a murderer out of me. Oh my beautiful God, one doesn't meddle in your business but why on earth do you create such people? Now what do we have to do to these *bulgur*, I don't know? Because of them, the apartment building is thick with the smell of garbage. The way things are going, no one will come in here. We'll lose our jobs, our daily bread. Child, spray a bit, okay?'

The sweet sugary perfume of the spray, with the picture of a deserted shore shadowed by palm trees and a turquoise sea, rained in particles on all corners of the shop and mixed with all the various smells. Cemal stole a glance at the cockroach in the hope that it would be poisoned by the room spray. However, not only was it not at all affected by the particles landing on it, it had even succeeded in climbing up to the top of the pile of rollers and was now getting ready to move onto the Brilliantine box next to it.

'God knows you're right, all your customers would run away,' the high-strung brunette jumped in, as she watched the Number 113 burgundy nail polish that had already dried on her toes now being put on her fingers. 'Of course you've grown accustomed to the smell because you're here all day long. Sometimes when I enter this apartment building, I feel suffocated by it.'

'The windows are wide open all day long, the breeze blows pleasantly and still the smell does not go away. They say it increases as you go up to the higher floors. Is that so Madam Auntie?' shouted the manicurist causing the nail polish to overflow.

'And the *bulgurs* across from us claim we take their garbage. Now look here, are you crazy? What would I do with your disgusting garbage?' Cemal intervened and looked sharply at the manicurist so she would understand his discomfort about her asking questions of the old woman at every opportunity.

'How so? What does that mean?' asked the Blue Mistress taking a break from bemoaning her new image that had just started to appear on the mirror. Like many other women who witness even just the trimming of their hair they had tried so hard to grow long, she too had already started to feel remorse even before getting up from the swivel chair.

'Oh, don't you know we're in dispute with the nutters at Number 4? And I thought there wasn't a person left who hadn't heard about it.' Cemal said. 'One day these people came and "Welcome!" I said, for why else does someone come to the beauty parlour? I thought they'd come to have their hair done, but apparently that wasn't their intention. This crazy woman in front, her stark raving mad husband behind her, their old maid older daughter next to them and the other old maid younger daughter behind them, all four of them were standing in front of me, out on a family campaign. First I didn't understand a thing from what they said. It turned out they'd tied up their garbage bags and placed them in front of their door and when they looked five minutes later, their garbage wasn't there! "Where's our garbage?" they said. "Meryem might've picked it up," I suggested. "No sir, the janitors had gone to their village that day." "The garbage men might have picked it up", I said. "What sort of a garbage man would enter the apartment building?" they retorted. "How would I know where your garbage is?" They obstinately maintained, "You took it, give our garbage back." What luck! Of all the places in Istanbul, we opened up a beauty parlour in an apartment building full of nutters!'

Absorbed in talking, Cemal suddenly realized he had moved away from his prey. Though he turned around scrutinizing the situation warily, the cockroach was nowhere to be found.

'For goodness sake, whoever took the garbage bag, took it. What's the big deal?' muttered the high-strung brunette, lighting a new cigarette.

'Hey, the incident isn't as frivolous as you think,' stated Cemal as he looked under, around and in the vicinity of the basket of rollers. 'The man's a paranoiac. His wife is even worse. Who knows what scenarios they invented in their heads? Something like the CIA took the garbage bags or the terrorists kidnapped them, this was on the tip of my tongue but I swallowed it, "Now look here, who do you think you are to imagine you might have your garbage stolen?" How sad! Being a poor *bulgur* but thinking yourself a blessing like beans.'

The pimpled apprentice started to collect the teacups accumulated on the counter, each stained by different coloured lipsticks. As Cemal stared fixedly at each teacup fearing the cockroach would emerge from under one of the saucers, his apprentice looked at the nipples of the Blue Mistress with a gaze just as fixed.

Since the Blue Mistress, finally rid of the plastic smock, was busy inspecting her new hair model, she was not aware of either the apprentice's looks or Cemal's anxiety. If only she could muster enough courage to one day have her hair cut very short...but the olive oil merchant would most certainly not approve of such a change. Far too many times he had said he liked hair long in a woman. God knows he was going to complain a lot at her trimming her hair even this much. She looked at her watch. She was late, very late. She still had a lot of errands to run. Cemal was standing right behind her with a bristle brush in his hand, she thought the anxiety on his face was due to her not liking the haircut, and because she wanted to please him and had also decided she should say her 'goodbye' in the same way she had been greeted, she fervently shook his hand, violating the customer departure custom of a women's hairdresser.

The Blue Mistress's hand had still not left Cemal's when the outside door opened harshly once again. As the bell shook mightily, with the yell of the watermelon vendor at the corner, who now seemed determined to suppress his competitor with the loudspeaker, a woman plunged in dripping with agitation all over. All heads in the beauty parlour once again turned to the door to see the new addition to their ranks. They looked and were left dumbstruck, as if frozen stiff by a new command. The door closed and the last remaining echo of the bell stopped by itself as it reached the rest with a puny sound. The new customer was none other than Hygiene Tijen.

Flat Number 1: Musa, Meryem, Muhammet

'No way, I won't go!' shouted Muhammet from where he had squeezed into. He then pounded his fist, as if it were responsible for all this, on the closest of the velvet sofas whose colour had first been egg yolk yellow, next sour cherry burgundy and then aquamarine, but now was ultimately a total mystery under these flowery covers. He would have preferred his kicks over fists, having lately made a habit of kicking everything he came across, but right at this instant the scrawny frame of his six years had been so tightly squeezed between the wall and the sofas that he was not even able to move his legs properly. Unable to free his body, he instead unleashed two of the longest barrages of swearwords he knew, tying one onto the tail of the other. Upon hearing him swear again, Meryem★ pushed with her feet all of the three sofas that were lined-up and pinned her blasphemous son to the wall, in the meantime guarding her swollen belly with two hands. Now literally cornered, Muhammet turned red with anger and opened his mouth to swear anew but did not dare go that far. As surrendering to his mother without resistance was a wound to his pride, he angrily bit the side of the sofa that had started to hurt his waist. The flowery cover protected the chair from all such outside pressures but maybe he could leave teeth marks if he bit hard enough...

★Meryem means Mary in Turkish and 'Meryem, Musa, Muhammet' is a trilogy referring to the three monotheist religions (Mary, Moses and Muhammet are the names of the family members).

The history of this scuffle that was repeated every weekday morning went back exactly five months and one week to the enrollment of Muhammet into the 1-G section of the only elementary school in the neighbourhood. All he could remember from the first day of school was the anxious mothers', distressed children's and sulky teachers' faces. With time, the mothers' anxieties, the children's distress and even the teachers' sulkiness had abated bit by bit, yet all these bits, instead of scattering away to eventually disappear, had altogether been transferred to Muhammet. Hence after five months, one week to the day, Muhammet was an anxious, distressed, sulky child who still did not want to go to school.

His starting school had coincided with his mother's sofa obsession. Around that time, Meryem had somehow heard that her cousin's son who resided in an Aegean town by the coast and made a living by repairing boats like his father and grandfather before him, had decided out of the blue to settle in Istanbul and go into the furniture trade. Within thirty-six hours of hearing this news, Meryem had arrived at her cousin's workshop and placed an order for some furniture, the colour and style of which she had not discussed with anyone else. The agreement was as follows: the cousin's son, who had not yet received his first order, was going to give her a family discount and Meryem was going to hand over her old sofas and a minimal payment. The thing neither side knew at the time was that Meryem was three weeks pregnant. This bit of knowledge was not as irrelevant to the situation as it might seem at first glance. For as it had been observed when she was with Muhammet, pregnancy made Meryem rather stubborn, quite apprehensive and a little 'bizarre.' When the cousin's son had finished the sofa set, Meryem's pregnancy had progressed two months and was going strong.

When the time came, she went to the workshop to see the finished work, looked at the colour of the sofas and threw up. Egg yolk yellow! When even the thought of egg yolks was sufficient to make her feel like vomiting, it was out of question that the sofas she was going to put in the living room be egg yolk yellow. When the cousin's son tried to contain the situation by reminding her that it was she who had chosen this colour, Meryem could not help throwing up again. She threw up so many times before noon that finally she got her way. The new agreement was as follows: the cousin's son who had still not received his first order was going to change the colour of the upholstery and in return, Meryem would give both her old sofas and more money than they had initially discussed.

Meryem's pregnancy had reached its third month when the cousin's son notified her that the sour cherry burgundy sofa set was ready. In the meantime her morning sicknesses had considerably diminished. Now she instead suffered from schmaltziness. When the time came she went to the workshop to see the completed work, looked at the colour of the sofas and started to weep. Sour cherry burgundy! When even the image of a single sour cherry fallen from its tree was enough to remind her of untimely death, the possibility of the sofas in her living room being sour cherry burgundy could not be even brought up. When the cousin's son tried to defend himself and reminded her that she herself had chosen this colour, Meryem could not help weeping again. That afternoon she cried so much that she finally got her way. The new agreement was as follows: the cousin's son who had not yet received his first order was going to change the colour of the upholstery and in return, Meryem would give both her old sofas and twice the money they had initially agreed upon. Only this time the most innocuous of all colours was going to be selected to guarantee customer satisfaction: aquamarine!

It worked. Two weeks later, when Meryem saw the aquamarine sofas she neither vomited nor wept. That night the cousin's son slept peacefully for the first time in days. The following day, he threw the aquamarine sofa set in a pickup truck and brought it to Flat Number 1, Bonbon Palace, with two skinny porters he hired at the last minute as his big and burly apprentice had suddenly been taken ill. Meryem had been waiting for them excitedly since early morning with her ear on the doorbell and her hand on her not yet too swollen belly.

In the fully crowded living room that was already small and had become almost impossible to walk around, with the arrival of the new sofas, the porters and the cousin's son jumped over the coffee tables and perched on whatever they could find to drink a cup of coffee to take away their tiredness. Then it was time to leave. The cousin's son put in his pocket the agreed fee, and made each porter take a large piece of the old melon pink sofa set on their back, thus heading toward the door in a convoy. Unfortunately, they then had to stop abruptly before they could take even a single step. Such instances happen every so often on the road as well. You see the vehicle in front of you come to a sudden stop and know instantly that the road is jammed, but being unable to see what had happened ahead, you have no idea what the problem is and are forced to a standstill. The cousin's son and the porters, who were now doubled under the loads on their backs, were slightly more fortunate. Even though they did not know the 'why's and wherefores' of the jam, they could see the immediate cause. Meryem stood at the threshold with ill-omened glitters in her eyes, her heavy frame and large belly, which seemed to have grown even more in the last few minutes, blocking the exit and not letting them pass.

Her husband Musa was the first to grasp what Meryem's problem was. He drew to the side with silent resignation and started to fathom the course of events. Musa had an ulcer of the stomach. Whenever he became irritated, his stomach started to burn sourly. So he had found the road to a serene life in accepting his wife as she was. He was particularly determined to avoid conflicts with her during her pregnancy. Yet, since he felt pity for the porters, he deemed they should at least be provided with some sort of explanation for the situation they were in. He began by saying simply, 'She cannot give up her old sofas. She cannot, I know.'

In point of fact, this last 'I know' was some sort of a forewarning. It was like suggesting 'Why don't you simply give up while you are ahead of the game!' Yet neither the cousin's son nor the porters could get the message. Accordingly, they put the sofas down and started to argue forcefully. Their steadily swelling anger, however, did not do anything other than make Meryem embrace her cause even more fiercely. The melon yellow sofas were indeed worn out but they had a common past with the family. The set had been bought when Meryem and Musa had finally moved out to their own house after spending five miserable years with the latter's mother and father. Muhammet's babyhood had been spent on them. The tiny pitch black hole at the corner of the double chair was a memento from the cigarette ash of a relative who had come to see the baby. That relative was no longer alive. Occasionally his scratchy voice smoked from the cigarette burn he had left behind. That is what the past was, that which you could not get rid of. The past did not resemble the crumbs spilled over a rug. You could not shake them out from open windows.

'Well, in that case, we're taking these new ones back,' said the cousin's son as he shouldered one of the aquamarine sofas. Taking his lead, the porters immediately reached for the other pieces of the set. Meryem looked at them with eyes filled with sheer sorrow like a small child witnessing the lamb she had lovingly fed for days now being taken away to be slaughtered. For the following hour, the cousin's son and the porters tried to persuade her in vain, the former furiously, the latter desperately, having now realized that they might not be paid in the end. Since it could not be decided which sofas were to go and which to stay, all throughout the steadfastly flaring dispute, everyone (except Musa) was left standing, which made them all (except Musa) even more likely to explode. Many times Meryem's eyes filled with tears, many times she felt nauseous. Considering her nausea, if not her tears, to be a message sent by the baby in her womb, 'See?' she asked, joining her hands on top of her belly, 'Even this unborn innocent's heart is not willing to let go of the sofas.' Joining her two skills to maximize power, she both cried and threw up so much that afternoon that by the end of the day the victory was Meryem's. The cousin's son was furious at himself for violating the oldest rule of trade history, 'Never conduct business with relatives,' and he and the porters, who were equally furious at him for his obvious failure, all left Flat Number 1, Bonbon Palace.

Even though indubitably victorious, an unexpected problem awaited Meryem. How they were going to place two separate sofa sets and their coffee tables simultaneously inside the already narrow janitor's flat with its low ceiling, was a challenge to the mind as well as being an eyesore but Meryem would not give up. Making use of every square centimetre available, she managed to make two three-seated, two double-seated and six single-seated sofas fit into the twenty-metre-squared living room by lining them up like a wagon with the coffee tables placed in between. Hence the largest mistake Muhammet had committed this morning when declaring to his mother his intention to not go to school was to take refuge behind one of these furniture wagons.

'You'll go whether you want to or not,' Meryem said as she continued to push the sofas with one foot and started preparing her son's lunch.

Once again she had made a toasted-cheese sandwich with a slice of white cheese, a slice of tomato and three sprigs of parsley in between. Depending on the day, she also put in a single fruit and just enough money, no more no less, to buy one bottle of buttermilk drink which Muhammet bought from the school canteen. Toasted-cheese sandwiches were prepared at the school canteen too and they were definitely much better and warmer than the home-made version, but even though he had told his mother over and over again not to prepare a toasted-cheese sandwich, not once had he been able to make her listen to him. If only she could be prevented from putting the tomato in and, if not that, at least the parsley, as he could not understand what that was doing there anyway.

However, whenever Meryem had her mind set on something, oblivious to all stimuli pointing in the opposite direction, she would simply hide like a sea-creature in the deaf silence of a cave, refusing to come out until the other side had totally given up. It was simply impossible for her to veer-off from these things she had learned at who-knows-what stage of her life: that toasted-cheese sandwiches, for example, were to be prepared with a slice of tomato and three sprigs of parsley. That is what she had been doing every morning for the last five months and one week, and today was no exception. Muhammet, however, felt as if it was not only this tomato and parsley that he carried to school every day, but also his mother's eye and ear. Should he ever not eat his sandwich or commit the much worse crime of skipping school, he somehow felt sure that this red eye of the tomato and green ear of the parsley would immediately break the news to his mother.

Until school started, it was not with fear but with love that he took pieces of bread into his hands. In those days, the two noses of the breakfast bread belonged to him. As Meryem gave the noses to her son, she did not neglect to take off the small piece of paper attached to either one or the other of the noses. She told Muhmmet that this notched piece of paper was a letter from the baker's daughter. The letter would be made to wait on the side until he had finished off his breakfast. Only then would Muhammet have gained the right to learn what was written in it. To that end, he would eat without any fuss. Even though he was forced to finish one boiled egg every morning, for the sake of reading the letter, he would complete his breakfast without a peep. And when the time came, Meryem took mischievous pleasure in clearing the table as slowly as possible to increase her son's curiosity, then poured herself a cup of tea and started to read, dissolving the words slowly in her mouth like a lump of sugar.

The baker's daughter was a lonely child; she had no friends or siblings. While her father baked bread at night, she would sit alone in between the flour sacks and secretly write a letter to

Muhammet. Her mother had died while she was still a baby and her father had remarried. The step-mother constantly tormented this tiny orphan because she had a stone instead of a heart. The poor girl escaped from the house at every opportunity to spend time at the bakery with her dear father. Sweet-smelling soft breads were prepared at the bakery, also crisp *simits*. As Meryem kept reading these, it never occurred to Muhammet to wonder how so much information fitted onto a piece of paper that was only one times three centimetres-squared. In the universe of nought-to-one years, bread was sacred and every piece of paper with writing on it remained an absolute mystery; as the abstruse magic of the two met on the nose of the bread, the baker's daughter would shimmer under a halo of sheer enchantment.

Muhammet wanted to learn everything about her: what the bakery looked like, what she did there, if she liked to sleep in the morning and be up at night when all children her age had to go to bed early, the games she played and, most of all, whether she was beautiful or not... Meryem described the girl as 'blonde and as delicate as a water lily that blooms in the water.' She kept her hair long. It reached her waist on each side in two braids. Muhammet, too, had long hair then. Those who saw him on the street thought he was a girl.

In her letters, the baker's daughter mostly talked about the people who stopped by the bakery all day long. Old people came, leaning on their canes; they dipped the hard biscuits they bought in their teas and dissolved them noisily in their toothless mouths. There were also the *simit* sellers, who came early every morning with round wooden trays on their heads. The baker's daughter wanted to be friends with them but some behaved rudely toward her and said impolite things. Still, there were some among them with hearts of gold. For instance, there was a freckled boy who could hop on one foot while whirling in each hand *simits* put onto two thin sticks. Muhammet was offended at the baker's daughter talking so frequently about the talents of this boy but wouldn't object. Then there were the pastry-sellers who stopped by with their hand carts. There were also women who came by to have pita-bread made at the bakery. They treated the baker's daughter well. They would always give her a pita before carrying their heavy trays back home. The baker's daughter would write these things at length, Meryem would read them one by one, time would flow by at a snail's pace. This halcyon innocence was going to be, however, roughly smashed to pieces in the fall when Muhammet was registered to the 1-G section of the neighbourhood's only elementary school. First his hair was cut. Now nobody could say he looked like a girl. Then the breakfasts got shorter, and after some time, he learned how to read and write. It was then that he had discovered those tiny papers stuck on each bread were actually the labels of the bakeries and there were no letters coming from the baker's blonde daughter. Since then, there were no more letters left to be read, nor that moon-faced girl to love. To learn to read was to lose forever the mystery of writing.

'No way, I won't go!' Muhammet yelled shrilly, unable to take his eyes off the lunch bag, but his voice was much weaker this time and within a couple of minutes, when Meryem heard a crushed moan like that of a puppy, she knew her son had given up and stopped pushing the sofa. As he emerged from his corner crestfallen, Muhammet threw his mother a vinegary glance.

Next to the huge frame of his mother, he was tiny like one of the dots on the letter 'Ö'. When his sibling was born, s/he would be the other dot. Even though Muhammet was only six years old and knew all kids his age were smaller than their mothers, unlike other kids, he had long known and accepted that he would always be smaller than his mother no matter how much he grew up, whatever age he reached, whichever unattainable future he accomplished. His mother, with her wide forehead that wrinkled up when angry, her round face with rosy cheeks amassed, her huge hazel eyes that grew wide when stubborn, her breasts swollen like balloons, her dimpled arms, her chubby flesh bulging from her thighs, her feet as big as a child's grave and her endless superstitious beliefs and unbelievable energy were all so big as to totally crush every obstacle into dust…and would always remain so…

Hence he put his toasted sandwich with parsley into his lunch bag, stepped on the flattened corpse of the cockroach he had crushed just this morning at the corner of the aquamarine double chair and, dragging his feet, set out on his way to school.

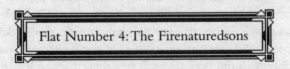

Upon entering Bonbon Palace, the inhabitants of the flat on the right, like all family residences on the ground floor, complained about being in front of people's eyes too much. All day long, the residents of the building and their guests of all kinds, as well as the door-to-door salesmen who always failed to read the written sign strictly forbidding their presence, could not help stealing a glance through the living room windows of Flat Number 4. With the snooping customers of the beauty parlour across from them added to all these people, the glances aimed at infiltrating the living room via its windows increased ten fold as did the anxiety of those inside.

Some of the families living on the ground floor might eventually get used to such traffic. There are even several among them who made the most of the situation of being continuously watched from the outside by continuously watching the outside in return – some sort of 'an eye for an eye' policy! Perhaps it is not a coincidence that the most well-informed peeping-toms of apartment buildings usually reside in flats at the entrance level...but the Firenaturedsons were not of this type. They could neither tolerate being seen by those coming to the apartment nor intended to spy on them. In their view, the world outside their house was a boundless terrain of everlasting trepidation. In point of fact, when the 'surname law' was promulgated in Turkey, if rather than letting each family make the choice, their characteristics were taken into account, the doorbell of Flat Number 4 would have read

'Everlastingtrepidationsons' rather than 'Firenaturedsons'.

All daylong the wide windows of the flat were tightly covered with different yet similarly impenetrable armour – first with cambric, then a sunshade of white cotton calico when the sun was up. Once it started to get dark outside, the thick velvet curtains of the same ashen-colour as the apartment building were drawn all the way across. It was then that the living room windows of Flat Number 4 hid from and guarded against the eyes of the outside world, like a vigilant animal camouflaging itself in the colour of the surrounding soil to avoid being noticed by its enemies. Still, even when all three drapes of cambric, sunshade and velvet curtains were fully drawn, there remained a sliver of light on the right. There at that corner sat fifty-six year old Ziya Firenaturedsons, who had planted himself at that spot ever since the day he was dismissed from the State Water Works for taking bribes. While reading the papers and watching television, drinking coffee and eating pumpkin dessert, he would occasionally peep from this sliver with great caution and case the surroundings with anxious and suspicious eyes, without quite knowing what to look for or why. At those rare moments when Ziya Firenaturedsons got up from his sofa, the retired, organic-chemistry teacher, fifty-five year old Zeren Firenaturedsons would replace him. She too would look out from the opening once in a while, but did so less to look outside than to check on the canary in its cage next to the window. The fact that this canary, unlike the preceding one, hadn't chirped even once, was a burning concern for Zeren Firenaturedsons. She kept saying she had to open the window for the canary to chirp but never found the courage to do so. The memory of that cursed morning when she found her first canary in its cage covered with blood was still too fresh in her mind. Though the criminals behind that deed had vanished when the wretched man called the 'Cat Prophet' had moved away from Bonbon Palace (taking all his stuff and entire tribe of cats with him) given all the street cats that roamed around wagging their tails, she worried to this day about the odds that her new canary would meet a similar end. She was particularly suspicious of that tar-coloured, grim-faced giant of a cat, with fur so fluffy it seemed it had skinned and donned the furs of at least four cats.

Actually Zeren Firenaturedsons did not have the slightest interest in either canaries or any other bird of breed until Zekeriya Firenaturedsons (thirty-three years old) broke his nose for the fourth time. A long time ago, when her son's nose was a pleasant protrusion on a soft cartilage that had not yet found its form, life was so nice and uncomplicated. Then, as he stepped into adolescence, the gentle curves of his baby face were totally wiped away and his nose somehow underwent an unexpected change, first insolently growing longer and then curving down. All the meanwhile Zeren Firenaturedsons had anxiously watched this transformation as if following the approach of a menacing stranger. She was very content with her own delicate nose; her husband's, though it might not be regarded as beautiful, was at least well-shaped. Given these facts, Zeren Firenaturedsons felt the need to climb further up the family tree as she firmly believed that all types of flaws in the world stemmed from the genes. In this vein, when she painfully realized that her son's nose had completed its transformation and would never again be as before, she started to search with a gene-map in her hand to at least find out the person responsible for this mishap. Going back systematically step by step, concentrating more on her husband's lineage than hers, she first reviewed the relatives she knew and when that did not turn anything up, combed through the old albums one at a time, only to return from her countless trips to the gene-map empty handed. With time, she gave up the search.

Then Zekeriya turned fourteen and smashed his nose to pieces when he took wings with the speed of puberty and flew down a hill on his bicycle. Upon receiving the news, Zeren Firenaturedsons felt a relief she could not confess to anyone. Despite her hopes that this unfortunate accident would be a new beginning, setting straight not only her son's nose but also his behaviour, everything had got worse afterward. With surgery, the cursory performance of which was quickly revealed, the nose that was already rather ugly achieved a hopeless crookedness and stayed this way. Curiously, Zekeriya's turn toward bent-and-twisted ways occurred around the same time. In the ensuing years, Zekeriya Firenaturedsons would part at every opportunity from the straight and narrow road his mother had placed him on, plunging one by one into all the turns he could find and continuously losing his way until he finally emerged a total source of embarrassment and torment. The year he broke his nose, he started to steal money from his parents; at age fifteen to dedicate his spare time to masturbation, at sixteen to see school as an arena where he could trample on the weak, at seventeen to smoke two packs of cigarettes a day and at eighteen decided to 'make it' in the quickest way possible, thereby sticking the nose that increasingly irritated his mother into every kind of filth that he could sniff out. When the outcome of his second nose operation was even worse than the first, Zeren Firenaturedsons' worries about her son peaked to the highest point while her expectations plunged.

With the strength Zekeriya collected during convalescence, at twenty-two he got mixed up with various parking-lot mafia, at twenty-three he became infatuated with a divorced bank clerk with two kids, at twenty-four he stabbed the bank security officer his former lover had sent after him and got arrested, at twenty-six he took a nasty revenge against life by breaking the nose of the president of the Association to Beautify Kuzguncuk (who had started to organize the neighbourhood inhabitants into a protest group against the construction of a parking lot in the back garden of an Ottoman mansion), at twenty-seven he went into hiding from his family, then, at twenty-eight, after the discovery of his hiding place, he was hurriedly married off to a relative's daughter the family elders had found suitable and produced a child that same year. Yet, according to the account of his willowy wife who often came round to the Firenaturedsons' flat to complain in tears, marriage had not straightened out his habits one little bit. Not that he wandered around outside day and night like before, but he had turned instead into a highly irritable nervous wreck. At the end of one of these nervous breakdowns, he had 'roughed up' an inexperienced woman driver who had bumped into his car at an orange traffic light, and after a terrible beating from the brawny husband the following day, had his nose rearranged once again.

During this time, Zeren Firenaturedsons had eagerly awaited the baby her daughter-in-law was pregnant with. For babies who are conceived when a conjugal relationship stumbles – coming to term while the marriage is still unable to get up from where it had fallen flat on its face – are like cement sacs: tiny cement sacs that plaster the visible cracks, keep the columns of the nest bound and fortify those marriages which are on the brink of collapse. When Zekeriya's baby was born, like every cement sac, it too had a mission, a double one: to prevent the destruction of first his father's nose and then his marriage.

It worked, at least for a while. Exactly one year and five and a half months passed without any incidents. Then came the shocking news which shocked no one. While carrying the baby carriage around in the house, Zekeriya had fallen down the landing of the stairs. Fully prepared to encounter the same scene for the fourth time, each more annoying but much less moving, Zeren Firenaturedsons went to the hospital her daughter-in-law had named on the phone in between sobs. She angrily stormed into the room and looked in bewilderment at her son who stood in front of her in excellent condition. A nose had indeed been broken in the accident at the house, only this time not Zekeriya's but that of the little one sleeping in the carriage sent down the landing. Upon detecting the bandages she had grown accustomed to seeing for years, right in the middle of her son's face, which she every time interpreted as a rebel flag waved against her rule, now being transferred to her grandchild's face, Zeren Firenaturedsons was convinced that there had been a grave genetic transfer somewhere and this defect would never be corrected. There and then she gave up all hope about her son and his bloodline.

The first thing she did when she returned to Bonbon Palace in hopelessness, was to shut herself in her bedroom and reorganize the drawer of the chestnut wardrobe in which she had kept her son's baby belongings. After all, whenever we decide to no longer love someone, we must first work out what to do with the belongings we have of theirs. Yet since Zeren Firenaturedsons could never and would not ever discard anything related to her family, the most severe course of action she could manifest was emptying out all her son's belongings to thoroughly examine each and every item before putting it away once again. As she went through the entire chestnut wardrobe, the culprit gene she had sought for years suddenly appeared inside an old etiquette book jammed behind one of the bottom drawers. A photograph had been wedged, who knows when and by whom, in the 'How does one talk to an unfamiliar lady in a train compartment?' section of the book that had an illustration on every page. The answer Zeren Firenaturedsons was dying to find out was hidden in this faded photograph. For the fourth male brother of her husband's grandfather – the effeminate, coquettish, worthless one who had constantly relayed gossip from one person to another and been primarily responsible for so many family fights so as to be remembered by all as 'Hoopoe' – also had a nose exactly like Zekeriya's. In the photograph taken in his later years, HoopoeHamdi, with a fedora on his head, a rather long cigarette holder in his hand, and smoking a cigarette while gazing dreamily into the distance over the shoulders of the family members, had given his profile to the camera as if to better highlight the ugliness of his nose. Zeren Firenaturedsons was not interested in the fact that the family dictionary had made a basic mistake, in that the bird called Hoopoe had never relayed gossip to anyone except when taking news from the prophet Suleiman to Belkis. The only thing that interested her was the man carrying this nickname. It was a terrible injustice that her one and only son, her firstborn, had seized, rather than those of his own father and mother, the nose of a senile elderly man whom he had not once met in his life and who possessed the most despicable genes in the whole family. What was even more terrible was the link of her one and a half year old grandchild to the same genetic chain.

With a sudden impulse, she upped and threw this ugly document and the etiquette book into the garbage. And in spite of the many complaints of the apartment administrator Hadji Hadji concerning the putting out of trash at inappropriate times and thus rendering the apartment's entrance an eyesore, she put the yellow garbage bag outside her front door.

Five, ten, thirteen...exactly seventeen minutes later, Zeren Firenaturedsons felt a deep remorse. Within a minute, it occurred to her that having until today carefully collected everything she had concerning her family, she should certainly have saved this old photograph regardless of its unpleasantness. When she reopened the door, however, the garbage bag had vanished. A story she had once heard from her mother suddenly came to mind. Her father and mother had placed the cat they had kept at home for years but no longer wanted into a sack, and had driven out as far as they could to leave this sac in some desolate field outside the city. Upon returning home at night, they had found the cat in front of the house indolently waiting for them. Now, as she looked at the empty space left by the garbage bag, Zeren Firenaturedsons caught the cold shudder her own mother had felt upon seeing that tabby in front of her. For the disappointment of seeing how something we thought we had gotten rid of has stuck to us, and the disappointment in observing how something we suppose we could get back anytime has slid away from our hands, are actually reminiscent of one another.

Similar things had happened in this apartment building;

garbage bags were mysteriously taken away from doors before Meryem had a chance to collect them. Yet since those bags had been of little concern to Zeren Firenaturedsons, the riddle of who took them and with what purpose had never intrigued her. Now she wanted her garbage back. Suddenly in her mind's eye the lost garbage bag turned into a sealed letter – one that was so personal it should never be seen by strangers. Our garbage is private as long as it is still in front of our door: it belongs to us, is about us. The moment it ends up in the garbage can, it becomes anonymous. Those who make a living from garbage can stick their fingers into the cans in the middle of the street or in the garbage piles that rise up at certain corners or in the dumps near the city, but only when they dare to open or even worse kidnap the garbage in front of our door, is it considered an invasion of privacy.

In the following hour, Zeren ran up and down Bonbon Palace looking everywhere she could think of, getting suspicious of everyone. At one point, guessing that the garbage bags in front of each door could all end up in the same place like streams that all flow into the same river, she went outside and rummaged through the garbage pile accumulating by the garden wall; but the ground had split open and the yellow garbage bag tied with a bow had slid within. Since the janitors were away visiting their village, only one possibility remained: the beauty parlour across from them! Yet she returned from her exploratory visit there with her husband and daughters empty handed and with shot nerves. As if it was not enough for the garbage bag to vanish with the photograph of Hoopoe Hamdi, she had received on top of it a bunch of insults from that shrew of a hairdresser Cemal.

It was some time after that incident that Zeren Firenaturedsons purchased a canary. Before the canary however, there had been fish of all colours and sorts...

Actually, Zeren Firenaturedsons hadn't the slightest interest in fish until the day when she finally accepted after many denials that her older daughter had neuropathy. She loved her older daughter; at one time she had loved her more than anything else. In the days when her son started to follow that crooked nose of his, she in turn had started to pour all her attention and love onto her older daughter. Back then, just as today, Zeynep Firenaturedsons (now thirty-one) was far more active and outgoing than either of her siblings. At age eleven, she wanted to be the principal at the school her mother worked at, a firefighter to spray all the water of the State Water Works where her father worked, bum-around like her brother, crochet lace like her younger sister and become an actor like the father of her best friend at school – all at the same time. Little had changed at age twenty-one. She still wanted to be more than the sum of everyone around her. Pulling the day apart into chunks of time and squeezing a separate occupation into each chunk, she had divided herself into many pieces, doing first one thing then another and, strangely enough, succeeding in most of them. Her intelligence was sharp enough to flatter her mother's genetic pride. Yet, she was just as unhappy. Whatever she possessed was far from being sufficient, in fact, nothing was sufficient. There was not a single thing in life that was complete; to her 'completeness' was just a hollow word in dictionaries. There was no sea, for instance; even within one sea, there were an infinite number of seas each one trying to flow in another direction. The height and frequency of the waves we saw reaching the shore was what remained of inter-sea wars. They arrived only to be decimated bubble by bubble, particle by particle. Likewise, there was no Istanbul. There were tens, hundreds, thousands, millions of groups, communities and societies. The 'pluses' took away the 'minuses', opposite winds prevented each other's drift and because no one group was strong enough to dominate another, the city managed in the end to preserve itself though it could not help being constantly diminished in the process. Just like the waves, Istanbul was what remained from the total: from what the rats nibbled on, the seagulls picked to shreds, the inhabitants shed, the cars wore out, the boats carried, the very first air breathed in by all, godknowshowmany babies born every hour...the remnants scattered and shattered, always lacking, never to be completed... Zeynep Firenaturedsons was twenty-two when she had her first breakdown.

Zeren Firenaturedsons was not at all affected by what the physician said as she took neither the physician nor his words seriously. There was no leaf on any branch of the family tree where one would come across such a disease. The mind of even the darkest blot, Hoopoe Hamdi was in excellent condition. That aside, her older daughter was the smartest, brightest one among her three children. The crisis she went through could be nothing more than late puberty despair.

Zeynep Firenaturedsons' quick recovery convinced her mother further that she had been right. Yet, as it soon became evident, this recovery was not permanent but temporary. From then on life for the older daughter of the Firenaturedsons would be divided into two seasons: when she was sick, it was as if she would never recover from her illness, yet when she was well, it seemed as if she would never be ill again. There was no middle ground. No one could tell when she would make the transition from one state to the other. The most evident difference between the two states was her reaction to bad news. When sick, she would only be interested in certain items of news, like a colour blind person only notices certain colours, and she would read the newspapers for this type of news. Street children who got high on paint-thinners, honour crimes, suicides, women forced into prostitution, suicide bombers, babies kidnapped from hospitals, youths taking overdoses, all sorts of tragic occurrences... In addition to the papers, she also carefully searched through the community news: uncovered sewer pits, burst water pipes, uncollected garbage, closed roads, ferocious pickpockets, pastry shops sealed up for filth, butchers selling horse meat, grocers marketing contraband detergent, parking lot gangs, old wooden houses mysteriously destroyed by fire, gas explosions, gas leaks... Unsatisfied with simply following this maddening news,

Zeynep Firenaturedsons loved to relate in fullest detail each and every item to whomever she came across. Since she did not come across many people, as she spent most of her time at home with her mother, she recounted the same stories over and over to the latter. When she was well, however, she skipped the amply illustrated news of doom. She was, subsequently, the only one among the Firenaturedsons who read the newspapers consistently.

Whenever the excited voice of her older daughter talking about catastrophes grated on her nerves, Zeren Firenaturedsons listened to the peaceful bubbling sound of the aquarium she had filled with colourful fish and phosphorescent accessories. Before the fish, however, there had been decorative plants of all kinds...

At twenty-three, Zelish Firenaturedsons was neither a bum like her brother, nor as intelligent as her sister. Actually, just as one could not say that since childhood she had looked like the other members of her family, neither could it be said that she was like them in type or disposition – and this difference became most striking when compared to her sister. Like a bulky, plump mushroom somehow grown next to a wild, rough plant with flowers that soothe the eye, and inured to the plant so as to suck all its sun and water, Zelish had attached herself to her sister perching on a corner of her life. She was mediocre and hesitant, lazy and inadequate. It was as if seeing her sister incessantly swing between two poles, intelligent and attractive at times, nutty and weepy at others, had confused her so badly that she had decided instead to stop somewhere in between, at a secure threshold. While her brother craved 'to be something', her sister 'to be everything', she for years had only wanted 'not to be'.

Among the Firenaturedsons, Zelish was the one least resistant to anxiety. For other family members, anxiety consisted of a menace coming from the outside. Even though its causes varied, the address remained constant and the world remained outside the thick, velvet, ashen curtains. Where that world was involved, each had their own concerns. Ziya Firenaturedsons was most apprehensive that the bribery trial would reopen to lead to his imprisonment, followed by his appearing in all the newspapers and becoming the talk of the town. The major anxiety of Zeren Firenaturedsons was her children, and after that came, in the following order: the growth of Islamic fundamentalism, being attacked by pickpockets on the streets and another earthquake in Istanbul. For his part, Zekeriya Firenaturedsons mostly feared failing in bed, being powerless in life, the people to whom he had gambling debts and, finally, fear itself. As for Zeynep Firenaturedsons, she was a pendulum that carelessly swung between fountains of apprehensiveness-anxiety-fear and fearless-carefree-untroubled seas.

Yet for Zelish Firenaturedsons, anxiety was something abstract. It was everywhere like air and almost as intangible: with causes far harder to identify than the reopening of a bribery case, being nailed because of a gambling debt or the coming to power of fundamentalists. To start with, anxiety was not external to a person but rather the very fauna in which s/he lived. For fear and anxiety and worry are nourished by 'the horror of the probability that everything could turn out to be different.' (Here are your house, friends, body, family... These are yours, but unfortunately they could all be taken away from you one day!) As for apprehension, that is fed by 'the horror of the probability that nothing could be any other way.' (Here are your house, friends, body, family... These are yours, and unfortunately could always remain the same!) When she was in middle school Zelish had been to her friends' houses a few times. These visits, which gave her the opportunity to see up-close mothers, fathers and families not at all like her own, were a turning point for her, as until then she had thought 'mother', 'father' and 'family' meant basically a carbon copy of the ones she had. The embarrassment she felt about her family grew over the years in folds like the interest rate of a slyly increasing fine.

The hesitant syllables of the stuttering physicist in the

schoolroom rang in the ears of Zelish Firenaturedsons: 'Lll–let us aaa–ttach two cups that bbb–both have equal amounts of lll–liquid with the sss–same density and at the sss–same level. Lll–let us www–wait for lll–liquid to transfer from one ttt–to the other.' Having said this he then added: 'Aaa–ctually let us not wait in vain. Ddd–don't forget kids, aaa–always from high to low and more to less... Otherwise, nnn–no transfer occurs between things that are at the sss–same level.' If that be the case, Zelish thought, the apprehension levels of both her house and the world outside of Bonbon Palace were one and the same. This made it impossible for her to muster the courage to escape from Flat Number 4 never to return. She had made numerous plans until now. However, since these had been plans to leave rather than to escape, she still had no idea about where to go and what to do if and when she left the house.

Anyhow, Zeren Firenaturedsons expected little from her younger daughter, whose only distinctive characteristic as far as she could determine was to faint on the spot when she saw blood or anything that reminded her of it. She compensated for the lack of the daughter she would like to have with decorative plants. The only problem was that they demanded far more sun than the rays that barely penetrated the curtains could provide.

As the curtains of Flat Number 4 blocked off the sun's rays, these decorative plants withered away one by one just like the glances of strangers. The fish in the aquarium also suffered huge losses over time. The canary was massacred by the tribe of the Prophet of Cats. Although there was a new canary in the same cage now, for some inexplicable reason, it had not chirped even once.

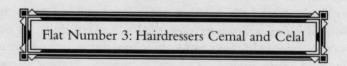

Upon seeing their all time favourite subject of gossip walk in, the people in the beauty parlour had plunged into the uneasy silence that is typical of those caught in the act. Encountering right in front of your eyes the person you were ruthlessly gossiping about a minute previously might lead you to suspect something mysterious is going on. Likewise, it seemed to the people inside as if Hygiene Tijen had heard the mention of her name from the spirit world. Still the reason for the nervousness they felt in front of her, did not solely stem from their inability to figure out how to straighten the facial expressions they had so carelessly slackened while gossiping. They were equally bewildered at seeing a person who had not stepped out of her house for months now, visiting a place that was probably one of the last locations on her 'list of potential places to stop by if and when the time is ripe enough to step out one day.'

The first to shake off this immobility was Cemal. He headed towards the door, saying in an almost merry voice, 'Welcome, come on in, Misses Tijen!' without even noticing how impolite it was for him to address by name someone he had not once before met. Such are the side effects of gossip addiction: if you wag your tongue too much and too often about someone, you might may well start to believe that you have known them personally for quite some time. Had Cemal's intimacy been reciprocated even the tiniest bit, he might have gotten so carried away with this delusion that he could have even reproached Hygiene Tijen, as he did to his regular customers, for not coming more often…but that did not happen. Giving him a once over from top to toe with a coldness that revealed she was not at all thrilled with this greeting, the woman facing him turned her head without saying anything and started to scrutinize everything. Her eyes got stuck one by one on the shorn hair on the ground waiting to be swept away, the threadbare towels that had lost their colour from frequent washing, the stains on the leopard-patterned plastic smocks tied to the necks of the customers, the thin crack on the wall-to-wall mirror, the dead mosquitoes lying around the edge of the counter adjacent to the mirror, the dust on the shelf lined up with boxes of the same brand hair gel, hair foam and brilliantine, hair-balls jammed in the hair brushes, the filling that was sticking out of the tears on the chairs, the shabbiness of the furniture and the bubbly water with doubtful contents on the three-layered manicure cart. The dissatisfaction she felt at what she saw was so deep and her desire to immediately leave the premises so evident, that Cemal, who felt both the place he worked in and himself demeaned, swallowed back all the cries of greeting that were on the tip of his tongue and was reduced to silence.

However, Hygiene Tijen did not, as Cemal had feared, turn her back and run away. After standing stock-still for a few seconds unable to move as if nailed to the spot, she cut her scrutiny halfway along so as not have to witness any further the hideous and slovenly world surrounding her and slid her looks outside the open window. There she saw her cleaning lady who had come down to the garden to collect the clothes. The woman, whose displeasure at being forced to collect so many clothes so meaninglessly thrown down could be read from her bleary eyes, had seen her at the same moment. Her nerves shot from cleaning all day long, she was so tired that she did not even have the energy to wonder what Tijen was doing down here. Leaving the laundry basket heaped up with clothes on the ground and with her elfin body remaining out in the garden, she slipped her head covered with a mildewed lemon headscarf inside the window of the beauty parlour and murmured in a dead beat voice: 'I'm going Misses Tijen, I've got a family to look after.' But even she had trouble making a connection between the situation and the words that had left her mouth, for she felt the need to add some sort of an explanation: 'This is the last basket, I gathered them all. I'll take it up right now and leave it in the house. I've already been up and down five times. Don't wait for me on Thursday. This neighbourhood is out of the way for me anyhow.'

Slightly crossing her eyebrows, Tijen gave a silent nod of approval. Even though her turbid facial expression did not reveal what she was thinking, the distress she felt at being here among people she did not know was too evident. She remained standing like that until Celal, eager to save her from this torture, drew near to mend the bridge his twin had tried to build but had smashed-up instead, and asked in a reassuring voice what she wanted done to her hair. It was then that Tijen turned to Celal, redirecting her glance from the space now vacated by the cleaning lady and muttered: 'Not me, my daughter.' Next, as if to make her point clear, she slowly drew aside.

Only then did those in the beauty parlour notice the little girl with curly, ebony hair and exceptionally white skin in contrast, with large eyes tinged with no other colour but black. Her hair was wet, with drops that flowed down from the zigzags of her hair to leave shallow puddles at shoulder level, she looked as if she had been caught on the way over in one of those drizzly summer showers.

While Celal was busy taking his young customer to the seat in front of the mirror, Cemal, resignedly enduring the treatment he had been subjected to by the child's mother, invited her to one of the sofas on the side. Hygiene Tijen did not sit down right away. For a few seconds she remained standing, stuck in her uneasiness. She then gave up and halfheartedly perched on the closest sofa she had been directed to. When the manicurist, whose habit it was to ask every customer if they wanted a manicure within thirty seconds of their entering the parlour, suddenly appeared at her side, Tijen was sitting still, her gaze fixed on a stain on the floor, her mind floating elsewhere. The moment she heard the question directed at her, however, she withdrew her hands in disgust, as if touched by an invisible rat, and hid them behind her. Utterly unprepared for such a brusque reaction, the manicurist returned to her seat flabbergasted but as soon as she sat down, a gnawing suspicion crossed her mind. Could she have called her 'Misses Hygiene' instead of 'Misses Tijen'? Could that be why the woman's face had soured all of a sudden? Thinking in this vein, it would not take the manicurist long to be convinced of having made a blunder. After all, the mind has a proclivity to pessimism. Whenever it wavers between two contradictory options, it tends toward the negative one. For a moment the manicurist thought she should go back and apologize, but the only thing she ended up doing was cowering uneasily behind the manicure cart and secretly glancing around to figure out if anyone else had heard her blunder.

In the meanwhile, Su, placed by Celal in front of the mirror right next to the old woman, kept rotating her chair to observe her surroundings with a genuine curiosity brought about by being at the beauty parlour for the first time. Unfortunately, she had to cut her study short since wherever she turned she would encounter female eyes staring at her and rouged lips talking about her. The only person in this strange place who did not inspect her with such a sticky stare, thought Su, was the old woman sitting by her side. She knew her. She was their next door neighbour whom she ran into from time to time and who was always so nice to her. Now, with her tiny, overly made-up face sticking out of the plastic smock covering her entire upper body all the way to her neck, the old woman looked like a bust placed askew on its base, impishly painted in all colours.

Noticing the girl's gaze on her, Madam Auntie turned aside and gave her a smile. It seemed as if she was on the verge of saying something but Celal appeared right at that instant with a rectangular wooden plank. Whenever a child came to the beauty parlour, the twins placed this plank on top of the arms of the chairs to extend the height of the small customer. However, as soon as Su had fathomed Celal's intention, she fervently shook her head from side to side, glancing all the while at the old woman. 'But I am taller than her!' she finally protested in a piercing voice. 'Why doesn't she sit on the plank too?'

The objection was more than enough to leave Celal, who had never been much of a speechmaker anyway, speechless. On seeing that in response to the girl's outrageous remark, Madame Auntie was so far from being offended that she was actually laughing, he handed the plank back to the apprentice without pimples. Right afterward, however, as if having sensed a secret wisdom in the child's words, he carefully observed through the mirror the reflections of his two unusual customers. Sitting there side by side in front of the wide and long mirror with leopard-patterned smocks around their necks, they were startlingly alike. In point of fact they stood on two opposite poles of time – one was eleven, the other seventy-eight, and yet both existed somewhere on the borderland of the human life-span. Su was mistaken. She was no taller than the old woman. Actually they were exactly the same height and maybe even the same weight. Uncanny as it was, that the frame an old person kept shrinking into would equal the frame a child had been growing into, they were like two elevators having fleetingly stopped at the same level while one was on the way up and the other down. After a second, an hour, a month... one of them would inevitably grow taller than they were at the moment, while the other would move correspondingly in the other direction, and no longer would they be alike. It was extraordinary that they had found each other, thought Celal, at this point of ephemeral equality.

Once he had found a resemblance between the old woman and the girl, it would not take Celal long to duplicate his love for the former by carving out a similar affection for the latter.

That is precisely why he personally undertook not only the preparation of the girl's hair for trimming but also the trimming itself. He let loose the thick, curly, ebony hair tied up haphazardly by a resin ribbon and brushed with care the strands that still had water dripping off them. In the meantime, he had not neglected to ask the child her name, for whenever adults embark on a communication with a child, the very first thing that occurs to them is to ask their name and then immediately afterward to praise it. 'What a beautiful name you've got!' Celal beamed but Su paid hardly any attention to his comment, having now plunged into an ad-filled woman's journal with wild hairstyles on every page. She would have remained glued to the journal for quite some time had it not been for her mother's bloodcurdling scream.

Just as dogs approach those most scared of them or as the hair falls in the soup of the one person at a dining table who will be most disgusted by it, so the cockroach Cemal had long lost track of had decided to enter none other than Hygiene Tijen's field of vision. The apprentice without pimples, determined to grovel to the bosses, immediately intervened. The bug was transformed under his shoe into a compressed residue of revulsion.

'These bugs have taken over everywhere,' Celal stammered, not knowing quite what to say next. Recently, he had been seeing creepy bugs around that he could not recognize at all. It was as if the variety of different breeds had increased along with their numbers. Some left a nasty smell when crushed. The apprentice ran to get the room spray.

'You need not wait, Misses Tijen,' wheedled Madam Auntie, detecting the horror that had appeared on the latter's face. 'Don't worry about your daughter. We'll come upstairs together.'

Hygiene Tijen was so desperate that she did not even wait for the offer to be repeated. In two seconds flat, she jumped over the corpse of the cockroach, left the price of the haircut on the register and reached the door. Before going out, she stopped for a brief moment to wave at the old woman with appreciation and at her daughter with affection.

As soon as she left, the manicurist, having sat stiff as a poker for longer than she could tolerate, jumped to her feet. 'The lady couldn't stand it!' she bellowed twisting her face into a sour expression. 'I bet she couldn't drink the coffee because she found it dirty. She must have disliked not smelling any bleach in it.'

The plump ginger-head and the blonde with the cast eye jumped into the tittle-tattle, Cemal turned up the volume of the TV when he saw the video clip he had been awaiting for days finally being broadcast, another round of tea was served to all customers, cigarettes were lit one by one and with amazing speed the beauty parlour became immersed in its usual languor. Having now gotten rid of the guilt of being obligated to look the woman who was an all-time-favourite topic of gossip in the eye, they had no difficulty in going back to where they had left off. This can be called the 'Full-speed, full-throttle return of the repressed'. Just as nature detests emptiness, so too does the gossip-machine crave the completion of the missing pieces. The fact that there was now a child among them did not stop the gossipmongers in the beauty parlour, nor did the fact that the child belonged to the person they were lavishly criticizing behind her back. For when women start gossiping, not for the simple sake of chewing the fat, but authentically, unreservedly and with all their heart, they tend to deem either their voices inaudible or their children deaf.

As for Su, it was hard to tell if she was aware of the innuendoes revolving around her mother's persona since she kept hiding behind that gaudy journal. On the page in front of her eyes stood the picture of a woman of mixed-race, who was naked from waist up and with her very short hair spiked and coloured in different phosphorescent hues.

'Do you like it?' asked Celal, upset about the talks and worried about the child. 'We can do your hair like that if you want. It would be a great hit at school.'

'No!' griped Su sullen-faced. 'My hair has to be shorter than that.'

'Come on, you don't have to have it so short. Let it grow a bit!' Celal objected.

Finally lifting her head from the journal, Su gave him an appraising look. An infinitesimal light furtively flickered and then faded inside the dark well of her eyes.

'No! Then my lice won't go away,' she protested, almost shouting.

The jittery brunette, all her permanent-wave rollers just removed, raised an eyebrow at the blonde with the cast eye. However, realizing she had an audience only goaded Su to increase her voice.

'The teacher called me at school. She had written a slip. "Take this, make sure your mother reads it," she said. Then they sent me home. My mother was very upset when she read it. She said I had lice. We went into the bathroom and washed it with medicine. We went through two shampoos. "You stay here," she said, I sat in the tub. Then she took off my clothes from the closet. She threw all of them out the window. She threw the sheets too, and my backpack, she threw that as well.'

'We didn't see a backpack,' the manicurist broodingly grumbled, with the discontent of someone who right after leaving the movie theatre learns that she has missed the most significant scene of the film.

'You probably picked them up at school. It happens all the time,' Celal said, trying to dismiss the matter lightly.

'I didn't pick them up at school,' Su shrugged her shoulders. 'Besides, there's no one at school with lice except me.'

The women looked at one another with meaningful smiles. It was scarcely news to them that Hygiene Tijen had adamantly sent her daughter to a high-priced school no one else could afford and, by spending all their money to this purpose, had totally wrecked not only her husband's nerves but also the foundations of her marriage.

'No one in the classroom has lice but me. Now it'll spread from my head to the whole school,' giggled the girl. There was a shadowy, blemished tinge to her laughter. It was blemished because it was a laughter oblivious to the reactions of the people around her, originating in her alone to then flow once again back to her, not knowing where and when to stop, and perhaps only indicating a starvation for entertainment. It was shadowed because it was a laughter accelerating at full speed as Su egged herself on, getting out of control as it gained momentum, bordering silently on pain. Her laughter was inconsistent and maladjusted, totally detached from the contents of her talk. It was too unwieldy, too heavy, too much for a child her age.

'My mother says the lice came from my father. He got it from his hookers and then when he cuddled me, I got it from him.'

As if all the windows had been simultaneously opened wide and an unbridled wind rammed in, the women lined up in front of the wide mirror shuddered from top to toe. For it is awesome to hear the most private family secrets spill from the mouth of a child, pretty much like reaping the fruits of your neighbour's garden without actually stealing them. Though there might be a crime, there is no criminal around. Since when is it considered a crime to softly pull aside and make way for the muddy waters that will flow anyhow? Likewise, the beauty parlour populace had backed aside, becoming entirely silent so as to let the child speak fully and freely. They writhed impatiently to hear more, as much as possible, without getting involved, mixed up or messed up. Even Cemal, despite his long-established inability to stay still for more than two seconds and his tendency to poke his nose into each and every conversation around him, managed to keep utterly quiet. Only Madam Auntie felt the need to take action to end this unpleasant topic, but since she could not quite figure out what to say, all she did was to warn Celal to finish his job as quickly as possible and then shrank back into her chair to stay stock-still. Lost in her thoughts, she pulled out the pendant inside her blouse and distractedly caressed the stern face of Saint Seraphim.

Su twirled her chair around in a full circle and, as if to

determine the impact of her words, took stock of everyone's faces. When she completed the circle and returned to her former position, her pitch black eyes met in the mirror the navy blue-grey eyes of the old woman which were glittering like a bead. As Madam Auntie delicately let out from her small, sharp nose the air she had drawn in with melancholy, she smiled with an embarrassment that contained an apology somewhere within. It was difficult to tell if she was apologizing to certain people present on behalf of the child for what she had told or, just the opposite, if she apologized to the child for the curious listeners surrounding her. Though unable to decipher the meaning of this nebulous smile, Su could not help but smile back at her.

Having now speeded up, Celal called both apprentices to his side for help. Within a few minutes, all three resumed work with apparent intensity and blow-dried the hair of both the old woman and the little girl. By having his two apprentices hold two oval mirrors to their necks, he enabled them to see how their hair looked from the back. Thus besieged with mirrors from both the front and back, the images of the child and the old woman multiplied while their similarities concomitantly increased and coalesced.

★★★

Yet when they said goodbye to Celal, who saw them off all the way to the door, and started to climb the stairs of Bonbon Palace, the age difference between them became woefully apparent. The child stopped frequently to wait for the other, sometimes descending the stairs to accompany her up. When they reached the third floor in this manner, Madam Auntie stopped to catch her breath. As Su leaned against the door standing on one leg as if she were punished, she used this opportunity to share more with her new elderly friend that she had started to relax with.

'Three girls in the class, they nicknamed me. Those name

stickers on the notebooks, you know, they wrote "LICESU" in capital letters on mine. My real name is Bengisu, I just shorten it.'

'You know, I too had lice when I was a little girl,' muttered Madam Auntie, in spite of her discomfort about the girl's laughter.

'Really? Did they nickname you as well?' said Su, while trying to figure out who the red-bearded, frowning 'grandfather' dangling from her necklace was.

'No, they didn't nickname me. We had a washer woman, she used to line all her children up and split their lice. She picked all my lice as well. My poor mother had a fit. She was a delicate woman, couldn't handle such things. That was the way she was brought up. What could she do? If a rose in the garden withered, she would take to her bed with grief, if she saw a dead rat, she could not recover for days. I guess she was born in the wrong age...'

The woman's navy blue-grey eyes became lustreless, if only for a moment. With the intuition unique to those who have long prohibited themselves from remembering specific events and mentioning certain names, she sensed she was about to enter the forbidden garden of her memory and withdrew immediately. As if sharing a secret, she teasingly winked at the child whose head appeared even smaller after her haircut.

'Don't pay attention to their calling you "Licesu" or anything else. Everyone gets lice as a child and not only as a child. People get lice when they grow up as well. How can you know who has lice and who does not? Can you see lice with the naked eye? Everyone claims to be clean as a whistle but believe me they too have lice somewhere in them!'

More convinced of the good intention behind the words than the words themselves, Su ran to ring her doorbell as soon as they reached the fourth floor. 'I'm baaaaack!' she yelled when the door opened. Though Hygiene Tijen looked worried that they were late, she seemed to have cleared away her earlier anxiety as she thanked her neighbour. 'It looks good, both short and very chic,' responded Madam Auntie.

Then they looked at one another with the stress of feeling obliged to say a few more things but not quite knowing what those could be.

'I would've invited you in but the cleaning is still not finished. Everything was interrupted when the cleaning lady took off,' stuttered Hygiene Tijen. The stressed, skittish woman at the beauty parlour seemed to have disappeared, leaving a timid, reticent copy in her place.

'Of course, of course, go ahead with your cleaning, but don't tire yourself out too much. You were exhausted today; lie down and rest a little. Anyhow, I have things to do.'

They had never visited each other's houses until then. They sometimes ran into each other at the door and exchanged a few courtesies.

'How can I possibly sleep!' Tijen broke in. 'I get headaches from this disgusting smell. My husband says I exaggerate. Do you think I do? You too get the same smell, don't you? Tell me, Madam Auntie, do you get the garbage smell?'

An indiscernible shadow crossed Madam Auntie's face. When she started to speak again, her voice was rough and rugged, just like her faded hands with the protruding veins.

'Years ago my brother travelled to Cairo. He said one heard a 'hum' as soon as one got off the plane. The hum of Cairo! Yet the airport was quite a way from the city. It turns out a city spreads its hum for miles. Just think, what kind of a city it must be, what kinds of people must live in it for them to overflow like that! Isn't our Istanbul like that, Misses Tijen? Though Cairo hums, Istanbul smells. Strangers are aware of its smell before they even approach the city. We can't smell it, of course. They say a snake likes milk a lot and finds milk through its sense of smell, but could it detect the smell of milk if it swam in the milk cauldron? Probably the Cairene wouldn't hear the hum and the Istanbulite couldn't spot the smell of his or her own cities – and these are such old cities. When I was young, I didn't know Istanbul was so old. Naturally, as it ages, the garbage increases. I no longer get angry. Neither should you be angry, Misses Tijen.'

Not knowing what to say Hygiene Tijen emptily blinked the round, long eye-lashed ebony eyes she had passed on to her daughter. Another prickly silence descended upon the two women. Such intermittently scattered silences are refrains in the conversations of those who are not used to talking to one another; they repeat themselves with set interludes. They uttered a few more words about garbage, a few more words about various other things and wished each other a nice day. The doors were carefully closed, with special attention being paid to not banging them loudly, but the women did not immediately get back to their own tasks. Both stood without a sound for about ten seconds becoming all ears to try to figure out from the noises what the other one was up to. No matter how hard they tried, however, neither could hear a thing.

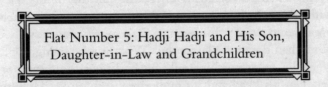

'Once upon a time there lived a much venerated saint....'

'But you said it was gonna be a real story this time!' yelled the seven and a half year old, 'Why did you start it again like a fairytale?'

Hadji Hadji pouted at the boy in anguish. Among his three grandchildren it was this child who upset him most, upset him like no other. He was not human, this boy, but a *jinni* disguised as human or, even worse, the mixed offspring of a *jinni* and a human being. That was why he had turned out to be so peculiar, with a head like a demijohn...but the moment the old man caught himself thinking of such things, he felt ashamed. He immediately repented and shooed such wicked thoughts away. Repentance had with time produced some sort of a spontaneous effect on him. Whenever ashamed, he would immediately repent, like a muscle spasm, with an urge almost as uncontrollable. He did so again, three times successively. First he repented for attempting to grasp and even question with his limited mind why Allah had created people as He had. After that he repented for having indirectly and inadvertently mistrusted his daughter-in-law's chastity by tracing the bloodline of his grandson to the *jinni*. Finally, he repented for having such dreadful thoughts about a little sick child. This last one, however, he had uttered out loud. The seven and a half year old narrowed his moss green eyes into a line and, as if he had understood something had been said about him, observed the old man even more carefully. Hadji Hadji hastily averted his eyes. Even if not a *jinni*, who could deny that this child was *jinn*-like.

Allah had conferred to his siblings all the beauty He had withheld from him, but then, to ensure justice, had bestowed upon him far more intelligence than his siblings, actually even more than the entire family line. What was he going to be like when he grew up? Not only his body, but the disproportion between his head and his body grew day by day. How much bigger could his head expand than the one and a half times its normal size it had already grown to? His hands could not bend back but twisted inside like a monkey's. How much longer could he live with these clawed hands and with the 'Ma-ro-te-aux-la-syn-drome' that no one in the family had even been able to correctly pronounce? Suddenly feeling a tug at his heartstrings, he forced his face into a smile.

'This isn't a fairytale, it's the plain truth,' he said with a gentle expression. 'The saint lived a very long time ago, that's why it came out of my mouth sounding like a fairytale. These things really happened. He even has a tomb. If you don't believe me, you can go and see it with your own eyes.'

The moment he said this he recognized what a 'gaffe' he had made. His oldest grandchild could no longer leave the house. It was to his best interest that he did not. Unlike his peers and siblings the boy's entire world consisted of this one hundred and five metres square house. With a compassion rolled up in mercy, the old man patted the child's puny back.

'This great saint, before he was a saint, used to be a dervish. When his Excellency Sultan Muhammed the Conqueror besieged the city of Istanbul, he immediately ran to help. They beat the city walls with canons. They fought for days but weren't able to get the Byzantine infidel to surrender. Then our dervish had an audience with the sultan. He said, "My sultan, give me permission to open a big breach in these walls so our soldiers can get in from that gap and snap off the infidel's neck like that of a chicken." The sultan looked at the ordinary, ragged dervish standing in front of him. What could such a meek man accomplish? He didn't believe him and expelled him from his audience. Weeks passed by and they still weren't able to take Istanbul. The great Ottoman army was exhausted from thirst and fatigue. Then the sultan remembered this dervish and beckoned him back to his presence. "Here is your permission, go ahead" he said. The delighted dervish kissed his Excellency Sultan Muhammed the Conqueror's hand and sleeve. He said his goodbyes to all the other dervishes. Then he walked around the city walls to think about which point of attack to pick and finally decided on one particular spot. The walls were thicker there and there were more soldiers to boot. For behind that wall was the palace of the Byzantine king. Then the dervish said, "Now throw me to those walls." They were of course surprised but still carried out his wish. They put the dervish in the cannon and hurled him.'

'Come on. They killed the man,' exclaimed the seven and a half year old.

'No they didn't! He is not like you and I, he didn't become a saint for nothing.' Hadji Hadji softened his voice for the sake of all he had repented a moment ago. 'They threw the dervish. With that speed, he went and attached himself to the walls. He didn't fall, that is. He opened wide his hands and feet and grabbed onto those thick walls like a spider. The Byzantine soldiers were teeming like ants there. When they saw the dervish, they threw poisoned arrows. Not one of them fell on the target. Next they showered flaming arrows. Wherever the arrows fell, fire erupted. They set the grass on fire, burned the trees, the whole place was in flames like doomsday, but nothing happened to the dervish. Not even a single thread of his hair caught on fire. He stood in the flames like a salamander. From afar he looked and smiled on the Conqueror's soldiers. There he prayed until night fell, performing the ablutions at sunset.'

'If he's glued to the wall, how could he perform the ablutions?' hollered the seven and a half year old in a shrill voice.

'He performed them with his eyes,' replied the Hadji Hadji now staring angrily. 'Your deceased grandmother, may she rest in peace, also performed her ablutions with her eyes. Those who can't bend down and up do so. Then when the dervish finished his ablutions he said, "My Allah, take my life and turn me into a void!" Allah accepted his prayer and lightning struck in the sky. Remember how the arrows of the Byzantines had been showered right onto him from up close and not even one had found its target? But now a faraway lightning came from the seventh heaven and hit him right on target. The dervish turned into ash. Then, where he had clung to the wall, a large hole appeared. The Conqueror's fighters could not believe their eyes. The hole they could not open for days was all of a sudden created thanks to the dervish. They immediately plunged in through that hole, put the commander of the infidels to the sword and took the city. When his Excellency Sultan Muhammed the Conqueror settled in Istanbul, he didn't forget the self-sacrifice of this dervish. He wanted to have a tomb built for him. Yet the dervish didn't have a corpse. "If there is no corpse, how could there be a grave? What shall we bury?' grumbled the soldiers."

The five and a half year old, who was accustomed to suck till the last drop the privileges granted to her for being the only girl and the youngest child, looked at her grandfather with eyes glazed in fear. In her ornate 'grammar bag', where she put the new words she learned every day, she collected some other words in a place separate from the others, in a wallet with snaps, for instance: 'spirit', 'doomsday', or 'ghost'; likewise: 'demon', 'devil', 'deceased', 'ogre' or 'hellhound.' She rolled in her little fingers the word 'salamander' she had just heard and placed it there as well. All these words had one meaning for her: *jinn*! As for what the *jinn* was, she did not fully know, but whenever she felt the need to know, she plunged her hand into the wallet with snaps, inside her smart ornate bag, randomly pulling out a word. Hence, somewhere in the recesses of her mind, the indistinct figure of a *jinn* that had so many different names though it did not exist, transparent like the gossamer wings of a fly, was nourished from all sides and constantly grew fatter, spreading every passing day like a shameless smokescreen to cover an ever larger terrain.

'They performed ablutions for him in absentia and then they took the empty coffin onto their shoulders,' continued Hadji Hadji after taking a small break to sip on his tea. 'They started to walk, but where were they to go? They could never decide where to bury him. However, at this point the coffin suddenly took wings! It started to move by itself, right in front of them. They crossed many rivers and hills, coffin in the front, mourners in the back, up and down six of the seven hills of Istanbul. When they came to the seventh hill, they looked and saw in a distance an empty grave: a grave dug deep and left open. The coffin immediately dashed in that direction, started to descend right onto the top of the grave and remained hanging in the air until one hand span from the bottom. Then a howling was heard from the grave…'

The five and a half year old gulped loudly, but deep in his trance, Hadji Hadji did not notice that detail. Whatever attention he had left he reserved for his oldest grandchild.

'They then lowered the coffin into this empty grave. After that they built a tomb over it. The saint's name became Father Void. The passers-by always recited a prayer for his soul.'

'But the man isn't even there! Don't they know the grave is empty? Who are they praying to?'

'Women who can't have children pay a visit to Father Void,' muttered Hadji Hadji pretending not to hear the question. 'If brides with empty wombs go to Father Void, pray, and then sit alone by his tomb all night long without falling asleep, their prayers will be granted at dawn. They'll give birth to a healthy child within a year.'

All three children reacted in their own way to these words. The five and a half year old reopened her wallet of snaps, gingerly placing 'void' among the words that corresponded to 'jinn.' The six and a half year old, who was particularly interested in all topics that could somehow be associated with sexuality, seemed more concerned with the brides' part than the saints. As for the seven and a half year old, he in turn had questions to articulate, objections to raise. Still, however, he did not say a word. It was time for the noon nap, and that, the kid reckoned, was far more imperative than identifying the numerous mistakes in the rationale operating behind his grandfather's tales.

Around these hours of the afternoon, time in Flat Number 5 gradually slowed down. The same things were always repeated every day in the same order. Early in the morning their mother went to work and their father to look for work. When left alone with their grandfather, every weekday morning without fail, an argument broke out among them regarding the television. Hadji Haji would rather not have the children watch much television but, if they did, preferred it to be one of those insipid children's programmes or even better, the cartoons that were simultaneously broadcast on a couple of channels. The kids however had a different choice, insisting on watching the morning programme hosted by a chatty and flirtatious person who wore outfits that, depending on the day, either left bare the red rosebud tattoo on her belly or the cleavage of her breasts. When their request was not granted, they either took out the battle-axe and went on the attack or became fussy and refused to talk to their grandfather. Hadji Hadji's reaction also varied daily. Now and then he put up with the situation and while the children watched the programme, he kept reading one of the four books he owned – a number which had remained the same over the years. At times he got hold of the remote control and, in spite of all the objections buzzing around him, fixed the screen on the first cartoon he could find. On other occasions, he tried to draw his grandchildren's attention away from the screen and wore out his imagination by concocting various games, each more strained than the other. Whatever he did, however, he could not wrest power away from them, especially not from his oldest grandchild, until noon. After that things got worse for the old man for they would, just like they had been doing every weekday for the last two months, pile up all the sheets, pillows and covers in the middle of the living room and start to create 'Osman'.

Two months previously, Hadji Hadji had read to his grandchildren the first three chapters of one of his four books entitled, 'How Was a Magnificent Empire Born and Why Did it Decline?' When he took a break, he got, as usual, three dissimilar reactions from his three grandchildren. The seven and a half year old had listened austerely, attentively and was now ready to voice a couple of issues of great interest to him: 'Grandpa, how many tents did the Turks have when they arrived in Anatolia?' 'A thousand!' Hadji Hadji hastily made up. Yet that response did little to satisfy the child's curiosity. 'About how many people in all were there in these thousand tents?' 'Ten thousand!' Hadji Hadji roared. The anger dripping from his response only provoked his oldest grandchild even more. 'When the Turks came with their tents, weren't there already other people in Anatolia?' 'No, there weren't, this land was empty, whoever was there had run away,' grumbled Hadji Hadji. 'Okay, did the Turks settle in the houses of those who had run away? Or did they continue to live as nomads for some time? Did they build their first cities out of tents? In that case would that be a tent-metropolis? How could one draw on a map a city that was peripatetic? How...?'

'Shut up!' Hadji Hadji had replied losing control.

The child had indeed shut up but all the questions that had accumulated on his tongue circulated in his mouth, moved up through the passages of his nose and climbed up from there to trickle into his teardrop ducts, so in his moss green pupils curious, insistent, accusing sparks of questions continued to light up and fade away like fireflies flitting about on summer nights.

In order not to keep looking at him, the old man had turned with a weak expectation to the six and a half year old, but judging from the indifferent expression on his face the only thing he registered from the story was that there were many concubines in the harem and it was not a good thing to be born as the brother of a sultan. With a final crumb of hope, Hadji Hadji turned to his youngest grandchild, the five and a half year old. It was then that the little girl, her face bright with excitement, jumped on her grandfather's lap, nudged him with her pinkish-white elbows and with the cutesy manner she assumed whenever she wanted anything from grownups, cooed: 'Come on, grandpa, let's build a tent too!'

Had Hadji Hadji not been so distressed with the apathy of his male grandchildren, he probably would have hesitated before jumping at this idea, but since with a sleight of his hand he had transferred all of his love to the youngest grandchild in order to punish the other two, he soon found himself among piles of sheets and pillows busily building a tent in the middle of the living room. They too would have a tent just like the dynasty of Osman.

Compared to the tents they later built, the first one was rather primordial. The grandfather and the child had produced a small, covered area by throwing a few sheets over the four chairs arranged in a square and then filling this area with pillows. Yet the tent, even in this simple form, had succeeded in drawing the attention of the other two who had not participated in the game and had, until then, suspiciously watched everything from the side. After a while, they could not resist and, dying to see this hidden, compressed world constructed in the middle of the living room, had parted the sheet intended to be the door and joined their grandfather who was sitting cross-legged on the pillows. Surprisingly Hadji Hadji felt swelling within him the type of pure pride he had yearned for so long. It was this pride or the possibility of it that had led the old man to wholeheartedly embrace this game. Yet how wretchedly shaky the foundations were, and how fragile the domination he had by chance established in the house, would become evident in no more than a day.

Around the same time the next day, the five and a half year old had placed herself in his lap in exactly the same manner: 'Come on, grandpa, let's make Osman!' When the old man heard the name 'Osman', his hair stood up as he had not yet been able to get rid of the fatigue the previous tent-exercise had produced on his out of shape legs and stiff back. Alas, neither his dulcet warnings nor his seething anger had been of much help in teaching the girl that the tent was not supposed to be called 'Osman'. Such was the girl's nature. Once she coupled one word with another, no authority in the world could sever this linguistic connection in her mind. Just as ghosts, spirits, ogres, hellhounds and the deceased were altogether lumped in the category of 'JINN', so too was the tent called 'OSMAN'.

After that Osman became an essential part of their lives. Now every day around the same time the children started to get antsy like drunkards awaiting their drinking time. Within half an hour, all the sheets, bedspreads, mattresses and pillows were piled in the middle of the living room. Even though Hadji Hadji hoped in vain that, with their record of getting bored with all the games they played, his flighty grandchildren would also get their fill of Osman, this was not to be. On the contrary, they gradually expanded the boundaries of the tent adding new rooms, sections and cavities, leading a blissfully nomadic life in an area of five and ten square metres. Osman was rebuilt at noon every day, stayed in the middle of the living room until late in the afternoon, and then when it started to get dark outside, was taken down in a flash minutes before the parents were due back from work.

There were a number of other incidents repeated daily without exception. For instance, the phone rang around the same time, around 11:45 a.m., after the last minute theatre-goers had settled in their seats for the noon show. Each time it was the oldest kid who answered the phone. He reported what they had done since morning, always giving the same responses to the same questions: yes, they had finished their breakfasts...no, they weren't being naughty...yes, they were watching television...no, grandfather wasn't telling a story...no, they hadn't turned on the gas...no, they didn't mess the house up…no, they didn't hang out of the balcony…no, they didn't play with fire…no, they didn't enter the bedroom…Allah was his witness that grandfather didn't tell a story…' and so forth…

Even though deep down the Daughter-in-Law was suspicious of her older son's honesty, never willing to call her father-in-law to the phone, she had to be satisfied with what she heard. Meanwhile, as the seven and a half year old held the phone in his hand and recited his usual responses with a suggestion of slyness in his voice, not even for a second did he take his eyes off his grandfather. He was more than aware of the continuous tension between the two adults and had long since discovered that he could bolster his power by favouring, as the occasion dictated, one adult over the other.

Not only did they have their meals inside Osman, but they listened to their bed-time stories there as well. Every day after lunch before their nap, new personalities joined them: coldhearted stepmothers, ill-fated orphans, hellhounds escaping from the bowels of the earth, bandits waylaying people, female *jinns* seducing men, bloodied fighters, certified madmen, poisonous rattlesnakes, spiteful hags with sagging flesh, malicious skeletal demons and ogres with protruding eyes…all crammed into the tent. Once they arrived, they never wanted to leave. As the concluding sentences of the fairytale still smoked in the air weariness descended upon them. Everyone curled up in their place. Hadji Hadji was the one to fall asleep the fastest and the easiest, followed by the five and a half year old and then the six and a half year old. As his grandfather's snores and his siblings' puffs filled the tent, the seven and a half year old got up quietly. First he stopped by his grandfather and watched him. He watched as if examining a creature he did not know, a tropical fruit he had not tasted or a clam filled with surprises, Hadji Hadji's round, greying beard rising and falling with each intake of breath, the amber prayer bead that had slid from his fingers, the greying hair creeping from his chest to his neck, his cracked lips, the deep wrinkles that had cut paths across his forehead... He had started to examine his grandfather two and a half years ago and was soon about to complete his discovery.

That mild, fragrant day when he had met his grandfather for the first time had been a turning point for the child, as it also happened to be the last day he was able to walk around outside. Then his illness had advanced so rapidly and had become so visible that he had never been out onto the streets ever again.

In the fading residues of that distant past, when he was still considered or at least looked looked like a normal child, when his father and mother had to go to the airport to pick up his grandfather, they had taken him along as well. Until that day, he had not heard much about the old man. All he knew was that his name was Hadji, he lived with his wife in a far away city, they had had a traffic accident when travelling to Istanbul to see their grandchildren for the first time and the grandmother had died in the accident. After losing his wife, grandfather Hadji had cried a lot, been hospitalized for a while and gone on the pilgrimage to Mecca as soon as he was discharged. Having now completed the pilgrimage he was coming back. This was all the seven and a half year old who had then been five knew about him. On the way to the airport, he had also acquired another piece of noteworthy information: from now on, grandfather Hadji was going to live in Istanbul with them.

The part of the airport reserved for the passengers' relatives was jammed. After descending from the plane and completing a whole bunch of bureaucratic procedures the passengers passed through the automatic door swishing open to be reunited with their awaiting relatives. As the kid waited in the crowd holding tightly onto his mother's and father's hands, he carefully looked at every person passing by. All these old men back from their pilgrimage were surprisingly like carbon copies of each other and the reason for this similarity was not only that they were all dressed in the same colour, were of the same age and height and possessed the same round, greyish beard. They also unerringly repeated, as soon as they went through the door, the same motions in the same sequence. When the door opened, they all narrowed their eyes as if suddenly encountering a beam of light, looked at the crowd, took a few steps in this state, then saw someone and dashed in that direction, put down the suitcases and exuberantly embraced the acquaintances who scurried toward them. In making their entrance, the elderly copied one another exactly, it was as if, rather than a plane load of different people, the same man kept walking in through the automatic doors again and again.

Then the door swished open one more time and through it entered a man whom he guessed, from his mother's and father's reactions, was his grandfather. This man, though dressed just like the other pilgrims, still looked like a stranger who had mistakenly become mixed up among them. It was as if he was not even old but was rather a successful imitator who had plunged into the changing room at the last minute to don the clothes of one of the others. He almost looked like them but was nevertheless an imitator because something was obviously missing. Blinking his moss green eyes, the kid looked once again and only then he grasped where the deficiency originated: this old man did not have a beard! Where there had to be a beard shone a dazzling white crescent curving up – the area within the crescent having amply received its share from the sun, the north of his face was pitch dark as night while the south as pallid as a cloudless morning.

The man with the 'unfinished face' had longingly embraced the grandchild he was seeing for the first time. Then he had sequentially embraced his son, again his grandson, the Daughter-in-Law, again his grandson, again his son, and then again and again his grandson. Meanwhile, soon everyone around them was embracing one another, the airport waiting area filled-up entirely with clusters of humans who cried, kissed, embraced and bumped into one another. When the elderly men returning from the pilgrimage had somewhat satisfied their yearning for one another, they became deeply occupied with introducing each other to their own families which this time around led to handshakes, hugs and embraces across the clusters. In that uproar, the kid passed around from one lap to another had registered another observation in his memory book: those 'Mehmets' returning from the pilgrimage were called 'Hadji Mehmet,' and the 'Ahmets' were called 'Hadji Ahmet.' On the way back, he had asked his father the question that had preoccupied him, 'If one had to go to the pilgrimage to deserve the name Hadji, how was it that his grandfather's name had become Hadji by birth, before going to the pilgrimage or indeed anything? And since his name was already Hadji, why on earth had he gone to the pilgrimage?' While his face was incomplete, it was as if his name was overly complete. 'You rascal!' his father had scolded him. As that was far from being a satisfying answer, it only helped to serve the kid's conviction that his grandfather was unlike any other grandfather. Ever since then he thought his grandfather was somewhat 'eccentric.' That the old man had been obliged to cut his beard because of a bad rash a day before his return from Mecca and had quickly grown it afterwards, thus after a short while looking like all other grandfathers at the airport, had little effect in convincing the boy to the contrary.

Now after all these years, even though he still studied his grandfather, he had begun to cut his examinations shorter with every passing day, mainly because he did not find him as interesting as he had in the past. Once bored of watching the old man, he got out of Osman without a sound and started to tiptoe around the house. To be up when everyone else was asleep was a terrific privilege. The house would then resemble the castle in 'Sleeping Beauty'. For, unlike his siblings, the seven and a half year old did remember the fairytales his mother used to tell them in the mornings long before she had started working at the cinema of a shopping mall. He recalled those fairytales and discerned the difference between those and the ones told by his grandfather.

While the others slept, he would go into the kitchen, light the oven, play with matches, leaf through the four books of his grandfather, the total number of which had stayed constant through the years, snack on junk food, go into his parents' bedroom and poke around the wardrobes, dump his mother's jewellery on the bed, count the money his father hid at the corner of the wardrobe...he made the most of doing everything that was forbidden. Then, when the others' waking up time approached, tiptoeing back into the tent, he lay down in a corner and patiently waited. He did not have to wait too long. Every day the garbage truck entered Cabal Street around 5:30 p.m. The voices of the garbage collectors, the clatter of the emptied cans and the grumble of the engine rose up from below. There were cars parked on each side of the road, so the garbage truck could not maneouvre easily and the traffic would be jammed for sure. As soon as the honks of the car horns reached Flat Number 5 of Bonbon Palace, Hadji Hadji was jolted out of his sleep, almost screaming. In point of fact, Bonbon Palace was one of the last places where this old man, who carried in the wrinkles of his forehead, his face and in his heart the traces of the traffic accident he had been through, could comfortably take a snooze.

The children also awoke with Hadji Hadji's scream. First the five and a half year old woke up, muttering fussily. Then the six and a half year old got up, lazily yawning. As for the seven and a half year old, he would not immediately get up from the place where he had laid down only a couple of minutes previously, but instead counted silently to twenty to give the others enough time to fully wake up. Then, standing up groggily he would rub his moss green eyes and, hiding the sharp glint within them, approach the open window and stretch his neck to look at the doors of the outside world filled with secrets which he deeply sensed could be much more horrifying than all the fairytales he had heard.

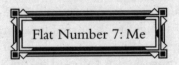

Flat Number 7: Me

Strange as it was, I woke up without the help of an alarm clock this morning. As if that was not astonishing enough, when I woke up, I found myself already awake. My eyes were open as if they had awoken by themselves and having once done that, had taken to wandering around the ceiling. For a fleeting moment I thought I was looking at myself from the ceiling. I cannot say I liked what I saw.

Whenever I fall asleep here, my legs spill over from the couch but this time I seem to have forgotten to take off my shoes to boot. My head had slipped from the pillow, my neck was sore. In the dent extending from the side of my mouth to my ear, I detected a bubbly, pasty spittle – befitting a dog gone rabid or a baby regurgitating the food just consumed. My shirt had wrinkled up on me, the pain of lying down lopsided had hit my back and my mouth was parched. I had also thrown up on the corner of the rug. At least I had thought of taking off my trousers, but as 'Ethel the Cunt' likes to articulate in yet another aphorism of hers: 'To be without pants while in socks and shoes can make a man only as attractive as a candied apple with the exposed parts all rotten...' or something like that. When viewed from this angle, perhaps I should consider myself lucky for waking up alone this morning, just like I had done for the last sixty-six days.

It is all because of this house. It has been two months and five days since I moved in here. I have come to realize that for all its abstractness and vastness the terms in which time is measurable are no more concrete and no less petite than mere driblets. I count up every day that has passed, every drop of it. By now I should have fully settled down and established some sort of an order in this house. Yet not only have I failed to settle down, I live as if I might pack up and leave any moment. As if to make moving out easier, the flat is still not much different from the way it was the day I moved in, with boxes piled up on top of one another, some opened but most only roughly so: a perfunctory, transitory dwelling amidst parcels yet to be opened...the fleeting order as evaporative as room sprays...a 'Lego-home' constructed of parts and pieces to be dissembled at any moment...When single, one lives amidst 'belongings-in-a-house'; one's past, trajectory, personal worth all contained in possessions that bear symbolic value. Upon getting married, one starts to live in 'a-house-of-belongings', established more on a future than a past, more on expectations than memories; a house where it is doubtful how much one personally possesses. As for divorce, depending on whether one is the person leaving or the person staying behind, it is like camping out all over again, only this time one either stays behind in a 'house-with-belongings-gone' or departs, carrying 'belongings-without-a-house'.

My situation is both, because of this house and because of 'Ethel the Cunt'. The day I had to move in here, no matter how hard I tried, I could not convince her to stay out of it and not mess things up by helping. When I had finally perched myself in the front seat of the truck belonging to the moving company that had agreed to transport the books, clothes and knick-knacks I had deliberately refused to let go from the tastefully decorated home of my marriage (as well as some cheap and simple furniture I had recently bought for the dingy apartment that would be the base for my post-marriage era); there right next to me was none other than Ethel. As if her presence was not alarming enough, she teamed up with the dim-witted driver, utterly stunning the man with the premium quality cigars she offered, preposterous questions she asked and the absurd topics of conversation she came up with – which included making a list of the most difficult neighbourhoods in Istanbul to move in and out of. When we had finally reached Bonbon Palace, Ethel meddled with the porters, running around excitedly in that hard-to-believe skirt of hers, which was no bigger than the size of a beggar's handkerchief, on that huge, hideous ass she so much enjoys exhibiting.

Shooting orders left and right, she instructed the porters where to put each box, how to arrange the book parcels and where to stack the common, slipshod packages of shelves of what was supposed to turn into a self-made library, which she herself had forced me to purchase from one of those huge stores in which families paid homage at the weekends. The porters were wise enough to know that it is the woman who has the last word in these matters and in their wisdom unashamedly ignored me, the real owner. All day long I do not remember them even once paying attention to what I said, except when the time came to pay them. It was only then that they favoured me over Ethel. Even when they accidentally banged the cardboard box packed with all kinds of glasses, cups, and goblets, the authority they addressed and the person they apologized to was not me, trying to mildly dismiss the incident, but Ethel who gave them hell about the probable damage they might have caused.

All day long, I had to stand at a corner and be content with watching what was considered appropriate for me. My exclusion reached its peak during the installation of the 180 x 200 cms, golden bow, system-orthopedic king size bed – one of the two hearty spoils I had wrested from my former house. When, after six tries, it had become only too evident that the bed would not fit the shapeless space of a room that Ethel had decided to make into my bedroom, an argument broke out among them. Ethel wanted the bed to be put in sideways and would sacrifice the showy headboard, if necessary. As for the porters, they were all for locating the bed head-on, even though there would then be no space left to move around.

Meanwhile, no one asked my opinion and if someone had, I would not know what to say anyhow. When they finally agreed to put the bed in sideways, still leaving no room to move, I did not object. That bed was too big for me at any rate. Accordingly, I have not slept on it once since I moved here. I am pretty much consistent in sleeping on this narrow couch that torments my posture and tortures my back. In the past, during her lengthy Masnawi season, Ethel had once lectured me about how Rumi had to reckon with his body. Though not in such a mystical manner, in these last two months I too have probably shown little gratitude to my frame. Still, like a desperate lover ever more attached to his oppressor or a despicable apprentice inured to scorn, I too cannot break away from this cruelly uncomfortable sofa. Before the end of the term, I should assign 'The Discourse of Voluntary Servitude' to the Thursday section.

The television oppposite is, no doubt, the main reason for my preferring this couch. These days, having given up regular sleeping hours, I seek refuge in television and can only sleep with it turned on. Likewise last night, back home so late and high, I must have turned on the television. Now on the screen some madcap of a young girl with a short, multihued shirt with tropical birds, a crimson rosebud tattoo almost as big as a fist on her bare plump belly and orange-coloured hair tied-up in handfuls with phosphorescent green ribbons, chirps with a glee not many people are bestowed with this early in the morning. Though the girl does not move her body around that much and talks with simple hand gestures, her breasts keep wobbling in that way particular to women scurrying to catch a bus at the last minute. This is not to my taste though. I have always gone for contrasts; I like them either as small as the palm in a big frame, or huge in a petite body.

Ten days later, when Ethel came to inspect the house and saw everything was as she had left it, she kept her comments to herself. Nothing had changed by the third week. Still not even a single package had been unwrapped, not even a single shelf mounted. When she stopped by one month five days later, I wished she would keep silent once again. However, with a disagreeable smile on her face and whilst clicking her long, brightly polished fingernails together, she blurted out in that particular manner of hers intended to stress the importance of whatever she was going to say, 'Look, sugar-plum! It's none of my business but you'd better stop treating your new house like you've treated your ex-wife. You neglect your house assuming it's all yours and will never go anywhere, but God forbid it too might be taken away from you, just like your wife was.' I did not respond. I have always hated long, polished fingernails.

Ethel uses her tongue the way a frog catches a fly. Whatever comes to her mind she blurts out and before the victim has even had a chance to get the message, catches with her harsh pink tongue the momentary bewilderment on the latter's face and then gulps it down with great pleasure, without even bothering to swallow. Although following the divorce I had barely hesitated in ending numerous friendships in my life, I do not know, and frankly do not want to know, why I am still friends with her. Not that I make any special efforts to see her, but I do not take any steps to stop seeing her either. The issue is not that I do not like her any longer, for I have never liked her more or less than I do now. If a bond has kept us together all this time, I do not think it is one of love, companionship or trust. Ethel and I are as compatible as each single wing of two different butterflies positioned side by side under a collector's magnifying glass. We are very much alike in our incompleteness and yet it is two different halves, with utterly distinct designs and colours that we eventually pine for. As we waft along with the wind, we have been coming together, even sticking together, but never in such as way as to complete one another. If I don't see her for a month, I barely miss her and am sometimes hardly even aware of her absence; yet, when we meet after a month, I do not feel the slightest distress next to her or ever think about cutting short the time we spend together. Ethel is Ethel, just as some things simply are what they are. In spite of this, or maybe precisely because of this, I see her more frequently and share more things with her than with anyone else. That is how it has been for many years. This loose relationship of ours may persevere as such or brusquely unravel one day like the nail of a haemorrhaged finger. At times I wonder, if such a thing happens, which one of us will be the first to realize and how long after the fingernail has fallen?

As I was getting up from the couch, my foot got caught on the phone cable. The receiver emerged from under my pillow, as if I had tried to squeeze the life out of the phone last night. It is so annoying, all the data at hand indicates that I was not able to resist calling her last night before I passed out.

Nobody would object to the fact that it is dangerous for drunks to drive. Making phone-calls whilst drunk, however, could produce even more deadly results than driving whilst drunk, and yet there are no legal procedures for dealing with this particular danger. Drunk drivers hit random targets, like an unfortunate tree that suddenly appears in front of them or an unrelated vehicle moving on its way...in these accidents there is neither purpose nor intent. Yet those who use the phone when drunk always go and hit the ones they love.

It is enough of a torment to realize that you've called your loved one when drunk, but it is even worse not to remember whether you called and, as you force yourself to remember, to try to convince yourself to the contrary. Since my divorce, this scene kept repeating itself at almost regular intervals but I had not yet called Ayshin on her new number. She probably does not even know that I managed to get this number. That is, of course, if we did not talk last night... I had to be certain. I pushed the redial button. One, two, three...it was answered on the sixth ring. There she was herself! In the morning, her voice always sounded as if it had come from the bottom of a deep well. She likes to sleep. Highly unattractive upon waking up, she cannot possibly come to her senses before having her filtered coffee. No sugar, no milk. Her second 'hellooo' sounded even more furious than her first. I hung up.

I tried to collect my thoughts. In spite of everything, there was still some hope. The fact that I called her did not mean that we actually talked. Maybe the phone was not answered. If Ayshin had answered the phone last night and said a few good or bad things, I would have at least remembered bits and pieces of what had been said. As I did not recall a single word, probably nothing worth remembering had occurred, but there was no way I could find solace on the bosom of this slim chance. The most plausible explanation for Ayshin's not answering the phone last night was that she was not home at the time. At that time, outside.... Outside, at that time...

On the bathroom floor lie two dead cockroaches half a metre apart. This must be two of my accomplishments last night but I cannot, in the doubtful records of my memory, come across any explanation regarding this matter. I take my shirt off. It is suffused with a sharp smell: an unbearable smell jointly produced by the smells of the deep-fried turbot, lots of side dishes, the *rakı* I drank and the premium quality cigars I smoked, all mixed up then totally dredged and made unrecognizable by my stomach acid. The washing machine is a divorce gift from Ethel. She has always been a practical woman, handy and generous. I throw my navy-blue linen pants into the machine as well. I have learned by now that for linens one uses the 40° temperature and the second short cycle, but even if I succeed in purifying myself from the unpleasant sediments of last night, it is amply evident that I will not be able to free myself from the disgusting garbage smell engulfing this apartment building. I am extremely regretful about acting so hastily during the divorce process in my search for a house. For the same amount of money I could have been living in a much more decent place if I had not, with the intent of getting away as soon as possible, attempted to land the first relatively cheap and adequately distant flat. I miss the comfort of my old house. The issue does not solely consist of my yearning for the lost comfort and the lost heaven from which I personally arranged my own downfall. The house actually belonged to Ayshin or, to put it more correctly, to Ayshin's family, but after a three and a half year long residency, I had thought the house was mine too until that unfortunate moment after gathering my underwear, books, lecture notes and razor blades when I went back for a last look to check if I had left anything behind. Such a puny little word: 'too!' Like a child enthusiastically expecting that what his brother has received will be given to him too: 'Me too, me too!' Yet it seems that in marriage, just as in sibling relations, one side gets more than the other, while people's traces can be removed from the places they lived, or sometimes even thought they owned, as easily as the string off of a string bean. What I find hard to take, what thrusts pains into my stomach, is exactly the part about the string. It upsets me to think that now Ayshin has a great time by herself in the house that was once mine too. One should of course be always grateful, for there is worse than the worse imaginable: she could be having a great time not all alone...

I took stock in the bathroom, freezing at times or getting scalded at others under the shower that either heated up so much that it then suddenly turned icy, or turned cold and then became boiling hot, managing never to end up lukewarm. Even though it was unclear how I had found my way home last night imbibed, it was certain that I had called Ayshin with my drunken jellyfish-head. Okay, what then? If we had talked, a memory, a moment should have been left behind. A sentence... As I soaped my face, the headquarters of my brain sent the news that a sentence fitting the description of the sought suspect had been observed wandering around and been arrested: 'Don't you see that I will totally cease to care about you if you keep calling like this? Before we lose our respect for each other...' I did not see anything. Even though I tried to open my soapy eyes for a moment, I again shut them when they started stinging from the soap. No, the information proved to be groundless. This was not the sentence I was searching for. I remembered. I had not heard this one last night, but earlier, sometime before Ayshin had tried to change her phone number.

I stepped out when the manic depressive shower started to push my endurance. The pain in my stomach was unbearable. The kitchen was not too small, but became rather narrow after the installment, right in the middle, of an impressive burly refrigerator more or less the size of the cottages that low-income holiday-makers perch along sea shores and fill up with their families. Rather than insisting on taking from my old house this American bullock, designed to satiate the tribal appetites of consumer society's nuclear families with their hangar-like homes, I should have gone and bought myself one of those box-like, knee-high refrigerators used in either hotel rooms or flats in Tokyo. I probably would have done so if Ayshin had not objected by stating 'It's too big for you.' I had heard this remark twice in a row: firstly, for the king-size bed and secondly, for the refrigerator. It was only then, upon realizing that what was too big for me was not that big for Ayshin, had I been able to surmise that there was another man in her life and my place would be shortly filled up. So even though I did not cause any difficulties on any matter and was more compliant and docile than necessary so as to hurry along the divorce process, no one, Ethel included, could make out my uncompromising stubbornness concerning the bed and the refrigerator.

My loot might have been substantial but it was totally hollow. It looked pathetic empty like that. Large refrigerators are distant relatives of those old locomotives who gobble-up coal all along the way; they are, just like them, never full and as they get filled, constantly want to be filled some more. Forget sacks of coal, mine is bereft even of a shovel full of coal dust. On the top shelf there was a box of opened cream cheese coated with a thin layer of mould, inside the door are five cans of beer and half a large bottle of *rakı,* in the vegetable container sat three tomatoes and wilted leaves of lettuce. That was all. Then, on the bottom shelf there was the mushroom pizza slice sent by that elderly woman neighbour. I had seen many who send puddings and the like, but had never before encountered one who made pizza and distributed it slice by slice. I was going to throw it away but forgot. Now, however, as the alcohol particles left over from the night slowly gnawed on the membrane of my stomach, I reached for the pizza slice with gratitude. It took three minutes to heat it up in the microwave oven and approximately thirty seconds to get it down my stomach. It was a bit stale but so what: it was great considering the conditions! Having thus appeased my stomach, just a tad, I embarked on preparing my medicine. This included a pot of skimmed milk with two heaped spoonfuls of Turkish coffee, one spoonful of pine honey, a generous quantity of cinnamon and a little cognac. This is my miracle medicine for hangovers, its curing power proven through experience. It may not suit every constitution. Actually every constitution should, through trial and error, develop its own cure. That is how I found mine. That day I made the proportions more generous than usual, as I needed to sober up as soon as possible. It was Thursday and since the beginning of the term, every Thursday afternoon I have taught the course I love the most to the class I love the most.

While waiting for the milk to boil, I looked through the brochures Ethel had thrust into my hand. Another private university was being founded in Istanbul. I had been aware of some of the details for a long time, like the long preparation process for example. What I did not know was that Ethel the Cunt was involved as well; she was actually at the very centre of it all and told me more than I ever wanted to learn at dinner. Only two minutes after we had met, she introduced the topic with a 'plop' and talked of almost nothing else until the end of the night when, under the weary looks of the skinny Kurdish waiter who could barely keep his long black eyelashes open, we wobblingly departed from the restaurant that had no other customers left except us. She kept talking continuously about how this university was not a financial investment but a moral one; how she had not so wholeheartedly believed in a project for quite a long time; she personally knew the founders and that she herself was actually one of the eight investors behind the scenes; she had enjoyed life much more since she got involved in this and that she was sure when she looked back in her old age this would be the job she would be most proud of in her life; about how they would educate a group of youth much more conscious and knowledgeable than their generation within five years at the most; how the size of this group of youths would increase from year to year and how they would altogether affect the fate of our haggard country. As she kept speaking, I kept on drinking. If I had drunk less, or more slowly, the summary of the night would have been something like this: Ethel talked, I laughed; Ethel got angry, I burst out; Ethel shouted, we fought. So in order not to cause a scene, not to muddy the waters for no good reason, and not to spoil the night, Ethel talked and I drank.

What upset me was more the perpetrator of the words than their content. Of course, Ethel the Cunt could go and talk about this bullshit with anyone she wanted, anywhere she wished, but of all the people in her life, she should not have acted like this to me. Not that I take it personally. The issue is not personal, but rather 'linguistic.' At dinner yesterday, for whatever reason, Ethel either decided to break our tradition or simply forgot the language we have been speaking when alone for as long as I can remember.

'Language' is one of the most nonsensical words in a language. It is by definition something more than the sum of all words but in the end it, too, is a word. Should there be the need for a connection with another word, you could say that the word 'language' is like the word 'meal.' There is just as little sense in labelling everything a 'meal' – which totally overlooks very different food mixtures with differences in taste, nutritional value and calories – as there is in labelling as 'language' all the expressions that play totally different tunes, talk about different words at random and emerge in different styles. I should of course add that in making this observation, 'linguistic' differences such as the Chinese cuisine, Turkish cuisine, Spanish cuisine and so forth are not even taken into account. Otherwise, I would have to multiply all these with a global coefficient. In short, hundreds of 'languages' reign even within a single 'language'. Just as we do not all eat the same 'meal' in a restaurant we also do not and can not speak the same 'language' with everyone all the time, and just as meals have residues, languages have remnants. A garbage dump language comprises words we not only do not use everyday but are reluctant to even pronounce, words we silently pass over, nonsensical words we keep to ourselves because they would not be proper, criticisms that come to the tip of our tongues but we lack the courage to voice, innuendos we slice into thin strips at the tip of our tongues to then gulp back, curses that blow up in our palate before we can take out the fuse and throw them away, expressions that are too loaded or jokes too light for our milieu. There might also be a remnant left over from the attention we pay, the tact we demonstrate and the care we take when we talk or write to others. We can call this a recyclable language of 'Solid Accumulated Waste (SAW)'; accumulated, if not in the basement or the attic or under the pillow, then on the nasal passage, in between the palate and under the tongue; a language which, once adequately accumulated, we fill into a bag, tie up and throw away to stop the smell and the stink.

I should say right out I never leave evidence of this language lying around and not only do I not use it in front of my students in class, I do not like to hear it from them either. Yet just like a teenager secretly smoking in a secluded spot without his parents' knowledge, I too am occasionally thrilled to 'sass' – as Ethel and I call it – in this language as I open my caché in a dark and dingy corner, unbeknownst to my moral principles and conscience. It is exactly at this point that Ethel's presence acquires significance. For 'sassing', just like making love or quarrelling, requires that someone else be there with you at the same time. You might smoke alone but to speak in this kind of garbage-language you definitely need a companion.

For years, whenever left alone, Ethel and I would speak, or used to speak until yesterday, in SAWish. Whenever we got together, without stating that one needs to be serious to call the other silly, without making any claims to be just or equitable, we loved to recklessly and coarsely belittle everything and shower this or that person with insults. Just like a bully brushing off an attack to then plunge into a fight by randomly pruning the noses and ears of his adversaries, we attacked social life with our cutting tongues and did our best to prune the maladies and blunders of whomever chanced to appear in front of us.

Who says you cannot make fun of other people's defects? With spears in our hands and waterproof goggles on our eyes, we would dive headfirst into the seven depths of the sea of flaws-faults-failures and bring each defect captured to land, with the intent of examining it at great length and tearing it to shreds. Sometimes, not content with this, with an appetite befitting calamari-lovers we would lift our catch up in the air and hit him against this or that rock for hours on end. In the final instance, no one escaped our tongues but some received from our shower of generalizations more of their share than others. Peasants, the lumpen proletariat, advertisers and academics, housewives and lawyers...all were a target, albeit for different reasons. Yet the diameter of our net was rather wide, enough to easily contain all sorts of people. There was a place for everyone there.

We pitilessly and coarsely belittled those we saw to be unsteady or those who attempted to look smart. We were irritated by those who cared about their appearance but totally drowned in derision those who dressed tastelessly as well; had no respect for the masculine heroes of the 'have-not's' but were beside ourselves with anger at the prima donnas of the 'have's'. We turned up our noses at those who feared death to then merrily trample on those who had no concern about death. We could not bear to read a poorly written article, story or novel but also slung mud left and right on those well written ones. We did not even take note of those who turned religious in the aftermath of a serious surgery or trauma but also carelessly cast aside the ones who remained at exactly the same level of belief either with or without religion, all through their lives. We did not forgive the decent ones because of their decency but also took the crookedness of the crooked and danced around with it. We threw on the ground and trampled on those guilelessly naive secularists who thought Christianity was less interventionist or Judaism less patriarchal than Islam; gleefully gnawed on those who were unaware of the variations within Islam but also bruised with cannon salvoes those who imagined themselves privileged for happening upon mystical movements; and tore to pieces those who, in the name of the trinity of 'Being, Becoming & Transcending Sainthood', sought alternative Indian, Chinese, Tibetan messiahs for themselves. We rammed into those breeders married with kids but laughed our hearts out at those who regarded not getting married a form of political resistance. We also covered in tar and paraded naked before us both those who perceived their heterosexuality to be a socially given 'for once-and-always' yet craved to take at least a petite bite of the apple of sodomy, as well as those who regarded their homosexuality as entirely an individual choice to then sluggishly sit in the oases of isolation, closing themselves off to all. We did not like those we knew personally but also expended recklessly those we knew intimately.

We did not feel the need to express all of these attitudes and beliefs at length and were content with using codes instead. With the meticulousness of the archivist, we one by one classified and filed everyone and everything. We were deliberately, recklessly unjust, to everyone and everything. In any case, if you combed through the section covering the letter 'J' of the basic illustrated dictionary of the SAW language, you would never come across either 'just' or 'jurisprudence', just as you would not be able to find under 'S', 'sacred or sacredness', or under 'E', 'exalted' or 'exaltedness'. As for injustice, the definition given in this dictionary is as follows:

1. To do wrong to that which is wrong (example: to take the fur coat off of someone in a desert or to take the wine glass in front of a pious person)
2. Indirect attribution that produces no harm (example: to spit at someone's photograph).

Whenever Ethel and I spoke SAWish, we committed injustice against this or that person in the second meaning of the word. We'd never sugar-coat our words when alone. Yet last night at dinner while Ethel the Cunt talked about her grandiose goals in relation to this private university to be founded in Istanbul, it seemed as if she had checked our mutual language into the cloakroom at the entrance.

'Don't you realize? Your all-time dream is finally becoming a reality,' she exclaimed as she held her jasmine cigarette-holder tightly between her teeth. No more political appointments from above, or the usual sterility and similarity that budgetary restrictions produce in state universities. Instead they will gather the highest calibre faculty in Turkey, recruit the most brilliant minds snatched away by the universities abroad, and bring to Istanbul lots of foreign experts from different corners of the world. 'Just think, we'll put a stopper on this chronic brain-drain, and within the first five years we will even reverse the current. Then Western minds will be at our service. We'll cure the inferiority complex of the nation,' she added with a giggle, as if she had made a witty, naughty remark.

Why she giggled like this was no mystery to me. I am actually used to Ethel's ascription of an erotic connotation to the word 'brain.' She was not much different back in our college years, harbouring a layered hatred of other women and a boundless passion for intelligent men... Now that I think about it, the large number of male students outnumbering the females and the 'brains' surrounding her must have played a considerable role in her decision to major, though she never intended to practice, in such a difficult field like civil engineering. In those days at Ethel's house, there was the pick of dozens – if calculated over the years perhaps more than a hundred – exceptionally intelligent male students from different departments. One could even argue that the Cunt made a substantial contribution to Turkish education if one considers the fact that this place operated like a kind of soup kitchen where these male students could feed themselves, or a kind of club where the members could utilize the library as they wished. Even though we may, as regular customers of this alms house, have appeared at first glance to be rather different from each other, we were very much alike concerning one matter: the way in which we invested in our intelligence. In those days, no matter which department or class they belonged to at Bosphorus University, all the male students who, in order to escape the complexes induced by the unjust distribution of life, successfully pushed their brains to the limits; would have definitely heard of Ethel's name and most probably touched her body. The overwhelming majority were those who had devoted themselves to read, study and research, having put their demands from life away into the deepfreeze of their expectations, not to be thawed out until the arrival of 'that big day.' Some of Ethel's aphorisms addressed this point: 'Just as the blind man perfects his other senses, so too the ugly male who goes unnoticed develops his brain.'

Among Ethel's favourites, in so far as they succeeded in developing their brains, were those male students who were either unable to establish relationships with women or were rejected by all the women they were interested in, subsequently giving up on love, practicing love and even making love. After those who were broke in terms of looks, came the chronically shy whose relationships with the fair sex had soured for one reason or another and others...These others included: asexuals who composed panegyrics, praises and poems to a life without contact; avant-garde marginals; overt or closet homosexuals; highly dignified critics; asocials who hated exams but whose greatest thrill in that period of their lives consisted of taking exams; those who came from the provinces and lost their way in Istanbul; those who could not leave their shells let alone Istanbul; valedictorians who managed to get an education despite coming from the wrong families, as well as those 'hidden talents' getting an education in the wrong departments because of their families; the rare geniuses of the natural sciences; the passionate orators of the social sciences...all the hopeless, unhappy, maladjusted, extremely intelligent young men who struggled to cope with society for various physical, financial, psychological or incomprehensible reasons were within Ethel's field of interest. If she had her way, she would not let any female brain enter her house...although somehow, sometimes, upon realizing that a male she cherished happened to have a girlfriend, she would not let on and invited them both. In spite of all this, for some reason, exempted from her notorious hatred for her sex were a few girlfriends left over from private school. One among these frequently stopped by the temple-house. She was so attractive that a comparison with Ethel could not even be considered: with long shapely legs, flawless milky skin, pearly teeth and breasts kneaded in accordance with the laws of dialectic: vibrant within the context of her large body yet tiny enough to fit into the palm...Yet she had one flaw. Like all women who lose their naturalness as soon as they become conscious of the admiration they arouse in others, she too assumed a forced toughness and made the common mistake of thinking that keeping a guy waiting in purgatory, neither too much at a distance nor needlessly close, would render permanent the attention she received. Even when telling people her name she sounded as if she thought she was doing a favour: 'Ay-shin!'

Oddly enough the other men in the house fell in love not with this arrogant fairy but instead with the hideously ugly Ethel. Actually many among them obviously liked Ayshin, yet 'like' is a flimsy verb. As expressed by a contestant in a highly-contrived contest, while listing his hobbies: 'I like to read books, listen to music, take walks and also long-legged, tight-hipped Ayshin.' Yet when the name of Ethel, the ugliest one of all time, came up, they would go full throttle beyond the liking phase and, burning up with desire, fall in love headfirst: either with her or her house – or both.

The temple-house belonged, not to Ethel's mother and father or any other Jewish family member, but to her personally. Whereas the band of students around her stayed at either their parents' insipid-looking homes, worn-out bachelor pads or in overcrowded dormitories where one could only be by oneself inside the wardrobes, the Cunt was the owner of a villa in which she lived all by herself. Though this alone sufficed to make the situation rather surreal, in addition her house was a dream world and just as dreams flirt shamelessly with the art of exaggeration, Ethel too was susceptible to overkill. With its garden overlooking the Bosphorus (every square of which was totally covered up with jonquils and jasmines, that in warm winds released delicately sweet smells at night overflowing with the scent of pleasure); its small but cute pool in which Ethel floated lanterns of all colours at night; its high quality drinks, tasty food and furnishings each more interesting than the next; its vast collection of records and rich library; not forgetting the premium quality cigars constantly being passed around; this place was almost like a miniature version of the world during the Tulip Period of the Ottoman Empire – the excess of which the contemporary historians had attacked with clubs and defaced with extravagant praise.

However, if you ask my opinion, it was not only the wealth that stunned the guests who came here; not the ostentation or the luxury either. What was even more striking was the 'endlessness' of it all. The dwindling cigarette boxes were immediately replenished, the collection of records was so vast you could not count them all, the library did not lose its splendour even though the borrowed books were never returned, and in spite of our eating in hoards, the kitchen cupboards never emptied out, the stock of delicatessen never diminished. We liked to joke among us that when the ground was broken for the villa, the venerated Saint Hizir happened to be one of the workers and had blessed this place: 'Let it multiply but never lessen, let it overflow but never spill.' Even the magical cave of the forty thieves, with its jars of gold, chests brimming with jewellery, bolts of satin and barrels of honey and butter could not rival Ethel's temple-house.

As much as the house was prosperous, so was our host generous. Ethel watched closely the things her cherished guests enjoyed. Her offers increased in accordance with how much she valued someone. For instance, was there someone among us who liked whisky? As soon as she learned about it, Ethel would fill up the drink chest with the highest quality whiskies. If another person liked puzzles, Ethel would order an acquaintance going abroad to bring puzzles each more challenging. Most of our time, however, we dedicated ourselves not to such games but to wearing ourselves out with various gatherings or 'get-togethers'. We would burrow ourselves in the comfortable sofas in the living room, eat, drink, smoke and 'sass' about this or that person, but mostly about each other. We would quickly free ourselves of our past, focus on who we were now, reveal our dreams and constantly debate with each other. Our host did not at all care about the content of our conversations. In fact, as individuals, I don't think she cared much about us at all. She liked the environment she provided for us…and she also liked fireworks. For each guest plunged into this place was like a firework speeding through the night's darkness. He would first glide with shaky, staggering steps and, when convinced he had risen high enough and adjusted to the environment, would burst with a magnificent bang and light the place up by scattering the colourful rays he had hitherto hidden. As we found our voices, became encouraged and burst out with explosions of our own, Ethel provided every comfort by constantly serving us. The genie in the lamp, the *houris* of heaven, even Peter Pan's fairy... none would have served their masters with as much devotion. Ultimately, sooner or later, all these guest-masters ended up falling in love with their host. Yet this also brought their downfall. Those who had the freedom to swim as they pleased in this vast sea, often moved so far away from land as to suddenly realize, upon looking back, that they had lost sight of the land. Ethel was no longer at their side; she had lost interest in them just when they had miserably fallen for her. The only drawback of being a guest at this house was the ease with which one overlooked the fact that both the guest status and also the visit were temporary. Hence each departing guest, just like the infinite replenishment of the materials of the temple-house, was quickly replaced with another. Saint Hizir's prayer for abundance was valid for Ethel's 'brains' as well: they constantly multiplied and never lessened.

As for me, I was the exception. From the beginning till the end, I was the only constant visitor of the temple-house; a type of honorary member. I was ambitious, more than was necessary according to some. My report card was filled with 'A's' for a couple of solid reasons. For one thing, I was tall (three stars), then wide-shouldered (three stars). I will not be as modest as to say I was 'considered handsome' for I was always the most handsome in the places I frequented (four stars) and I was extremely impatient and 'difficult' (five stars). Unlike the others, I had choices. I certainly enjoyed being here but could have left at any moment. I could have gone and not returned. Ethel was too well aware of this. That is why I was so dear to her. The seed of discord in the middle of heaven. My presence enchanted Ethel and disquieted her guests. Little did I care. Being considered a threat by other males was old news to me. If I had cared about these types of looks, I would have done so much earlier: back when walking the distressed corridor of an eleven year old. With a plate filled with wedding cake in one hand and only underwear on my wiry body, I had almost collided by the kitchen door with my stepfather, I was so relaxed and hungry with the warmth of the wedding night. Until that moment, the poor man had always seen me as the older son of the woman he was going to marry, a boy who had problems but was in essence hungry for love and needy of compassion. I should not do him wrong, he wanted to be a father to me: a talented sonny bestowed by God to a childless, fifty year old man. Yet on the morning of his wedding night when we unexpectedly met in the hall, with my facial features inherited from my father, my half-nakedness that revealed I was about to leave childhood and my tremendous appetite revealed by my filling up my plate (signalling also that I would be getting bigger very quickly), I must have seemed far from being the 'sonny' he envisioned. An apprehensive gleam flickered and faded in his pupils. The bad thing was that my mother also realized this, and did so without losing any time. It was as if she had found the remnants of that look when she swept the floors the following day. This did not bode well for anyone because my mother was one of those women who took the tensions that ricocheted among the men in her family, established fickle and knotty alliances and always turned them to her advantage until the last drop; one of those whom whom, without knowing his name, made Bismarck's soul rejoice... She turned her older son against her younger one, the younger one against her late husband, her late husband against her new husband and her new husband against her two sons...

Hence I was rather used to unvoiced maliciousness. I did not care about the looks of others. I was Ethel's favourite and Ayshin's lover. I was fond of hanging around the temple-house but that was all. I had other alternatives and more important things to do. As I said, I was ambitious, very ambitious. Not wasting a moment after graduation, I started the doctorate in England and finished it here in Istanbul, in a field that signified nothing to my family: political philosophy. Ayshin too had passed, on her second try, the sociology assistantship examination. We looked good together. Ethel barely caught up with us. When she finally managed to graduate, she made brazen oaths about never entering through the gates of the university ever again and then burnt her diploma with a ceremony at a party she threw in her temple-house. Then, while Ayshin and I gradually built a decent life for ourselves, Ethel destroyed hers with startling speed. First she stoped living as a clan. Then she left that villa and moved into a penthouse that, when compared to its predecessor, was very spacious and cute but was undistinguished. She no longer gathered everyone in her house, spent most of her time not by drawing attention in large crowds but instead by putting up with the whims of her lovers in crowds of two, and though she devoted all her money, love and energy to them, was still not loved the way she wanted. We heard that her congregation was not happy with her behavior, but Ethel was not happy with them either. She grumbled behind their backs at every opportunity even though she knew it would eventually reach their ears.

'Since you have read more books than I did and chose to become social scientists, could you please solve this little puzzle for me? If you observe a wide range of countries all around the world, from the most democratic to the most oppressive, you'll find in all of them quite a number of writers, painters and the like among the Jews. It's as if whatever the circumstances, they somehow find a way to develop their brains. With the exception of one country! In Africa, the Middle East, the United States, Europe, Russia...just keep on counting...in all these countries... Only in Turkey something went wrong with the Jews. For whatever reason, in Turkey they didn't feel the need to use their brains as much.'

'You're mistaken,' objected Ayshin frowning. 'Many of my friends are Jews.'

Ethel giggled ruthlessly. She never forgave such mistakes. I however was split in two. One part of me had relished the naïvety Ayshin had displayed in defending Jews in front of her Jewish friend – this must be the part of me in love with her. My other half had looked at Ayshin with the anger I felt toward those who tried to roll up the qualities they acquired thanks to their family trees, the exceptional family structures they were born into, the elite schools they attended and the things life had bestowed upon them which they then tried to pass as merits they themselves had developed – this must be the part that made her fall in love with me.

Yet Ayshin must not have been aware of either Ethel's solid reaction or my bifurcated one, for she plunged into her assertion full force: 'They all entered good university departments. Many of them received very wonderful grants and they've now risen to quite good positions.'

'And I tell you this,' Ethel had said, clicking her fingernails again. 'You talk about occupation, I, talent. You mention career, I genius. Economists, academics, lawyers, surgeons...I beg you, please put these aside and move on. I'm talking about something else. Why don't the bohemian, bibulous poets or hedonists, the perverse or even better gory film producers and such emerge from among them? Why don't my people make music? And on those rare occasions that they do, why is that that they always sweetly sing the syrupy traditional songs of our Sephardim grandmothers and can't come up with something totally wicked, like a protest song?'

'My people' was the final stage: against Ayshin's insignificant defense, Ethel's regal attack. Whenever the location of a group is debated between someone belonging to that group and someone not, the patent right always comes smack onto the agenda: the end of the road, the dry well of all debates, the last curtain...when everyone withdraws to where they ultimately belong, the married to their family-homes, the peasants to their village-homes... At that point I lit a cigarette, having drawn both of them into my own vicinity, and sat back. It did not make a difference to me. Both of them were, at the same time, *my women*.

Men committing adultery find *quality* significant: they enjoy receiving from another woman love that is in essence different from what they receive from their wives. Yet women committing adultery find *quantity* significant: they enjoy receiving from another man love that is more than that which they receive from their husbands. Cheating on Ayshin with Ethel flattered my vanity. Those days, I very much enjoyed observing their differences. As to whether Ayshin cheated on me or not, I never attempted to find out.

'Okay, but these are so for a reason,' Ayshin had spoken up, by no means intending to give up. Then she had gotten down to business and commenced with a detailed explanation. Trying to employ objective expressions, she had talked about the shaky psychology of being a minority, the constant insecurity generated by the crisis of belonging and the domination nurtured not by concrete threats but by abstract tenets. She did so neither to be a smart aleck, nor to display her interest in talking big. She talked like that because this was the only language of debate she knew. Yet debating in an academic language is like going to bed with a woman who does not put a drop of drink into her mouth. You can rest assured that she will remain standing until the end of the night, never go overboard and never lose it. Yet you have to accept upfront that you would not be able to relax around her, let out wild yells, hit bottom, pass out in each others arms; in short, that you would not have any fun whatsoever.

'What you say is nice but totally useless,' Ethel had remarked, girding up the swords she had just sharpened. 'If gloomy writers, slovenly producers or socially undesirable painters had emerged from among the Jews in Turkey, do you know what explanation the generations succeeding us, say fifty or a hundred years later, would've given? Exactly the same ones you used just now. They would've said, "Yes, so and so was a great artist or thinker. What made him so great, what separated him from all the rest?" Then they would've started to count the reasons you gave: the psychology of being a minority, alienation from the language, insecurity, being unprotected and so on. Thus everything you now see as an obstacle would have become a cause for difference, for privilege even. This is how these things operate. If a lame man can't dance, we say, "Of course he can't dance, he's lame!" but if the same man is an expert dancer, then we say, "Of course he has to be better than others, for he's lame!"

Ayshin had flinched, as if avoiding a pushy salesman, shaking to one side then the other both her head and hands. I knew that motion too well. It meant, "Thanks, but I'm not buying that nonsense." During our three and a half years of marriage, she would conclude almost all our arguments with the same gesture.

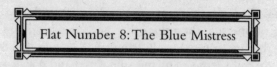

Flat Number 8: The Blue Mistress

Shooting up the stairs, The Blue Mistress unlocked the door of Flat Number 8 panting. She was very late. As if it weren't annoying enough that the visit to the beauty parlour had taken so long, she had also spent too much time afterwards shopping. Once inside the flat, she emptied the contents of the shopping bags onto the kitchen counter. The food could wait, her appearance could not. She dashed into the bathroom. While brushing her teeth, she scrutinized the waves in her hair with discontent. This new style had seemed much nicer in the mirror down at the hairdresser than here in her bathroom. Being one of those women who sometimes envied curly hair and sometimes straight, but in each case only ever on others, her hair had all this time been oscillating, unable to lean in either direction. Now that chatterbox of a hairdresser had upset this delicate balance, making it far curlier and trimming it far shorter than she had asked for. She stole another glance at the full-length mirror while taking her clothes off in the bedroom. Though her hips had somewhat widened lately, she was still fond of the way she looked. If only those cuts were not so visible... She applied a handful of foundation cream, the same colour as her skin, managing to conceal the scars once again.

The drawers opened one by one and she paused for a fleeting moment but did not have to ponder for long over which underwear to pick since it seemed to make no difference to the olive oil merchant. That had not been the case in the beginning. Back in those days, he wanted her to wear the naughtiest underwear possible, buying it personally as a 'present' to her. He always chose the same colour: a lucid, brilliant, infinite sky blue. The Blue Mistress liked this colour, she really did, except in panties or bras. When it came to the underwear in her gift packages, she felt uneasy about the incongruity between the docility of their colour and the licentiousness of the intention behind. A garter could be as desire-inducing a colour as cherry, as carnal as black or as deceptive as white; even violet in its flirtatiousness or pinkish in its hypocrisy...but it could not be a lucid, brilliant, infinite sky blue. Fusing that specific hue with those specific intentions was pretty much like diluting milk with water, or even worse, adding milk to *rakı*. Not that it wasn't possible for a man to enjoy both, just as long as he refrained from drinking them simultaneously. Of lambs turning into wolves or wolves into lambs, she had seen plenty, but it was the ones trying to be both lamb and wolf at the same time who spawned the worst monstrosities while believing themselves to be innocuous in the meantime.

It was the half-lamb/half-wolf who had harmed her the most – even more than those who liked to remind her of the unsurpassable border between women-to-marry and women-to-bed. Such men lusted after what they vilified and vilified what they lusted after. The Blue Mistress had once seen a hoodwinker on the street tricking the passers-by with three tin cups on a cardboard box. As he changed the places of the cups, the bead hidden in one of them was displaced too. At the onset it was in the first cup: 'Be ashamed of your desires!' In a flash it moved into the second cup: 'Be ashamed of the woman you desire!' Then, in one move, there was the bead again, now under the third cup: 'Desire the woman who brings you shame!' That, in turn, meant that sooner or later these men would start to scorn the women they slept with.

In order not to repeat this vicious pattern, the olive oil merchant kept seasoning their affair with spices that would outweigh both the zest of desire and the tartness of shame.

Always a prolific diary-keeper, the Blue Mistress had written down when she had first met him: 'If someone awakens in us a desire we'd rather not have, we try not to like that person. However, if that fails, we then seek something likeable in him, something good enough to make the desire for him less bothersome, more endurable.' It was akin to wearing a celestial glove, of lucid, brilliant, infinite sky blue, so as not to have to touch muck or mess while enjoying rummaging through the debris.

In the spice basket of the olive oil merchant there wasn't the slightest trace of lust. All sorts of other things were present there but for some reason during the past few years he had always fished out the same spice: compassion. He felt compassion toward the Blue Mistress: *she was not the type of girl to live a life like this.* Then there were times when he felt compassion toward himself: *he was not the type of man to live a life like this.* Too often he talked about *Kader* as if she were a wicked whore. As for the Blue Mistress, she regarded this lust covered with compassion like a dirtied, mud-covered slice of jellied bread lying on the ground. She had no appetite for it. At times like this, she likened her position to her hair. On the one side was the wife of the olive oil merchant, smooth and even like straight hair, on the other was this whore called *Kader*, bumpy and imbalanced like hair with permanent wave. Then there she was, in the middle of the two, swaying toward either end…semi-wife, semi-whore…both blue and a mistress…

She knew how heartbreaking it had been for her parents when she had left home for good but still could not help but suspect they had also been relieved deep down. They were both nice people but the nets they repetitively threw into the sea of parenthood rarely turned up anything decent. Though never at ease with their love and hardly able to bear their attention, this ingratitude of hers was hard for even her to handle. She could have gotten a better education if she had so wanted, could have at least graduated from high school, but after that 'incident', she had felt barely any desire to return to school. Before she knew it, the scar on her face had drawn a hair-thin boundary, first between her and her peers, then between her and the age that she lived in. She had to leave that house. If given a choice, the only place she would like to go was, undoubtedly, the universe that her grandfather inhabited…a grandfather whom she loved dearly, lost too early…After losing her *dede*, tracing the jumbled footprints of people from all walks of life in Istanbul, she had tried to track down those that belonged to the dervishes.

Hard as it was she had managed to find them – scattered here and there on the two sides of the city and gathered, like moths attracted to light, around their own *dedes*. She had joined them. For two years, she had participated every week without fail in the sermons of three separate religious orders in Istanbul, seeking solace in the resemblance between the words she heard from their sermons and those she had heard back in her childhood from her own *dede,* but it had not worked. It wasn't that the words were not reminiscent of those of her grandfather's, for they were. Nor was it that the people who uttered them were not sincere, for they were. Still, for some reason it just did not sound the same. Little by little she came to realize that in these meetings it wasn't the talks that she was really interested in but the chants that followed. She would sit side by side with the other disciples while the *dede* talked, but rather than be all ears like the rest, she would withdraw behind a solid deafness. Only when the chant started would she reopen the sealed gates of her ears. How profoundly she loved that moment, that true and total desertion of the body, again and again, sealed in the infiniteness of repetition. It wasn't the words articulated there but instead the beat of the drums and the notes of the underlying melody that took her away. However, no matter how far she swerved she could never quite shake that old feeling of incompleteness. After a while she had started to feel like a hypocrite. Why had she insisted on being one with those she felt so apart from? Every chant attended left her yet another mile away from the other disciples. Just as she had been unsuccessful in reciprocating the love of her parents, neither had she found peace next to those who constantly preached peace.

'I don't know how to be satisfied with what I have,' she had solemnly confessed to herself, 'because I'm not able to show gratitude.' Surprisingly, rather than causing offence this confession had relieved her. She had been suffering from the malady of those who, while still children, realized how extraordinarily beautiful their childhood is; the malady of those who started life with the bar set high... Thereafter, all the people she met were destined to remain in the shadow of her *dede* while even the most pleasing things in her life would embody a harrowing sense of absence. Such incompleteness, however, was utterly unbeknownst to others, and therein resided the problem: *the absolute wholeness of good*. Those who unreservedly believed in their own goodness and the superiority of their morality were doomed to failure far more than the bad for they were so smug in their completeness. There were no leaky roofs in the edifices of their personalities, no crumbling floorboards, neither a hole to be filled, nor a notch to be fixed. The Blue Mistress had found them incomplete in their gorged fullness but being unable to express this, she had gradually recoiled from the good, distancing herself step by step from their learned codes and credo of goodness. It was thus that she had started to suspect somewhere in her innermost soul she was inclined to depravity and immorality. Before long, she had entirely cut her ties with all three religious orders. Be that as it may, moving away from the believers had not once shaken up her beliefs. Faith for her was not living in accordance with the unchangeable rules of a commanding God or joining the ranks of a conscientious community, but rather a sunny, dulcet childhood memory. And as her childhood memories with her *dede* were the best moments of her life, she had steadfastly, doggedly remained a devout believer. Even when not as full of faith as she had been in her childhood, her faith had still retained a childish side.

Yet there was neither a house she wanted to return to and nor did she have enough money to continue on her way. It was during those days that she had started to get used to the attention of men as old as her father and managed to not remain indifferent to the attention she had got used to. These men who thought they had everything, discovered at one point the incompleteness embedded in their lives and thereafter became eagerly attracted to her as if she and only she could right that wrong. In any case, being a mistress was a good start in terms of getting away from the humdrum wholeness of the good. She was first blue, then a mistress, but there were also periods when she was thrown around in between the two. When the olive oil merchant rented Flat Number 8 of Bonbon Palace, she had finally stopped fluctuating between being blue and a mistress to become both. As soon as the man provided her with a house, his manner had drastically changed, becoming visibly coarser. For he was that type. He was an LTCM of the SDEM section and the WCWL sub-section, and he naturally acted in accordance with that.

There lives on earth another type of creature whose world is as crowded as that of humans and that is at least as complex: bugs. They have succeeded in spreading everywhere and stay alive in spite of everything. They display a magnificent variation, even a particular type of bug can come in ten further varieties, sometimes even reaching thousands. It is assumed that the sum of all bug types is more than one million at present. In spite of this harrowing complexity, the scientific world does not stop classifying them. It divides them into their upper categories, classes, lower classes; upper sections, sections and lower sections. A tree worm, for instance, belongs to the bug category, 'changeling sub-class, sheath-winged upper-section, different-stomached section, plant-eater sub-section'. The overwhelming majority of the disappointments women experience in their relationships with men originate in their unwillingness to accept that, like bugs, humans too come in types and therefore the men they are with also belong to a type – with only one difference: a bug cannot leave its type and make the transition into another type. A horsefly, for instance, cannot at any stage of its life turn into a praying mantis. It stays the same. However, Adam's sons and Eve's daughters can indeed accomplish this transformation. The trademark of a human is the faculty to deviate from what it was originally, to betray its own type. Accordingly, the table of modern human types is less complex but much more convoluted than that of the primitive bug. Nevertheless, making the transition between categories is not easy. After all, in order to preserve their stability and maintain their existence, not only do all types make, without exception, their members exactly like each other but they fix them in that guise as well. The olive oil merchant belonged to upper category of the men's type, 'Long Term Complainers about Marriage', was on the 'Can't Quite End Marriage' team and also in the 'Want Change Without Loss' subsection: a harmful type whichever way you looked at it.

'You are my betrothed,' he had said as they silently drunk at the *rakı* table they had, on their first night in this house, set together. He liked to drink and often drank at night. He was not one of those who made do with a fistful of appetizers, half a mould of cheese and a slice of melon. Instead he always insisted on having a table filled to the brim. It couldn't be ready-made either, everything had to be prepared at home from scratch. Chicken with ground walnuts was his favourite dish. That night, whilst using a piece of bread to wipe off the last crumbs of chicken with ground walnuts from his plate, he had remarked: 'Our religion permits it as well. As long as you are fair enough, you can have up to four women.' The Blue Mistress had tittered, a bristly, edgy snigger. He had grimaced. She had left the table: unlike the olive oil merchant, she did know the mentioned verse of the Qur'an in its entirety.

Choosing a gauzy green dress from the wardrobe, she dressed in no time, then ran back to the kitchen to open the packages from the grocery store. First she placed the hummus in a bowl, decorating it with mint leaves. Next, she arranged the other appetizers on plates: dried bean stew, eggplant purée, green beans in olive oil, liver with stewed onions… She lined up the cheese pastry on one side, planning to fry it when he arrived. There was also the Russian salad Madam Auntie had sent yesterday with the janitor's son. This she actually had found rather odd. The Blue Mistress had never before seen a housewife sending Russian salad to neighbours and the like, but she guessed that the olive oil merchant might enjoy it on the *rakı* table. She could place it on the table as if she had prepared it herself. After inspecting the plates for the last time, she crumpled up the packaging paper into a ball and threw it in the garbage; then tied up the garbage bag and took it outside. It was then that she recalled the conversation at the hairdresser. She had not mentioned this to anyone but her garbage had also been stolen a couple of times from her front doorstep. Inspecting the garbage bag suspiciously, warily, she took it inside again to put it out later when Meryem was due to come to collect them.

The delicacies she had prepared the Blue Mistress then carried to the table with the azure tablecloth. She set the napkins that matched the tablecloth in colour, then the plates and the glasses. She took out from the refrigerator the *rakı* she had seasoned with ground mastic and poured it into the crystal water pitcher with the turquoise handle. Finally, she poured into a maroon bowl a small amount of the heavy-smelling olive oil the merchant had brought and sprinkled it with red pepper, sweet basil and thyme. Though it was still early, she could not resist lighting up the lily-shaped candle that floated on a glass bowl half-filled with water. With a soft, satisfied smile, she scrutinized the table and then everything around. She liked her house. If only this horrendous smell of the apartment building could be gotten rid of …

She lit a green apple-scented incense stick and placed it in the middle of the living room. As the smoke delicately dissipated in the air, she sprayed, first on herself and then at all the corners of the house, half a bottle of perfume. Recently she had started to spend a considerable amount of her money on perfume. As the smell of garbage circumnavigating the apartment building had augmented, so had her perfume expenditure. She frequently stopped by the stylish store at the end of the avenue, always buying her bottles of perfume from the same place even though she knew too well that she did not have the same standards of living as the women shopping there. She liked fruit smells the most: mixtures of peach, watermelon and papaya. She had no clue what papaya was but found the name cute.

The perfume she bought lasted at most ten days. She poured the different scents everywhere; on her clothes, onto the pillows and sheets, the curtains and the armchairs, her toys of all sizes and types, and on the evil eyes she hung all around the house. Instead, she could have saved up this money, or she could have bought long-lasting things for herself. The merchant must have realized the wastefulness of his little mistress for he had reduced the amount of pocket money he gave her. Yet the Blue Mistress kept on doing things as she pleased. She did not know and did not try to understand why she behaved like this. The only thing she knew was that if the money she received were five times what it was now, she would purchase five times as many bottles of perfume.

The table looked fine, tasteful and refined. She sent a message from her cell phone asking him when he was going to come. While waiting for the response, she pushed on the remote and randomly turned on a channel. On the screen appeared two women throwing resentful looks at each other. One of them, the one with the fashionable lavender suit and four strands of pearls, crossed her hands on her chest and snorted: 'Admit it Loretta, I'm the one he loves.' The long haired brunette wearing a dress that reminded one of a field of daisies with one such specimen also placed on her hair, opened wide her green eyes, pronouncing syllable by syllable: 'But you do not love him.' Pulling on her necklace almost to its breaking point, the other one replied: 'That doesn't concern you Loretta, it doesn't concern you at all.'

'May stones as big as Loretta rain on your heads,' grumbled the Blue Mistress. Even though 'Loretta' was as of the same type of word as 'papaya', it did not sound as cute at all.

As she reached for the remote, her cell phone beeped, delivering only a single word: 'Night.' Such a long, abstruse slice of time. She heaved a sigh, changing the channel. A middle-aged woman with a wide forehead and a chubby face, who either had not considered or did not much care about removing that moustache of hers, was listing the ingredients for cooking *spinach au gratin*.

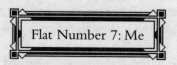

Flat Number 7: Me

I went out to the balcony and lit a cigarette. The balcony is the only place I enjoy in this house. It is almost detached from the house inside; whatever attachment it has to the flat seems fortuitous, as if it doesn't really belong here. I notice a brick-coloured bug wandering on the iron grills. My presence annoys it and its presence annoys me. There are bugs everywhere. They spread out from the kitchen cabinets, under the refrigerator, the cracks on the tiles…

For a fleeting moment I ponder calling Ethel to ask her help to find out whether I had talked to Ayshin or not the night before but I soon decide against it. Since I already had had more than my fair share of the Cunt's whims, to ask her for Ayshin's new phone number, asking once again for help, would be of no use other than further inflating her already over-inflated ego. I can't stand hearing her grouse one more time: 'I'm going to lose my best girlfriend because of you sugar-plum!' If it were up to me I am sure I'd have done both a great favour by putting an end to that gangrenous relationship of theirs but why bother?

This twosome, the closest of buddies in high school, used to meet without fail once every two weeks to dine, always at the same type of restaurants. After our engagement, it hadn't taken Ayshin long to convince first herself, then me, that I'd better join this uninviting routine. In order not to upset the balance, Ethel too had started to bring her partners to our meals. Before long, these partners were gracing our table one after another, with no apparent consistency or similarity among them, like the winning numbers in a lottery. Before we found the chance to get acquainted with one number, another one would have already replaced him. During that period, Ethel's love affairs were so slapdash and so fugacious that we did not feel the need to hide our amazement when a lover succeeded in attending three dates in a row. Such exceptional partners we would inspect all throughout the meal with an admiration mixed with awe. During that three and a half year long parade of lovers, Ethel introduced us to partners of all kinds and sizes. If there was one thing all these men had in common, it should have been their incapability to bring to a close what they had started. All were allergic to anything conventional, obsessed with being original by doing things never done before and had ambitious projects which they had abandoned halfway through for one reason or another. They happened to be enormously enthusiastic about a myriad of projects, the only problem being that they could not flesh them out any further than the beginning phase. Like mussels in their shells, they had gotten stuck in their half-developed projects, waiting for someone to pull them out by their hands to continue on. It was precisely at this stage that Ethel the Cunt appeared, plunging in and randomly pulling them out with her long fingernails painted in harsh colours. What she did not like she threw back in the water; after all, Istanbul was a huge mussel field and she was an accomplished mussel-hunter.

There was an edgy young scriptwriter, for instance, who must have been at least ten years younger than Ethel. He was working on a script he assured us must be sent to European producers as he resolutely believed those in Turkey were not worthy of him. The scenario was definitely ready, he claimed, if only he could decide on how to end the film. We dined with him once. While Ayshin grumbled and Ethel giggled, the two of us put our heads together and — as we downed *rakı* with ice, proceeded from cold to warm appetizers, from warm appetizers to the main dish, and from there to dessert and coffee – came up with a total of four different endings to his film, all of which we were particularly proud of. Then there were the other lovers: a photographer who nursed amazing grudges against the managers, workers and even the readers of all the journals he worked for; a haughty advertiser who saw no harm in claiming that everyone who kept a television at home was an idiot; an amateur actor who did not find any play staged in Turkey successful and therefore went from door to door seeking a sponsor to establish his own theatre company; a foul-mouthed satirist who had a reputation for leaving everything he started halfway through and thereby speeding up the bankruptcy of all journals he became mixed up with; an alcoholic psychiatrist who had as his patients all the intellectuals of the city, who kept going to him even though everyone knew he could not hold his tongue when he got drunk and happily divulged his patients' innermost secrets... At times, I could not help thinking that Ethel brought these men to eat with us just to upset Ayshin. If that were the case, she certainly succeeded. Even though Ayshin never thought of ending their friendship because of this, she always had a grisly opinion about the life Ethel led. She knew I did not approve of Ethel's ways either. What my wife did not know, however, was that disapproving of a woman's habits was no obstacle to sleeping with her.

Ethel was actually a threat to all her partners. She would help them out, pouring money on them, all the while flaring up that spark of 'I wouldn't be the man I am if only my circumstances were different' ready to char the wooden cottages of their characters. As soon as these men – who for one reason or another had repetitively failed to accomplish their goal but accepted both themselves and their fate as given – bumped into Ethel at an unexpected turn of their lives and were pumped-up with money and flattery, they would abandon their life-long projects to go after far more avaricious ones. Shortly after that Ethel would abandon them without notice, just as she had done years ago to her guests in the temple house. As she did not love herself, she did not love the men she turned her lovers into either. However, there was one among them who did not fit this pattern and whom Ethel cherished like no other...

He was a *ney* player. In the days when the principal Mawlawi order had bifurcated over the debate, 'Is it permissible for male and female dervishes to whirl together?' he had taken issue with both sides and retreated into his shell, ever since that moment devoting half his day to seeking refuge in sleep and the other half to escaping from his dreams. How exactly and on which part of the day Ethel had met him I had no clue. The only thing I do know for sure is that she had once again plunged her hands into the water to pull out yet another mussel and, as soon as she parted the shell to look inside, had encountered what she least expected: a shy pearl! For a while she gave to him what she had given to others: financial help, excessive attention, suffocating love...but unlike all the others, there was no visible change in the nature of this heavy-eyed, big-nosed, absentminded Mawlawi. In the guy's calendar of life, the longest time period was one day. Whenever Ethel tried to plan something, say go on a trip in a week's time or get married in the spring, the only response she got from her lover was 'Let's see what that day looks like when it comes.' From his perspective, one could not reach days, let alone land up on them; rather days came to people and, when they did, always brought something along. He was the most unambitious, uncalculating, un-future-oriented man and the only anti-*tarikat tarikat* master I ever knew. He would no doubt have replaced my place on the throne in Ethel's harem had he not taken off from us so suddenly.

'You and I are standing by the seashore. We dangle our feet into the water, Ethel. You are saying, "Come on let's swim together out to the fifty-fifth wave. Look how appealing that wave is!" And I ask you "Which one?" Before I can even finish my question, the wave you had pointed out changes place.

Look, it's no longer where you said it was! Now it isn't the fifty-fifth but perhaps the thirty-fifth one. It keeps coming closer. That is, it moves toward us by itself, and as it draws near, it brings many things along with it. The sea being what it is, you are left with only two options Ethel. You can either forget about the waves and dive into the sea to become a drop within or sit by the shore and simply wait. Watch the waves get smashed as they hit the shore, each turning into a drop in front of your eyes. Life is lived in one of two ways, if it's to merit the name. You either render yourself invisible within life or render life invisible within you.'

Poor scandalous Ethel! It must have been the curse of all the lovers she had frittered away. As she listened flabbergasted to the dazzling words of the Mawlawi, she kicked me under the table, throwing me despondent looks begging for help. Though she sure could manoeuvre around all the ins and outs of the language of the mundane, when confronted with these spiritual abstractions she was as inexperienced and helpless as a child. After a while, she started to blame herself. *She should have known this language.* How she repented now turning her nose up at her grandmother's attempts to teach her the basics of Jewish mysticism. To make up for her shortcoming, she started to read in a frenzy, devouring first the books given to her when she was a child and then others. Her increasing interest in the Kabala was a bridge she hoped would lead her to all those things her dear *ney* player kept prattling on about. She wouldn't go around without at least a couple of books to hand, including, for sure, a copy of the Mathnawi. Frequently stopping by a senile bookseller in Beyazit, she parleyed with the man behind the counter in whispers, as if tracking down an arcane hand-written manuscript, and each time emerged from the store with bags full of books. So seriously had she let her heart be captured that she was ready to go anywhere and even settle wherever her lover wanted. Ethel the ugly crow, while gliding guilelessly in the sky, had all of a sudden spotted something shiny down on earth, and now wanted to grab it, whisk it away and make it totally hers. *Why didn't they wander, say for a couple of years, around the most mystical cities of the world, like Jerusalem, Tibet and Delhi, or go in search for the lost tomb of Shams?* I have seen people mess their minds up but Ethel had literally lost her identity. Yet however much she tried, she could not convince her beloved to go on these exotic trips. The serene Mawlawi was as inclined towards the idea of taking a trip as a cat to the activity of taking a bath.

Be that as it may, this young man who was so unwilling to go anywhere turned out to be too much in a hurry to change worlds. A week before New Year's Eve that year, he was one of the four victims claimed by the bomb that had exploded in one of the garbage cans on Istiklal Avenue – an explosion for which no revolutionary organization would claim responsibility. I do not think Ethel cried so much for anyone, not even her own mother and father, though perhaps with the exception of the older brother she had lost to suicide when she was fourteen...he was the only person she might have loved so intensely...

I got married to Ayshin two months and two weeks later. Ethel attended the wedding alone.

A day before the wedding, she was lying down stark naked. Parading in front of my eyes all of her fat body, so big, belligerent and bulky. When her body turned into a heap of raw white meat, that hairy reddish birthmark spreading from below her neck to the top of her breasts was even more pronounced. She could have had this removed if she wanted. Just as she could have gotten rid of her body fat, fixed up her nose or nipped and tucked parts of her body like everyone else. Women as ugly as Ethel and just as rich spent everything they had on plastic surgery, cosmetics and clinics to become beautiful. As for Ethel, she had put her entire wealth into the service of her ugliness. Not only did she not try to beat her ugliness, she did not even care to spruce it up and hide it away either. The doors of the wardrobes taking up two of her bedroom walls were covered with full-length mirrors. After making love, she had the habit of stretching out on the bed lost in watching herself. At times she looked at her reflection with such desire that I wondered what she saw there. As she displayed her body, she acted less like a woman who wanted to be desired than a man desiring what he regarded. It was as if being admired meant nothing to her; her aim was simply to display with the intent to startle. Even so, while the victims of a flasher ran away screaming, those of Ethel kept coming back to her bedroom with their own two feet. There were, of course, exceptions: the Mawlawi *ney* player was one and so was I.

'Oh sugar-plum, you're making a gross mistake. You're gonna regret it. I've sullenly accepted the very fact that from here on life won't bring me anyone better than you and that's precisely where your problem lies. You haven't yet realized I'm the best you'll ever get. Well, what's there to be done, except to wait for you to see the truth? Keep roving around, fondle a few more asses, crumple a couple more times. Then you'll finally pull in and admit I was right from the start,' she had glibly stated. 'Sooner or later you'll hit your head against the wall, lamenting, "Why didn't I get married to Ethel then?" Look, I mark it right here,' she had flashed a grin as she marked a jagged thin line on the side table, making it screech with her long fingernail painted in glittering cobalt. Affixing a cigarette on her jasmine wood cigarette-holder, which she constantly lost only to replace it with a new one, she had then waited for me to light it up.

'Why? Is it because you are the richest woman I'll ever encounter?'

I probably could not have fathomed how well-off she was even if I had the inventory of her worldly possessions. Though the rich are never able to get this, there is, in the mind's eye of the non-rich, a threshold at which wealth gets riveted. Once that threshold is surpassed, no matter how much you go over it, it is bound to remain the same amount: a lot! Just as the folk tales of the penniless fix the wealth of a merchant in the chimerical cornucopia of the number '1000', Ethel also, if you had asked me, owned a 'thousand' properties.

'No sugar-plum! Not because I'm the richest woman you'll ever encounter but because I'm bad. Of course, not any worse than you, but with badness there can't be an amount, can there? Wickedness is no flour we can measure by the cup. Let me put it like this: you and I are of the same breed but poor Ayshin isn't one of us. Okay, she may not be a good person, but she isn't bad either. She is at most a capricious young lady; the one and only daughter of her elite family, a little too much of a straight arrow and, I should confess, at times a bit too boring and all, but certainly not bad. And do you know what the saddest thing is? As you rough her up, she'll try to defend herself. She'll first compete with you logically, strive to make a case; then frustrated she'll burst into tears and end up believing she's suffered terrible injustice. Whenever you make her miserable, shred her self-esteem to pieces, she won't even realize that the issue at hand isn't really what you are arguing about. You know as well as I do that Ayshin too is one of those types. The type eager to bow down before God without getting to know the devil first...'

Ethel loved this remark and uttered it repeatedly. I suspected she had stolen it from one of her bright men – maybe it belonged to the *ney* player – but it suited her well. Those who were eager to bow down before God without getting to know the devil first; those who never wondered about the source of the gale of destruction breaking the fruit-filled branches and destroying the flower beds of the garden they had fortunately been born into, never to get a glimpse of the world outside; were outrageously confident that they lived in the most habitable place on the face of the earth. Not once did they worry about how many rooms or exits there were in the house they lived in, and did not, in spite of the noises they heard day and night, find it necessary to go down and unlock the old, musty door on their pantry floor. The types who think they are right basically because of the rights they were granted... Ethel was not mistaken. Ayshin was indeed one of those.

What is so distressing is that I had frequently remembered these words during my marriage, but had not confessed them to Ethel so as not to further stroke her ego that already wandered onto the summits. Last night while we drank together, however, I was careless enough to let this already stale confession slip out. She listened to me with barefaced pleasure. When she got up I watched her huge ass sway as she wobbled to the bathroom, suspecting all the while she was aware that I was watching her big ass sway as she wobbled to the bathroom. She has the ugliest ass I have ever seen. No way can it be groped; there is no shape that it fits into. Like a gooey, soggy jelly, Ethel's ass is less solid than fluid, if you just let it flow, it might just as well drain away. I have seen much fatter asses and more formless ones as well, with cellulite, pimples, wounds, hair that has grown more than necessary or in wrong spots; but all had something, one thing that turned me on. Ethel's had not…none whatsoever…

Once back at the table, luckily Ethel seemed to have overcome the delight of my confession as she delved again into the topic of upmost interest to her these days: the university project. At long last she let out the morsel of information she had all this time hidden from me. They had made an offer to Ayshin as well, and she had accepted. Though she knew I would never ever, even if I were desperate for money, work at the same place as Ayshin, she continued to insist as she kept looking right into my eyes: 'Come on sugar-plum, why don't you have faith in my word once in your life. Join us, come to this university. You can philosophize as much as you want; no one will meddle. We are ready to serve your brain professor.'

That obscene association the word 'brain' assumed in the Cunt's mouth aroused me. Bizarre as it is that even though during my marriage to Ayshin, Ethel and I had been screwing regularly, we had not once slept together since my divorce. I do not remember why we returned apart last night. I don't even know how I got home. Maybe Ethel played a game wheeling in at the last minute, but I don't think so, that wouldn't be her style. At the most, she must have seen I was too crocked to wind her up and decided to drop me off home. That is more Ethel-like.

I stretched my legs to the rails of the balcony and lit another cigarette. The brick-coloured bug remained under my foot. It had had a chance to escape but it did not. Down below on the street I noticed a skinny, swarthy woman throwing garbage bags onto the pile in front of the garden wall. Just at the same time a fuming voice roared from somewhere in the lower flats. The woman stood still for a couple of seconds and then, heedlessly, absentmindedly, as if in a dream, scampered back and hared away. This place pisses me off. I have to get out of here one way or the other. Perhaps I liken Bonbon Palace to myself – a disgruntled apartment that bitterly misses the prosperity it was once accustomed to. I need to move somewhere else but do not have the money. All throughout my marriage, Ayshin and I had maintained a division of labour, the absurdity of which I can only now comprehend. Since the house we lived in belonged to her parents and therefore to her, I paid all the other expenses. How scatterbrained of me! I do not have any money saved 'on the side' either. When faced with unexpected expenses and the need to pay rent, my salary shrivelled ridiculously. I could no doubt borrow some money from Ethel, but that I won't do. Such a move would only upset the symmetry in our relationship. I'd better start making some money soon.

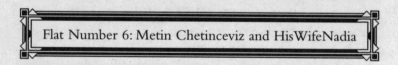

'That's none of your business Loretta. I tell you, none of your business.'

'You are wrong honey!' bellowed the woman with the daisies, narrowing her eyes with rancour. 'Everything that concerns him concerns me too.'

'Everything that concerns him concerns me too,' repeated HisWifeNadia, trying to pronounce the words in Turkish exactly as she had heard. The soap opera she watched was called 'The Oleander of Passion' and it had been broadcast every weekday afternoon for the past two and a half months. At the outset it was broadcast before the evening news, but once it had become indisputably obvious how slim its chances were of becoming a hit, the scheduling had been altered in a flash. Now in its place was aired some other soap opera, one far more ostentatious. Unlike its precursor, this soap opera had been so successful and drawn so much media attention from week one that quite an uproar revolved around it, especially when the leading actors were flown to Istanbul to sign photographs for their fans after a glitzy press conference. However, HisWifeNadia was not interested in either this or indeed any other soap opera. It was only 'The Oleander of Passion' that mattered to her. Every afternoon at the same hour she took her seat on the divan with the burgundy patterns on a mauve background, the re-upholstering of which she constantly postponed, and watched the soap opera while simultaneously doing some other work. Depending on the day,

she would have a tray full of rice or beans on her lap to sort and shell, look at old photographs in old albums, try to do crossword puzzles with her limited vocabulary in Turkish, reread the letters from her great aunt or write her a response. Yet every so often the tray would become weighty, the puzzle unsolvable and the sameness of the photographs and the dullness of the letters depressing. At such times, HisWifeNadia would scurry to the kitchen to get a few potatoes and, as she watched the soap opera, would craft yet another potato lamp. Though the whole house was filled up with these lamps, she still could not keep herself from making new ones. Anyhow, given the frequency of power-cuts at Bonbon Palace, one might need a potato lamp any time.

As to why she could not watch 'The Oleander of Passion' without doing something else at the same time, there were a couple of reasons behind that. Firstly, she found the soap opera so mind-numbing that she could barely bear it without some sort of a distraction. Secondly, when she kept herself busy with another task at the same time, the hidden discomfort of having become a hackneyed viewer of a hackneyed soap opera tended to diminish. Perhaps most importantly, however, by keeping busy with other things she could prove to herself how much she disparaged not only the soap opera, but also that leading actress of it, namely Loretta.

'The Oleander of Passion', like all other soap operas, was broadcast on weekdays only. However, despite the fact that all the other soaps were constantly in the public eye, via fragments from upcoming episodes and gossip from the real lives of the actors saturating the papers, not a single line – good or bad – had yet appeared about either 'The Oleander of Passion' cast members in general or Loretta in particular. It was not only the newspapers that remained so indifferent on this matter. Among the acquaintances HisWifeNadia had made in Istanbul, there was not a single person who had heard of the programme, let alone become a regular viewer. It was as if the entire country had unanimously pledged to feign ignorance of 'The Oleander of Passion'. The fact that nobody took the soap opera seriously did not by any means please HisWifeNadia. After all, for the vilification of anything to have any value whatsoever, the thing sneered at should at least be of some value for some people in the first place. Under these circumstances, it was neither gratifying nor consequential to vilify Loretta. Thus, HisWifeNadia kept her thoughts to herself. No one knew anything about her obsession with this soap opera: not even her husband…least of all him…

Be that as it may, the fact that the papers mentioned nothing about the future episodes of the 'The Oleander of Passion' did not seem that awful to HisWifeNadia. There wasn't much to pry into anyway since almost every forthcoming event, including the most imperative secrets, were already revealed in the early episodes. As such, perhaps the real riddle was less to find out what the ending would be than to find out how the already proven ending would be eventually arrived at. If there was anyone who still did not know the mysteries woven in the soap opera it certainly wasn't the viewer but rather Loretta herself. In the fire that had erupted in episode five, she had lost not only the mansion she lived in, along with her title of a lady, but her memory as well. Ever since then, she had been struggling to recall who she was and mistaking an unknown woman for her mother. She could not even fathom that the famous physician whose photographs she kept seeing in the newspapers had once been, and actually still was, her husband. Since her condition had worsened in the ensuing episodes, she was now about to be checked into a clinic – a move destined to complicate things further given the fact that her physician-the-husband/husband-the-physician happened to work there.

Deep down HisWifeNadia was fond of being so well informed about all these things that still remained a mystery to Loretta herself. Whenever the latter made a wrong turn failing to spot the truth behind the intricacies she faced, HisWifeNadia was secretly thrilled. At such moments, her life and the one in the soap opera would sneak into one another.

Between these two entirely dissimilar universes it was Loretta who stood out as the common denominator, the passageway from one to another. Physically, she was there in the life of the soap opera; and vocally, she was here in the life of HisWifeNadia. Ultimately, there were two distinct women around: the Latin American actress who played Loretta on the one side, and the Turkish speaker who voiced Loretta on the other. Though none of them was named Loretta in real life, in her mind HisWifeNadia had identified both with that particular name. She had no problem whatsoever with the first Loretta, the Latin American actress being of no concern to her. Her foremost target was not the Loretta she watched but the one she heard. It was that voice that she had been after for so long; a voice with no face…a velvety, dulcet voice that came to life in a knobby, peach-puff kneecap… Nonetheless, since every voice required a visage and every visage a voice, as she stood watching 'The Oleander of Passion', the voice she heard and the face she saw would so easily blend into one another that HisWifeNadia would soon miss the target, shifting her focus from the woman doing the voiceover to the Latin American actress on the screen. Then she could do little to prevent herself from watching the soap opera with a twisted gaze; taking pleasure in the scenes where Loretta was in pain and feeling distressed whenever things went well for her.

The Loretta on the screen was a slender brunette with jade eyes and long legs. When she cried, tears round as peas rolled down her cheeks. As for the woman who did Loretta's voiceover, HisWifeNadia could not quite surmise what her body looked like since she had not been able to eye-her-up thoroughly on that ominous day when the two had ran into each her. She must be one of those ephemeral beauties, HisWifeNadia guessed, as fleeting and frail as a candle flame. Shine as she might with the freshness of youth at the present, her beauty would be tarnished sooner or later, in five years at most. When that day arrived, she would have to pull herself together and stop going after married men. Still, five years was a long time – long enough to cause HisWifeNadia anguish, as she had to face the prospects of all the things that could happen until then.

It was a pure coincidence that had made HisWifeNadia aware of Loretta's voice three months ago. On the morning of that ill-starred day, she was in the kitchen once again to cook *ashure*. Even though she had considerably improved her culinary skills since her arrival in Turkey, her *ashure* was still not as good as she – Metin Chetinceviz more precisely – wanted it to be. Countless experiments had all ended up in flop. There was either too much or too little sugar or some ingredient missing altogether, and if not these, even when everything was mixed in properly, something would go wrong in the cooking phase. When cooked for an adequate amount of time, she would remove the *ashure* from the stove and dole it out into frosty pink cups. Desperate to have made it right this time, she would take great pains to garnish each and every cup with pomegranate seeds. In the beginning there was a time when she used to overdo this, dissatisfied with the hackneyed decorations of Turkish housewives. Longing for novelty, instead of a dash of grated coconuts, roasted hazelnuts or powdered sugar, she would sprinkle a few drops of cognac or place sour cherries fermented in rum. Back then she was interested more in the legend of the *ashure* than in how the Turks consumed it.

The *ashure* in the legend was the epitome of a triumph deemed unachievable. All the creatures boarding Noah's ship in pairs to escape doomsday had cooked it together at a time when they could no longer endure the journey, when they were surrounded on four sides with water and were in danger of extinction given an empty pantry and with a long way still to go. Each animal had handed over its leftovers and hence this amazing concoction had emerged by mixing things that would otherwise never match. Though there was not much doubt as to what modern-day *ashure* was composed of, still the components of this dessert weren't entirely evident, and extra ingredients things could be added into it any time. It was precisely this lack of a fixed recipe that made *ashure* so unlike other desserts. Neither the ingredients were restricted nor the measurements fixed. As such, it ultimately resembled a cosmopolitan city where foreigners would not be excluded and latecomers could swiftly mix with the natives. *Ashure* was limitlessness generated by limited options, affluence born from scarcity and vast assortment burgeoning out of extinction.

About all these HisWifeNadia wrote at length to her aunt – an elderly spinster with legs covered with purplish varicose veins and hair as red as hell. In her letters HisWifeNadia wrote extensively about how drastically she had changed since her arrival in Turkey, how much time she now set aside to cook and also how she had come to acknowledge her aunt's analogies between meals and the verses in the sacred book. Her aunt was highly pious and just as good a cook. She resolutely, if not condescendingly, believed these two attributes of hers amounted to the same thing since 'The kingdom of heaven is like unto leaven, which a woman took and hid in three measures of meal, till the whole was leavened' (Matthew 4:33). The meals she cooked for her family, she placed upon God's table and watching her children gobble them down she felt blissful as if it were He who had been fed.

'There exists a command of God in every meal we consume,' the aunt was fond of claiming. 'Needless to say, that is with the exception of the slapdash meals invented by those messy women who apparently have no time to cook and mistake freedom with neglecting their homes, preferring the praise of their bosses to the gratitude of their children!'

Now in her letters to this aunt, HisWifeNadia wrote that among all the food of the world, if any were to be likened to the Tower of Babel in the Holy Bible, it had to be this *ashure*. Just like in the Tower of Babel, in the pudding cauldron too, miscellaneous types that would otherwise never come together managed to mingle without fusing into one another. Just as the workers at the Tower had failed to comprehend each other's language, so too did each ingredient in the cauldron retain its distinctiveness within that common zest. The fig in the *ashure,* for instance, though subjected to so many processes and boiled for so long, still preserved its own flavour. As they boiled there on the stove, all the ingredients prattled on in unison but each in its own language.

Hence supplementary ingredients could be incessantly added to this totality. If there was room in *ashure* for garbanzo beans, why not add corn as well? Where there was fig, there could be plum too, or why not peach alongside apricot, pasta in the company of rice…? In her first few months at Bonbon Palace, HisWifeNadia had for a reason still unknown to her fervently busied herself with such experiments. Yet, ramming each time into Metin Chetinceviz's fierce retorts, she had in next to no time exhausted her daring to experiment with further combinations. Whatever the legend of Noah's Arc and the adventure behind it, when it came to putting the teachings into practice, *ashure* turned out to be a highly unadventurous food. It did not welcome innovations. Her aunt, though never in her life having cooked *ashure,* must have arrived at the same conclusion for she had felt the need to caution in her letters that just as one could not modify the verses of the Bible as one pleased, it was better not to play with ingredients freely either. Eventually HisWifeNadia had given up, starting to cook the *ashure* in line with the routine. Be that as it may, perhaps because deep inside she still pined for a boundless variation and had never been able to make do with the ingredients in hand, the end product had failed to meet her expectations all this time.

Nonetheless, there was one occasion, that ill-starred day, when she had inexplicably been satisfied with her *ashure.* Having finished the cooking, as usual, she had put the cauldron aside to cool off, prepared the frosty pinky cups and started waiting eagerly for her husband to come home. Now that she had accomplished the outcome she had craved for so long, she expected to finally receive Metin Chetinceviz's appreciation. Yet, she had soon noticed that stinking amber briefcase of his was not in its place. That could only mean one thing: Metin Chetinceviz was going to head to his second job this evening, from which he would probably return around midnight. Her achievement at *ashure* had excited HisWifeNadia so much that she couldn't possibly wait that long. Hence she decided to do something that had never crossed her mind before: to pay a visit to Metin Chetinceviz's workplace with a cup of *ashure*.

Though it had been four years since she had arrived in this city, Istanbul remained a colossal mystery to her. She had seen so little of the city so far that she had no sense of the direction in which its streets lay nor any sense of its structure in her mind. Her ensuing audacity might therefore be attributed to nothing but ignorance. In such a state she headed to the studio on the Asian Side. Though crossing the Bosphorus Bridge had cost her two hours, finding the address turned out to be unexpectedly easy. She left her identification card at the entrance, received information from the receptionist, got in the elevator, went up to the fifth floor, walked to Room 505, peeped inside and stood petrified. Metin Chetinceviz was there sitting knee-to-knee with a woman; he had placed one hand on the knobby, peach-puff kneecap of the latter which puckered like a blemish too timid to come to light. As for his other hand, he employed that to rotate a tiny coffee cup, as he told the woman her fortune. It must have been good news, for a dimpled smile had blossomed on the latter's face. Fixated with her husband, HisWifeNadia was not able to eye-up the woman as much as she would like to. It wasn't so much the fact that she'd been cheated on which rendered her speechless, rather the affectionate expression on Metin Chetinceviz's face. Neither the woman in the room, nor the hand caressing her knee seemed a sight as horrid as the affectionate expression upon her husband's face, so dulcet and tender, so unlike her husband.

Up until now, HisWifeNadia had forgiven each and every one of Metin Chetinceviz's wrongs and in her jaded way endured his never-ending jealousies, callousness, even slaps, believing that he did it all involuntarily, almost against his own will. Yes, her husband treated her in an awful way occasionally – that is, frequently – that is, constantly – but this was because he did not know any better. To sustain a flawed marriage requires, in essence, rather than an obstinate faith in marriage a faith in obduracy as such. We can endure being treated brutally by the person we love, if and only if, and as long as, we can convince ourselves that he knows no better and is unable to act in any other way.

'Love is nothing but neurochemical machinery,' Professor Kandinsky used to contend. 'And the most faithful lovers are simply bird-brained. If you meet a woman who's been married for years, still head-over-heels in love with her husband, be assured that her memory works like that of a titmouse.'

According to Professor Kandinsky, for love to be immortal, memory needed to be mortal. In point of fact memory had to be fully capable of incessantly dying and reviving just like day and night, spring and fall, or like the neurons in the hypothalamus of those teeny-weeny titmice. These birds with their simple brains and with bodies just as frail had to remember each year a bulk of indispensable information, including where they had hidden their eggs, how to survive the winter chill, where to find food. As their memories were not large enough to shelter so many crumbs of information, rather than trying to stockpile every experience by heaping up all items of knowledge on top of one another, every fall they performed a seasonal cleansing in the cavities of their brains. Hence they owed their ability to survive under such convoluted conditions, not to adamantly clinging on to one fixed memory, but rather to destroying their former memories to create fresh new ones. As for matrimony, there too, just like in nature, being able to do the same things for years on end was only possible if one retained the ability to forget having being doing the same things for years on end. That's why, while those with weak memories and messy records were able to bandage much more easily the wounds inflicted throughout the history of their affair, those who constantly and fixedly thought about the good old days and yearned for the wo/men they married were bound to have a tough time in coming to grips with the fact that 'today' would not be like 'yesterday'. The miraculous formula of love was to have a mortal memory, one that dithered and wavered incessantly.

Yet, that day standing by the door with two cups of *ashure* in her hands, HisWifeNadia had not been able to thwart a particular scrap of information long forgotten in its return to her consciousness. She had remembered. As she stood there watching her husband flirt with another woman, she had recalled how doting he had once been toward her as well, that is, what a different man he once was. Even worse than remembering this, was the observation that his tenderness was in fact not a thing of the past and that he could still behave courteously. He was perfectly capable of acting, if not becoming, altered. If Professor Kandinsky were here, he would have probably found the incident too preposterous to bother with. The aptitude to renew memory by erasing previously stored knowledge was a merit germane to the tiny titmice, not to unhappily married women.

HisWifeNadia had then taken a step inside, her gaze irresolutely wandering, if only for a minute, over the lovers still unaware of her, still reading fortune in a coffee cup giggling and cooing. As she gaped, first at both of them and then the woman alone, she had found herself immersed in a scientifically dubious contention which was once of profound concern to her:'If and when you look attentively at someone unable to see you, unaware of your presence, be assured that she will soon feel uneasy and abruptly turn around to see her seer.'

However, before the other woman had a chance to do so, it was Metin Chetinceviz who would notice HisWifeNadia standing there. With visible panic he had jumped to his feet. Struggling hard to adjust his gleefully relaxed body to this brusque shift, he had hobbled a few steps only to make it as far as the centre of the room, where he had come to a full stop. In an attempt to make his body a *portiere* drawn in between the two women, he had stood there wriggling for a moment, not knowing which side to turn to. Not only his mind but his face too had bifurcated as he struggled to simultaneously give a cajoling smile to his lover, whom he had always treated gently, and frown at his wife, whom he was used to treating coarsely. Unable to cling on to this dual mission any longer, he had grabbed his stinking amber briefcase, along with his wife's hand and hustled both outside. Their quarrel that night had been no shoddier than the ones before, except that it had lasted longer. HisWifeNadia had hitherto been afraid at various instances that her husband might kill her, but now for the first time she had felt she too could kill him. Oddly enough, this gruesome feeling had not seemed that gruesome at all.

What *was* truly gruesome for HisWifeNadia was to know nothing about this other woman. Since she had no acquaintances among Metin Chetinceviz's colleagues, getting this precious information would be more arduous than she thought. Startlingly, she could not even describe her to anyone for however hard she tried, the woman's face remained hazy in her memory. Still not giving up, she had made oodles of plans each more complex than the previous one, and kept calling the studio with new excuses under different names each time. When unable to attain anything like that, she had started going to the studio every day, wasting four hours on the road, just to patrol around the building. She sure knew that her husband would break her legs if he ever spotted her around here but even this dire peril had not urged her to give up.

'The gravest damage psychopharmacology has wrought on humanity is its obsession with cleansing the brain from its quirks.'

According to Professor Kandinsky, the human brain functioned like a possessive housewife priding herself on her fastidiousness. Whatever stepped inside its house, it instantly seized, remarkably vigilant of preserving her order. That, however, was no easy task since, like many such possessive housewives, so too did the brain have several unruly, cranky kids, each of whom were baptized under the name of a distinct mental defect. Whenever any one of these kids started to crawl around, sprinkling crumbs and creating a mess all over the house, the brain would crack up with apprehension, worrying about the disruption of her order. It was precisely at this point that psychopharmacology stepped into the stage. To solve the quandary it tried to stop the toddling child and, when that failed, it took the child by the ear and dragged him outside: 'If you wish to control uncontrollable movements, stop movement altogether! In order to prevent the damage thoughts might generate, bring your patient to a state where he won't think anymore.' Hundreds of drugs and dozens of practices aimed repetitively at this result. The world of medicine, notorious for deeming the physician who invented lobotomy worthy of a Nobel, muffled ear-piercing screams into an absolute silence, and favoured death over life by taking from the brain's hands the boisterous children whom she indeed found troublesome but held dear nevertheless. According to Professor Kandinsky, there was infinite gain in acknowledging straight out that one could never entirely get rid of his obsessions and all attempts to the contrary were bound to cause far more damage than good. There was nothing wrong in entering into the brain's home and playing according to her rules, as long as the movement inside was not curbed and what was hers was not appropriated from her.

True, the brain could not tolerate seeing her order being upset. Nonetheless, since there was more than one room in her house and more than one memory within her memory, she could certainly confuse what she put where. The interior was like a multi-drawered nightstand. In the top drawer were the undergarments, in the drawer below the folded towels and the laundered bed sheets under that. In this scheme, wherein the place of every obsession and each mania was pre-determined, one should not strive to fully get rid of a fixation somehow acquired. One could, with the aid of science or deliberate absentmindedness, take something out of its drawer and place it in the one above. After all, the fastidious housewife the brain was, it would certainly search for a towel in the fourth drawer, and not in the fifth one where the undergarments were. 'Carefully fold the towels you took out from the front lobe and then leave them in the subcortical centre. Do not ever attempt to wipe out your obsessions for it is not possible. Rather, suffice to put them at a place where you cannot find them. Let them stay in the wrong drawer. You will soon forget. Until your brain accidentally finds them again one day while searching something else…'

Though she was well aware of making her professor's bones shudder in his grave, HisWifeNadia had still refused to take her obsession from its corresponding drawer and put it somewhere else. In the following days, she had made frequent calls to the studio her husband worked in, keeping it under surveillance for hours on end. Finally, one day a voice she had not heard before but recognized instantly, intuitively, answered the phone. It was her. 'Hello, how can I help you?' she had asked graciously. 'Who is this?!' HisWifeNadia had exclaimed in a voice devoid of fury but blatantly shrill. So harshly and snappily had the question been posed that the other, taken unaware, had immediately told her name. Often, identity resembles a reflex – becoming some sort of an involuntary reaction to a stimulus. That must be why, when asked to identify themselves, quite a number of people end up involuntarily introducing themselves rather than asking back, 'Who the hell are *you*?'

Upon hearing the name pronounced, HisWifeNadia had hung up on her. Once having learned the name and workplace of her competitor, it had been painless to discover the rest. Before long she was holding two bunches of information about the woman whose details she now had in her possession. First of all, just like Metin Chetinceviz, she did voiceovers on TV. Secondly, she currently did the voiceover for the leading character in a soap opera titled 'The Oleander of Passion'.

On the following day, before the news was broadcast, HisWifeNadia had sat down in the divan with burgundy patterns on a mauve background – the reupholstering of which she constantly put off – and watched in complete calmness an episode of 'The Oleander of Passion'. When it was over, she decided that she simply loathed it. The plot was so absurd and the dialogues so jumbled that even the actors seemed to be suffering. Nonetheless, the next day and at the same time, there she was once again in front of the TV. Ever since then, with every passing day and every concluding episode, her commitment, if not immersion, had escalated. Academics researching housewives' addiction to soap operas tend to overlook this, but there can be a variety of reasons for becoming a viewer, some of which are not at all palpable. Before she knew it, HisWifeNadia had become a regular viewer of 'The Oleander of Passion'. Soon the soap opera occupied such a prominent place in her daily life that she could barely endure the weekends when it was not broadcast. She hardly questioned her fixation and barely attempted to overcome it. She solely and simply watched, just like that…and months later, as she sat there watching the eighty-seventh episode, she could not help the voice and image of Loretta jumble in her brain.

Though 'satisfactory failure' was an oxymoron, there could still be unsatisfactory successes in life. Professor Kandinsky was fond of saying he was both 'unsatisfied' and 'successful'; which was better off than many others, he would add, especially those who were both satisfied and successful: for that specific condition was germane to either the dim-witted or the exceptionally lucky. As excess luck ultimately stupefied, the end result was the same. Nevertheless, toward the end of his life, the professor too had tasted a breakdown. Both the dissatisfaction and the failure grabbing him stemmed from the same cause: 'The Theory of the Threshold Skipping Species,' a project he had been working on for four years.

Even when wiped out by a catastrophe, bugs still retained

an amazing immunity to anything that threatened them with utter extinction. Around 1946 they seemed to have been resilient to only two types of insecticides, whereas by the end of the century they had developed resistance to more than a hundred kinds of insecticides. The species that managed to triumph over a chemical formula skipped a threshold. Not only were they unaffected by the poisons that had destroyed their predecessors, but they ended up, in the long run, producing new species. The crucial issue, Professor Kandinsky maintained, was not as much to discover how on earth bugs acquired this particular knowledge as to discover knowledge *in its entirety*. According to him, those premonitions that were a long source of disappointment for the Enlightenment thinkers, who regarded the social and the natural sciences as one totality, would be realised in the century that was just arriving, along with its catastrophes. Humans too were sooner or later bound to skip a threshold. Not because they were God's beloved servants, as the pious believed, not because they possessed the adequate mental capacity, as the rationalists assumed, but mainly because they too were condemned to the same 'Circle of Knowledge' as God and bugs. The societal nature of bugs' lives and the intuitive nature of human civilizations had been attached to each other with and within the same durable chain: *sociobiology*. Consequently, just as artists weren't as inventive as supposed, nor was nature aloof from craftsmanship. To stay alive, whenever they could, cockroaches and writers drew water from the same pool of knowledge and intuition.

'I doubt if they have read even the first page,' Professor Kandinsky had roared when the news of his report being rejected had reached him. It was a week before his death. They had sat side by side on the steps of the little used exit door of the laboratory where they worked together – a colossal building where Russia's gifted biologists worked systematically for thirteen hours a day. Yet from a distance, it was hard to tell how huge it was for it had been built three floors under the ground. Since the feeling of being among the chosen brings people closer to each other, everyone inside was highly polite to one another. Only Professor Kandinsky was unaffected by the molecules of graciousness circulating in the air. Not only did he decline to smile at others but also sealed his lips except when forced to utter a few words. He had little tolerance for people, the only exception being Nadia Onissimovna who had been his assistant for nine years and who had won his confidence with her submissiveness as much as her industriousness. Professor Kandinsky was as cantankerous and reticent as he was glum and impatient. Deep down, Nadia Onissimovna suspected he was not as grumpy as he seemed, and even if he was, he had probably turned into a wreck of nerves only as a result of conducting electrically charged experiments day and night for years. Even back in those days she couldn't help but seek plausible excuses for the coarse behaviour of those she loved.

'They don't know what they're doing to me! Failure isn't a virus I'm acquainted with! I have no resistance to it.'

Two security guards were smoking further down by the grey walls surrounding the wide field of the laboratory. The gale was blowing so hard that their smoke could not hover in the air for even a second.

'Some nights I hear the bugs laughing at me, Nadia, but I cannot see them. In my dreams I meander into the empty pantries of empty houses. The bugs manage to escape just before the strike of lightning or the start of an earthquake. They migrate in marching armies. Right now, even as we speak, they are here somewhere near. They never stop.'

A week later, he was found dead in his house: an electrical leakage, a unfussy end… Nadia Onissimovna always reckoned he had died at the most appropriate moment. Fortunately he would never learn what had happened to his laboratory. First, the experiments had been stopped due to financial restrictions and then numerous people were fired. Nadia Onissimovna also received her share of this turmoil. When she met Metin

Chetinceviz, she had been unemployed for eight months.

Metin Chetinceviz was a total nuisance, one of the last types a woman would like to fall in love with. Unfortunately, Nadia Onissimovna was so inexperienced with men that even after spending hours with him, she had still not realized she was with one of the last types a woman would like to fall in love with. Anyhow that night, she had been dazed by the incomprehensible enormity, the bold crowds and the ceaseless booming noise of the discotheque she had stepped into for the first time, had thrown up all the drinks she had and was therefore in no condition to realize anything. She was there by chance; having been dragged by one of her girlfriends, from whom she hoped to borrow money by the end of the night. Metin Chetinceviz was among a group of businessmen coming from Istanbul. By the tenth minute of their encounter, before Nadia Onissimovna could comprehend what was going on, the tables were joined, women she was not acquainted with were added to these men she did not know, and a deluge of drinks was ordered. While the rest of the table rejoiced in laughing at everything, she had shrunk into one corner and drank as never before in her life. A little later, when everyone else scampered onto the dance floor in pairs, she saw a swarthy man sitting still, distressed and lonely just like her. She smiled. So did he. Encouraged by these smiles they exchanged a few words. Both spoke English terribly. Yet English is the only language in the world capable of giving the impression that it might be spoken with a little push, even when one has barely any knowledge of it. Thus in the following hours, rolling their eyes as if hoping for the words they sought to descend from the ceiling, snapping their fingers and drawing imaginary pictures in the air with their hands; doodling on napkins, sketching symbols on each other's palms, giggling whenever they paused; opening up whenever they giggled and continuously nodding their heads up and down; Nadia Onissimovna and Metin Chetinceviz plunged into one long, deep conversation.

***

'Rather than marry a Turk, I'd lick a crammed-full ashtray on an empty stomach every morning.'

'You can lick whatever you want,' Nadia Onissimovna had replied impishly. "Not that which goeth into the mouth defileth a man; but that which cometh out of the mouth, this defileth a man."'

'Do not recklessly scatter in my kitchen the teachings of Jesus as if they were epigrams of that untrustworthy professor of yours,' her aunt had bellowed, as she blew on the ladle she had been stirring for the last fifteen minutes in a greenish soup.

'You know nothing about him,' Nadia Onissimovna had muttered shrugging her shoulders. 'Only prejudice…'

'I can assure you that I do know what I need to know, honey,' her aunt had pontificated sprinkling salt in concentric circles onto the pot. 'And if you had not wasted your most beautiful years chasing ants with a good-for-nothing nutter, you too would know what I know.' She pulled a stool by the oven and, jangling her bracelets, kept stirring the soup. Due to varicose veins, she could not stand up for more than ten minutes. 'At least you must know that Turks don't drink wine,' she said with a distraught expression, but it was hard to determine what distressed her more, the subject matter or the soup's still refusing to boil.

Desperate to object, Nadia Onissimovna had started to recount, though with a dash of exaggeration, the whiskies, beers and vodkas her future husband had consumed at the discotheque, refraining from mentioning how he had mixed them all and the outcome.

'Whisky is another story. Do they drink *wine*? Tell me about that. No, they don't! If they did, they wouldn't have destroyed the fountain of Leon the Sage when they captured Zavegorod. The fountain gushing wine for three hundred years was raised to the ground when the Turks got hold of it. Why did they destroy that gorgeous fountain? Because it gushed wine instead of water! The Turks tore down its wall with axes. Idiots! They thought they would unearth a cellar crammed with barrels of wine somewhere down there but you know what they found instead? A bunch of grapes! Hear me well, Nadia, I say a bunch of grapes! And only three among them had been squeezed. Apparently with only one grape, wine flowed out of the fountain for a century. What did the Turks do when they saw this miracle? Did they appreciate it? No way! They demolished the walls, broke the fountain and even destroyed the grape bunches. They don't honour wine, don't honour things sacred and don't honour the sage.' Still grumbling she had shaken the ladle toward her niece. 'They don't honour women anyhow!'

***

When coming to Istanbul, Nadia Onissimovna had not fantasized at all about the milieu that would be awaiting her. In spite of this, she couldn't help feeling disappointed when she saw Bonbon Palace for the first time. Not that the apartment building she was going to live in from now on was more dilapidated than the ones she had lived in so far. If anything, it was more or less the same. That was the issue anyhow, this *sameness*. For moving somewhere brand new only to encounter there a pale replica of your old life is a good reason to be disappointed. To top it all, there was neither a sandy beach nearby, nor a job for an entomologist, but the gravest problem was Metin Chetinceviz himself. For one thing, he had lied. He did not even have a proper job. He made a living by doing minor voiceovers at irregular intervals for various TV channels. In addition, he occasionally went to weddings, circumcision ceremonies or birthday parties of affluent families to perform the shadow theatre Karagoz. He kept his reeking leather puppets in his amber coloured briefcase, but lately Bonbon Palace had started to stink so awfully that the smell of the leather puppets was nothing compared to the smell of garbage surrounding the apartment building.

To cap it all, HisWifeNadia soon realized how badly mistaken her aunt had been. Metin Chetinceviz glugged down low-price low-quality wine at a rate even the miraculous grapes of Leon the Sage could not compensate for. When drunk he lost not only his temper but also the ability to work. If doing a voiceover, he forgot the text; if performing with the shadow theatre, he stirred up a ruckus by making his puppets talk gobbledygook, peppered with slang and slander. At the weddings he attended, as he played the puppets, behind the shadow screen he gobbled down every drink in his reach, causing a disgrace by the end of the day. Once he had been kicked out for hurling from the mouth of the puppet named 'Hacivat', lascivious jokes and loutish insinuations about the groom in front of the guests. Since those witnessing his scandals never gave him work again, he incessantly had to set up new job contacts.

Still Nadia Onissimovna did not go back. She stayed here at Bonbon Palace. Even she herself could not fathom when and how she had internalized the role of a housewife she had started performing temporarily, with the idea that this would only be until she found an appropriate job. One day the writing on a wedding invitation captivated her attention: 'We wish Metin Chetinceviz and His Wife Nadia to join us on our happiest day.' She stared at the letter blankly, there and then realizing that she was not 'Nadia Onissimovna' anymore, not 'Nadia Chetinceviz' either, but 'HisWifeNadia'. Though shaken by this discovery, she still did not attempt to make any significant changes in her life. The days had for so long been impossible to tell apart, as if they were all photocopies of a particular day now long gone. She cooked, cleaned the house, watched TV, looked at old photographs, and when bored, she made something other housewives might not know much about: potato lamps that lit up without being plugged in. Both Professor Kandinsky and his 'threshold skipping species' had remained behind in another life.

'Why can't I remember my past? I wish I knew who I was. Why can't I remember, why?' moaned Loretta spinning in her hands the daisy which was in her hair a minute ago.

'You're searching for it in the wrong drawer, honey! Look at the one below, the one below!' yelled HisWifeNadia, without noticing that she repeated the gesture on the screen, spinning in her hands the latest potato lamp she had fabricated.

It was precisely then that she heard a sound by the door. He was coming. Earlier than usual today. He would probably munch a bit, take a nap and then go out again in the evening, taking his smelly briefcase with him. You could never tell when would he come or leave, but no matter what hour of the day it was, he never cared to ring the doorbell.

As the key wiggled in the lock, HisWifeNadia grabbed the remote and switched the channel. When Metin Chetinceviz appeared at the door, Loretta had already been replaced by a cooking programme. A woman with a wide forehead, round face and a remarkable moustache was busy tasting the *spinach au gratin* she had just removed from the oven.

Flat Number 1: Musa, Meryem, Muhammet

Keeping an eye on the door for Muhammet's return, Meryem embraced her swollen belly with her dimpled arms and heaved a deep sigh. That day, she had again had success in sending her son to school but god knows what he would look like when he returned home. In the beginning Muhammet used to tell her in great detail everything that happened in school, be it good or bad. Yet he had sunk into arrant silence over time. What her son did not put into words, Meryem heard anyhow from his troubled eyes, or the split seams and ripped out buttons of his school outfit, or the bruises on his arms. As she listened her worries soared. The thought that somebody might be hitting her son, be it a child or a grownup, killed her; his own father had not yet given him a flick. Only Meryem, she alone had slapped him a few times, may Allah forgive her, and occasionally pinched him too but that was different. As a matter of fact, ever since she had discovered that others had been 'roughing-up' her son, Meryem had refrained from even this minimal disciplining. When in her mind's eye she saw children raining blows on her son, her blood boiled. There was a time when she thought it was nothing other than a simple scuffle among children and yet weeks and months had passed without any change for good. What infuriated Meryem the most was not so much her son's being smacked by his peers as seeing how he gradually became indifferent to torment.

As to why her son was relentlessly bullied she had a hard time unravelling. Was it because he was a janitor's son? But she had sounded out the neighbourhood kinfolk who held the same job and found out that their children faced no such calamity at school. What else then? Muhammet was neither fatter nor uglier nor more dim-witted than the other kids so why couldn't he struggle against the wicked? In despair she eyed her swollen belly. The answer, she knew too well, was right under her nose: it was because of Musa. Blood takes after blood, they said. Muhammet was his father's son, brazenly compliant and docile. Even a wee bit of his mother's splendid bulk had not been bequeathed to him; he was so tiny, so short and wiry. For years she had force-fed the boy five times a day, making him eat a soft-boiled egg every morning, but to no avail. Not only had he not put on weight or grown taller, he still looked at least two years younger than his peers. True, Muhammet had always been petite, but his frame had shrunk visibly since he had started elementary school and thereafter to butt into the barricade of his peers' scorn.

When Muhammet put on the school outfit that was tailored a size larger so that he could still wear it in the years to follow, and shouldered that huge knapsack of his, so noticeably did he dwindle that everyone who saw him in that state scolded Meryem for not waiting another year before sending him to school. When next to his peers Muhammet's runtiness became all the more striking as if he was held under a magnifying glass. He was the smallest child in his class and, of course, in the entire school. Had this been the only problem, Meryem would not have made such an issue of it. She would have simply patched over her yearning for a son as robust as a pine tree and awe-inspiring as a sultan's skiff; one who could squeeze the water out of a stone and make whomever he frowned at shake in their shoes, yet at the same time possessed a heart so soft to take care of his by then senile mother. Despite Meryem's visions, not only had Muhammet proved to be his father's son in terms of physical frame, he had started to acquire the latter's habits as well. Oddly enough, even though from cradle to school he had been glued to his mother and had an at-all-

times-asleep-or-sleepy man for a father, as soon as released
from his mother's wings, the person Muhammet ended up
taking after was none other than his father. That was what
troubled Meryem the most. After all, she firmly believed that if
Musa had a roof over his head and a job to keep him fed, it was
all thanks to her. Musa had hitherto been able to stand on his
feet precisely because he had handed himself over to his wife.
What if his son was not so lucky? What if life did not present
Muhammet with another Meryem? Then there was no way
could he survive in Istanbul. This city would give him a
beating worse than the one he now got from his peers.

Lost in her thoughts, Meryem started to grind her teeth.
This she did rarely now, only when truly distraught or
confused. Yet as a child she used to grind her teeth so much at
nights that would wake up everyone in the household. Her
great grandmother was alive then; alive and so old that her
emaciated body had been entirely cleansed of the dual malady
of angst and haste. One day she had sat Meryem down to warn
her that only when she learned to be patient could she ever
leave her teeth alone, otherwise she would be of no use in life,
and just as she robbed people of their sleep today, she would
rob them of their peace of mind tomorrow. The way to learn
to be patient was through learning how to fill up a 'patience
sack.' This required an empty sack, which should be left
somewhere high, tied sidewise to the end of a stick like a
banner. Meryem, who was no older than Muhammet at that
time, had listened to this counsel attentively and fast as a rabbit
climbed up the roof of the coal cellar in the garden, where she
hang an empty sack to a broom with great difficulty. As the
wind blew, the empty sack would accumulate various things
inside, filling up bit by bit in time. As such, the only thing
Meryem was expected to do was wait without doing anything
and as she waited, to make sure she did not forget what she was
waiting for. This was what they called 'patience.'

Yet even at that age Meryem was impulsive, not to mention
alarmingly impatient. Whenever faced with a challenge, she

would do everything in her power to beat it. Filling up the 'patience sack' had been no exception. In the days to follow, she would check the sack first thing in the morning only to come down the ladder disappointed each time. The burden of not doing anything was so unbearable that each night in her sleep she would carry buckets of soil to fill sack upon sack. As this dream labour had made her teeth grating even worse than before, the nights had turned into a nightmare for the entire household. Her great grandmother was despondent, her grandmother baffled and her mother infuriated. All three women kept talking about a prophet named Eyup.

'OK, I'll wait, but tell me for how long?' Meryem wanted to know. 'Until the sack fills up by itself,' suggested her great grandmother; 'Until you are ready,' snarled her grandmother; 'Until the sack is filled and you are ready,' concluded her mother. In the meanwhile, her father, sick and tired of the four generations of women at the house and this sack business of theirs which was getting nowhere, had already brought down the wooden ladder. 'Waiting without doing anything' counting for nothing in her book, Meryem had only been able to endure two weeks without climbing to look inside the sack. After two weeks, when no one was at home, she had carried the kitchen table out to the garden, placed a chair on top, hopped onto the roof of the coal cellar and stuck her head inside this sack of patience. Then and there she had seen the outcome of what they called patience: dry leaves, thorny shrubs, broken branches and two dead butterflies...such were the rewards of those who endured: either a handful of dry twigs or the lethal wounds of the prophet Eyup...

That was it. After that day, she had stopped peeping into the sack and had never given it a second thought. Waiting leniently was not meant for her. Had that not been the case, Meryem would not have married Musa but waited instead for Isa, her favourite among her other suitors, to return from Istanbul. However, instead of waiting for Isa to come back 'godknowswhen', she had decided to come to Istanbul herself and to this end married Musa, dragging him along. Unfortunately, once they were back in the city things had not gone at all as she had expected. Realizing Musa wasn't going to be able to cope with Istanbul, Meryem had found herself remembering after all these years her great grandmother's Patience Sack. There was no way she was going to sit back and wait for the wind to fill up the sack, Musa to mature and life to bring them a few dead butterflies or dry twigs. Instead she would take charge of their destiny. As for Musa, his wife's industriousness, enterprising skill and willpower would leave a chilling effect on his nerves, rendering him more and more weak-kneed, sluggish and pessimistic. Subsequently, once in Istanbul, Musa and Meryem had turned into two opposite tides, just like the waters of the Bosphorus. This contrast in their dispositions was further reflected in their appearance. In the years to follow, while Meryem, tall and big boned to start with, gained day by day more and more weight, Musa shrunk like a hand-knitted sweater laundered in the wrong cycle.

Not that Meryem expected anything from her husband, having by now resigned herself to the man he had become. At night, half an hour before the arrival of the garbage truck, she collected the bagged trash from the flats of the Flea Palace and distributed in the morning their bread and newspaper. The latter she finished early in the morning so there would be time left for her scuffle with Muhammet, as well as for fortune-telling. She lingered before work while having her coffee, but once she got going, did not easily stop. Five days a week she went to five different flats for housecleaning. Though by now in the fifth month of her pregnancy, the sum total of her activities had not lessened a bit. Perhaps she now went up the stairs more slowly but that was all. Her energy resembled her weight; however much she ran around it didn't decrease a bit. Similarly, her fortitude resembled her energy; like a machine in perpetual motion she kept turning her own wheel.

Every so often it occurred to her she would actually be better off without Musa. Had she received the news that Musa was dead hit by a car, she would of course have been distraught with sorrow but her life would not go astray; in point of fact, it would not even change. Yet if she were the one hit, Musa would be smashed to smithereens as if the car had hit not his wife's body but the mainspring of his own life and livelihood. Though Meryem struggled hard not to think such inauspicious things, she couldn't help doing so…and the more her pregnancy moved ahead, the more fixated she became on the ghastly thoughts parading full force in her mind.

Lately she had been more and more scared of outlandish apprehensions, having nightmares upon nightmares, waking up every morning her heart pummelling, agonized by the thought that something ominous might happen at any moment. Given her score in the Patience Sack episode, how could she be expected to wait passively for evil to come her way? Thus she took precautions. If researchers conducting ethnological analyses on the birth customs and beliefs in Turkey had, instead of surveying each and every village and town, simply come across Meryem, they would indeed have obtained the same data with much less expense and effort.

Meryem's package of precautions concerning birth came under three clusters:

1) Never do those things that should never be done.
2) Be careful in doing those things that need caution.
3) Do those things that are felicitous as much as possible.

Those 'things that should never be done' had no explanation and no justification for their categorisation. Just as one should not clip nails at night, one should not interpret dreams then either. As the mysteries of dreams are barely comprehensible even in plain daylight, how could one possibly interpret them in the darkness of the night? Meryem never left her nail clippings around, always throwing them into the toilet to make sure no one else would get hold of them. Likewise she frequently checked and collected the hairs on hairbrushes and then burnt them. If a single strand of her hair accidentally fell some place outside her house, she would immediately pick it up and put it in her bosom. She was particularly sensitive about hair and nails, holding the belief that these were the only two things in the human body which continued to live for sometime, even after the body they belonged to passed away. According to Meryem you shouldn't take a knife from anyone's hand, leave a pair of scissors open, bring to the tip of your tongue the name of the living while passing by a cemetery, speak of animals in a room where the Koran was kept, mumble a song and if possible, you shouldn't even open your mouth when waking up to go to the bathroom where the *jinni* gather at night, or kill spiders...The list of the things you should avoid doing extended interminably and births were accorded a special place on this list. Women had to be watched both during pregnancy and for forty days after the birth and the plasma of the baby needed to be buried deep under earth. Though Meryem had not been able to convince that spectacled, cold fish of a physician to dig a hole for Muhammet's plasma in the garden of the hospital where she had given birth, thanks to the goofy nurse she had eventually emerged triumphant. Deaths, too, were as sensitive as births. When visiting someone on their deathbed, Meryem addressed the patient by different names one after another to bamboozle the Angel of Death. If she still could not fool *Azrael* and the patient died, she would give away every single item of the deceased's clothing to a peddler of old clothes whom the former had never met. If the peddler committed the mistake of uttering a few words of courtesy about the departed one, she would instantly take the clothes away from him to give them to another.

After all, anonymity lay at the essence of the profession of peddlerhood. On a peddler's cart one should never know which goods were left by whom, in point of fact, one should not even think that they once upon a time belonged to someone. The noble task of delivering familiar clothes to unfamiliar people was incumbent upon the peddler. Ultimately, while those who gave away these clothes needed to get rid of their past, those who purchased them didn't want to know anything about that past. In between the two groups of people crisscrossed the peddlers, cleansing personal items of all the memories they had gone through and the poignant ends they had met, so that they could start life anew. That's the way it had to be so that the old could yield the new and death engender life. Actually, if asked to name the most consecrated professions on earth, Meryem would name the peddler before the teacher or the physician. Not that she wanted Muhammet to become a packman but she sure felt deep affection for these men carting away the remnants of a dispersed home or a departed acquaintance, to then bring from afar others' goods, and thus steadily, spontaneously mixing up bits and pieces of Istanbul's seven hills and motley communities.

As for the 'things-that-required-care', it was better not to do them at all but if you had to you should at least take precautions. One should refrain from sewing a cloth on a person, for instance. Alternatively, one should bring an object that could counterbalance any misfortune the needle might bring. That's why whenever Meryem sewed a cloth on someone's body, she would put a wooden spoon in her mouth. If she accidentally broke a mirror, she would instantly go and buy another one, and since fire could be fought with fire, smash that mirror into pieces as well. Nonetheless she would rather have as little contact as possible with mirrors, each being a silvered sealed gate to the unknown. Since she deemed it inauspicious to see one's image repeatedly, the only mirror in their house always faced the wall. As for normal doors, she paid great care when passing through them. Even cemeteries did not scare her as much as thresholds. When passing through a door, she would never ever step on the threshold, opening her legs to the widest step possible and always with the right foot first. Differentiating her right from her left was a constant concern for her anyhow. When at the table, she would place a piece of bread to her right side to feed the eyes of those who coveted the bounty of their table. Reserving her left hand for the dirtiest jobs, she took great care to turn from her right when someone called her name on the street, hung up her clothing from right to left as if writing in Arabic and always made sure she got up from the right side of the bed. Though this inevitably meant that Musa would have to get up from the left side, he did not seem to care about this as long as his sleep was uninterrupted.

All day long, Meryem collected premonitions and read signs. It was good portent if her right eye twitched but she instantly got wary if her left eye did so. A ringing in her right ear was good news but she would start to worry about her fate when the ringing was in the left one. Itchy feet was a sign of a journey on the way, itchy palms meant money and an itchy throat suggested a tight spot. If she got goose bumps, Meryem suspected that *jinn* were nearby. As for tea leaves…if an unexpected tealeaf escaped the sieve and appeared in her tea, Meryem would expect a visitor that same day. From the leaf's shape, she would try to surmise the identity of the guest and from its colour their intention. If a dog howled after midnight she forlornly concluded someone would soon be dead. Yet she was no longer as resolute about this matter as she used to be since a dopey, skin-and-bones medical student had moved into the flat across from hers with his ogre of a dog.

Meryem resorted to the coffee cup in order to find out the calamities beyond her grasp. Morning coffee was reserved for fortune telling and night coffee for the simple pleasure of drinking it. Recently she had formed the habit of topping-up her night coffee with three thimblefuls of banana liqueur. It was that Blue Mistress in Flat 8 who had introduced her to this liqueur business. There were all types of liqueur there, lined up with olive oil bottles of all sizes. She had made Meryem taste each and every one. The raspberry was scrumptious and the mint left a pleasant freshness in one's mouth, but it was the banana liqueur that Meryem had relished the most and could have drunk in heaps if only she weren't concerned about harming the baby. Mistaking Meryem's hesitation for fear of sin the Mistress had chuckled: 'Who says a liqueur is an alcoholic drink?!' Meryem had instantly grabbed on to this explanation: a liqueur was not an alcoholic drink after all. 'If you like them so much, go ahead and take the banana liqueurs with you,' the mistress had urged. Her man brought new ones anyhow. Meryem had seen him a couple of times: old enough to be her father and married on top of it. She had made no comment on the matter, however, for she considered private matters truly private.

Yet there were other things she could hardly stay away from no matter how much she tried. The evil eye, for instance; it was like an echo. Just as one could not detect the original voice behind an echo, one could not track down the source of the evil eye either. Fearing an attack from four different directions in forty different ways, Meryem had equipped every corner of the house with preventive measures. On the walls, she hung evil eye beads, prayer placards, horseshoes; she sprinkled and scattered holy water from Mecca, salt lumps or blessed black cumin seeds under the pillows, behind doors and especially in Muhammet's pockets; she kept tortoise shells, crab legs and horse chestnuts over the thresholds, and had charms written on almonds, dates, copper plates, all types of paper and animal skins. By now both Musa and Muhammet had become accustomed to living with this ever expanding hodgepodge concoction of items, most of which constantly changed location. Still, none of these precautions could ease Meryem's fear of the evil eye even a wee bit. At different times during the day, when a sudden sorrow settled in her heart, she instantly broke a plate inside the kitchen sink. If hot water cracked a glass cup, she concluded the curse of the evil eye was on her family and spun salt over fire. When she bumped into someone whose eyes looked menacingly blue, she surreptitiously covered Muhammet's face with her hands and if Muhammet happened to be away, closed her own eyes thinking of him. The thought that the curse of the evil eye might touch upon her son terrified her. Thus ever since he was a baby, Muhammet lived his life going around with amulets pinned to his undershirt and blessed black cumin seeds in his pockets; finding papers covered with Meryem's scrawl under his pillow; getting under a sheet once every ten days, its four corners held by four women while melted lead in cold water was poured over his head to break a spell. Muhammet would readily endure all of these things as long as he was not forced to eat eggs.

Having spent the interval between six months and six years being spoon-fed a soft-boiled egg every damn morning, Muhammet had a small problem with eggs. What he found even worse than their taste was their shells being used as complaint petitions. Every morning, once the egg was eaten and the shell was sparklingly clean inside, Meryem had penned on the shell whatever complaint had been left over from the day before: 'Yesterday Muhammet lied to his mother, but he will never ever do so again,' 'Yesterday he did not want to eat his egg, but he will never ever do so again,' 'Yesterday Muhammet cursed the auntie who poured the lead, but he will never ever do so again…'. These empty egg shells were each time thrown to the birds so that they could take these complaints to the two angel clerks recording on their celestial registers all the sins and good deeds committed on earth. Until the day he started elementary school, every morning before breakfast Muhammet would peek out of the window to see his winged informants. Yet each time he did this, the only species of birds he could spy were either the screeching sparrows perched upon the branches of the rose acacia in the garden or the ugly crows recklessly hunting the streets. There was also the caged canary inside the window of Flat Number 4 but that bird could not even flap its wings, let alone fly.

It was the seagulls Muhammet was suspicious of. He spotted them as they dug into the garbage bags accumulating by the side of the garden wall. In the damp breath of *lodos*, they drew circles as they descended onto the trash piles and it seemed to

Muhammet that each time they chanced upon a precious piece of information they would then glide into the sky squawking with pleasure. At nights, they gathered together on the roofs to watch the sins committed in the apartment buildings of Istanbul. Unlike his father, seagulls never went to sleep.

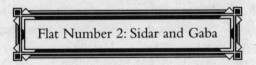

Flat Number 2: Sidar and Gaba

He opened the door with a grim look on his face. It was not screwing up the anatomy exam that upset him so much, but the fact that he had taken the anatomy exam in the first place, knowing only too well he would screw it up. He now profoundly regretted that when waking this morning, on realizing the alarm clock had again failed to go off, rather than hitting the pillow he had scurried out of the house and paid for a cab to boot. He even more profoundly regretted that after the exam he had joined his friends, who were clustered like pigeons flocking to wheat, to learn how each had answered every single question, to then complain unanimously about the instructor and then the whole university structure. To top it all off, once having joined them, he had ended up spending the entire day in cafés amidst non-stop chatter. Now he regretted all the energy he had so lavishly squandered. Energy, Sidar reckoned, was a finite commodity, like an eye lotion in a tiny dropper. Accordingly, he spent no more than two drops a day, one to wake up in the morning and the other to go to sleep at night.

Closing the outside door behind him without turning on the hall light, he found himself engulfed in darkness. He must have forgotten to draw the curtains back when he left hurriedly in the morning. Not that it would have made much difference, as its miniature windows were at ground level, this squat, narrow basement floor could get only a morsel of light. Cursing the dim-wit who had placed the switch two metres further in from the entrance, Sidar wobbled in. He could not get far, however, as his passage was blocked by the hefty silhouette emerging behind him. As the two bumped into one another, Sidar lost his balance, lurched forward hitting his head against the thick pipe passing right through the middle of the living room. Scared out of his mind, he reached the switch…and frowned at Gaba…Having got what he wanted, Gaba, on the other hand, was happily chewing on the *simit* he had snatched from his pocket.

Rubbing his head Sidar reclined on the sofa. Since the dirty, dusty pipe passed right through the middle of the living room – which also served as his bedroom, dining room and study – just at his ear level, he kept banging his head at the same spot. Just this morning, while rushing to leave the house he had bumped his head again, and if it went on like this he would soon have a bump there. Fortunately, as soon as he stretched out on the sofa, his grumpiness faded out. He so much enjoyed being at home. Here he could stay away from the turmoil that plagued every corner in Istanbul; as long as he was home, contrary to the world outside he could remain entirely still and utterly calm, just like Gaba did when his hunger was fully satiated.

It was particularly during late afternoon periods that the insularity reigning in Flat 2 became all the more blatant. Around this time every day, an excruciating mayhem swallowed Bonbon Palace. As the immediate surroundings assumed the hullabaloo of a fairground – synchronized by the brazen honks of the cars caught in traffic, the howls of the children playing at the park and the yells of the street peddlers – the mélange of sounds seeped in through the cracks and crevices of Bonbon Palace, getting hold of each and every flat except this one. It wasn't only the clamour that failed to penetrate Flat 2; the heat waves could not break through either. Getting almost no sunlight, the house was cool as a cellar during the summer when all other flats burned up. Likewise, the sour smell of garbage tormenting all the other residents was least detectable down here.

The truth is that when Bonbon Palace was built, Flat 2 had been designed not as a residence but a storage area, and had been used as such for many years. However, after the death of the owner, when the control of the apartment building had passed onto his daughter who had preferred to take care of everything from afar, this place too had received its share in the changes that occurred, each more problematic than the former. During the disarray that had prevailed, such huge fights had erupted when each and every neighbour attempted to pile their unused personal belongings up in this narrow space, that no one had the good fortune to use it for a long time. In the end, upon the instructions received from France, this stumpy, narrow, single-room basement floor was rented out at half the amount of rent of the other flats. From then on, a myriad of people had taken shelter here: people blatantly different from one another but with poverty and bachelorhood in common. Among these were, in the following order: a local radio news announcer living on chicken sandwiches three times a day; a depressed accountant whose best friend had snatched away his entire bank account along with his wife of eight years; an army deserter who turned the TV on full blast during Ramadan making everyone listen to sermons and hymns; a fishy fellow whose job no one had been able to guess at or dared ask about and a droll artist who used the place as an art studio painting the legs, ankles and shoes he watched from the window. Among all the tenants Flat 2 had seen thus far, the Cat Prophet, who had moved in next, was the one who had left behind the most in terms of traces and smell.

After the Cat Prophet, Sidar had appeared with his St. Bernard breed dog. As he, unlike the previous tenants, barely had any belongings, though it had for so long been accustomed to being chock-full, Flat 2 was now going through the most barren phase in its saga.

Gaba was such a bizarre dog, a walking contrast when compared with his breed, famous for their ability to go for days without water and food, to sense impending danger and make life safer for their owners, trace narcotics stashed away in secluded corners, rescue the victims trapped under debris and keep faithful company to the children, the blind and all those in need of aid. If there was one thing in the world Gaba could not possibly stand, it was hunger. His was a bottomless stomach and a never-to-be-satiated appetite. If left without food for a couple of hours, let alone a day, he would create havoc by chewing on whatever came to its paws, be it an anatomy book, a wooden chair or a plastic pail… He would pull all sorts of tricks just to get an additional morsel. Once having filled his stomach, however, he would lay in the corner, huge, fuzzy and dead still as a stuffed bear, with no trace left of the 'oomph' from a moment ago. Perhaps because he withheld even a dab of enthusiasm for food from all other spheres of daily life, there was no activity he enjoyed, not even being taken out for walks. Sidar might have suspected Gaba was going deaf with age if it weren't for the fact that he did not seem to experience any difficulty in hearing sounds that were of significance to him, such as the rattle of the dog food poured into a bowl, the crackle of a tin can being opened or the footsteps of Meryem bringing bread in the morning.

Deep down Sidar felt guilty. Having shoved this majestic dog of the Jura Mountains into a dingy basement in a dilapidated apartment building in one of the most jam-packed neighbourhoods in Istanbul, how could he expect him to behave normally? If the truth be told, part of this guilt stemmed from his guess that all the pastries with opium poppy and cakes with hashish he had made Gaba eat – at first simply for the fun of it and then because he had become addicted – might have a role in the dog's lassitude, not to mention the impact of the second-hand smoke all throughout these years. Such were the brief contours of the pangs of conscience that gnawed Sidar deep inside.

Gaba was matchless in the eyes of Sidar, 'the one and only'. Actually there was only one of everything in this house: one Gaba, one Sidar, one computer, one sofa, one chair, one

armchair, one table, one lamp, one pot, one sheet, one pencil…
When an item was worn out, the book had been read or the
CD had become tedious; only then was a second item acquired
and the old would be either immediately thrown away or
chewed to smithereens by Gaba.

Yet the plainness of the place came to an abrupt end at the
ceiling as if cut off by a knife. Onto the surface of the ceiling
Sidar had posted, nailed, taped or pinned on top of one
another black-and-white pictures clipped from various
journals. These included: some of his parents' letters, Nazim
Hikmet's 'My Funeral Procession', fanzines he had gathered
from here and there, fanzines he had made himself, strips from
Art Spiegelman's 'Maus', a gigantic Dead Kennedys poster, the
picture of a ship trying to make its way through fog (taken
from an old photograph and used as a menu cover at a
restaurant he had dined in a couple of times upon his arrival
in Istanbul never to visit again after getting used to the price
difference between Istanbul and Switzerland and realizing how
expensive it was), pages torn from the 'Batman: Dark Night'
series, a black T-shirt with the 'Receipt for Hate tour of Bad
Religion' printed in front, an anti-drug campaign poster with
letters made with pills writing '*Ma Vie Peut Etre Differente*',
photographs of Gaba as a puppy, the enlarged photocopy of
Goya's 'Boogeyman Is Coming', collage with quotations
plucked from Cioran's essay on Meister Eckhart, sketch of the
health goddess Hygieia with her rounded breasts, soft belly and
the big snake she wound around her necklines from Allen
Ginsberg's 'Kaddish', a sign that instructed: 'A civilized person
does not spit on the ground. You should not either!'(a placard
he had painstakingly removed one night when stoned),
Wittgenstein's photograph taken right before his death, a faded
picture of Otto Weininger, a poster of Spiderman squatting
down to watch the city from the top of one of the towers of
the World Trade Centre, right next to it a photograph of the
moment of explosion when the second plane dove into the
towers on September 2001, words from a song of the band

This Mortal Coil, self-portrait of the Turkish philosopher Neyzen Tevfik with a tag saying 'Nothing' hanging on his neck, newspaper clips about Robbie Fowler, midterm exam with 'COME AND SEE ME IMMEDIATELY' written on it with red ink, a faded computer print-out of Leonara Carrington's 'Zoroaster Meets His Image in the Garden', collages made with all sorts of prescriptions and Xanax boxes, an advertisement with the writing, 'Do not fool around with your son's future. Circumcision requires sensitivity. Sensitive is our middle name. Leave us all your circumcision business,' as well as a passport picture of a bushy-moustache, beetle-browed Scientific Circumciser (a poster he had chanced upon while wandering around the streets of Fatih and, being unable to remove it from the wall, had to go and personally procure it from the address written on it), cassette covers of Kino recordings he had once made, photograph of the ash-bone-tar train wreck which became the collective grave to four hundred people in Egypt on February 2002, notes of Walter Benjamin from the 'Moscow Diary', reproductions of William Blake's drafts of 'Songs of Innocence', cartoons of Selcuk clipped from 'Maniere de Voir', one of Freud's later photographs wherein he did not stare into the camera, engravings from the Lisbon earthquake/Istanbul postcards, a family picture taken exactly thirteen years ago at the Haydarpasa train station before leaving Turkey, notes with phone numbers or messages and last but not least, the silver necklace with a black-stripped transparent stone which was a souvenir from Nathalie whom he was tired of loving though whose love he had not tired of.

When Sidar had moved in, like all other urbanites he had the habit of decorating his walls with cherished pictures and posters. Before long, however, Gaba had rendered this impossible. On the way from Switzerland to Istanbul the dog had passed out in the train compartment in which he had been leashed, let out a terrible howl as if his flesh was being torn out and refused to calm down, even though food was placed in front of him every ten minutes. By the time his paws touched the Istanbul soil, his nerves were so shot that he was too confused to know where to look or who to bark. Finally, when stuck in this tiny flat, he had developed the habit of attacking the walls and started to chew any kind of paper he could find, due to hunger or irritability induced by love of his homeland. In desperation, Sidar had then begun to move his pictures and posters a bit higher. Yet 'a bit higher' could not be high enough for Gaba whose height, when standing up, was taller than the Turkish national average. Bit by bit, all pictures and posters escaping Gaba's sharp teeth, like refugees heading for the hills to flee from the warfare in their country, kept constantly climbing north to finally transcend the boundary of the wall, rushing altogether into the lands of the ceiling. Sidar had enjoyed this unexpected innovation so much that he had expanded the business over time and filled his topmost part with all types of visual and written material he held dear. Lately, this daily increasing bedlam had, like a vigorous vine, started to branch out into the kitchen ceiling on the one side and the bathroom ceiling on the other.

When stretched out on his back onto the only sofa in the living room with a rolled cigarette in hand, Sidar would fix his eyes on this ceiling for hours. While the smoke circulated in his blood full speed, the ceiling would acquire an astounding vivacity. At such times, Wittgenstein's black and white picture reddened, as the philosopher's face blushed; the miniature figures in the cartoons of Selcuk hopped and jumped around the ceiling; Spiderman dangled from a thread climbing up and down; the coronas in Blake's drafts started to blink as if relaying messages in code; Carrington's hairless magician melted into his own image and disappeared; Goya's bogeyman all of a sudden took the white sheet off to reveal his face; a cruel smile appeared on the Scientific Circumciser's face; Hygiea's breasts heaved with excitement; the figures on the photograph at the Haydarpasa train station one by one withered away. Before long, Sidar would feel the blood in his veins, as well as the two droplets of energy he possessed withdraw from his body, and he'd abandon himself in a woozy, puffy sea of ecstasy. When Gaba too came along and curled under his legs, the Flat 2 and its two inhabitants swimming in composure would form one flawless whole.

There existed only one thing that Sidar enjoyed ruminating: death. He did not do so consciously; in fact, consciousness was not at all the issue here, for he didn't invite the thoughts, rather they flocked to his mind on their own. His obsession with death was not a choice; he had been like this since childhood. He found death neither scary enough to grieve, nor grievous enough to be scared of. All he wanted was to understand it fully, truly. Whenever he met new people, before anything else, it was their attitudes towards death that would arouse his curiosity: whether they were scared of death or not, had lost someone close, had someone die before their eyes, had ever felt they could kill someone, did they believe in the afterlife... There were so many questions he had to ask, but seldom could. He had long before succumbed to the convention that he must hold his tongue on this particular subject. However, whether he could fall in love with a woman or not, feel comfortable at someone's house, liked a character in a film, how he regarded the author of a book he read, what he thought of the singers he listened to...it all depended on their relation with death. He could appreciate some bastard solely because he had died beautifully or just as well turn up his nose at a dignified person if he had met an ordinary end. Since his interest kept whipping up his knowledge and his knowledge his interest, Sidar possessed a magnificent archive of death in his mind. He never forgot where and how book characters, film stars, national heroes, philosophers, scientists, poets and especially murderers had died. This curiosity of his had cost him dearly at high school wherein all his history teachers hated him: 'Alexander the Great, oh yeah, he met his end with such a debauched illness: he either burst or, after a two day long feast thrown in his honour, got diarrhoea.' His interventions in the philosophy class were no different: 'But in his letters to Voltaire, the same Rousseau had mentioned with gratitude the Lisbon earthquake that killed hundreds of people. Such occasional cleanings, he thought, were necessary in terms of population quantity and quality.'

The nuggets of knowledge Sidar thus scattered would wreak havoc at each lesson. Upon learning Alexander had breathed his last due to diarrhoea, his greatness tended to wane and his reputation dwindled considerably. In the student's minds, Rousseau turned into a modern age terrorist while his philosophy fell on deaf ears. When confronted by death, the credibility of a religious scholar notorious for advising his disciples constant abstinence who himself could not make it to the morning after a night of gorging, the respectability of a well-esteemed elderly politician taking his last breath in the nuptial bed the same night he took a new wife half his age, the command of an Ottoman sultan who raided taverns hunting and hanging all those who drank even a drop of wine only to meet his own end through cirrhosis, and the esteem of a scientist squished like a bug while trying to cross a street without looking...all perished drastically... The deaths of the East were at least as preposterous as those of the West. In fact, death itself was preposterous.

'Since you seem to be paying no attention to my third and final warning, could you please step outside the classroom?'

His teachers never shared his views. Each time he would be thrown out of the classroom but unlike all the other male students who were ejected from the classroom, he would never become a hero in the eyes of the female students. Probably because girls, just like the teachers, did not find death preposterous.

Sidar had expected things to be different in Turkey. After all, dying was easier here; deaths occurred in larger numbers and life was shorter. Alas! Hard as he tried, his remarks on death were largely dismissed. At first he suspected it was because of his Turkish, perhaps he could not properly express himself. However, due to the dogged efforts of his mother — who had worked as a Turkish teacher until the day they were forced to escape out of the country and who had been worried her son would become alienated from his native tongue through being carried away not only by the French but also the Kurdish his father had tried incompetently to teach him – the long years Sidar spent away from Turkey had caused his Turkish to regress only a couple of steps. The issue was not how he expressed himself but what he expressed. Sidar had detected a number of differences between Switzerland and Turkey on the subject of death, and each point was written on a tiny piece of paper among the bedlam on the ceiling:

1. People in Turkey did not like death to be brought up as a subject (just like in Switzerland)
2. Whenever people in Turkey brought up death, they talked about the actual dead rather than the insubstantial idea of death (somewhat different from Switzerland)
3. People in Turkey were not able to distinguish death as something abstract (quite different from Switzerland).

Yet Istanbul, unlike its inhabitants, was not a bit bothered about the allusions to death. On no account did she shun this subject. At one of the lessons he had not been thrown out of, Sidar had listened attentively to how in the West the fools were put on ships and sent away from the cities. He likened the cemeteries in Switzerland to those ships with unwanted passengers, albeit with one difference, they had cast anchor, unable to drift away. All the same they were just as much insulated from city life. One could go visit the cemeteries at any time but the graves themselves often disembarked to become a part of the city. However, Istanbul had either forgotten to assign its ships to the graves, or the graves had escaped from their ships to disperse into the streets with turbans on their heads and marble stones on their arms. They were everywhere. Scattered all over the city like pollen strewn by the wind. At the corners where local markets were set up every week, in the midst of shopping malls, in swarming streets, on roads off the beaten track, in fields where the children played, on slopes overlooking the sea, in courtyards of dervish lodges; next to walls, hills, hedges, far and wide they popped up in front of the people in the shape of a tombstone, vault or numerous graves squeezed in between apartment buildings. Pedestrians passed them by as they strolled, scurried, promenaded, shopped... In this city, the dead resided side by side with the living.

Hence after a thirteen year interval, Sidar had spent his first year in Istanbul discovering graves and cemeteries. Sometimes he would consciously stroll around desolate neighbourhoods for this purpose alone, at some other times he would accidentally come across a cemetery and wander off into it. Walking around non-Muslim cemeteries had proved to be far more difficult than the Muslim ones since almost all of the former were surrounded by towering walls and were closed except on certain days. Once when in the garden of a Greek church he had asked what the relief of strewn pomegranate seeds on a tombstone meant and what the writing under it was, the custodian had hopelessly bobbed his head from side to side. He could not read a single word of Greek. Anyhow, he was not Greek but a Gregorian Armenian; for years he had worked at this church during the week and went for religious service to his own church on weekends. Since that encounter, Sidar had stopped presuming that all the people he saw in the Greek cemeteries in Istanbul were Greek, the ones in the Jewish cemeteries Jewish, or the Assyrian ones all Assyrians...

With their low walls and permanently open gates, the Muslim cemeteries were easier to roam. Most of these were badly neglected; it was as if it was not the lives of Muslims that were mortal but rather their cemeteries. Especially the more recent ones gave the impression that they might at any moment get up and migrate somewhere else. Sidar had until now met all sorts of people while walking around these places. Coarse guards, men who read the Qur'an for money by the graves, slovenly kids with pitchers in their hand who followed the visitors to fork out some money, those who came with all their family and filled baskets as if for a picnic, those who arrived alone and were for hours lost in thought, drunks who imbibed nearby at night, pickpockets who mushroomed wherever there was a crowd, clairvoyants with young, old, urban and rural women as followers... Over time he had learned to differentiate them. The habitual visitors of the Muslim cemeteries fell in two groups: those who came to leave a trace and those who came to follow some sort of lead. The former visited their relatives at regular intervals and then departed leaving behind their prayers, tears, pitchers full of water and flowers. These were harmless, self-contained people when compared to the latter. Those who came to follow some lead or another were rather sinister. They came to steal goods, milk people out of their money, cast a spell, gather signs... That is, they came to get something from the cemeteries and did not leave until they got what they had come for. Those who acquired a profession, wealth, status or a past from the cemeteries were included in this group, as were all soothsayers, the insane, thieves...and also Canadian gynaecologists.

He had met the Canadian gynaecologist and his charming wife, who did not seem to have any knowledge whatsoever about either Turkey or the Turks, at one of the Muslim cemeteries while they were searching the grave of the man's Turkish grandmother. The young couple had gone around for hours with a cemetery guard eager to help, and as they were on their way out to try their luck at another graveyard, Sidar had not been able to resist asking why they had undertaken such an endeavour. 'So that I have a family tree to give to my future children,' the young man had said, his eyes shining. Meanwhile his wife, as if holding the thing called the family tree in their hands, had softly crossed her fingers on her breast and smiled as she lifted her hands up like branches.

Sidar had remembered the brass picture frame in the shape of a tree at their house, one of the few pieces they had taken with them when they escaped from Turkey. It could fit a total of ten photographs, in round frames big as plums, hung from five separate branches, two on each one. His mother had somehow decided to hang here the pictures of all the family members, starting with her own mother and father. As filling out all the frames had become a problem, as they were unable to reach ten in this manner, they instead exceeded this number by leaps and bounds upon the inclusion of distant relatives. To solve the issue the photographs of the two cousins they loved the most were included. As the frames were too small, each photograph had to be carefully cropped, leaving only a tiny head behind. The heads of the family members had swung on that brass frame for years like the fruits of the mythical Vakvak tree with fruit shaped like humans that, upon being plucked, rotted away in screams.

I do not share the same blood as you. My birth into your family is just a coincidence. I am one of those children who are given life to rock to sleep the fear of mortality. I am one of those children you abandon to produce yet another one upon realizing you still could not escape death. I scatter my semen to the ground. I do not want to fertilize anyone...and, that being the only way not to end by chance lives started by chance, I bless not you, but suicide...

His interest in death had incited further rebukes from Istanbulites. The people he consulted instead of giving him an answer almost always counselled him to recite the opening chapter of the Qur'an. This he did not do, as he did not know how to recite anyhow and not only did he not know much about Islam, he did not intend to learn anything either. He did not think that any religion had the right to expect obedience from him as long as it continued to ban suicide.

Still he was not as ignorant about Islam as he thought. Every now and then he realized he knew things he didn't even know he had learned. For memory is like a cyclist going downhill fast against the wind: all sorts of knowledge carried by the wind hangs onto you, gets inside your mouth or into your hair and sticks to your skin... Bits and pieces of prayers, the pillars of Islam, sections from the prophet's life; he knew all these, though rather feebly. They say that any language learnt as a child will never be forgotten. Sidar was not so sure about that but he could easily defend the claim that the religion learnt as a child will never be forgotten.

When he walked around the cemeteries, he was forced to leave Gaba at the gates. Upon his return, he found him either snoring away or eating a *simit* off the guard's hand. As he was penniless and also because the bus, minibus or cab drivers were largely unwilling to let Gaba in, they often returned home on foot. Neither did they pay anyone a visit, nor did anyone visit them – with one exception. Only once had they entertained a guest in their house and a female to boot…

Sidar had met her at one of the bars on Istiklal Street. She was the friend of a friend of a friend he had recently met. Other than her coppery hair, the girl had two instantly noticeable characteristics: her eyes and a talent to imbibe beer like a sponge. When the bar had closed down late at night, on her own she had followed Sidar to Bonbon Palace. Once inside, she had scrutinized the flat in a vain attempt to find an item that could be a rapport between the guest and the host. There was no object to talk about. Thank goodness there was Gaba.

Spotting the hazelnut wafer the girl offered him out of her purse, Gaba had sprinted toward her rolling like a ball of fur. Like all burly creatures, he was unaware of more refined techniques of expressing his love. The two of them had tumbled around the floor together in some sort of a game invented there and then. Meanwhile Sidar had watched them from aside, scowling at Gaba's unexpected vigour and ogling at the girl's belly appearing every time her T-shirt slid up a bit. Then suddenly, like the men in the 'Tales of a Thousand and One Nights,' who go mad with anger when the woman they had their eyes on is interested not in them but in an animal, he had interrupted the game, chased Gaba away and drawn the girl to himself. Just like her belly, her breasts too were milky white. They shivered when kissed.

Shut in the bathroom Gaba had stumbled headfirst from the crest of glee he had climbed just a moment ago. After a while, his bewildered barks had turned first into angry growls and finally into an endless howl. As the girl had shared his sorrow, Sidar had the most spoiled sex ever, coming in castrated ecstasy.

When the door opened, Gaba had refused to move an inch, lying there down by the toilet, indifferent and immobile, as if hadn't been him scratching the door and making all that noise all this time. There he stayed that day, the following day and the day after that. Desperate to win his heart Sidar had bought his favourite foods, sacrificing part of the money put aside for the electricity bill. Gaba had reluctantly smelt the meat, cheese and sausages placed in front of him and remained glued to his spot by the toilet, all the while shooting daggers with his eyes. Only three days later, upon sniffing the roasted rabbit that had cost the rest of the money Sidar had put aside for the electricity bill, had Gaba finally returned to his old self. Sidar listened to his dog's slurping and munching with a grin on his face as if listening to enchanting compliments. The fear of losing Gaba had been so unnerving that he had decided never again to bring another guest into this house.

He had remained true to his word. Meddling in love affairs did not match the life he led anyway. One needed a decent life for such things; it required time, money and energy. He had no money. His energy was limited. As for time, it was becoming short. To dodge his fixation with death, the year 2002 seemed an appropriate time, through its completing a circle – by moving from the nothingness of zero to the amplitude of two only to follow the same path back – and the earthquake ridden Istanbul, which smelt as rankly of death as 18th century Lisbon, seemed the most appropriate place. Inside his head, just at the spot where he kept banging on the dirty, dusty pipe crossing the living room, Sidar carried his rage like a malignant tumour fattening day by day, making plans to die soon.

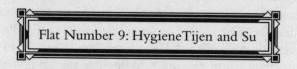
House cleaning sessions fall into two types: those that stem from yesterday and proceed into tomorrow and those that have neither a yesterday nor a tomorrow. So utterly different they are from each other in terms of both causes and consequences that where there is one not even the name of the other comes up. Accordingly, women who do house cleaning also fall into two types: the traditionalists, with a strong awareness of yesterday and tomorrow, and the radicals, with no notion of either.

When the traditionalists clean their houses, they know too well that this will be neither the first time nor the last. The cleaning done at the moment is an important and yet ordinary hoop of an extended chain that advances at regular intervals. The last house-cleaning stint has usually been done only a week (or fifteen days) previously and will be repeated within a week (or fifteen days). Hence every cleaning-day is part of a solid routine and more or less the same as the one before. It always commences and ends in the same way: first the windows are cleaned and the rugs shaken out, then the floors are swept, starting always with the same room and proceeding in order. The furnishings are dusted without altering priorities, the kitchen always receives great attention, tea and meal breaks are taken at approximately the same hours and finally, in the last phase, the cleaning is completed when the bathroom is given a once over. Since the traditionalists have such firm ties with the past and their confidence in the future is just as strong, there is no harm in leaving the unfinished parts until the next cleaning episode.

The cleaning of traditionalists is not a bustle performed in the name of keeping the house in order, but the very mark of order itself.

As for the radicals, in the eyes of these who are less in number and more scatterbrained, every cleaning operation is unique and absolute. It does not matter one single bit if they have done cleaning fifteen days, a week or even a day ago. Since there is not, in the map of their lives, even a single suspension bridge connecting the two separate cleaning days, the cleaning of the past remains there. Thus they always go through their houses as if they had never gone through it before. They set on the task as if held responsible for cleaning it for the first and the last time, as if making a damp den, long uninhabited by anyone except the genies, liveable. It is hard to predict when and where they are going to commence cleaning since any impetus at any moment can incite them into action: be it a melon seed stuck on the switch, soot on the curtains, lime traces in the sink, oil drops on the table cloth, forgotten liquid at the bottom of a glass that has turned mouldy, a bit of mud on the floor…the tiniest detail can suddenly provoke the radicals to launch an all-out cleaning stint. As such, all cleaning activities are different from one another as no one, including themselves, knows where to start and how to proceed. Actually at the outset they might not even be conscious of embarking on yet another cleaning mission. They could find themselves cleaning the whole kitchen when they are supposed to be simply washing a glass, the whole bathroom when scrubbing the sink or the whole house when wiping the switch. Their cleaning has neither a 'before' nor an 'after'. For the traditionalists housecleaning is one of many such bouts of activity, for the radicals it is the one and only.

Rather than bringing order, the cleaning done by radicals is the very reason behind the chaos in the house.

Hygiene Tijen was one of the radicals. Perhaps she had always been so, but her radicalism had reached in the last three years a level that was worrisome to those around her. Not only was she capable either by herself or with the help of a cleaning woman of turning the house upside down at any time, she could also devote her entire day at other times to scraping off the burnt oil deposits wedged in the handle of a single pan. Stain or rust, dust or soot, crumb or residue, mildew or dirt; she couldn't stand to see any of these. When she deemed an object could not be cleaned enough, she had lately acquired the habit of opening the window and throwing it out. Staunchly believing that filthiness was an invasion by microbes, what she really wanted to get rid of at such impulsive moments was not the objects she threw down, but the microbes emanating from them. The tiniest amount of dirt would never stay still but would generate microbes that every minute increased three, even five fold. So she immediately threw this hive of microbes out of the house. Not only the residents of Bonbon Palace but also quite a number of pedestrians happening to plough the street at the wrong time had been witness to Hygiene Tijen's catapulting of items. First she had thrown a burnt-out pot out of the window, upon failing to cope with the feeling that she would never ever be able to remove the tarry marks that betrayed the snow white rice. Then, she had hurled out an old rug after whisking it for hours upon becoming anxious that she could not at all get rid of the dust in the tassels. Yet just like her cleaning, her way of throwing out items also lacked consistency. When she hurled an object, sometimes she would utterly forget about it, abandoning it in the garden to its fate, whereas some other times she would instantly regret her actions and ask for it to be returned. Then, it fell either upon her daughter, husband or the cleaning lady on duty to go down to pick the item, since she hadn't stepped out of Flat Number 9 for about four months.

There was only one person who could keep up with her pace: Meryem. Their relationship was a perpetual ebb-and-flow. With her constant bagging and caprices Hygiene Tijen too often offended Meryem who, though not at all irked by the amount of work piled in front of her, was extremely sensitive about how she was treated. When Meryem quit, Tijen would hire other daily cleaning women in rapid succession, ending up woefully yearning to get Meryem back and eventually managing to do so with pleas and a wage increase. These days Meryem had again signed an armistice. Though they were at peace now, Hygiene Tijen was worried about the advancing pregnancy of her most trustworthy sanitary soldier. She would evidently have to stop working before long, at most in a couple of weeks.

However, the sour smell of garbage engulfing Bonbon Palace worried Hygiene Tijen even more than the thought of being left without Meryem. She could not stand this smell. Like never before, nowadays she regretted marrying her husband heedless of her parents' advice and thus having to forego a considerable inheritance, as well as the prosperity she once used to live in. Along with the garbage smell, her misery also escalated day by day. Every morning as she opened her eyes into this smell, she felt like throwing up and slammed open all the windows, without realizing that in so doing she scared everyone below into thinking that a new set of items would start to rain down. Before long, unable to judge if the open windows decreased the smell inside or not, she would close them all again and repeat this pattern at least ten times a day.

Hygiene Tijen's nerves, which were already strained to their limits by the garbage smell, had entirely snapped the moment she read the letter sent by the school administration. The teacher writing the letter requested that as a favour to the other children Su should not be sent to school until it was ascertained that she was rid of her lice. Since that day, the washing machine worked non-stop. Su's clothes were all kept in bleach and a feverish cleaning routine reigned in the house. Hygiene's soldiers were fighting a war at dozens of fronts against an enemy immensely fecund and invisible to the naked eye. Yet the cleaning militia, too, were everywhere. Each had taken up a position at a separate location. There were cleaning fluids, some in spray form, some liquid and still others you left to dry (with separate ones for the windows, metals, wood, marble and tiles); brushes, a different one for the sink, toilet and the tub; lime removers, rust removers, stain removers; floor wax, silver polish, sink drainer, toilet pump; a vacuum cleaner (with different hose accessories for liquids, dust, curtains, armchairs, rugs, corners, air filters), carpet-sweeper, mop, duster, pail, brush, sponges and coated sponges (separate for smooth or rough surfaces); detergents with cider, lemon, lilac and pacific islands smells; throat searing disinfectants; cloths for the floors, walls and dusting; moth balls, lavender pouches, garment bags, soap pieces…all had been mobilized and, along with special shampoos from the pharmacy, were defending Flat Number 9 of Bonbon Palace against lice shoulder to shoulder at every possible corner.

'Please grandpa, pleease...' repeated the seven and a half year old while looking sideways at his siblings.

The other two children were glued to the TV. Though the programme they watched had ended about ten minutes ago, they had not yet been able to detach themselves from the vacuum left by the coquettish announcer with the rose bud tattoo. Still, Hadji Hadji considered the demand of her older grandson the joint wish of all children. 'Well, okay, let me tell you the tale of the fisherman Suleyman then,' he said, as he put aside his four books – the number of which had not changed in years – the second one entitled, 'Interpretations of Dreams with Explanations.'

'During the old days in the Ottoman Empire, there lived in a cottage a fisherman named Suleyman. He was so poor his hands had not touched money even in his dreams, but he had a golden heart. He lived alone without getting mixed up in anything, not hurting even an ant. Those were the most wretched days for the Ottomans. It was the period of 'The Rule of Women', a time when the country had hit the bottom. The concubines in the palace pulled a thousand tricks every day. So many innocent souls were strangled because of them. The bodies of the victims were thrown into the sea from the palace windows. The corpses would bloat in the water for days, sometimes getting caught in fishermen's nets.'

The six and a half year old, unable to adjust to the spirit of his grandfather's tale after the vivacious morning programme he had just watched on TV, swallowed hard as if to get rid of a bad taste. The little girl right next to him had bent her head down, thrust out her lower lip and sat still, almost petrified.

'One night, Suleyman went out fishing. Luckily, oodles of fish were caught in his net, but he was such a soft-hearted fellow that he was unable to kill any and instead returned them one by one to the water.'

'What kind of a fisherman is that?' croaked the seven and a half year old.

'So Suleyman was going back to his cottage empty handed,' continued Hadji Hadji, having no intention to quarrel with him this morning. 'But all of a sudden he noticed a white protrusion on the water. Though it was dark, there was a shadowy moonlight. He paddled in the direction of this shape and when he was close enough, saw a corpse floating on the water. Had he been some other fisherman he would have just let it float there, feedng the fish, but being the good man that he was Suleyman could not do so. After some struggle, he pulled the corpse into the boat with the help of his oar and uncovered it. What did he see but a young and very beautiful woman! There was a dagger thrust right between her two breasts, and yet, if you looked at her face, you would think she was alive! She smiled sweetly, as if not at all angry at her murderers. Her lips were like cherries, her eyelashes arrows, her nose an inkstand; as for her hair, it curled all the way down to her heels. Our fisherman Suleyman could not take his eyes off this beauty.'

The ringing of the phone ripped the story apart. The seven and a half year old grabbed the receiver with hands that were becoming more contorted and inward curling by the day. *Yes, they had finished their breakfast. No, they were not being naughty. Yes, they watched television. No, grandpa was not telling them one of his tales. No, they had not turned on the gas. No, they did not mess up the house. No, they did not swing from the balcony. No, they did not play with fire. No, they did not go into the bedroom. He swore it was true that grandpa was not telling a tale.* His mother must have had a gnawing suspicion that day since she insisted: 'If your grandpa is telling you kids a tale, just say: "It is warm today." I'll understand.'

The seven and a half year old turned and intently looked at the old man who was looking intently at him. Without taking his eyes off the old man, the child murmured distinctly: 'No, mom, it isn't warm today.'

He placed the receiver back. Waiting for a couple of seconds to pass so that he could enjoy this game he played every day, he tilted back his large head the growth of which could not be stopped and urged with an indistinct smile, 'Come on grandpa, continue!' Only this time, his voice sounded not as if he were making a request but rather as if he were giving his approval.

'Fisherman Suleyman could not possibly leave the corpse of this mysterious beauty back in the water,' continued Hadji Hadji, trying hard to beat the distress of taking refuge in his grandson's compassion. 'He took her to his cottage and watched her all night long, heartsick with sorrow. At dawn, he dug up a deep grave in his garden. He did not at all want to part with her, but nothing could be done about it. The dead are under the earth and those alive over it. This is how it will be until the Day of Judgment when we will all gather together.'

'Couldn't he just not bury her?' blubbered the five and a half year old.

'No!' jumped in the seven and a half year old. 'If you don't bury a corpse, it'll stink. It'll smell so awful you can't stand it.'

'But it smells awful here too,' whined the other one, thrusting her lower lip out even further.

'Maybe there's a corpse in here too. Did you ever open the closet and look inside?'

'There's no corpse here,' roared Hadji Hadji seeing daggers in front of his older grandson. 'It just smells of garbage. No wonder it stinks when the entire neighbourhood dumps its garbage in our garden! Yet, as the building administrator, I'll certainly find a solution to this problem. Don't worry.' He sat the little girl on his lap. 'And listen, the beautiful woman in the tale had not died anyhow. Before burying her in the soil, fisherman Suleyman said, "Let me remove the dagger on her breast" The moment he took out the dagger, the woman moaned. She had not died after all. The dagger had reached the bone but not the heart.'

Trying to find solace in this unexpected explanation the five and a half year old gave a crooked smile. She cowered on her grandpa's lap, and certainly would have felt a lot more comfortable had she not felt her older brother's gaze upon her.

'Our death is written on our foreheads. Even if they thrust a dagger to your heart, you won't die if it is not so written on your forehead. When the poor woman came back to life, she asked fisherman Suleyman for a cup of water. Then she started to talk. Apparently she was a concubine at the palace. The sultan liked her the most. The other concubines were so green with envy and their hearts were so tainted with evil, they had decided to kill this innocuous soul. Buying off the harem eunuchs, they had made them stab the beautiful concubine's white chest. She told this story in tears and then said: "If you take me back to the palace, our master the sultan will surely reward you with heaps of gold." Upon hearing all this, our fisherman Suleyman became lost in thought. He didn't want gold or anything. He had fallen in love. That night this beautiful concubine slept in his bed in the cottage but fisherman Suleyman slept outside in his boat. Some time in the middle of the night the devil approached him. "Don't take the woman back," he hissed, "How could one take such an attractive woman back? Let her be yours. She could stay here, wash your clothes, cook for you and be your wife." That's exactly what the devil whispered.'

Hadji Hadji silently studied his grandchildren as if expecting them to put themselves in the hero's shoes. Yet, that pertinacious smile on the face of the six and a half year old hinted his mind was not on the moral dilemma of the tale but on the parts that promised sexuality. As for the five and a half year old, she was busy adding another word, 'concubine', into her wallet of words newly learned. Once again, the seven and a half year old was the only one left. When his grandfather's eyes turned to him, he slurred sarcastically, 'Of course he didn't take her back.'

'Of course he took her back!' thundered Hadji Hadji. 'He personally delivered her to the palace. The sultan was delighted. 'You can ask for anything from me,' he declared, but fisherman Suleyman asked for nothing. He left the palace gates as poor as he had entered them.'

There ensued a prickly silence. Finally convinced that the tale was over, the six and a half year old hollered: 'I'm so hungry!' The five and a half year old, closing the wallet in her mind, jumped off her grandfather's lap: 'Osman first, Osman first!' While the pot warmed up on the stove, they set upon building their tent, piling sheets, pillows and bedspreads in the middle of the living room. Only the seven and a half year old, he alone kept sitting where he was, maintaining his composure. He had picked up an illustrated novel and pretended to be reading it with interest, but his moss green eyes, that looked contracted as they failed to keep up with the growth in his head, were fixated on his grandfather and siblings. Every passing day, he detested them more.

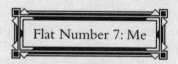

Flat Number 7: Me

Ants raided my balcony today — or perhaps it was just today that I *noticed* ants had raided my balcony. They never remain still. In step with commands that only they can hear, in orderly russet strips they now march back and forth between the dark fissure at the wall and the hot dog I had forgotten on the coffee table. I cannot figure out where they came from and how on earth they made it to the third floor. This apartment building is teeming with all types of bugs. At nights they keep me company whilst I down a few drinks.

My father's curse, I guess. Either his curse or his genes. Back in those days when I assumed my drinking had nothing to do with his, I thought my father's greatest problem in life was not to know how to drink. Ever since I realized how badly my drinking habits resembled his, I started believing instead the problem was not his drinking but his not knowing when to stop. He couldn't break it off, it was that simple. At the outset, he couldn't possibly foresee where to stop and once he arrived at that point, he would have gone too astray to care about stopping. After he had polished off a few, it didn't take him long to pick up the pace. Before long his bloodshot eyes searched for a road sign. A clear sign, a concrete warning: 'Slow down, fine gravel at ten metres!' or 'Slippery surface! Sharp turn! Graded road!' It was at those times that he needed most someone to come forth and tell him how he looked from the outside. Only we could do that, being closest to him, but we never really tried. Both my mother and I would take our place at the table with him, fill our plates with appetizers, peel apples, dice oranges, make lanterns out of orange peels and simply wait for what was going to happen to happen. My mother had convinced first herself, then me, that my father should not be disturbed while drinking. She was so diffident when she was around him, and perhaps rightly so, but even at that age I knew this was not the only reason for her behaviour. Though it certainly pained her to witness my father's collapse, I couldn't help but think that she also secretly, unknowingly enjoyed it. Observing him squander every night the grandeur he would not even momentarily be bereaved of during the day gave her pleasure. That is why she set those *rakı* tables lavishly garnished with appetizers and *mezes* each more delicious than the other every night... Every night for twelve years...

After all, my father was too much of everything. He was too handsome, too dexterous, too pedantic, too intricate, too egotistical, too unflappable, too frivolous...too much for me and my mother; too much for the housing complex we lived in, the army he served at, the towns he was appointed to, the animals he failed to heal...too much for the life he led...I cannot tell for sure if there ever was a time when I loved him, but I do remember being proud of him once. As a kid I was proud of him because he was tall and handsome, far too much. Back in those days, oodles of stories circulated about children being kidnapped and raised by the gypsies and I remember thinking of my father being one of the kidnapped kids thereafter accidentally mixed in with us. He was so unlike everyone else. We all had similar features, brownish hair, average height and the same laughter. When annoyed we averted any eye-contact, even our stormiest moments looked composed, so patient, ordinary and meek we were, men and women all the same. However, amidst us there he was, with a height that did not fit through doors, a head of hair that turned burning blonde under the rays of the sun, piercing hazel eyes that darkened when sad and always looked you directly in the eye as if to get you to account for your actions, a temperament that swayed between opposite poles and a checkered record of outbursts, flaws and failures piling up day by day along with his sins.

If my father had not been so handsome, robust and self-assured, my mother would have probably been more at ease. That malicious angst furtively gnawed at her bliss and cast shadows in her eyes – shadows that could be deciphered even in her engagement photos where she stood fretfully smiling on his arm, wearing an aquamarine engagement dress with a huge synthetic magnolia attached to her collar. She must have abhorred the hypocrisy of time. First having me, next my brother, then two miscarriages one after another, and finally the daughter she so much wanted, raised spoilt and turned in the end into a replica of herself… I have always found pitiable the way in which middle-aged women who were once beautiful vent half-coyly, half-superciliously, how beautiful they were in their youth, showing every one, each and every time the same old photographs to make their claim credible. Even more pitiable than that is when their children, especially their sons, show the same photographs of 'my-ma-was-so-beautiful-when-young' in a rather coy, but mostly supercilious manner to their own acquaintances, especially to the women they fall in love with. As for us, because of my father, or maybe I should say thanks to him, neither my mother could play this game, nor my brother and myself.

If my father were, could ever have been, any different, my mother would have probably found it easier to come to terms with the evanescence of youth – just like all those housewives around her with their two or three children, middle income, middling life and the poison of their many compunctions seeping out from either their tongue or their gaze. Those women and their husbands were normal. What was far from being normal was my father's condition. They were married; their lives, children, money, home, frustrations and past were all identical, but the passing years had treated my mother and my father very differently. While my mother had soon become worn-out, my father would even decades later still look as young and robust as he had been in their engagement photos. I can't blame ma for failing to bow to the ephemerality of her youth when next to her was a youth that never faded. There was nothing she could do, and in the fullness of time the lenses through which she viewed herself became more and more hazy. Since the photographs she could have otherwise exhibited to prove how beautiful she had once been were bound to disclose not only the drastic change in her but also the complete lack of change in my father, unlike the other housewives with two or three children, middle income, middling life and the poison of their many compunctions seeping out either from their tongue or their gaze, my mother kept no photo albums in our guest room.

Being too busy priding in and imitating my father, for a long time I must have failed to notice my mother's fretful nature. From every new branch of age I perched on over the years, I watched my father with admiration. When he put on his uniform, his face acquired a deliberate toughness, just like those of all the other soldiers. Yet, unlike them, his was a deliberation that could dissipate and a toughness that could thaw at any moment. The clues of this transformation were already there during the day. That stern stare of his – which glazed over as if he needed to prove that he took care of animals not because he was fond of them but simply because it was his job to do so – would soften, if even for a moment, when he healed a colt, relieved the pain of a cat whose jaw had melted in the acid-filled hole it had tumbled into or gave a weasel attacked by dogs the final peace it yearned for. At any one of those moments, I could perceive how bored he was from incessantly taking off and putting on two contradictory faces. A contradiction reflected in the two professions he carried out simultaneously: veterinarian and soldier.

As he ran around all day long hurling orders left and right with that impressive air of his, he awakened among women an admiration tainted with envy and among men envy tainted with admiration. Yet inside the uniform he wore he kept another personality, as if carrying around a baby porcupine he could not heal: someone who purported to live beyond sorrow and pleasure, was scared silly of death, could not bear to afflict or be afflicted by pain, could not easily recuperate when confronted with injustice, someone who knew, not rationally but intuitively, that he was doomed to screw up sometime somewhere; someone unsteady and tender, troubled and untrustworthy, pessimistic and enraged, aggressive and alcoholic… As long as the sun was up in the sky and he was doing his job, he could indeed hide the baby porcupine. He was so captivating and striking at such times that even my mother liked to grab one of us three to stop by his workplace with any old excuse. Both my siblings and I were thrilled to be next to him during the day. Alas, these were the times when we saw him the least. Then night would come along and, as his aura would lose its sparkle and his face its appeal, my father would metamorphose.

My mother had made a division of labour the rationale of which I could never grasp. According to her scheme, while my father drank each one of us had certain tasks to perform and roles to play. My brother and sister were to quietly watch television and go to bed early, whereas my mother and I were to stay at the table and act as witnesses. Since my father hated to be alone at the *rakı* table, we watched him in shifts. First it was my turn. As soon as he sat down at the table, I took my place across from him. My mother would then be busy deep-frying the pastry, mixing the sauce of the meatballs or carrying out to the table the appetizers each prepared in a more burdensome fashion than the other. Meanwhile, I would remain at the table and answer my father's questions. He always asked the same questions, which were all about school, and always cut short my answers to tell his, which were all about life. That wouldn't offend me at all. As a matter of fact, this first phase of the evening was the most enjoyable time of my father's soliloquy. When halfway through the first glass, he would be so cheery and chatty that, even though I knew to the letter what was going to happen soon, I couldn't help but feel blessed to be there with him. Then my mother would come and sit next to my father with an expression that barely revealed her thoughts, and as they started chatting about the events of the day in a muttering, monotonous voice, I would go to my room to do my homework. Two or three hours later when I returned to the table, time would have elapsed, my mother's eyes would have drooped with sleep and the chat would have long come to an end. Thus begun the third and final phase of the evening – the phase when everything gorgeous rapidly rotted…the phase wherein the baby porcupine scuttled over the table and I, upon touching its quills, got offended…

Depending on the day, my mother would either walk around the house grumbling, curl-up crying next to my sister and sleep there that night or, if all was fine and dandy, wash the dishes in the kitchen humming a cheery song. However, whatever she chose to do, she'd never return to the table, delegating to me the task of keeping my father company until the very end of the third phase. Yet this was the longest part, the longest and indisputably the most gruelling. The ice in the bucket would have now turned into a lukewarm, cloudy water afloat with cigarette ash and breadcrumbs, the meatballs at the plate would be cold and congealed, the fine-chopped onions in the salad a smelly squander, the ashtray filled to the brim; the leftover appetizers would have lost their delicacy, the sliced melons their freshness and my father his grandeur.

When I think about it after all these years, it seems bizarre that even though I was the only one among the three siblings who witnessed our father's most disgraceful moments, it was again I who took over his bad habits. My younger brother drinks and smokes once in a while, only when he has to mingle with drinkers. As for my younger sister, she ended up becoming one of those women who never frequent smoke-filled locales, who sulk when someone smokes around them, regard a drunk with dismay, an alcoholic with disgust, and a hobo by changing their route; deeming in the final analysis every drunk an alcoholic and every alcoholic a vagabond. To top it all she transferred these festering habits to her little daughter in their entirety. Whenever I attempt to light a cigarette in their house, my little niece reacts like a tiny robot whose buttons are being pushed, and, wrinkling her nose in visible repulsion as if she had just seen a dead rat, starts to deliver a memorized speech about the dangers of smoking. It boils my blood to see people, especially kids, embrace with such rehearsed passion a statement that is not even their own. At their house there isn't a single ashtray I could use. Inside the ostentatious walnut cupboard in their living room, in addition to all sorts of hefty drinks with different glasses for each type of drink, there are dozens of porcelain, marble, crystal, silver, gold-coated, steel, bronze, wood, beaded, miniature painted, marbled, statue-like, toy-like, kitschy or far too classy ashtrays bearing the emblems of the resorts and foreign cities they have visited as a family; but when it comes to flicking the ash of my cigarette, there is not a single ashtray in use. I wonder, from among her three children, did my mother keep me away from my siblings and close to my father at nights because among her children it was only I who resembled him? Or, on the contrary, did I, among the three children end up resembling our father because she kept me away from my siblings and close to him at nights? Put differently, is this my father's curse for the day I left him prone and alone at the table during yet another 'third phase' wherein I could no longer stand his offhanded and uncouth words? Or is it because ultimately he and I are simply the hoops of the same genetic chain where numerous, industrious genes in tidy strips march on ad infinitum in accordance with pre-determined codes?

I must have been twelve or thirteen. When my brother had the mumps, we shut ourselves in the house for days, forever stuffing ourselves with *oleaster*, watching TV glued to our seats and only ever getting up to go to the bathroom. In one of the old Turkish movies we watched back then, the leading actress, who was secretly in love with the man her sister was about to marry, vomited blood onto snow-white needlepoint bordered handkerchiefs and was diagnosed with tuberculosis. During the scene where the physician told her she would die soon, my brother and I had burst into laughter spewing out *oleaster* dust. The film was outrageously ridiculous and just as surreal; it belonged to a stale age and was miles away from credibility. It was no more possible to believe in the death from tuberculosis of the actress on the screen with a face paled with make-up, hair whitened with flour and eyes sloppily empurpled, than it was to believe in the death from cirrhosis six months previous of our father

Toward the end of the film, my mother came back from the market with my sister. Since neither had had mumps, they were supposed to stay away from my brother. Still, my mother sat right in between us with a doting smile. Holding our hands in between her palms, she muttered in a hesitant yet composed voice that she was about to remarry. On screen the actress with the tuberculosis stumbled down as she tried to descend the stairs to join the crowd celebrating the marriage of the man she loved and her sister. She collapsed coughing. My brother and I bent double in laughter, my mother laughed too. Still standing by the door my sister stared at my mother with astonishment soon replaced by tears. We chuckled again, but this time my mother did not join in. Tilting her crumpled face, she blew her nose into her needlepoint bordered snow-white handkerchief. Perhaps there was no handkerchief after all but it has been seared as such in my memory because that was the way I wanted to remember it. All the *oleaster* dust we had been spewing out lifted off with a sudden gale and swirled and swirled in the middle of the room like a gauzy snowstorm escalating in anger until no one could see one another anymore; it then drizzled down, forming a canopy over us all, delicate and yellow. Like everything, everything was surreal.

When someone in the family dies unexpectedly, his belongings render surreal not only death or the God who deems that death befitting but also the lives of the ones left behind. Since my siblings had spent less time with my father and had not seen him surrounded by his belongings in his nest as much as I had, they probably did not experience this alteration as much as my mother and I. When night fell and the table was set, my mother would involuntarily start cooking her usual appetizers and I would take the same place always at the same hour, with a stale sense of duty. It was then that my father's belongings prevented us from acknowledging that the emptiness which sat on the chair across from us was death, and death was real. It was not only his emerald-green spiral striped *rakı* pitcher, his leather wallet embroidered with a horse's head or his chiselled lighter, that always flickered unevenly even when its gas had been refilled and its flint changed, that prevented this. Nor was it his snuffbox embossed on the lid with a purple-bodied and russet-winged owl, whose mistakenly connected eyes made it appear neither ill-omened nor wise but bewildered at most. As long as the living room and the house stayed put and we were unable to leave, there always would be a surreal side to my father's death. Eventually, when it became only too apparent that just as we couldn't move into another house, neither could we fend off this confusion, my mother and I ended up in a tacit partnership that involved our dressing up the ghost of my father and making it sit down at the table with us at night. Yet this secret collaboration which could have brought us closer, in the end, irretrievably separated our paths.

For what she did next was nothing other than being a complete spoilsport. As she served my father's ghost at the table, she increasingly depicted him not as he had been but as she had always wanted him to be. Being the good housewife that she was, she aspired to sweep away from our collective memory all the traits of her dead husband she had never liked in the first place. When she had finished with her sweeping, sitting at the table with us was this facsimile of a man as colourless and lustreless as a droning elegy – a man who had always worked for the good of his family, had no other luxury than sitting down with his wife at night to down a glass or two, kept whatever venom he might have to himself, never faltered, never complained; it was if he hadn't been made of flesh and nerves. My mother so loved this bogus apparition, and so wholeheartedly believed in it that when she decided to remarry six months later, the man she chose as husband for herself was exactly the same as the ghost at the table.

All through this period, every crumb of information she swept outside her memory I collected one by one, less because of my devotion to my father than because of my fury towards my mother. In the end, however, the alternative ghost I had tailored did not turn out to be any closer to truth than the one she had created. All in all, my father was neither as distinguished as my mother later convinced herself, nor as ignominious as I claimed in contrast. Still, both of us tenaciously embraced our respective delusion. In point of fact, it cannot be considered total deception since we were merely covering up each other's partial unfairness with our own partial righteousness. It was as if the same cadaver lay in two different graves: buried in one grave were my father's mornings, and in the other, his nights. Whenever we wanted to recall his memory, my mother visited one grave and I the other.

Years later, when Ayshin had conducted with a British colleague a survey in three Istanbul neighbourhoods on how popular Islam shaped everyday life, she had mentioned in surprise seeing two graves for the same saint, a fact that none amongst her sample groups found odd. I did not either.

It was at around this time that I finally surrendered to the unremitting requests of both Ayshin and my mother to meet one another. On our way back from a visit to my mother, Ayshin – apparently unable to identify the 'father' she had heard about from me with the 'first husband' she had heard about all day long from my mother – had already reached the conclusion (as always happens in such situations) that one of us was lying and that this lie was addressed especially to her. After a brief hesitation wherein she tried to track down the *real* personality of the deceased, she drew the conclusion that I was the one who lied and did so solely to justify 'my condition.'

What was meant by my 'condition' was my escalating alcohol consumption. What Ayshin did not know then was that I did not have such a problem until we got married. Not that I blamed her or our marriage. I cannot determine a starting point anyhow. The only thing I do know is that after a while, my life drew a circle of allusion returning to the beginning and I found myself on the chair my father once sat on. However, there were significant differences. Ayshin was not like my mother. She did not set lavish tables for me and neither did she remain passive. She pretended to take 'my condition' lightly and then was offended; she approached me compassionately and then was offended; she got upset and then was offended; she threatened me and then was offended; she belittled me and then was offended; she supported me and then was offended; she abandoned me and then was offended; she returned to me and then was offended... She tried hard in every way she could think of to fight my drinking, with frequent intervals of being offended. I too tried hard to please her. I guess I felt grateful to her, especially at the beginning. Her interventions verified the fact that unlike my mother, she didn't enjoy seeing her husband stumble and nor was our marriage like that of my parents. With genuine gratitude I struggled and everything went well for about five months. I managed to cut down the drinking. Yet before long, this most praiseworthy progress turned me into my own rival. At first when I overdid it, then when I drank a bit too much, and finally whenever I drank, she rebuked and sarcastically scolded me for my inability to repeat my earlier success. 'We know you can do better than this,' said Ayshin, 'We know it, don't we?'

There is something in this 'we' that is like the sour core of a sweetly sucked candy...a dulcet magma...a scorching, burning, conquest-obsessed lava sprouting from a single source to spread to every corner, taking everything in its way under its coattails until there is no being left outside itself... God talks like this in the holy books; addresses as 'we' when narrating all the acts of creation, destruction, punishment and reward. Mothers too talk in the same format with their children. 'Are we hungry?' they ask, or conclude, 'Though we have been naughty today, actually we are well-behaved.' Despite the fact that the decision reached and the choice made belongs solely and entirely to them, they annex into the borders of their own existence that of the other as if there were not two separate personalities out there. The 'we' formula employed by God in the Qur'an, by mothers when addressing their children, and by Ayshin when referring to my drinking problem is not '(We = I + You)', but '(We = I + I)'. To remain outside of such a sweeping 'we' is simply impossible.

I could not remain outside either. Consecutively, repeatedly I stopped drinking numerous times in rapid succession, first with enthusiasm and perhaps a bit of success, subsequently with a somewhat slackened interest, then with weakened effort, and towards the end, with no hope. Each time we prepared new calendars together: calendars where days, rather than years constituted the turning points, where time was measured by promises that could not be kept. In neat squares we would draw monthly calendars box by box. Whenever I deviated from the plan, I would convince Ayshin with great difficulty not to indicate it on paper like a stain but rather prepare a new one from scratch. To my calendars, each trivial event presented an appropriate opportunity, every special day a genesis. Thus when I received my doctorate, on New Years' Eve, on my thirty-third birthday, on the first snow of the year, when we survived in one piece the traffic accident that totalled the front of our car, on our wedding anniversary, on Ayshin's thirty-first birthday, when I learned my thesis director had lung cancer, on the night when my sister and I brawled raucously at long last spilling our guts out, on the day when I received the news about my stepfather's death, on all sorts of gatherings acknowledging the value of life, on the pretext of Ayshin and I going out of Istanbul for the weekend, on roads, parties, hotels, shores… I ga-ve up, ga-ve up, ga-ve up drinking, each time zealously supported by my wife….

I achieved success but not enough. Since I had once managed not to put a drop in my mouth for weeks, every glass I had thereafter inevitably meant a move backward. I myself was the role model I craved to be; the ideal which slid out of my palms like a slippery soap, whom I kept chasing after but could not seize even when I caught it by the trouser leg was me. After a while, Ayshin too started to confuse what was 'insufficient' with what was a 'fiasco'. From that point on, the reason for her interventions tended to be blurry. Her worrying about my health was no longer the reason for her to force me to compete against myself. Words and actions lost their primary meanings; through convoluted ways, everything became the indication of something else. My calendars were each a barometer now. Ayshin measured how much I loved her by the number of days I spent without imbibing. Yet when love is the issue, numbers and proportions only cause trouble. 'Very' became such a feeble adjective whenever 'more' was do-able. I loved Ayshin very much but *we both* knew I could do better than that. Somewhere along the way there had been a misunderstanding, leading Ayshin to believe that it was necessary for me not to reduce drinking but to stop cold, and that I could only reach this goal with the help of love, *her* love. If I could ever accomplish this it would be 'for her sake.' I was trapped. She had initially wanted me to reduce drinking for the sake of my health, then for the sake of our relationship and next, before I knew it my drinking had become not my problem but hers.

On one of those days, I drew a huge crimson 'X' on my calendar. This latest re-birth which had by chance fallen on the 22nd of the second month was in two ways different from the previous ones. First, while hitherto I had honestly stopped drinking, now I was stopping drinking honestly. Second, unlike my previous oaths, I remained true to this one till the end. From 22/2/2001 to 22/2/2002 when the court divorced us in one hearing, I did not put a drop of alcohol into my mouth in Ayshin's presence.

She watched for a while this brisk, definite development with a contentment marred by incredulity. Still she did not go any further, playing the detective to uncover the truth. Even though she constantly kept me under surveillance while I was with her, she did not once pry into what I was getting up to in the shady zone outside her field of vision. I wonder if the saint with two graves had ever crossed Ayshin's mind during those days, for at this juncture my circle had rotated once again and, just like my father, I had assumed two separate personalities in two separate parts of the day. There was a clear difference between the two of us however. My father was teetotal during the days and drunk at nights. With me, it was the opposite, as necessitated by my circumstances: I was sober during the nights and drunk during the days.

The human body shelters within it a clock that works not only from right to left, but also the other way round. It all depends on how you set it up. I had become fully adapted to the new system within at most two weeks. Not having regular work hours at the university was a blessing. During daytime I did not miss any opportunity that came my way and went around constantly drunk, but at night as soon as I went home I sobered up as if hit on the face with a pail full of ice water. I stayed sober during the nights and right after Ayshin left for work in the morning, started drinking at breakfast. In the last analysis, day or night did not make much of a difference: to properly manage one, I needed to mess the other one up. Contrary to what I had feared, this particular arrangement did not weigh heavily either on my stomach or my conscience. Perhaps one gets used to anything as long as he knows there is no alternative on the horizon.

When making this arrangement, however, I had simply

overlooked the fact that everything has a life cycle of its own – a hint my father knew all those years. The morning hours were not apt to hide secrets away. Not only because we mingle with others all day long or have duties to perform in full view of everyone, there is something else in daytime, intrusive and insidious, transforming the city into an open forest of unseen creatures. The moment I placed a few crumbs of secrets into a tree hollow, somebody would snatch it away. Wherever I turned my head, I saw among the branches, twigs and leaves that surrounded me hundreds of eyes dazzled by the sun; a harsh beam of light which made it impossible to comprehend who was looking from where and with what intent. In that suffocating brightness of daytime, I wobbled amidst whispers, unable to distinguish the faces behind the voices. I could sense that others caught the smell of liquor on me, and every so often my tongue stumbled at words or my mind was distracted. I could sense it all but never could I discern who around me knew of my secret and to what extent.

It was precisely at this juncture that Ethel came and perched amidst my life with all her weight. We had not been seeing each other for two years. After losing the Mevlevi *ney* player and hurling enough poison to last me forever over my decision to get married to Ayshin, she had gone to the United States to settle down there with a bright, versatile Pakistani brain surgeon. Then she returned, just as suddenly and impetuously as she had departed, barging into my life fortuitously at a moment when I needed her or someone like her the most. I had forgotten that Ethel's greatest pleasure in this life was walking with her muddy feet on the priceless carpets in the spotless living rooms of women like Ayshin. She was quick to make me remember that. It didn't take her long to discover my addiction and when she did, she neither disparaged me, nor put me on trial, nor suffocated me with questions that already had the answers within.

Instead she handed me an expertly drawn map – created in how many years on what kind of a life experience I still cannot fathom – so that I could wander around in the forest of bodiless eyes and faceless sounds with minimum damage. This chart of hers was so technical. It included short liquor breaks adjusted to my work hours, one shot of hard liquor hidden in fancy thermoses, tiny clues about what would suppress the smell of the particular drinks, reinforcing drugs that would help me collect my thoughts, antioxidants, vitamins, minerals, artichoke tablets to appease my liver… With the seriousness and perseverance of a seasoned trainer coaching for the international games a young athlete with measly means but boundless dreams, she prepared the best possible program available under the circumstances. In fact, she did much more than that. All during those years, at every single opportunity she kept me company and drank with me.

One of the gravest strokes of misfortune a married woman could face at a time when her husband is searching for ways to trample on the rules and prohibitions set by her is for life to present him with an accomplice in the guise of another woman. Once such a chance event occurred, I instantaneously found myself in a room filled with contorted mirrors that made Ayshin appear far more distant and Ethel much closer than they actually were. Perhaps, however, the outcome was not as clear-cut as I believed it to be. After all, when Ayshin initiated divorce months later, the reason behind this decision was neither Ethel nor my infamous addiction.

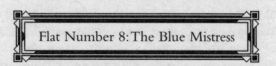

Flat Number 8: The Blue Mistress

The Blue Mistress had been sitting without taking her eyes off the thin, crimson stripes of peppered oil oozing from the half-eaten, half-messed-up chicken with ground walnut. There was nothing she could do. She did not even want to talk, let alone raise objections. There wasn't much to say anyhow. She had been caught in the ultimate trap of mistresshood: children!

Being the mistress of a married man is to know too much about what should remain unknown but not know what to do with this surplus knowledge. Mistresses are cognizant of the most hidden, most shameful secrets of certain members of the same sex who they have never met before and are probably not at all likely to meet hereafter. While spouses know little about them and are most probably not even aware of their existence, mistresses have long since gathered by the armloads all sorts of information...thorny, meaningless, morbid details... If the aforementioned have the habit of plastering their faces with cream before going to bed at night, for instance, a mistress will even know what this cream smells like. Likewise they would know the latter's taste in clothes, their devotion to make-up, the type of mothers they were, the sort of jewellery they wore, at what time they went to bed and got up, their eating habits, unceasing curiosities, hideous obsessions, frigidities, hypocrisies, complexes, and also, what their possible reaction would be *if they learnt the truth*. Mistresses know all the answers without having asked the questions about these kinds of things. They do not seek confidential secrets, rather secrets come to them. They come because in order to provide their mistresses with evidence of the kind of pandemonium they live in, men who are 'Long Time Complainers of Marriage Who Still Don't End Marriage,' and 'Want Change Without any Loss', throw about headlines each more blatantly provocative than the last, like a crummy, popular daily newspaper ends up goading itself while trying to inflame its readers' emotions. Contrary to what spouses suppose, those who grumpily, maliciously gossip about them are not the mistresses but their husbands in person. Mistresses are just good listeners. Not only do they not make the slightest effort to learn more, but also, as long as they are confident about their power and content with their privileges, they do not even touch these armloads of unpleasant knowledge heaped onto their laps. They get to probe, pardon and protect their foes who in the meantime would not hesitate in drowning them in an inch of water.

However, even Achilles has a heel and even on satin sheets there is a mothhole at some spot, an air hole that deflates all the power of mistresses with a hiss. From the moment they have a mistress, men who are 'Long Time Complainers of Marriage Who Still Don't End Marriage' and 'Want Change Without Any Loss' start to love their children as if they have never loved them before. It is a sincere love and just as pathological. Just like Adam has covered his nakedness with a grape leaf, so too do the 'LTCM' men of the 'SDEM' team and 'WCWL' sub-team cover all their shortcomings with their love of children. As years move along and the number of mistresses increases, their fondness for their children spreads far and wide. Just like Eve was obliged to obtain herself the same grape leaf, so too are the mistresses bound to appreciate their lovers' attachment to their children, an attachment that steadily increases in folds, getting more sensitive with each fold and acquiring immunity in the process.

The Blue Mistress lifted the gaze she had fixated on the thin, crimson oil stripes oozing from the chicken with ground walnuts, half-eaten half-messed-up, and looked at the olive oil merchant with a weariness bordering on fury. The man's twelve year old daughter had taken to bed with a fever. He had been snapped at by his wife when he had attempted to scold her for neglecting the child: 'If you love your daughter so much, try not to go to your mistress tonight!' Having been until that point confident of hiding his illicit affair from his wife, the olive oil merchant had been truly flabbergasted. A dreadful brawl had then erupted in the house and the sick child had heard *everything*.

The Blue Mistress got up from her chair and gave the man a warm hug. She told him in a cruelly soft voice there was nothing to worry about, his daughter would get well soon, and her broken heart could be easily mended since the kid loved her father very much. She had uttered exactly what was expected, not a word more or less. The olive oil merchant looked at his mistress with a sour gratitude. He seemed more comfortable now that he had heard exactly what he expected to hear.

As the Blue Mistress saw him off all the way to the door, the olive oil merchant smiled for the first time in hours. 'Well done,' he murmured just when about to go out, pointing at the table left behind.

'It wasn't I who made them,' shrugged the Blue Mistress, 'I bought it all from the market.' From her voice, it was hard to tell whether she was enraged or not.

The olive oil merchant stood still for a moment. From his stare, it was hard to tell whether he was surprised or not.

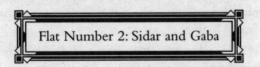

Flat Number 2: Sidar and Gaba

In the lassitude canopying Flat Number 2, entirely severing it from the world outside, Gaba snored away, each paw pointing in a different direction. Since he had curled himself not only within the serenity taking over the house but also on top of his housemate, there was no way Sidar could budge until Gaba woke up. Not that Sidar minded that. He loved to stay still without achieving anything, not even trying to, with barely any energy, feeling slightly zany and slovenly, embraced by aimlessness, next to the being he loved the most in this world…to stay just like that, simply and purely stay… He too slid into sleep.

In a wide, weed-filled garden framed by an ornate steel railing, Sidar stood gazing at an amber-haired young girl who had wrapped herself in silvery tulles and stretched out on a *chaise long*. The girl looked astonishingly like one of his sisters but was more beautiful. She had been motioning him to come hither. Sidar checked Gaba sleeping away at the entrance. Though he knew only too well that Gaba should not be left there alone, he pushed open the humongous entrance gate without taking his eyes off the girl and plunged in. Though the garden was greener than it appeared from the outside, the pool at its centre was for some reason bone-dry. Bugs the size of fists wandered around in it. The girl got up smiling and Sidar suddenly saw that she was much, much taller than him. What's more, the girl did not stop growing, as she stretched toward the sky. The shoes she wore had towering heels. The girl suddenly stumbled and while trying to recover her balance, she stomped her foot on the ground, making a noise that sounded like 'Tock!' 'Don't!' Sidar exclaimed, but this plea of his created just the opposite response from the girl, for she started to stamp her feet like mad: 'Tock, tock, tock!'

'Stop doing that. Are you nuts? Stop it!' Sidar yelled, worrying that Gaba might wake up. He turned back to check him, but the humongous gate with the steel railings that only seconds previously had been cracked open was both closed and now very far away. As the girl kept hopping, 'Tock, tock, tock,' what Sidar had feared happened. Gaba started to bark, tearing himself apart. Throwing the girl a bitter look, Sidar ran hurriedly toward the gate. At the same moment he found himself running dazedly toward the door in Flat Number 2 of Bonbon Palace. There was an ear shattering noise all around. While Gaba barked, the door jolted; while the door jolted, Gaba barked some more.

When Sidar had finally opened the door, standing in front of him was Muhammet, proud to have made his kicks talk. The child gave him a once over from top to toe and held out a napkin-covered plate: 'Madam Auntie sent you this.'

Sidar rapidly rid himself of his grogginess and smiled brazenly. A joke had come true. The traditional *halva* that old women neighbours distributed from door-to-door had reached him just at the right time, just when he was yearning for sweets after an acid trip. Sidar and his friends had termed this among themselves: 'Tradition infiltrating the unconventional.' He thanked the child, stumbling over his words in delight, grabbed the plate and slammed the door on him. Having caught the smell of the recently delivered food, Gaba had stopped barking, waiting eagerly with his wet nose in the air. Sidar winked at him teasingly, lifted the napkin and stood dumbfounded. What faced him was not *halva*, but two floured cookies. *Floured cookies with the ends slightly crushed and the powdered sugar on top spilled*. Sidar's face paled.

He had remembered.

Flat Number 7: Me

As I sat on the balcony sipping my drink, 'Why don't you think of something to stop these folks?' Ethel asked, grabbing the railing with fingernails painted a hue of dried apricot. Where she pointed, I spotted a headscarfed woman throwing her garbage by the side of the garden wall.

I shrugged. It doesn't make any difference anymore if I open or close the windows. With the weather warming up every passing day the garbage smell gets worse. If exposed to this malodour on the street, one walks faster, if in the car, one rolls the windows up. However, if the house you live in, the morning you wake up into, the night you sleep through, the walls, the windows, the doors and every direction you turn to stinks, then you are trapped. There is no way of stepping outside the yoke of smell. Every night when I return home I encounter yet another warped garbage hill by the side wall of the apartment building. Every night a brand new garbage mound awaits me comprising of stuffed plastic bags of all sizes marked with the emblems of the grocers and markets in the neighbourhood, bags with their tops tied but for some reason always with a hole or slit at the bottom, cardboard boxes tossed here and there, items that once belonged to godknowswhom, and black clouds of buzzing flies landing on and taking-off from the leaking watermelon juices and scattered scraps. Cats too… dozens of cats loom hither and thither… some skinny, some chubby, all indifferent to passers-by, bedridden in their foul-smelling kingdom, basking all day long over, inside and under the garbage bags, as their number increases incessantly, alarmingly...

I watch the garbage hill at various hours of the day. Before noon there already is a substantial pile, which mounts further during the rest of the day. Close to dusk, two gypsies, one juvenile, other elderly, arrive with their handcarts and pick at the garbage. They load tin cans, newspapers and glass bottles into separate sacks to take them away. Life down there seems to be based on endless repetition where each part complements one another: the cats dig up what the flies have set their eyes on, the gypsies pick on what the cats have dug up, the garbage truck that enters the street every evening at the rush hour takes away what remains from the gypsies, what the garbage truck scatters, the flies, cats and seagulls swipe at once again. Within this ceaseless rotation whatever diminishes is speedily replenished, never letting that sour smell fade away.

'What do you want me to do?' I asked. 'Should I stand guard by the wall?'

'Do something so drastic that they'll never again want to dump garbage here. Come on sugar-plum, use your brain! You'll think of something,' she said once again finishing her *rakı* before I did.

I leaned back lighting a cigarette. Oddly, there are no ants tonight. As the smoke coiled like gauze in the air, out of the blue, an idea as tiny as a louse crossed my mind.

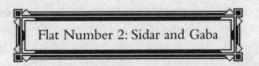

Flat Number 2: Sidar and Gaba

Watching Gaba lick the crumbs of the floured cookies with his rough, rose-pink tongue, Sidar couldn't help recalling a particular day of his childhood. It was a snowy Saturday. They had paid a visit to grandma, as they always did on Saturday mornings, but this time for some reason their visit had been shorter than usual. Ever since they had left the old woman's house, his mother and father had been walking arm-in-arm, murmuring reticently. Sidar, whom no one expected would grow up to be so tall and lanky back in those years, was covered in layers of clothes, lolloping like a cabbage; his reindeer-motif wool beret pulled down to his ears and the same coloured scarf wound around his neck. As the distance between him and his parents who were coming at a snail's pace from behind extended, Sidar took the liberty of tramping through all the puddles on his way. He could thus estimate the graveness of the quiet quarrel between his parents. The only thing adults need to do to make their children sense the inauspiciousness hovering in the air without explicitly declaring the news is simply to not get angry at things that always anger them. Accordingly, Sidar had fathomed something was wrong. For him to be convinced this day was like any other day, he first had to find a deep, dirty mud puddle to march in, and upon doing so, be rebuked by his mother and conceivably slapped by his father.

Before long he came across what he wanted, a russet, murky hole full of mud, the depth of which he could not possibly estimate. Doggedly, almost blindly he stomped in it and would have simply spurted ahead had he not heard an indistinct growl right at that instant. He flinched, checked the surroundings but couldn't see anyone. It was as if the voice had come from under his feet...as if the mud had been hurt... Perhaps it was a warning urging him to stay back. Perhaps this hole in front of him was one of those infamous death holes the municipality dug up to then forget to refill: a brown, bottomless dirty death hole... It frightened him, but the fear of death, Sidar sensed for the first time, was not that frightful. He moved forward.

His heart pounded wildly. How deep was the hole, where was its bottom? Perhaps in a step or two he would be swallowed up... In his mind's eye he visualized his death, the hole gulping him up, leaving behind nothing but his red deer patterned beret. He imagined his mother and father passing by the hole, still talking fervently, then returning down all the roads they had passed searching for their only son. The more he thought about it the more he took pleasure in making everyone pay for past offences: slanders that had hurt him, squabbles that had injured him, the injustices he had been subjected to... It felt good to envisage how his friends and relatives who had been separately responsible for each one of these slights would repent upon learning he had died.

Yet before he was able to arrive even at the midpoint of his dreams, he had reached the end of the puddle. He grudgingly stepped out and still stomping his feet, dropping burly mud drops, he turned the street corner only to stop there flummoxed. Right across from him, by the sidewalk, lay a puppy. Those blaring sounds had emanated not from the death-hole of the Istanbul municipality but from this puny, black-eyed puppy. It had no blood on its coat, no visible cut or wound. The wheel tracks of the minibus that had sped over it were not detectable. Sidar's face paled. Realizing that the death he had lavishly dreamt of a minute previous was now so close and yet so external to him, he felt stupid. All these visions that carried him away were incongruous and all the aspirations he set up futile.

The only things that were real to him at that moment were the mud left on his trousers, which was already drying up, and the pain tormenting this puppy. The rest was entirely meaningless. He had a family but was lonely; he was constantly belittled by everyone and he in turn constantly belittled everyone; he did not know how to be happy and did not think he could learn it either; he had turned eleven but was still a child in everyone's eyes; no one asked his opinion on anything and even if they did, he did not have any opinion anyway.

No doubt he should have returned and asked for help from his parents or else, moved forward to help the puppy himself, but he could do none of these things. He nervously thrust his hands into his pockets and simply waited. The sour despondency of his parents was approaching step by step from the back: this was life. In front of him, a puppy speedily slid from pain into oblivion: that was death. As for Sidar, he did not want to join either side; he would stay as far away as possible from both the death that excluded him and the life from which he had excluded himself. If only he could withdraw behind his eyelids the way he had hidden under the coat, gloves, beret and scarf. Lost in his thoughts it took him some time to realize what the soft thing in his left pocket was. It was a floured cookie.

'The girls will stay with me,' grandma had remarked broodingly that morning. 'But the male child, he has to be by the side of his father.'

When Sidar had entered the kitchen, the two women had their backs to him. They were doling out the freshly baked floured cookies into the porcelain plates lined up on the counter. 'Don't leave me without news,' grandma had mumbled. 'But as soon as your new phone is connected, call a candy store first thing.'

When a new phone was connected at a new house, whom one called first determined all the rest. That was why, with a new phone, before calling friends and relatives, one had to randomly call a candy store so that all the following calls made from that phone would end sweetly. After having talked to a candy store, one could call a bank, foreign currency bureau or a jeweller to bring in money for future phone calls, a real estate agent to bring in a house, or a car dealer to bring in a car and the like, but possessions and such did not matter that much. What really mattered was for the things to run sweetly. Accordingly, while calling all others depended on one's own pleasure, calling the candy store was some sort of a duty.

Sidar had been bored stiff there, as he was every Saturday morning. Fortunately they had not stayed for long this time. While the adults had become wobbly with emotion and the children had still not comprehended how different this Saturday morning was from others, they had all been swept toward the outside door with the current of such incessant farewells that it was uncertain who kissed whom and why. The only thing apparent was that the girls were to stay behind with the grandmother. Sidar had no objection to this. He was so pleased to learn that he would be spending the weekend away from his sisters' yakking that he had not even objected to his mother's instruction to put on this beret which was made for a girl. However, just as he was about to leave in that covered, wrapped-up state, his grandmother had pulled him to herself fast, stuck him onto her breasts that touched her belly and keeping hold of him tight like this, she had crammed things into his pocket. 'You'll eat them on the way,' she had snivelled as she sniffed her red nose and pointed with one arm to some place in the sky as if the road she referred to was up there somewhere. In that state she had remained stock-still at the threshold, like a burly statue of a woman turned into stone. With her blocking the door in this way, all family members had lined up next to one another along the narrow corridor like forgotten clothes pinned up on a clothesline and left to freeze outside in the cold of the night.

Always confused when confronted with excessive expressions of love, Sidar had finally succeeded in escaping the mangle of grandma's breasts that smelt slightly of sweat, intensely of lemon cologne and a whisk of fresh baked bread. That was the exit. From that moment on they had been wandering the streets, he in the front and his mother and father at the back.

★★★

As soon as the puppy spotted the floured cookie Sidar took out of his pocket, it stopped wailing. They stood eye-to-eye for an awkward moment. Sidar felt a hatred surge in him; he couldn't help loathing the animal. Here it was on the verge of death and yet the desire to devour a damn floured cookie flickered like a flimsy flame in its already lustreless black eyes.

A couple of minutes later, his father and mother turned the corner. They approached and saw their son indifferently munching on a cookie in front of a dying puppy. Confronted with such cruel insensitivity, the nerves of both adults, which were thoroughly stretched under the influence of the topic they had been talking about, completely snapped. While his mother yelled at him, his father slapped him on the face.

At long last his wish had come true. Both his mother and father seemed to have turned back to their normal selves. Still however, that malignant feeling pulling Sidar apart inside had not lessened a bit. As he started to weep, it was neither the slap nor the rebuke that had hurt him so badly. In truth, on that last Saturday morning in Istanbul, his conviction that the life he had become accustomed to would forever continue the way it was, had perished for once and all.

That same night Sidar travelled on a plane for the first time in his life. He would with time comprehend why his mother and father had become so agitated before going through passport control and why they had left Turkey in such a hurry. At the end of the trip which he spent watching the charming flight attendant smiling the same smile at everyone, when the plane started to descend, he saw under him a city that scattered bright lights without shadows into a calm darkness: Switzerland!

Two months later, when they had left the school dormitory set aside for those seeking political asylum and settled into the dwelling they were going to share with an Assyrian family similarly in asylum, the first thing his mother had done was to run to the phone. She had talked with her daughters in tears, constantly repeating the same sentences over and over again; not a patisserie, not a candy store, nor a chocolate factory... Perhaps because they had used their new phone to call their family first, and to hold a most doleful conversation, throughout the long years that followed, at every single call they received they feared the worst news from Istanbul. Even when grandma died five years later and the girls also arrived in Switzerland this barely changed. In all the phone calls to ensue, there was some news from Istanbul and if not that, certainly a mention and a steady, thorny anguish.

Be that as it may, Sidar was the only one of the family to return to Istanbul, after eleven and a half years and one day...

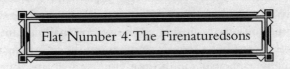

Flat Number 4: The Firenaturedsons

Shut in her room, sitting cross-legged on the carpet next to the cockroach she had squished, Zelish Firenaturedsons had for the last half hour been staring at the mirror she solemnly and dolefully held, as if some grave injustice had been inflicted upon her by the face she saw there. Until some time ago her face had been as pallid as if she had run into a ghost at night and as round as a pastry tray. Yet, for about five months now, it had been spotted with tiny, ruby blisters as if she had had a heat rash without knowing. The dermatologist with bleary eyes and hearty laughter they visited, diagnosed them as being neither adolescent acne nor an allergy but instead *psychosomatic*. Under extreme anxiety, he had maintained, the skin could transform itself into a red polka-dotted tablecloth. Chuckling at his own joke, the physician had given Zelish a whopping slap on the back and thundered in his bass voice: 'For goodness sake, if you get so anxious at this age, you'll end up racking your husband's nerves when married. Relax, my daughter, relax!'

If there is one thing in this life that starts to multiply out of spite and proliferate all the more the moment it is intended to be reduced, it must be anxiety. Even fear has an ending, a saturation point. When that particular point is reached, even if one were up to the neck in fear, one would and could not be frightened any longer. Excessive fear anesthetizes itself. As for anxiety, that is the venomous water of a bottomless well. It has neither an overdose nor an antidote. Just as much as the source of fear is concrete and evident, the source of anxiety is vague and abstract. As such, even though one would have no trouble determining the reason behind fear, there is no way to detect the cause for constant anxiety. Given that, warning an anxiety-ridden person who is already worn out from battling not some corporal enemy but a chemical one, about the menacing things that might happen if she did not appease her anxiety, would solely serve to create just the opposite effect, rendering her all the more anxious.

Not only did Zelish Firenaturedsons not know how to relax, she did not think she could ever learn either. Finding out that the cause for all these blisters was not a particular allergy but an ambiguous anxiety had simply heaped more angst upon her pile of angst. There was no soap, cream or lotion on earth that could heal her. Anxiety had no cosmetic solution. The blisters hitherto confined to her forehead and chin had since then increased twofold, spreading all over her face.

All of a sudden she overheard some music seeping through from the flat downstairs. Getting down on her knees, her face turned to the dead cockroach, she glued her ear to the floor. By now she had formed the habit of eavesdropping on the flat below at various times of the day. Her room was right above the living room of the wiry guy residing in the basement flat. At times she heard this strange 'tap' and 'rap' as if he had been walking on the ceiling or was taken hostage downstairs and was trying to climb up...or perhaps he was sending her a coded message... Once she had even heard moans jumbled-in with dog barks. That day she had patiently waited by the living room window to see what this female guest looked like. She had seen her. A petite girl with short, spiked, coppery hair and loose, baggy pants that looked like they would fall off at any moment. As soon as she had left Bonbon Palace, the girl had lit a cigarette there in the middle of the street. She didn't seem to have any blisters and thereby no anxieties.

'Every human being spends life searching for her own image,' wise men said, 'To become one with her and to find herself in her.' But even if that were the case, just as the Tuba tree in heaven had turned upside down with its roots up in the air and branches under the soil, so did certain mirrors turn what was sought upside down. In the girl who had left Sidar's house, Zelish Firenaturedsons had seen the opposite of her image. If only she could, she would entirely do away with herself and be converted into her.

'What the hell are you doing on the floor?'

Zelish Firenaturedsons bolted to her feet and frowned at her brother who had dashed into her room without bothering to knock on the door first. Zekeriya had come to dinner that night with his wife and child. In slow, heavy steps Zelish left the room in silence. She found everyone seated around the table in the living room having their soup while watching the news. At one end of the table stood three pieces of the coffee cake the old widow at number ten had sent them.

As Zelish perched on the chair at the corner, the TV screen caught her eyes. A sixteen year old mother who had left her three-days-old baby in the dumpster of a supermarket was trying to hide her face from the cameras. The luckless baby had slept in the barrel among the litter quietly all day long and only when it started to wail at night had it been noticed and saved by passers-by. The policemen who took her to the station and fed her had named the baby-from-the-garbage '*Kader*'.

All of a sudden Kader appeared on the screen, her tiny face flushing crimson. She kept crying and crying, turning a deeper and deeper colour with each cry. Zelish Firenaturedsons broke out in a sweat. The baby was so red. Though she tried to release her glance from the pressure of that nasty colour, it was too late. As baby Kader was being passed around from the lap of one policeman to another, all darkened – and the darkness was a vivid red.

Zelish Firenaturedsons had fainted.

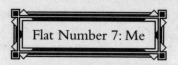

Flat Number 7: Me

Awakened with the squeal of the alarm clock at 5:45 a.m., the idea I had relished so much last night now seemed pure nonsense. I would have hit the pillow and gone back to sleep if only I could. Instead I got up and looked out the window. It was still dark outside. That was when I felt like trying my plan out. At least it would provide me with something to laugh about with Ethel the Cunt. Taking the bag I had prepared at night, I slipped ghost-like down the stairs. The apartment building was dead silent. As soon as I opened the building door, the cool morning breeze hit my face – and then the subtle garbage smell. It had started already. Who knows, maybe my plan will have some use. If I succeeded in convincing even one person not to dump their garbage here, I would have considered myself as having served not only the residents of Bonbon Palace but the entire city.

In all its forlornness, for the first time since I had moved here the street I lived on looked gorgeous to me. Two sturdy street dogs sprung from the corner. They advanced zigzagging from one sidewalk to the other, got in front of each other; slowed down upon reaching the garden wall, sniffed at the garbage reluctantly and failing to come across anything worthy, trudged away. As I looked after them, for a fleeting moment I felt someone's eyes on me. Yet when I turned around Bonbon Palace was in utter darkness with the exception of Flat Number 9. A shadow rapidly passed by the living room windows of the top floor. The lights of all the rooms in the direction the shadow moved were lit and then for whatever reason were turned off in the same order. I felt awkward. As I cased my surroundings, the silliness of what I was about to do upset me. Still, something in me refused to give up. My plan is pure nonsense but perhaps it is better that it be so. At times the only way of stopping ongoing nonsense is not to fight it back with rational rules or despotic prohibitions but to launch back some thing just as nonsensical.

As I got on the sidewalk and faced the garden wall, a grim pair of eyes accosted me. I had seen this cat before. It stares at humans with such pure hatred. Disturbed by my presence, it got up and walked to the end of wall with klutzy steps from where it continued to watch me. Taking the paint can out of the bag, I opened the lid with difficulty. When buying the paint the day before, I had asked the salesclerk for 'Muslim green' to match the occasion but what emerged from under the lid now was downright pistachio green – certainly not an apt colour for otherworldliness. What's more, another nuisance struck me once I faced the wall with the brush in my hand. I sure knew what sort of a message I wanted to write but hadn't given much consideration to how to phrase it most effectively. A bread van passed behind me noisily, continuing on its route after leaving a crateful of bread in front of the grocer opposite. Realizing what little time I had left before the whole city woke up, I hurried to write the simplest expression that came to my mind, going over every letter twice. As I worked conscientiously, the bastard cat watched my every move, swinging the tar black tail it had dangled off the wall.

When finished, I stepped back and examined my handiwork. It was not bad. Though the pistachio green was far too vivid and I had apparently failed to centre the writing, it still was all right. Large and legible enough to be perceived from even the middle of the street. I winked at the cat, collected the paint and the brush and returned to Bonbon Palace.

Just as I was about to enter, someone was getting ready to go out.

The aged lady at Number 10 was the last person I expected to see at this godforsaken hour of the morning, but it was as if she too felt at least as uneasy about this encounter as I did. While I tried to hide the contents of the bag in my hand, the ones in hers caught my eye. She was carrying four large bags that seemed empty. Her bags as light as a feather, she as light as a feather... I held the door open for her. Crowning that quizzical smile of hers with a polite, 'Thank you', she embraced her tiny frame and slithered away.

As soon as I entered the house, I went out on the balcony. Though I had intended to perch there to see with my own eyes the effect of my writing, the sleep I had left incomplete came and captured me like a clingy creditor.

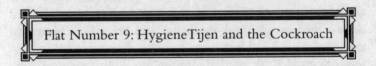

Flat Number 9: Hygiene Tijen and the Cockroach

After checking one by one the kitchen, living room, corridor and the back room, Hygiene Tijen finally turned off the lights and lay down on the bed exhausted. In the dead-calm of the darkness, sliced by the gradually dawning day, she turned and gazed with curiosity at the body next to her as if she saw it for the first time. She indeed gazed, but what she saw there was less a body than numerous infinitesimal bits and pieces. Her infatuation for cleaning, having long progressed to a chronic level had after a certain phase affected her eyesight like some insidious disease. Her eyes now subtly sliced-up everything she regarded, dividing the whole into pieces, the pieces into details and the details into bits. When she looked at the rug in the living room for instance, she perceived not the rug but its designs and the stains sheltered in those designs and the specks of dirt hanging onto those stains. While her eyes had become sharp enough to see indistinguishable details and hunt down the parasites invisible to the eye, she conversely had lost the ability to grasp anything in its totality. As such when she turned around in the bed and stared at the body next to her, she did not see her husband but the two drops of dried saliva by the corner of his mouth, the sand that had accumulated in his eyes, the food sediments on his teeth, the nicotine yellowing on his fingertips and the dandruff at the roots of his hair. In a flash she turned her face away so as not to have to see this any more but was too late. The disgust had already set in.

Disgust is no ordinary feeling, distributed lavishly to all

living creatures on earth. To bein with, it is exceedingly particular to humans. Women are disgusted more often than men, and among women, some more so than others. Whenever Hygiene Tijen was disgusted, the sides of her mouth turned down, her legs got stuck stock-still and her whole body first got a subtle tickling sensation and was then covered with an intensifying itch. She curled into the foetal position, scratching herself non-stop while the feeling of disgust prickled her toes, spreading from there to the upper parts of her body in wave after wave.

So far, she had become disgusted an infinite number of times for all sorts of reasons, but this time she felt a tingling not only on the tips of her toes but also on her temples. The tingling increased in a couple of seconds to cover her entire head; it then ran down her neck, squeezing left and right as if passing through a bridge and as soon as it left the bridge behind, started to descend in splintered, orderly strips. Behind this swiftly mobilized army was none other than Hygiene Tijen's brain. Predicting well ahead the possible perilous consequences of Hygiene Tijen's sudden disgust for her husband, her brain had acted on its own.

For sometimes our brain grasps before us the likely results of the action we are about to take and, if it deems necessary, sets about taking precautions of its own accord. Hygiene Tijen's brain too had independently decided to take over the way things were going as it could envision that this disgust did not resemble the preceding bouts and that, when she started to be disgusted with the man she had once married, risking a confrontation with her own parents, the issue could transform into an interrogation of an entire life. During the following couple of minutes, Hygiene Tijen experienced a peculiar, terrible cramping in her stomach. For it was exactly at this region that the rebels fighting in the name of 'Disgust-for-husband' and the forces of 'Devotion-to-husband' confronted each other. It was the latter that emerged triumphant. The brain had successfully put down yet another mutiny. Now relieved from her stomach ache Hygiene Tijen breathed a sigh and headed to the bathroom dragging her feet. She turned on the light. The surrounding area was snow white. She poured a few drops of bleach on a paper towel and thoroughly wiped the toilet seat. As she peed she scrutinized everything around. There was nothing within an eye range that could pierce through the absolute dominance of white, her favourite colour.

There was an aura of a certain colour surrounding each and every person, according to a brochure she had once seen – the brochure of an organization established in California where the members called each other not with their names but colours, held hands to form colour scales like impressive watercolour sets, but ultimately had to disband when the members started to separate into factions based on their hues. Perhaps the reverse was also true. Perhaps, 'There is an aura of a certain type of person surrounding every colour', and if that indeed is the case, the aura of people surrounding the colour white will no doubt be comprised of housewives. White confers pride and dignity to housewives. To Hygiene Tijen it only conferred comfort.

After flushing the toilet, she dripped a few drops of bleach on a paper towel and wiped the seat. Having thus embarked upon the task, she also cleaned up the toilet cover, under it and around it; then the toilet paper and towel hooks, the sink, the tub, and unable to stop herself, pulled up the washing machine to mop behind it. Just before she got out, she turned around half-weary half-content to take a look at the whole bathroom one last time. She closed the door behind her, but stood still. For the brain does not always go in the front but occasionally comes from the rear like this. Hygiene Tijen's brain too had decided with a lag of few seconds that it had seen something black, pitch black, wandering somewhere within the whiteness covering the entire bathroom. She reopened the door; she was not mistaken. A black and disgusting antenna was rapidly making way on the white tiles. Her heart in her mouth, Hygiene Tijen drew closer with cautious side-steps and only when really close could she distinguish that the thing she had been looking at in its details, but had failed to see in its entirety, was not a black and disgusting antenna, but a black and disgusting cockroach.

Before she let out a scream, the black, repulsive owner of the black repulsive antenna had already vanished into a hole on the bathroom wall.

Flat Number 1: Musa, Meryem and Muhammet

Because of the squabble inside, Musa woke up earlier than usual this morning. As soon as he entered the living room he spotted Muhammet there, squeezed between an armchair and the wall. Pretending not to notice the plea for help flickering in his son's eyes, he sat down at the breakfast table. Grudgingly shovelling into his mouth a lump of cheese, he reached for the teapot only to let go of it even more grudgingly. Alas, the tea had gone cold again. Though he pointed the teapot out to his wife, Meryem, too busy pushing the armchair with one leg while stuffing parsley twigs into half a loaf of bread, paid no attention to him. Sullenly bowing to the fact that he had to take care of himself, Musa's sluggish gaze scanned the surroundings and, passing at a tangent to his son's despondent stare, inspected one by one the armchairs, coffee tables and chairs weightily lined up. Having thus drawn a complete circle in the living room, he finally focused on his wife once again. Meryem's belly seemed even bigger this morning.

Gobbling half the cheese on the plate, three slices of bread and all the olives left in the bowl as fast as he could, Musa left the house without a word. At this hour of the day, as the only place he could think of going was the grocery store opposite, that is where he headed. The grocer – who was notorious for sitting hunched-up on the same stool and in the same spot, all the time spying on the passers-by – hadn't arrived yet. Like many a grocery store in Istanbul, in this case too, what made the store different from others was less the qualities of the groceries sold than the traits of the grocer. So profoundly had this identification of shop-with-owner been internalized by the hunched-up grocer himself that for a long time he found it impossible to accept the simple fact that his store could open in his absence. Nevertheless, ultimately facing the risk of losing customers if he kept on closing the shutters every time he went to the mosque to pray, he had been forced to entrust the store to his freckled apprentice.

The apprentice happened to be his brother's son, but since the hunchbacked grocer was a firm believer in the need to keep kinship and trade apart just like water and oil, he treated the youngster not like his nephew but as an apprentice ought to be treated. As for the boy, on no account could he work out how on earth this uncle of his, who bombarded him with callous orders and icy scoldings six days a week could then on the seventh day, on a Sunday family visit, turn into an utterly different person, bringing him chocolates he would not even let him get near to in the store. On such Sundays, whenever his uncle asked – as if they had just run into each other for the first time in weeks, as if it wasn't him who had sworn at the boy only that morning in the store in front of everyone – 'Tell me, my nephew, what do you do in your spare time after school?', at those thwarting moments how desperately the boy wished to vanish from the face of the earth. The acrimony of the past Feast of Sacrifice was still seared fresh in his memory. On that day, all their relatives gathered together, sacrificed a bulky ram early in the morning, then spent the entire day gulping down tea, almond paste, roasted meat, yogurt soup, wheat boiled with meat, yogurt drink, rice and meat sausage, apricot compote, meat pilaf, tea again, baklava with pistachios, semolina dessert for the spirits of the dead, grapes, watermelon, again baklava with pistachios and coffee; only to end up suffering from severe indigestion at night. The next morning, when the boy had arrived at the grocery store later than usual and still drained of colour, his uncle had yelled at him, crowning his reprimand with a sermon on an apprentice's responsibility to go to bed early and rise early. Unable to match in his mind's eye the jittery grocer at the store and the fatherly uncle he ran into on family occasions, the freckled apprentice had in the fullness of time started to perceive them as two distinct persons. This apparent solution, however, caused a few problems of its own: each time his parents asked him to deliver a message to his uncle at the store something inside the boy seemed to short-circuit, for he always forgot to do so.

When Musa approached the store, the freckled apprentice had placed the Book of Quranic Verses on the counter, and with one eye on the door and one hand in the peanuts case, kept wolfing nuts while memorizing sections of the Qur'an.

Not at all used to getting up this early, and apparently disappointed to see the apprentice instead of the grocer, Musa thought, why not distribute the bread of the apartment building himself this morning? The moment he took a step toward the glass cupboard where the breads were lined-up, however, he stopped, highly perplexed. In a daze and almost frozen to the spot, what he looked at from that angle was the garden wall of Bonbon Palace, which he soon pointed out to the freckled apprentice. The two of them stood side by side, studying the pistachio green writing there.

'I hope Meryem won't ever see this,' Musa exclaimed. Then, as if sharing a joke with himself, he chuckled, displaying his rotten teeth.

'Why so?' the freckled apprentice grimaced, having just missed the nut he had flung in the air.

'Why so? Why do you think? Simply because she'd accept it as true!'

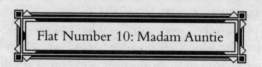

Flat Number 10: Madam Auntie

Having emptied every single one of the bags she had brought in, Madam Auntie opened the double doors and stepped onto the balcony. The roofs of the apartment buildings across were dotted with hordes of seagulls, all staring in the same direction, all similarly sullen, as if compressed under the weight of the same cryptic contemplation. Her eyes fixated on them, Madam Auntie distractedly caressed the pendants on her two necklaces, one of which she never took off. On the long chain there hung a key, and on the short one, the austere face of Saint Seraphim.

Istanbul, she thought, resembled a woman heavy with child – a woman who during the last months of pregnancy had put on far more weight than she could carry. With every step, the swish of water rose in waves from that belly of hers, long swollen with grandeur. Though she constantly devoured whatever she could get hold of, she was no longer able to tell how much of what she ate benefited her or the crowds of teensy, touchy and voracious beings growing within her body day by day. How desperately she would like to, if only she could, get rid of this excruciating burden. Instead all she could do was to simply swell up throughout the centuries. The comestibles which she consumed in one gulp were transported to her by ships and boats, cars and trailers, shaky-legged porters and caravans, their tails long lost on the way. Had she, with this insatiable appetite of hers, not been able to spurt anything out, Istanbul would have long before blown up, taking the life of both herself and those dwelling in her. Auspiciously she could always spew things out. She purified her worn-out body, just like a person would use expectorants to oust putrid gases, bodily fluids and vomit in order to live and keep living. Istanbul poured the pus oozing from her festering wounds into hills of garbage. That she could still persevere, she owed to the garbage mounting in piles upon piles even when buried deep in holes, emerging from its ashes even if burned shovel by shovel, never to wane even when carried far away. It was thanks to the glorious garbage that Istanbul could still carry on.

As such the garbage dump was not an end. Life did not terminate there but merely changed form and essence. The items thrown in the trash, as if churned out from the invisible walls surrounding the city, were then dissolved into their components, sorted out, burned up, pressed, buried – yet they never wholly perished. Like a fugitive on the run, the garbage ultimately sneaked back to Istanbul – through the soil, water or at times air. With the help of the garbage-gatherers, the *lodos* or the seagulls.

The seagulls seemed to be of the same opinion as Madame Auntie. These theoretically carnivorous, originally directionless birds had in time become so accustomed to feeding on Istanbul's trash that they had fully integrated into this everlasting gastral circle incessantly begetting waste from life and life from waste.

Every night and every morning, Madam Auntie sat on her balcony looking far and down on the russet hill where the shanty houses with cursorily painted facades had been heaped to the brim while she listened, as attentive as a silence-worshipping seagull, to the hum of the city flocked together by the gale only to be scattered by it once again. In this final stage of her life, if she were offered a chance to be born again wherever she pleased and as a different species, Madam Auntie would no doubt choose to be born here in Istanbul, only this time, disguised as a seagull.

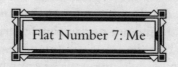

Flat Number 7: Me

It was almost noon when I woke up. Thrusting into my briefcase today's lecture notes, as well as yet another Kierkegaard for Ece, who apparently preferred to borrow them from me rather than purchase her own, I rushed out. While I was leaving my flat, the neighbour at Number 8 was going into hers. In a hurry, as always. She seemed to have done something to her hair. It was better before but she still looked fetching, indeed very fetching. She greeted me warily with a nod, averting her eyes. Yet I caught that glance in her eyes. She is not as timid as she seems to be. Neither is she that indifferent to the world around her. Down on the ground floor, the door of Flat Number 4 was ajar. That nasty woman was standing at the threshold, asking Meryem to do her chores. Upon seeing me, her lips twisted into a galling smile.

'Professor, did you hear what happened to our apartment building?' she blurted out. 'It turns out there was a holy saint in our garden!'

I had completely forgotten about it.

'I am not at all surprised,' I said, not losing my cool. 'It is a well-known fact that there are countless graves left from the Ottomans, as well as the Byzantines, at various corners of Istanbul,' I added without taking my eyes off my watch. 'Are we to claim that all the dead in this city lie within the existing cemeteries? Of course not!' There must be still thousands of undiscovered graves. What could be more natural than the fact that some of these graves belong to people regarded by the populace as holy saints?

Zeren Firenaturedsons inspected me from top to toe, trying to grasp whether I was making fun of her or not. When she pouts, the creases on her forehead make her look even more edgy. 'Academics!' she heaved a sigh, and as if with this single word the whole conversation had turned to her advantage, she crossed her arms on her chest, remaining silent. So did I.

Zeren Firenaturedsons' thorny stare stirred toward Meryem, standing next to us, listening to our conversation with a look of anguish and tightly closed lips as if worried she might let slip a word she'd rather not. For a fleeting moment it seemed to me that upon hearing my response a gleeful glint glimmered in the depth of her eyes, but the very next second, hurrying to get rid of us both, she grabbed her list of chores and scurried out ahead of me.

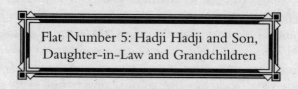

Flat Number 5: Hadji Hadji and Son,
Daughter-in-Law and Grandchildren

'But grandpa, what if I step on them by mistake?' exclaimed
the five and a half year old.

'If you step on them, the genies will get into you. They will
twist you out of shape,' roared the seven and a half year old.

'Like you've got a giant head!'

Hadji Hadji intervened: 'Don't talk like that with your older
brother. Neither the genies nor Allah will like those who don't
respect their elders.'

The five and a half year old tilted her head, tugging her
pinky-ginger pleated skirt. Utterly immobile for a while, from
the corner of her eye she then looked at her older brother only
to see the other pouting at her. Without a sound she slid closer
to her grandfather.

'The genies have a sultan. They call him Beelzebub. Never
do they dare to disobey his orders, but there are times when
they get involved in all sorts of intrigues without his
knowledge. The genie gang comes in all types. The genies are
like humans, some are good, some wicked. Some are devout,
some infidels. There are three types of genies: firstly, there are
some in the form of snakes or bugs, secondly are those in the
shape of wind or water and last but not least, there are those
who take the form of humans. It is this last group that is the
most menacing of all! You can never tell if they are really
humans or genies. They throw weddings that last until dawn,
eating, drinking and dancing to the rhythm of drums and
zurnas. If you ever happen upon a genie wedding late at night,

you should instantly turn your head. Don't ever try to sneak a look! When you get up to go to the bathroom at night, don't ever take even one step without uttering Allah's name aloud! Particular attention needs to be paid to thresholds because that's where the genies like to linger. The only way to eschew the genies is to not do anything without uttering Allah's name. If you forget to do so, the genies will surely reach you and meddle with your life!' repined Hadji Hadji, leaning his aching back on one of the pillows piled up on the couch to build an Osman afterward. The little girl next to him cowered and moved in tandem, as if glued to the old man.

'The most horrible one is the "Crimson Broad". When she haunts a woman who has just given birth, she'll never let go of her prey. All night long, she mounts the new mother's chest as if riding a horse. Only at dawn does she leave the poor thing drenched in sweat and fear, but the next night, she's back there again, this time attacking the cradle, throwing the baby up in the air like a soccer ball.'

'Oh I remember her,' the seven and a half year old blurted out, eyeing his siblings, 'She came to their birth!'

'Of course, she would! If, instead of having the birth her way, your mother had called for your deceased grandmother, there would be no quandaries. Your grandma, peace be upon her, would certainly have managed to get rid of the "Crimson Broad", but the poor soul passed away without seeing her grandchildren.'

Deeply vexed by their grandfather's response, the five and a half year old and the six and a half year old grovelled at once. While the little girl's lower lip drooped down, the boy had started to suck his thumb which was already thinned out from constant sucking.

'And you better be cautious about the "Black Congolos" too, the most merciless of them all… She disguises herself as an aged woman, wandering on the streets, waiting for her prey at street corners. She asks questions to the passers-by: "Where are you coming from?" and "Where are you going to?" she inquires. "Which family do you descend from?" she further asks. If you stumble upon "Black Congolos", you have no other choice than to respond to her questions by using the word "black" each time. Say, for instance, "I am from the black ones" or "I come from the black town". Only then will she leave you in peace. Every so often she asks for an address. If you don't know the address, I pity you. She takes out her cane, whacks you on the head and beats you so bad that...'

His words were ripped apart by the ringing of the phone. The seven and a half year old reached for the receiver with no hurry. Yes, they had finished their breakfasts. No, they were not being naughty. Yes, they were watching television. No, grandpa was not telling tales. No, they were not turning the gas on. No, they were not messing up the house. No, they did not hang off the balcony. No, they did not play with fire. No, they did not go into the bedroom. Really, grandpa was not telling a tale.

However, that day his mother must have been in need of confirmation for she insisted: 'If your grandpa is telling tales simply say, "The weather is cold," and I'll understand.'

The seven and a half year old hesitated for a moment. A nocturnal gleam slid from his moss green eyes. There followed a prickly silence. When the gleam had disappeared, he had already changed his mind. Without feeling the need to lower his voice or take his eyes off his grandfather, he answered in an indifferent voice: 'No, mom, the weather is not cold. However, grandpa does keep telling us creepy stories.'

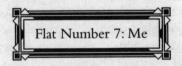

Flat Number 7: Me

'You seem to be in good spirits today, Professor,' Ece sitting at the front row twittered in the most glib voice she could manage. She was dressed in pitch black from top to toe, as usual: black lipstick, black nail polish, black eyes made to stand out with black eye pencil. I took out the copy of 'Sickness Unto Death' from my briefcase and placed it on her desk.

'I have indeed come to class in good spirits, but whether I'll still be in this state when we are done depends on you. Let's see if the articles have been read,' I said, proceeding with a typical introduction to a typical Thursday lecture.

'We have read from, "In Praise of Folly", by Erasmus. The part where he mentions Fortuna we compared to Machiavelli's Fortuna. Entirely read, analyzed and memorized!' Ece spoke up.

'Fine, then can somebody please tell me what sort of a thing this Fortuna is?' I asked, taking pains to address not Ece but the whole class.

'For sure, a female,' Ece raised an answer, apparently pleased with trampling whatever prudence I maintain. 'In both Machiavelli and Erasmus, Fortuna is personified and feminized and because she's a female, it's no big surprise that they don't find her reliable. The church fathers shared the same opinion – and we Turks are no different. We say destiny is either blind or a slut. If blind, she can't see what she distributes to whom, so can't be expected to be fair. If a slut, she'll have nothing to do with fairness anyhow. At times there's a wheel in her hand. At other times she herself forms a wheel by swirling her skirts.

Hence the expression 'Wheel of Fortune'! There is no way of knowing when or where she'll stop, bringing who-knows-what to whom. According to Machiavelli, Fortuna controls half of our lives and there's nothing we can do about that part. However, it is possible, even if only partially, to make Fortuna obey our demands. Since each and every one of the fountainheads of political philosophy happen to be male, it looks like in the persona of Fortuna they are unanimously searching for ways with which to bring women to their knees.'

'Huh? So this Fortuna you are talking about is our good old *Kader*?' Cem blurted out, apparently having not the slightest problem in revealing his ignorance on the assigned articles.

In the ensuing fifteen minutes or so, constantly interrupting each other's sentences, they talked about our good old *Kader*.

'I think it's really cheap to criticize Machiavelli from the standpoint of contemporary feminist paradigms,' said the curly-haired girl with the glasses whose name always escaped me, and who I knew did not like Ece one wee bit but for some reason always sat behind her. 'The issue is, do you think you're living a life that's been drawn up for you ahead of time? Has your life been determined a priori? That is the question we need to ask. In struggling against *Kader*, the man's clearly coming to terms with religion. Neither Enlightenment nor progress would've been possible without breaking away from Fortuna, or bringing her to her knees, if you will.'

Ece stretched tautly as she crossed her legs. She does this repeatedly, knowing too well the beauty of her legs. So far, I have not seen any colleague suffer serious academic damage for getting mixed up in some sort of a love affair with a student. If someone is hunted down for this reason, it is because he would have been hunted down in any case. At any rate, I do not reciprocate Ece's interest in me. Not because I am worried it would reach my colleagues' ears. What really matters is not what the academics pretend not to know, but what the students pretend to know, for female students always talk. They can never hold their tongues. Each one has a close friend to confide in, each confidant another one of her own, and so it goes. Complete disenchantment! All of a sudden you are not the 'esteemed, unknown' professor you once were, always watched by prying eyes from a distance, but an ordinary mortal whose weaknesses, lunacies, baloneys and fixations are paraded in front of all. To be with a young girl could indeed provide a pleasant boost to self-esteem for middle-aged men, but that comes at a cost: it is a shaky status bound to shatter any time. It might easily capsize at the very first flick. Then, all the letters you have written, the confessions you have made and the secrets you let slip will altogether vex you. Your sexual performance will be the talk of town and before you it, know you'll have become the butt of all jokes. It is not worth it. I never considered any female student of mine to be worth all this. Not even Ece.

'Why don't we just simply confess that we can't control our lives? I may be held responsible for what I do but I can't be blamed for what I spark off,' Ece said, watching my every move all the while. 'I'm from birth the daughter of this or that person. I can choose neither my father nor my nation and certainly not my religion or language. If they'd asked my opinion, I'd have preferred to have been born in another environment; if refused the alternative, I'd rather not have been born at all. It's that simple. If you had been born somewhere else, rather than a scarf on your head you would have had a cross on your neck,' she poured out. Though she had turned back, it was not clear as to which one of the three headscarfed girls she had addressed her words.

'I too believe in destiny', answered Seda, always sitting in the middle of the always together headscarfed threesome.

'But that's not at all what I'm talking about,' grumbled Ece the blabbermouth. 'You believe in a divine justice. Things are what they are at the moment but you think some day everyone will be held accountable for what they did in life. The debauched will be punished in hell, the gullible rewarded in heaven and so on. You retain a notion of justice in your mind.

Otherwise your faith will smash to smithereens. Fortuna is exactly the opposite. She has nothing to do with the other world, so solidly mundane!'

'Frankly guys, I have a hard time understanding why you got so hooked up on this Fortuna,' interjected Cem, bringing his chair closer to the wall as if getting ready to flee through the window. 'The real question is not Fortuna or anything similar but concerns the very difference between a line and a circle. If you believe this life you are living is a line, you might just as well presume you'll triumph over the past, reach the future. However, if it is a circle which your life resembles, rest assured that there is no such thing as 'progress'. Are you at peace with recurrence or not? That's the fundamental issue. A man like Machiavelli can't be at peace with recurrence because that requires acceptance of the sullen fact that the life you live now, you'll live again and again, that tomorrow won't be any different than today – exactly the same question as Nietzsche asked of Rousseau. When you're alone, at the loneliest hour of your life, say, if all of a sudden a teensy weensy devil descends all the way from hell and exclaims, 'Have no fear, I guarantee you, there is no such thing as death, if anything, there is only recurrence. Every single thing you've lived until this very moment, you'll live all over again. Then again and again. Forever…' how would you feel then? How many of us can tolerate living our lives over and over again? Those who can put up with Fortuna's whims will never go mad. It's that simple. To endure life, a man like Machiavelli has to cut the circle somewhere and transform it into a line. Only then can the idea of progress surface, and along with it, the notion of individualism.'

I looked at my watch; five minutes left to the end of the second hour. 'Once again you manage to surprise me with your ability to deviate from the subject matter,' I muttered as I took out my pack of cigarettes, indicating a break. 'Next week you'll have completed all the readings and we'll only talk about what you've read. No one will blabber without proof.'

During the third hour, I lectured and they listened without a comment. While everyone else took notes, Cem looked out the window and Ece munched half a pack of bitter chocolate. A speck of chocolate, almost black, stuck there on the side of her lip like a naughty mole.

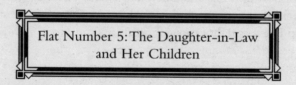

Flat Number 5: The Daughter-in-Law and Her Children

'Mom, why are you taking us with you?' whined the five and a half year old.

'Come on, isn't this great? Don't you want to see where your mother works?' the Daughter-in-Law said, as she held more tightly onto the hands of the two children forcing them to adjust to the speed of her footsteps. How on earth she was going to restrain the kids at the box office all day long she hadn't quite yet worked out, besides which she was afraid of angering her boss, but she was too high-strung to think rationally after the fight with her father-in-law. As they neared the end of Cabal Street, she slowed down and looked back over her shoulder. The seven and a half year old was two metres behind them. Despite the inquisitive looks of some passers-by, he seemed remarkably happy now that he had stepped outside Bonbon Palace after two years.

Soon the lump of anguish the Daughter-in-Law was used to savouring whenever she watched her older son chased away the wisps of worries pullulating from her mind. Though she knew too well that her oldest child would be the shortest to live with her, among all her children it was he that she was most deeply attached to. Children born with a lethal illness, unlike their peers and siblings, belong only to their mothers and always stay as such.

At the corner of the Cabal Street, just when she motioned her older son to hurry up, a swarthy, skinny hand slowly tapped the Daughter-in-Law's shoulder.

'My child, how can I get to this address?' It was an old hunchbacked woman, bent double inside a beige-coloured raincoat worn to shreds. In her callused hands she held out a wrinkled piece of paper. She looked lost.

Taking no notice of the horror on the faces of her two children, the Daughter-in-Law let go of their hands and concentrated on the address on the paper. Unable to decipher the scrawl, she returned it to the old woman, shaking her head.

'Mom, you couldn't answer the question!' the five and a half year old squeaked. Teardrops pitter-pattered down her cheeks. The six and a half year old was no better. Simultaneously sucking the thumbs of both hands, he persistently repeated the same words: 'How can you not know, how can you not know?'

'She could not,' roared the seven and a half year old as he approached from behind, quick to grasp the situation. The instant he reached the end of his words, the other two started wailing.

'What on earth are you talking about? What is it that I didn't know?' the Daughter-in-Law stuttered bamboozled, staring first at her children, then at the old woman walking off. But instead of a response what she got from her children was some more sobs and the squishy sounds of a frantically sucked thumb.

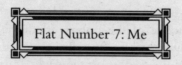

Flat Number 7: Me

It was hard to find a table at the bar, with the usual Friday night throng. When a table finally did become free somewhere in the middle, I grabbed it, ordering a double right away. I took it easy with the second *rakı*. Only after the third double, did the Cunt show up at the door, with an ear-to-ear grin. There had been a traffic jam, she said. However, this information was offered less as an explanation for her delay than as some useful detail in her account of the soccer game she and the cab driver – fortuitously fans of the same team – had listened to as they inched through the traffic on the way here. Though 2-0 behind in the second half of the game, they had finally won 3-2. Failing to see the slightest indication that Ethel minded being fifty minutes late for her appointment with me, I did not say anything either. In point of fact, I cannot deny how impressed I am with her soccer knowledge (the depth of which had been tested by experts many times over), her endless yakety-yak with cab drivers and her getting to know at each restaurant we dine the names, family trees and topmost worries of all the waiters serving us within the first ten minutes, to then convert every order into an opportunity for a chat…just as I am impressed by her refutation of womanhood on all occasions with an in-your-face attitude… She had always been like this. The high school friendship of Ayshin and Ethel was, to all intents and purposes, thesis-antithesis rapport, and this vivacious essence revealed itself when I came between them. I doubt Ethel's love for soccer would have reached such sky-scraping levels if Ayshin had enjoyed soccer the least bit or supported a team just for the sake of it.

'I've come up with the ultimate solution to the garbage problem of Bonbon Palace,' I muttered as I filled her glass. Then, slowly and assuredly, I told her about the writing I had written on the garden wall. She can't have been expecting to hear such nonsense from me, for at first she looked dumbfounded, if only for a few seconds, and then she made me tell the whole story all over again, as she tossed out hearty laughs. The more I narrated, the more hilarious I too found the story. Goading me to describe myself as I stood there at the crack of dawn in front of the garden wall with paint and brush in hand, she burst into laughter. She had either got drunk quicker than usual tonight or had come to the appointment already high. We left toward one o'clock. Ethel shook hands with all the waiters one by one and said her farewells. Nor did she neglect, in accordance with the information she had acquired from them, to send her regards to their families, concluding with comforting speeches about their respective worries. When we had finally reached the street and somewhat sobered up with the night breeze, she insisted that I show her the writing on the wall.

We jumped into a cab. Ethel's convulsive laughter, which had rolled out back in the restaurant and shot up a notch while we were walking on the sidewalk, turned utterly hysterical in the cab. Giggling non-stop, she launched attack upon attack, all the while attempting to undo the buttons of my trousers while my hands struggled in vain to shove hers away. I soon stopped resisting. As her fingers wiggled to fondle me, I kept under surveillance the driver who looked barely of driving age. The man's beardless face being devoid of any expression whatsoever, there was no way of telling whether he could see what was going on in the back or not. In the meantime, Ethel had reached her target, having enough of an opening to insert one hand once the third button was undone. I was just about to cover with my jacket what her hand was up to when a hoarse yelp escaped my mouth. How I hate those razor-sharp fingernails of hers. At the same instant, a crooked smile dawned on the driver's face, revealing his awareness of what was going on. Brusquely grabbing Ethel's hand, I freed myself from the Cunt's claws. She flinched, grumbling and grimacing, and instantly lit a cigarette. The driver, who now seemed to be a close observer of all the attraction and repulsion going on at the back, intervened with perfect timing and asked us where on earth we were heading. Blowing a circle of smoke from her jasmine *chibouk*, Ethel cheerily exclaimed:

'We are going to pay a visit to Bonbon *Dede*! The holy saint of the broken-hearted, of all those separated from their beloved and notorious for screwing everything up!'

The driver, whose youthful appearance I realized stemmed more from a lack of facial hair than age, shot both Ethel and me a nervy glance as if weighing-up how grave things could get. However, Ethel would not leave the man alone. Offering him a cigarette, she catapulted questions at him, asking where he came from, if he believed in saints or not, if he was married or not, if at some time in the future he had a daughter whether he would educate her, whether he would renounce his son if the latter ever turned out to be homosexual, and finally, asking which soccer team he supported. As luck would have it, they supported the same team.

'Once I picked up a couple, no less nuts than you two,' the driver said the moment he found a lull amidst the deluge of questions. Ethel released another chain of guffaws, accompanied by wheezing coughs as if she had a fish bone stuck somewhere in her throat.

'Back then I was new to nightshifts and wasn't yet familiar with the night-time customers. So these two get in, quarrelling non-stop. The woman keeps yelling and hurling insults. The man doesn't do zilch to appease her. Instead he too slurs back, and they utter such slanders, I'd better not repeat those now! Still, it is obvious they are in love. It turns out the man is going abroad to work. The woman doesn't believe he'll ever come back. 'If you go you won't ever return!' she says, weeping hard.

Then, before I know what's happening, she starts punching him. Dead drunk no doubt. Anyway, we head to the address they gave. The plan is to first drop the woman off and then the man. So we go to her house but she doesn't budge, she doesn't want to get out of the car. "Come on," she shrieks all of a sudden, "Let's go visit Telli Baba!" Glued onto the seat, "I am not going anywhere before I see Telli Baba!" she insists. In the end the man gives in, as for me I am already convinced. Telli Baba is a long way out from there, but does she care? Back in those days I used to say, "No way, I'll never work at night." So you see how one changes his mind in the fullness of time. Anyhow, they didn't want to take another cab, instead they offered me twice as much as the normal fare. So we sped off in the middle of the night. Once there we pulled over, the woman got out, opened her purse, groped for something and then got lost in the dark. The man and I, we're waiting in the cab. After ten minutes or so, the woman comes back crying, says to the guy, "Bend your head!" The guy obeys and she pulls out a handful of hair. The guy hollers, in pain, they then have another fight. Thank goodness the woman leaves again, finds a piece of cloth from godknowswhere, ties the man's hair to the tree, prays, sits down, prays, gets up. So we let her do whatever she wants. In the end she calms down a tad. "Next time I'll come to Telli Baba with my wedding veil," she murmurs. The man softens. They embrace. They ask for my name and phone number to invite me to their wedding.'

'I am sure they got married and then strangled each other in next to no time,' Ethel bellowed, jerking her head toward the driver while launching another attack on the buttons of my pants.

'No sister, it's even worse,' the driver grimaced, shaking his head wisely. 'Two years later, winter time, during such a blizzard, you couldn't see a damn thing. Doesn't this man get into my cab again? Only this time with a different woman! Was she his wife or lover? There was no way to tell. I instantly recognized the guy. He recognized me too. We both felt awful.

He looked away, I looked away. The woman next to him had no idea what was going on. She was blubbering and blubbering to deaf ears. Before we could move even ten metres, the man stopped the cab and jumped out. The woman dashed straight after him flabbergasted.'

Joining her hands on her lap, Ethel heaved a doleful sigh. If I could only have a wee bit of an understanding of when and why the Cunt is moved. An unwieldy silence engulfed us. No one uttered a single word until we turned the corner of Cabal Street, but as soon as we came to a stop in front of Bonbon Palace, embracing her stunted joy Ethel bolted from the car. Unable to resist her pushiness, the driver too got off. At 1:30am, there we stood, the three of us lined-up reverentially, and gaped at the writing on the garden wall.

'UNDER THIS WALL
LIES A HOLY SAINT
DO NOT DUMP YOUR GARBAGE HERE!'

'How does it look?' I asked the driver.

'It's OK, I guess, but off centre, brother,' he said with an expression so subtle it was hard to tell whether he was joking or not. 'I don't like the colour either.'

Ethel doubled up as if about to throw up. In a flash, she let go of herself, bursting into laughter until she was in tears. She caused such a ruckus that the lights of a few flats in the apartment block went on. The driver on one side and I on the other, we pushed the Cunt back into the cab. On the way, her steadily decreasing chortles were replaced by steadily escalating sobs. It had been a long time since I had last seen her go to pieces like this. When we reached her house, I did not feel like staying with her. She passed out the moment her head touched the pillow anyhow. The cab waited downstairs. On the way back I sat in the front. The cab fare had shot up. Ever since my divorce, half my salary goes on rent and the other half on such nights of carousing. I offered the driver a cigarette. He first lit mine, then his. Now that the garrulous, raucous female had got out of the car, a brotherly silence echoed around us in her absence.

'Sorry about the fuss,' I muttered.

'No problem, brother,' he shrugged, 'I wish things like this were our only troubles.'

While waiting at a red light, right out of the blue, anguish began to surge within me. A police car sped by. Ahead of us ran a garbage truck with two lanky garbage men holding with one hand onto the back of the truck, their other hand swinging free. As they passed under a streetlight, their pale faces emerged from the dark, if only for a few seconds. The two garbage men were quizzically smiling at each other, or so it seemed to me. There were no other vehicles around. The moment the light turned green, my anguish really took off. I asked the driver to steer in the opposite direction. Ten minutes later we were in front of Ayshin's house. I did not get out. The curtains were drawn, the lights off. As I stood there staring at my old house, the smooth-faced driver waited patiently, without a word.

On the way back, we turned on the radio. Oddly enough I enjoyed every single song that was played. Finally, as the cab-fare gained another zero, we reached Bonbon Palace. Under the headlights, we jerked our heads out the windows on each side, feeling the need, for some reason unknown to us, to look at the writing on the wall once again.

'Hey brother, now that you've written this thing, have you ever wondered what'd happen if someone believes it?' the driver asked as he gave me the change.

'Oh, come on, who would believe in that?' I chuckled. 'Even if they do, so much the better. Hopefully they'll stop dumping their smelly garbage here.'

'Yeah, okay,' he slurred, his fingers tautly rubbing his upper lip as if pulling on an invisible moustache. 'It's just that this city's folks are a bit bizarre. Especially the women, they are truly wacko brother, you've seen it yourself. Basically what I'm asking is this: what if someone earnestly believes in this writing of yours?'

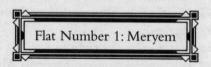

Flat Number 1: Meryem

Faith, like a train schedule, is essentially a matter of timing. The grand, rounded, ivory clock at the train station chimes at various specific hours of human life. The train leaves at specific hours. There is only one run before noon: those who have internalized a belief system while they are still children get on this one. There is another train that leaves in the afternoon, carrying along the troubled passengers of teenage years. After that there is no other direct run until night. Only then, when the first pressing regrets crop up in one's life and the unfeasibility of redeeming past wrongs is acknowledged; when even the most strongly built nests begin to topple and the first serious health complications occur; the train leaves for the third time. For some unknown reason, the passengers of this train get on it at the last minute. Then as midnight draws closer, after critical surgeries and on the verge of near-death experiences, there are two more runs, one right after another. These happen to be the most crowded runs. Without stopping at any station, they go directly to God on the intercession express. Unlike the daytime passengers, the nocturnal ones, so as not to miss this last chance, appear at the station way too early. Then, after a long wait when the clock finally strikes midnight and the circle is complete, from that swarming crowd only a handful of non-believers are left behind.

Being a passenger of the earliest train, Meryem's faith was not only far less calculated than that of others but also less 'by the book'. It's hard to tell, if she would have done the same thing had she not been pregnant at the time when the writing appeared on the wall. Since pregnancy rendered her a bit bizarre, early that morning she went out into the garden with an empty jar in hand to collect from the soil of the nameless saint. Not that she really believed there was a genuine saint buried in the garden, but as that university professor had stated, given the fact that under all these Istanbul sidewalks rested ancient graves, one could not predict what would emerge from where. If the writing turned out to be bogus, she would be left with just a jarful of soil, that was all. However, if there really was a saint under the rose acacia in the garden of Bonbon Palace, then there was only one request she would like to make to him: to infuse Muhammet with courage, even if it were only a morsel.

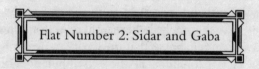

Flat Number 2: Sidar and Gaba

When the doorbell rang, Sidar scurried to answer it, hoping that Muhammet had once again brought them something to eat. However, when he opened the door, there in front of him stood not the little emissary of Madam Auntie but the nutty girl with the coppery hair. Either the girl had drastically changed since they had last seen one another or Sidar's memory of her had gone awry, but her eyes were just like he remembered, so beautifully solemn. She barged in with a bewildering smile and without waiting to be invited. As if tired she tottered unsteadily towards the couch and asked her host, still standing fixed on the spot, for something to drink. Sidar shuffled to the kitchen scratching his head. He opened up the only bag of coffee in the cupboard and poured the water heated up with the only pot in the house into the only mug on the shelf.

'Aren't you going to have one too?'

'Later,' Sidar shrugged. 'There is only one mug in the house anyhow.'

Three hazelnut wafers emerged from the girl's backpack, immediately arousing Gaba's interest. Still, however, he refused to move an inch.

'What was the dog's name?'

'Gaba,' Sidar grumbled, suspicious of having already told her this in their previous meeting.

'What does it mean?'

'Gaba is the abbreviation for gamma-amino-butiric acid –

which is an inhibitor nerve transmitter, something to do with the anxiety centre of the brain. Anti-convulsants, anti-anxiety pills and of course alcohol slows the Gaba receptor down. Consequently, you feel less anxious.'

'Cool! So you can speak German like your mother tongue, right? How long did you stay abroad?' the girl enthused before lying back on the couch. Upon seeing the ceiling, she fluttered her eyelashes in astonishment; then not knowing what to say, she fluttered her eyelashes some more.

'French,' Sidar corrected her tensely. Apparently the girl did not remember a word he had told her before. If she didn't care for the answers why on earth did she ask these questions? Besides she looked too sleepy to grasp a word. Her eyes were on the verge of closing while listening to the second, at most the third response. For what reason did she pose one question after another when it was all too obvious that the answers would remain incomplete, and that even if she learned the most that she could in the least time possible, she would have only attained straggly parts and smoggy pieces, not even the dimmest silhouette of the entirety of his life. The simple desire to get to know a person is a hollow pledge and a life-size burden! It requires that a person listen and observe, poke and sense, unwrap and amass for nights, weeks, years; to be able to peel off scabs and endure seeing the blood ooze from underneath. If a person is unable to put up with all this, it is much better, and certainly more honest, to throw in the towel straight off.

Not that I am a hitherto unappreciated treasure, locked in a chest awaiting exposure to sunlight. The answers to all the questions you ask about me are more or less already hidden inside you. I do not want you to desire to discover me or to even think you can do so. We do not have to know one another when we know so little of ourselves. Collecting information about others is like gathering food from garbage. What's the use of rotting the supplies in our brains if we are not to savour them in time?

A clipped snore interrupted the course of Sidar's thoughts. The girl had fallen asleep with her mouth agape. Taking a last puff from the cigarette he had rolled up at noon, Sidar curved up next to his guest. Watching them fretfully from where he had crouched down Gaba must have been finally convinced that nobody was out to get him for he hobbled closer. In a single breath, he wolfed down the hazelnut wafers, then, still licking away, he too came and curved up on the couch. As the headlights of the cars outside penetrated the petite windows spurring shadows on the wall, all three of them drifted off into three separate dreams.

Flat Number 8: The Blue Mistress and Me

Tired of criss-crossing a path between the kitchen and the living room, the Blue Mistress threw a last look at the table. Everything seemed ready. She lit the lily-shaped candle floating in the water-filled glass bowl and placed blue napkins next to the blue plates. They had agreed to meet at seven. The doorbell rang at ten to seven.

'Welcome,' she chirped. Though she was already wearing high heels, she instinctively felt the need to rise up on her toes. 'Do you always arrive early like this?'

'I tried hard not to, but it turns out that it takes three and a half steps to get from my flat to yours,' I said smiling.

'Of course, your legs are so long,' she cackled, blushing at the end of her sentence, as if she had made an erotic remark.

We stood up by the entrance in a daze germane to people who, after long desiring each other, come to a sudden halt the moment they notice how close they actually are to obtaining what they have so badly craved. Though the intensity and frequency of our acquaintance had been limited to running into each other now and then, and chatting about this and that, I had long been aware of how deeply attracted she was to me. Hers is a face that cannot mask secrets. Still however, I hadn't been expecting this 'thing' between us to run its course so speedily, so effortlessly...

Taking her face between my palms, I caressed that tiny, azure *hizma*. 'I've made chicken with ground walnuts,' she breathed when she drew back, trying to urge me to continue not from

319

where we left off kissing, but where we had been reservedly conversing. 'I hope you'll like it.'

Oblivious to her forged reticence, oblivious to the dinner table, I steered her inside into the bedroom. To my surprise, she was at ease. So was I. Couples wise enough not to harbour future expectations from one another keep little back when making love. Nevertheless, late at night when we sat down at the table, it felt as if, though devoid of a common future, we might have shared a common past, as if we had been living together for a long time, sharing the same house...and it seemed to me we both enjoyed this illusion deep down... For regardless of where you stand on the matter, a man abandoned by his wife and a mistress unhappy with the husband of another have a communal need in the worst way; to be assured that their constant disappointment with the marital institution does not stem from their failures, and that they could make it work with another person.

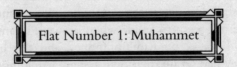

There were seventeen steps on the stairs at the entrance gate of the school. Upon reaching the sixteenth, counting out loud, Muhammet turned back with a wee bit of hope...but once again the miracle he ached for failed to happen. His mother did not disappear. Instead there she was waiting tenaciously at the same spot, leaning against the bolted garden gate with her swollen belly and all her weight, looking after him with the touching melancholy of someone at the dock saying farewell to her beloved on the parting boat. The moment she saw Muhammet looking at her, Meryem's face lit up with a smile compounded from a third each of compassion, pride and tenderness. She flapped both arms simultaneously, gesticulating with some sort of a peculiar athletic motion. Seeing that much of an effort there one would think she were trying to grab her son's attention from amidst an immense crowd. Yet, since the last weeks of the second semester, she was the only mother among all mothers of the eight hundred and forty-eight kids in the elementary school who insisted on bringing her child to school in the mornings and waiting at the gate until the bell rang – a policy she had been pursuing since receiving the news that Muhammet played truant. This, in turn, meant there would from now on be a twenty-five minute delay in the distribution of newspaper and bread to Bonbon Palace. So far nobody had complained. Madam Auntie did not buy bread anyhow, she seemed to nibble like a bird. As for Hygiene Tijen, every morning from her window she lowered a basket into which the grocer's apprentice left one of those breads that came wrapped-up, touched by no one. The Blue Mistress did not eat bread, so as not to gain weight, and the bachelor professor at Number 7 did not seem to be expecting consistent service since even he himself did not seem to know when he would come in or go out. Sidar, because he had no money, and the hairdressers, because they had set up their own system, would not mind this delay. That left only two flats and Meryem was definitely not going to risk her son's education for the sake of those two.

Shrivelling more and more with every wave of his mother, as if he was being hammered on the head, Muhammet finally reached the seventeenth step and billowed through the pitch black door of the primary school. The lunch bag in his hand got heavy, his backpack even more so. He looked around in vain for something to kick. As the ring echoed in the hall for the last time, he entered into his classroom to take his place among the thirty-two students.

Contrary to his fears, the first class passed without a single incident. The bully of a bench-mate in front had turned his back at him, fully concentrating on the writing on the blackboard, looking utterly unruffled; as if it wasn't him who had made a habit of slapping Muhammet at least twice a day. Muhammet eyed gratefully this back that was twice the size of his. He just wished it could always stay like this. If only he could be bench-mates not with this overgrown child but with his back instead. Dropping his shoulders, he crouched behind the sturdy back and, with the comfort of knowing he would not be spotted from this angle, surveyed his surroundings. The windows of the classroom were painted grey halfway up to prevent the students from looking outside but from the fissures and flakes on the painting one could still spot the blue sky. Then he turned his gaze to the puffy ribbons of the girl at the board and the sharp, pinkish fingernails of the teacher whose veins would swell up whenever she yelled. He thought that the girl at the board and the teacher matched well. After all, if the girl failed to give the right answer and the teacher yet again stuck one of those long fingernails of hers into the unsuccessful student's earlobe, there would be no big difference: the girl's ears were pierced anyhow. In spite of this, the ones whose ears were pulled the most happened to be boys. Until now, Muhammet's ears were pulled a-plenty, and each time he cared less about the pain than ending up with his ears pierced against his will. Having lived the first six years of his life on earth long-haired like a girl, he did not want to spend the rest of his life with his ears pierced like a girl. Hoisting his fears up the flagpole, he inadvertently flinched and it was precisely then that whatever happened happened. The back next to him abruptly turned around, now transforming into a chubby, beet-red, sulky face. Grinning insolently, his bench mate bulldozed Muhammet.

Since the very beginning of school, every day without exception, Muhammet had dreamed about running away. Yet as he gritted his teeth in pain now it was not fleeing the place that he pined for but to perish altogether. If only a disaster would happen right at that moment, a real bad earthquake for instance, so that the earth would split open, leaving not a single stone upon stone or a head on a body, smashing to smithereens the grades in the teacher's notebook, the gold stars of the girl at the board and the limbs of his bench mate, along with his elbows, slaps, insults…if only they would scatter on all sides never to unite again…

While Muhammet had closed his eyes and was dreaming about the worst possible disaster imaginable, a siren ripped the air apart. There was some scurrying and dash outside in the hallway, doors were banged. They all stood still as the teacher stared at the students and the students stared back. In next to no time the door was harshly shoved and in walked a dainty woman with piercing glances behind her pince-nez. She smiled first at the teacher, then at the students and, with a courtesy filtered through a fine sieve, 'Dear teacher, beloved students…' she bayed as if delivering joyful tidings, 'This is an earthquake drill.'

As soon as the dainty woman finished her sentence, three men looking startlingly alike, all stout and with droopy moustaches, dashed into the room. They had chick-yellow helmets and T-shirts with 'Negligence kills, not earthquakes' written on them. Remarkably agile, they took out one by one the various tools they had brought in their bags and hung posters of all sizes on the board hooks. Curtains were drawn shut and a slide machine started to light up the wall. Muhammet caught his breath as he followed with excitement the slides brought to life one by one with the dusty beam of light slashing through the darkness.

After the last slide was shown and the curtains pulled open, the dainty woman clapped her hands to announce how the drill was to take place. There would be two phases. During the first phase, the students were required to cower under the benches and, pretending everything around them was shaking violently, wait there calmly and courageously with their heads in between their arms. As for the second phase, that was meant to teach them how to evacuate a building in the shortest possible time. So the siren pealed, and all thirty-two of the thirty-two students went under the wooden benches giggling non-stop.

Muhammet rolled up into a ball to squeeze inside the morsel of space left from his bench-mate. Minutes later, he too got out from under the bench with the others to line up in pairs to evacuate the classroom. Yet since his bench-mate did not care to hold his hand as bench mates were supposed to, Muhammet could not join the chain of children. The two kids standing up at the corner away from the others must have drawn the attention of the dainty woman for she suddenly blundered out in a voice bubbling with delight, 'Will you two please come this way? We were looking for two brave boys.'

While all the other kids flowed out into the hallway streaming in perfect order, Muhammet looked longingly after them, his eyes brimming with anxiety. When the classroom totally emptied out, he realized the dainty woman and the teacher had departed too. Before he could find something to kick at, to diffuse the resentment of being left out of the game, and alone with the bully of a bench mate to boot, the three moustached men snapped into action. One picked up a stretcher, the other took out a longish rope and the third unfolded a blanket. They then laid the children down on the stretcher side by side, enveloped them in the blanket and tied them up tightly. Of the four separate ropes, two were fastened onto hooks and dangled down from the window, while the other two were tied to the doorknob of the classroom.

'Don't be afraid,' rasped one of the men and then let his voice dwindle as if letting slip a secret: 'We are going to lower you down from the window.'

Five minutes later, when Muhammet had finally mustered-up enough courage to open his eyes, he found himself sixteen metres above ground on top of a stretcher with his arms and legs tightly tied up inside a smelly blanket side by side with the boy he liked the very least in this world. All the children had gathered in the garden, watching them from below, cheering in unison. The sky was a clear blue; a lumpy cloud swayed lazily above. As the ropes were loosened from above, the stretcher came down in jolts, but no matter how much it was lowered, it never seemed to get closer to the ground.

'I bet you must be shitting in your pants,' his bench-mate croaked. So close was the boy's beet-red face that Muhammet inhaled the smell of his breath. He opened his mouth to declare that he was not afraid at all, but before finding a chance to say anything, spit rolled into his mouth. The other boy burst out laughing. Wriggling to get rid of the spit in his mouth Muhammet managed to spew out, only not to his right into the open space, but to the left onto the face of his foe.

This was not something the other boy had expected at all. Once he had got over the initial confusion, he counterattacked by replacing the spit gun with a spit machine gun. Though they had meanwhile dropped closer to the ground, none of those clustered below seemed to be aware of what was going on up here, three and a half metres above ground, 'Now watch what's coming,' the beet-face snarled. 'You'll descend in the middle of everyone with green sputum on your face!' Muhammet hurried to avert his head but was too late. He felt a globule stick onto the middle of his forehead, stay still for a second or two, slowly ooze down, and then start sliding toward his nose. He almost threw up. The stretcher went down another half a metre. Now one could clearly see the faces of those down below. The children were gleefully cheering-on their heroes sent from the sky. Struggling in vain to free himself from the straps, Muhammet felt like crying. Though he tried hard to convince himself that the liquid on his nose could not be sputum and that the beet-face had bluffed, little did he succeed. The stretcher slid down another half a metre, the cloud wafted and Muhammet made a wish: that if the earth ever had a post, it had better collapse now and bring on the end of the world... Before he could complete his wish, however, both children were brusquely hurled, as if to fling them out of their places, first to the front, then back and then again to the front. Screams rose from below, Muhammet closed his eyes, the rope on the left side broke off and the stretcher turned upside down, nose-diving to the ground from a height of two and a half metres. The beet-face let out a wail.

'Are they dead? Are they dead?' shrieked the classroom teacher with the pinkish fingernails, the veins swelling up on her neck.

As the earthquake officials tried to rein in the children who flocked around the victims like chicken running to feed, one of those with the droopy moustaches turned the stretcher over carefully only to meet two pairs of eyes opened wide as saucers, one with pain, the other with fear.

'Is there sputum on my face?' asked Muhammet when he succeeded in breathing out a sound.

The official, ashen with worry, gazed at the child's face distractedly, almost dreamily, and shook his head. It was then that Muhammet felt a surge of vigour inside. It had been a bluff after all! Once the ropes were untied and the smelly blanket lifted, he sat up on the stretcher with pride. While the beet-face whose leg had been broken was carried off to the hospital with the same stretcher, Muhammet was enjoying the sweet syrupy taste of bravery for the first time in his life.

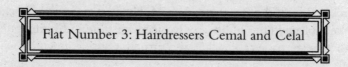

'Oh, I'm dying to learn about the man who put up the saint writing on the wall. Is he pulling one over us, or has he lost his mind, if only I could tell! I swear to God, I can't wait to see what's going to happen next. Last night, my good old *bulgur* didn't appear. I have been waiting for her. I guess I've gotten so used to her dumping garbage into our mouths, I'll miss the woman if she doesn't show up anymore. Could it be, I wonder, that she has taken that writing on the wall seriously. Not that it's impossible. This place is Turkey! The West long finished exploring the moon; they are now busily dividing Mars up into parcels and will soon clone humans. What about us, what have we been doing in the meantime? Finding holy saints in our backyards! Bless him, but is he a saint or some sort of a flower that sprouted from the soil? After that we ask in vain why on earth the European Union does not take us in? What would they want us for? Only when they are running short of saints will the Europeans ask us to join.'

A few flimsy giggles followed but Cemal did not seem to be offended at all with such limited backing from his audience.

'I swear to God, it wouldn't come as a surprise if one of these days we had a red alarm meeting at Bonbon Palace: an emergency meeting with a special 'holy saint agenda', in the house of our building manager Mr. Hadji Hadji! Sonny, why don't you spray a little!'

The pungent smell of the bug spray they had amply used last night all over the place had still not dispersed. In the morning, they had encountered dozens of dead bugs on the floor. All were swept away and dumped into the garbage can, before the first customers showed up.

'So here we are in the flat of Mr. Hadji Hadji, sitting around the table side by side,' Cemal voiced his vision as he emptied the wicker basket for rollers and turned it upside down. 'We are all there, nice and neat, in full gear. I tell you, even Hygiene Tijen has managed to make it out of her haven, perched at the corner of a chair, ready to explode at any moment.' Cemal took a hairspray with gilded trim and placed it on one end of the basket. 'And here is that penniless student in the basement, next to him that overgrown dog of his. Not that they care about the saint, these two are there to fill up their stomachs *gratis*.'

He stuck a fine-toothed comb through a hole in the basket and right next to that, to represent Gaba he placed a chunky, carroty, notched hair-roller.

'Oh, what is being served?' marvelled the blonde with a cast eye who came to have her hair dyed once a week, never convinced that she need not have it done so often. She was now inspecting the wicker basket curiously, as if waiting for a thumb-sized child to spring out of it to entertain her.

'You seem to have confused this meeting with a tea-party, honey,' snapped Cemal. 'We are talking about a serious apartment meeting here.'

'But if you're making up a story, we would like to hear the details too,' protested the Blue Mistress from the corner where she sat.

'All right, all right,' Cemal thundered, feeling no need to hide his pleasure in managing to attract the Blue Mistress's attention. 'So be it. Mr. Hadji Hadji's daughter-in-law has baked us a spinach *börek* and they serve a *samovar* of tea with it. Are you satisfied now?'

'Yes, yes,' nodded the women, chuckling, but no sooner had they given their consent that an objection was voiced: 'No, it's not okay!' It was the clerk of the Criminal Court, whom everyone deemed the most informed woman of the neighbourhood, making money out of putting down on paper the most criminal features of people's most private lives. Once a month she dropped by to have her hair coloured dark chestnut. When certain of being the centre of attention, she leaned back and superciliously recited the data in hand: 'For one thing, the daughter-in-law works at the box office of a movie theatre from early morning till late evening five days a week. She has no time to roll the dough into pastry. Even if she did have the time, though, let me assure you she still wouldn't do so. That woman must have more affection for her sins than for her father-in-law. She wouldn't even lift a finger for him.'

Cemal frowned at this over-informed customer of his. 'If that is the case, there is no pastry at the table. Just pure, plain hot tea. Okay? Can I now please continue onto the main subject?'

'But it doesn't make sense,' said the Blue Mistress with her sauciest smile, determined to force the limits of Cemal's fondness for her. 'Then there would be a logical flaw in the story. You had claimed that the student in the basement and the huge doggie were there to gorge themselves. Now you'll have to oust them.'

Cemal stared crossly at the chunky, carroty, notched hair-roller and the thin, long fine-toothed comb as if deciding upon their fate. 'OK, I surrender,' he bumbled, giving a wink at the Blue Mistress. Running to the kitchen he returned with half of the *simit* he had bought in the morning and placed it on top of the roller basket. 'For this special meeting, our respected manager Mr. Hadji Hadji has picked up a box each of sweet and salty canapés from the patisserie. He has also lined up sesame sticks into oval plates. Is this pleasing enough? Now are you all satisfied?'

'Yes, yes,' chortled the women, looking at each other and then at the Criminal Court clerk for a final approval.

'Frankly I would never believe, not in this life, that that stingy man would go to this much expense but let's assume he did, for the sake of the story,' decreed the woman, lifting up an eyebrow plucked dreadfully thin.

Now that he had full permission, Cemal excitedly plunged into the game, lining up all the remaining neighbours. The no-alcohol, extra-volume hair foam with nourishing vitamin B was the university professor at Flat Number 7; the hair dryer was Madam Auntie at Flat Number 10; the electrical hair-curler was the Russian housewife in Flat Number 6; the colouring brush and the pair of scissors were the husband and wife heading-up the Firenaturedsons family across from them and the manicure file was their young, despondent daughter.

After a brief pause, Cemal found the brush with the bone handle to be suitable for the manager. Lastly, he fetched the transparent, glittery container with bright blue gel inside: 'And this one here is the graceful young lady in Flat Number 8,' he cooed. As the Blue Mistress responded to the compliment with a composed smile, all the other women stirred nervously in their chairs.

'Oh, I shouldn't forget to place Celal and me. We of course have to be the same.'

From the haircare set on the shelf, Cemal picked two multi-vitamin sachets of hair repair with keratin, locating them side by side. 'Yes, this is exactly how we've lined up. Mr. Hadji Hadji explains why we're having this special meeting,' he grabbed the brush with the bone handle and coughed pretentiously to silence his audience. 'In case some of you have not seen it yet let me inform you all a saint's tomb has been found in our garden. Given this situation, we urgently have to make new arrangements.'

'Hmm…but sir, can a holy saint sprout from earth like a flower?' spoke up one of the multi-vitamin hair repairers with keratin. Turning to his customers over his shoulder, Cemal footnoted with a whisper: 'That's me!'

'Yeah, we guessed so,' chorused the women.

'You, as individuals, are free to believe or disbelieve. We are not obliged to convince you of the saints existence either. However, if you want democracy to flourish in this country, you are bound to show some respect to other people's beliefs,' decreed the brush with the bone handle. 'If we are all of the same opinion on this matter, there are specific agenda items we have to settle without further ado. The very first item on our agenda is the following question: whose holy saint is the one lying in our garden? You can't just call it such and be done with it. Every saint helps a certain segment of the populace in our country. Some are the saints of the sailors at sea; others care for the soldiers on land. Several saints heal women who cannot become pregnant, several others help the lepers. One should always go to a saint relevant to his particular problem. If the old maid mistakenly pays a visit to the Saint of the Bedridden, the most she can obtain will be an extra hop and a jump.'

'Someone should record all this in the minutes,' piped-up the clerk of the Criminal Court, lifting up her other eyebrow.

'All right,' said Cemal, and after brief consideration, appointed the manicure file for the job. 'Write this down missie, the first item on the agenda is to find out whose father this honourable saint is.'

'How do we know that? Maybe the saint is a woman,' objected the Blue Mistress.

'Nonsense,' roared the brush with the bone handle.

'Why? Couldn't a woman be a saint?' the Blue Mistress asked obstinately, without taking her eyes off the gel container that represented her. And since she had the floor to herself, she delivered a speech there and then: 'Plenty of pious people have emerged from among women. Let's first count the exalted Ayse and Fatma. Then there is Rabia, for instance. Of course, Mother Kadıncık is also notable, as is Karyagdı Hatun. There is Huma Hatun, the mother of Sultan Mehmed the Conqueror. Mevlana's mother, Mümine Hatun, is another example...not to mention the 'Seven *Filles*.'

The women lined up in front of the mirror turned to the Blue Mistress in bewilderment. She had too much knowledge on religious matters, way too much for a mistress. Cemal seemed to be the one who was most impressed. He gaped at her with adoration, as if the matchless concubine Canayakın who had stunned everyone in the audience of Caliph Harun al-Rashid with not only her beauty but also her wisdom, had been reborn in – of all the places in Istanbul in the year 2002 – Bonbon Palace.

'Then jot down this, missie,' proclaimed the brush with the bone handle to the manicure file. 'Our first agenda item is to find out whose father or mother this holy saint is. In order to carry out the necessary research, we hope our honoured university professor will not withhold his valuable help from us.' The extra-volume, no-alcohol hair foam with nourishing vitamin B, kind of stirred. He seemed pleased with the esteem bestowed upon him.

'Now let's proceed onto the second agenda item. Ladies and gentlemen, now that there is a saint in our garden, we have to confer extra care on our everyday manners. With this purpose in mind, I myself have prepared a list, a list of things we must strictly refrain from doing. With your permission, I'm reading aloud:

"*Article 1:* At night-time, residents should not extend their feet in the direction of the holy saint. Those beds with the foot side facing the garden have to be turned around immediately.
Article 2: Residents should not go around naked in their flats.
Article 3: From now on, rugs and carpets needing to be whacked should not be hung outside the windows facing the garden and nothing should be flung down from these windows either.'"

'But how could that be?' squawked the gilt-trimmed hairspray.

'Please do not interrupt!' scolded the brush with the bone handle.

"*Article 4*: From this time forth, no clothes shall be hung out to dry from the windows facing the garden.

Article 5: From this day forward no hair shall be cut within the boundaries of this apartment building."

'But sir, please take some pity on us, if we don't cut hair, we'll go hungry. This is our livelihood,' spoke up one of the two multi-vitamin hair repairers with keratin. Cemal whispered another footnote winking at his customers: 'That was Celal!'

'We guessed so,' trolled the women in unison.

'It absolutely can't be done. Don't forget that of all the flats in this building it is yours that happens to be the closest to the grave of the honourable saint. As such, the deepest reverence is incumbent upon you. You can no longer open the windows to sing popular songs, shake out hair or clip nails, just like you cannot cut hair or pluck eyebrows whilst looking at the tomb of the saint. If you cannot abide by the rules, go open your beauty parlour somewhere else.

"*Article 6*: From now on, the flesh, hair, feather and the like of animals such as horses, donkeys shall not enter into this apartment building…and this includes dogs as well…"

The fine toothed comb blurted out from the top of the roller basket: 'And why is that so, may I ask?'

'For the very reason that according to our religion dogs are reprehensible,' snapped the brush with the bone handle. However, realizing at this point he had barely any knowledge to support his claim, Cemal stared at the Blue Mistress for help. She spoke up as if waiting for an opportunity: 'See the Araf sura in the Qur'an: if you go at it, it breathes dangling its tongue, if you let it loose, it breathes dangling its tongue. In addition, let's not forget that Mevlana too calls human greed canine.'

'None of these apply to my dog. Gaba isn't Turkish. He's Swiss!' shouted the fine toothed comb.

The women lined up in front of the mirror looked at the chunky, carroty, notched hair roller in sympathy.

'But Mr. Hadji Hadji, as you already know the "Seven Sleepers" in heaven had dogs as well,' said the Blue Mistress, taking pity.

'Okay, okay,' the brush with the bone handle surrendered. 'But from now on, that dog will take a bath every day. There won't be even a single flea on it. No fleas in the apartment! Needless to say, no lice either. We've got to get rid of these bugs as well. All the flats will be fumigated from top to bottom.

"*Article* 7: From now on beggars, vendors, garment peddlers, pastry sellers and such shall not be let into the building."

'Very appropriate, sir,' chorused the husband and wife of the colouring brush and pair of scissors.

'And last but not least…

"*Article 8*: From now on, the garbage of Bonbon Palace shall be collected regularly. A circle with a thirty metre diametre shall be drawn around the holy saint and not a bit of garbage will be dumped within. Maximum attention will be paid to keeping the apartment building sparkling clean. It shall be spick and span all around. Whatever needs to be done to get rid of this disgusting smell engulfing Bonbon Palace shall be done at once. All this time we've been suffocated by the putrid smell. Let's at least make sure the praiseworthy saint doesn't suffer the way we did."

Cemal suddenly realized he had forgotten to include Meryem. He quickly placed an eyelash curler onto the basket. However, just as he was getting it ready to speak up, an ear-splitting noise broke out in the back. Celal, whose face revealed how little he had relished the ongoing game, had dropped a hairdryer. When all the eyes turned on him, he flashed crimson with embarrassment. Without picking up the dryer, he hurried to the door stammering: 'I'm going out, I need to get some air.'

'With all due respect, Cemal,' said the blonde with one eye cast, once the door closed behind Celal, 'There have probably never been twins with as different dispositions as you two. If you had at least one single thing in common, for God's sake.'

As a bristly discomfort fell like drizzle on the parlour, each and every one of the performers around the basket turned into the inert items they once had been.

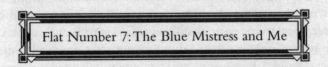

Flat Number 7: The Blue Mistress and Me

I sure hadn't been expecting the Blue Mistress. It turned out she had applied bug spray all over her house, so she asked if she could stay at my place until the smell faded away. I told her I was eternally grateful to the bugs. She laughed. Her grin curled into a quizzical smile, when she caught sight of the mammoth plate of cheese and smoked salmon on the table inside.

'I'm coming into money,' I said. 'Meryem stopped by this morning. The woman at Number 9 had sent her as an emissary. She wants me to give English lessons to her daughter. I wasn't interested at first. The last time I had given such lessons I was a student myself, but then, for some reason unknown, the woman offered a hefty fee per hour.'

'It's probably because she hates the idea of her daughter going out of the apartment building.'

'Whatever! We'll have the lessons at their house.'

'Perhaps she preferred to have the teacher from within the building,' she beamed before gulping down a large piece of cheese. 'Or perhaps, she too has fallen for you. Just like me!'

When she smiles the scar on her left cheek becomes more visible. I like caressing that scar. Slowly, I pulled her hand and dragged her inside. I like the taste her tongue leaves on mine.

'Do you know I was raised by my grandfather,' she mumbled as she grabbed my fingers stroking her cheek and lifted them to her lips. I lit a cigarette and leaned back. I've always enjoyed pillow talk. Thanks to the Blue Mistress, I had started after all that time to sleep again in the bed that was 'too big' for me.

'He was such a witty, well-bred person. My father and mother never got along, there were always rows at the house. They got divorced when I was four years old. Both got remarried within a year. Then my grandfather said to ma: 'Let me look after this poor child. You set up your house, come and see your daughter whenever you want.' Ma accepted. I'm so glad she did. I loved grandpa immensely. If he had not passed on at such an early age, I would've been at an utterly different place now. Anyway, after grandpa died, I was left alone with grandma. I liked her too, but not the way I liked grandpa. I returned to my mother's house. Everyone makes fun of Mrs. Tijen for not being able to leave her house, yet I, at such a young age, almost never left the house, not for two long years, would you believe it? Not because of a cleaning sickness or anything like that. Frankly, I don't know why I couldn't leave. I wouldn't even step onto the street, let alone go to school. Not that I wasn't curious about the world outside, but I guess I pined for a different sort of place. Both my mother and stepfather tried hard to encourage me to go out. Odd isn't it? Normally youngsters feel restricted by their parents. It was just the opposite at our house.

Anyway, one morning around the breakfast table, my mother and stepfather were talking about how to pay the phone bill, I heard myself say: 'Give it to me, I'll pay it'. Their eyes were wide with astonishment, I took the bill and threw myself outside. It had been so long since I had last left the house, I swear I wobbled like a drunk at first. I entered the post office. There was a line. I kept waiting and waiting, finally only a few people remained in front of me. That's when I first saw him. He was the officer taking the bills, behind the glass. He wasn't handsome like you, but his eyes were one of a kind. Could one's pupils be tinged mauve? His were. When at last it was my turn, he asked for the bill, I held it out. He gave me back my change, stamped the bill, and then looked at me carefully as if he wanted to see through me. I felt a chill run down my spine. 'Have a nice day', he said. I couldn't breathe a word. In that state I found myself back home. Next morning, I rushed outside early, straight to the post office. There was a line even at that hour. When it was my turn, with my heart in my mouth, I held out the already paid bill. He looked at me perplexed, and I too looked at him to see if his pupils were really mauve. They indeed were. The people waiting behind me started to grumble. He had a hard time hiding his amusement.'

I couldn't help thinking of Ayshin. In her entire life, she will never fall for a man just because his pupils are tinged mauve. Ayshin's love is like the helm of bureaucracy. She files her correspondence, makes calculations, keeps records, deducts the expenses from the income and thus maintains a colossal archive. She never forgets a quarrel; not only does she not forget, she makes sure it is not forgotten as well. If we were married, I wondered for a moment, would the Blue Mistress be like her? Not likely. There is a stupendously rowdy, almost animal-like aspect to the way she relates to life. She is only twenty-two years old, though, conceivably she'll change. Maybe as soon as she gets married, she too will rapidly turn into some replica of Ayshin.

'What happened after that?' I asked.

'The rest is rotten. We went around together. My mother was mad but who listened to her? I couldn't really tell if I was in love or not but I must have fallen badly for him. He wanted to get married right away and though I didn't, I guess I lacked the courage to say no. It was a capsule of a neighbourhood, wallowing in gossip, how can you not marry the man you date? Anyway, we got engaged and that's when he started to change, becoming a different person almost. He was such an unhappy soul. I was unhappy too, possibly, but my despondency was targeted at myself alone whereas his was targeted at everyone but himself…not that he was malicious… That was the problem at any rate. He wasn't a sly man, but the man he was died to become one. He would not utter a single pleasant word to me, not any longer. He was constantly complaining about the post office, its managers and, of course, bills. Still that was not the reason why we separated.' Her lips curved into an edgy smile. 'You know, it was actually a horse that caused us to separate?' Watching the confusion on my face she gave another laugh, this time even edgier.

'One day, while strolling together, I saw a horse and carriage. You may find this silly but I'm gonna tell it all the same. You see, grandpa was a remarkable man, so out of the ordinary. 'If you can't manage to die before death, the life you live and the death you die will be nothing but an obligation,' he used to say. He cared for neither the *houris* of heaven nor the flames of hell. He had this habit of saluting every single animal he saw on the street. "Perhaps that's an old friend of yours there, it would be awfully impolite not to pay your respects," he would claim. "When one departs from this life, he doesn't actually leave, but comes back to earth, at times as a human, at other times as an animal. Every time we take on a different form, whether it's a donkey, swan, butterfly or frog, it's all up to chance. No need to become embittered…" To prevent such resentment, our memories instead of our souls will die upon death. So that we won't be able to keep track of all the creatures we had previously been. You know the most vivid incidents from my childhood were when grandpa and I used to wander the streets greeting every animal we met. We would yell greetings at cats, dogs, sparrows, donkeys and crickets. "How do you do my dear friend?" shouted grandpa and I imitated: "How do you do my dear friend?" How fun it all was!'

I gingerly caressed the roundness of her belly, now hidden under the sheet tightly wound around her.

'Anyway, as soon as I saw this horse on the street, I unconsciously greeted it. When he saw me talking to the horse, the Mauve Prince started to make fun of me…mocked in such awful ways, hurt me so bad… He kept going on and on. In the following days, whenever he saw a donkey on the road, he would sneer: "There, run, kiss the hand of your grandfather!" It was then that truth struck me: I didn't love the Mauve Prince! The things that I cherished were of little value to him. "How am I gonna spend the rest of my life with him then?" I asked myself. Upon hearing of my decision to break up with him, he refused to take it seriously. "Oh, you are so touchy," he smirked, thinking my mood would change in a few days and when he saw that it did not, bullying was his next move. Such threats! One night, we were having dinner at home; he came to the door, stinking drunk. He hurled insults at my stepfather. Then he grabbed me by the arm and pulled me outside. He smelt so strongly of liquor, it was as if he'd fallen right into the bottle. "Hey, look here, if you leave me, I'll cut up your face!" That's exactly what he said. "Don't bother, I'll do it myself," I replied. I know you won't believe me. I can't believe myself either. I don't know why I spoke like that or why I did what I did. I was seventeen years old then, but it still happens to me from time to time. Whenever in pain, I do such things without thinking…harming myself…Not intentionally; afterwards I'm amazed, I say, "Goodness how did I do this?" But my mind is blank while doing such things. You know what I mean? If I gave a thought to it before doing it, I probably couldn't do it, right?

I smiled. One end of naivety leads to negligence, the other to innocence. The negligence part can be flawed but there is probably not much in this world as alluring as innocence.

'My mother and stepfather were listening from behind the door, ready to intervene if something happened, fearing harm from the Mauve Prince. They had no clue what I was about to do. Of course, I didn't have a knife or anything. There was only this steel pin in my hair bun – sharp enough – back then my hair was so thick, no other hairpin would do. Anyway, that's what I used to slash my left cheek. Though I couldn't see my face at the moment I could see the Mauve Prince's: ashen with horror, almost lemon yellow. He started yelling and shrieking to stop me. My mother ran to the noise, she too let out a scream. Only then did I understand I must be in pretty bad shape, cut up bad. My stepfather started hitting the Mauve Prince, thinking he was the one responsible, and the other didn't even defend himself, as he was still in shock! While my stepfather was giving him a thrashing, my mother and I jumped in a cab, straight to the emergency room. I was amazed that it didn't hurt at all. Apparently pain only comes later. There was a fatherly physician at the emergency room, almost a soulmate of grandpa. He talked sweetly, amiably, trying to get information out to learn who had done this to me. When he sensed the truth, he was livid with rage, but even his rebukes were sweet, I tell you. They gave me narcotics, sewed up the wound. Just as I was leaving the hospital, he held my hand. "My crazy little girl, now that you have transcended the threshold of sanity and sliced up this beautiful face of yours, do not ever go back to the meadow of reason and common sense. What is even worse than slicing up your own face without remorse is the remorse that follows. In that case you'll really suffer and suffer for nothing. So be true to yourself, remain as crazy as you have been once the sutures are removed, promise?" I promised. We shook hands. It was lucky for me that he did such a neat job. Any other doctor, I tell you, would have sewn my face up like a sack. Still a scar remains, that doesn't go away.'

I didn't know what to say. Her story was not quite what I expected to hear. To fall in love with a person is tantamount to retrieving repressed stories from their house of sorrow – stories that have never seen daylight. As for staying in love, it is to nose-dive, once having heard those stories, into the house of dreams of your beloved only to stay put even upon encountering other stories that are far worse. I had acted impetuously concerning the Blue Mistress. She was not blue. At least, her blueness was not as lucent as it seemed at first glance. I pulled her toward me. She snuck closer, fidgeted until she had made her head comfortable on my chest. Then she silently, softly let herself go.

'I loved the Mauve Prince because of who he was but then he pretended to be someone else. Never lie to me, please?

Everything should be what it is!'

I just nodded. A person who claims to abhor lies, if not telling one herself will inexorably bring bad luck to those around her, just like a smashed mirror. One who asks never to be told a lie actually yearns for it. It's similar to showing a gun in a film – sooner or later it has to be put into use. Still, I did not want to demur. Before long, she fell asleep under the light seeping through the window. She was not that beautiful but her face had a sort of magic. Watching her always gave me great pleasure.

I got up. Groping around for something to wear in the dark, I turned on the lamp. The sheet covering the Blue Mistress had slid across, exposing her right leg. Only then did it occur to me for the very first time that we had always made love either in the dark or half-dressed; her naked body still remained a mystery.

The upper part of her leg was covered with scarlet stripes of scars. Lined up vertically next to one another like those five line clusters of lines we imagine are used in prisons to count the passing, not-passing days. I took a closer look. The majority did not seem to be very deep, as if slashed open in a hurry. However, one among them was quite deep and seemed to have been opened more recently, having had no time yet to heal.

★★★

02:22 a.m.: She turned onto her face with a clipped moan. I covered her body and turned off the light. *Rakı* would have gone down well at that moment. As soon as I turned on the kitchen light, several cockroaches vanished like greased lightning. Sooner or later I too would have to have the house fumigated. I sliced plenty of white cheese and melon. On the cheese, I poured the olive oil the Blue Mistress had brought and thyme, a great deal of thyme. The olive oil merchant would probably not want to know that the bottles he carried to his little mistress were consumed by another man.

I stepped out to the balcony. Careful not to squash the cluster of ants busily shouldering home the bulky corpse of a black beetle, I pulled my chair closer to the railing and lit a cigarette. How many more cuts were there on her body? I did not know what had opened up those wounds... Was it a razor or a knife? Or a hair pin? I glanced at the garbage bags piled up by the garden wall down below. Nothing had changed. The sour smell of garbage was still with us.

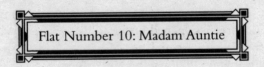

Flat Number 10: Madam Auntie

Madam Auntie had been waiting for hours by the seaside together with collectors like her. With each gust of *lodos*, that enraged southwest wind, the waves brought bits and pieces, torn sails, broken oars, compasses with shattered pointers, rudders that had lost their course, the letters spilled from the names of the boats left behind from those voyages that were never to reach a port of tranquility and those travellers long disembarked.

The sea, once satisfied with playing with those plastic balls or inflatable beds the waves had long ago snatched away whilst you were on vacation and the straw mats or hats the wind had carried far away from their rightful places, brings and delivers them all to different shores.

Next to collectors like her, Madam Auntie was waiting to collect what the sea would ferry to the shore.

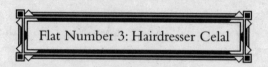

Flat Number 3: Hairdresser Celal

As soon as Celal left the beauty parlour, he blasted through the back streets right out to the avenue. After walking for about fifteen minutes in the crowd without a destination in mind, he entered a street lined up with five bars looking exactly alike. Though it was not at all his habit, he felt like having a beer. From among them, he chose one randomly and dashed in. Inside it was crammed full. He headed directly to the table closest to the door, as it was his habit to be as close to the exit as possible, asked for a beer, and also fries from the gaunt, runty waiter with gestures that displayed not only his distaste for his job but also the fact that his mind was occupied elsewhere.

As Celal waited to give his order, he spotted at the table across a swarthy man with three rings in three different shades of purple under his eyes, who either could not stand still or was simply on the verge of collapsing onto the table. The man's eyes were fixed on the *rakı* in front of him. Though not taking a single sip from his glass at present, it was only too evident that he had already had more than his share. He had not touched the fried anchovies either.

'Why-the-hell-are-you-star-ing-at-me-mate?' croaked the man all of a sudden, slurring the words hoarsely. Celal shrunk in his seat not knowing what to say but thankfully the waiter sprung up by his side at precisely that moment. 'Take it easy on him, brother,' the waiter advised, his attention fixed on the passers-by scurrying on the other side of the windows, as if he would like to be there among them rather than here in the bar.

'A harmless fellow. Just feeling down today.'

The beer was decent enough, the fries not at all. There were lengthy strings of mayonnaise and ketchup spurted all over them. Mayonnaise was fine but Celal couldn't stand ketchup. He got angry at himself for not having warned the waiter. Fidgeting edgily he turned aside so as not to have to face the table across.

One of the four strapping men at the next table had lifted his thumb up, as if trying to hitchhike from where he sat. He was a scary, brawny man with a hooked nose and a bottomless craving to have his opinions confirmed by others, given the frequency with which he asked 'Isn't that so?' Guzzling a swig of beer, he wiped his moustache with the back of his hand and blitzed his friends: 'What's up? Why are you all silent? We aren't the type to chicken out and run away! Isn't that so?' He brought down the blunt knife smeared with hotdog dressing he was holding, right in the middle of the table with a bang. 'You want a bet? Be my guest. This is how I make a bet, my man. We are no kids who'll bet on two marbles, three bottle caps, isn't that so? If I lose, I'll chop off this thumb and leave it at the table, but if you lose, the same rule goes for you, isn't that so?'

To this end, the knife on the table must not have been impressive enough, for he snapped the blade of a pocket-knife out in a flash, placing it next to the other one. Then he once again lifted his thumb up in the air, frozen like a statue. As the others gawked at the squat and chunky thumb aimed right at them, a chill swept over the table.

If it were any other time, afraid of a row Celal would have left the place, but today he felt like drinking. So he stayed and continued to drink in spite of the provocations of the drunk at the table across from him, the ketchup on the fries and the thumb terrorizing the next table.

Unused to alcohol, his eyes turned bloodshot before he was halfway through the second beer. Fixating his glance on the stains and cigarette burns of the tablecloth, he heaved a deep sigh. Why was his twin so different from him? They did not have one single thing in common. Why were they not alike in any way? And if they were so very dissimilar, why did they still work together? By the time the third beer had vanished, he had reached the decision to part ways with Cemal.

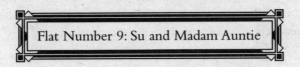

Flat Number 9: Su and Madam Auntie

Su was going to have her first English lesson tonight. 7:00 p.m. was the time agreed upon. She looked at the glow–in–the–dark watch her father had given her as a birthday gift: 4:35 p.m. There still was a lot of time. Bored stiff, she wandered around the house wherein everything had turned white. Her mother was sleeping, having once again spent the night awake and cleaning.

Opening the windows she peeped at the children playing down on the street. Though she watched them with interest, it did not even cross her mind to join them. She wouldn't want to be among them even if given the chance. Like all lonely children who had not a friend outside of school or buddy at home, who had mastered the art of being as well-behaved as expected and as docile as was not expected and who were now searching for ways to subvert the art, she too looked down on the street games with a hidden fury. Exceedingly careful not to make a sound, she sneaked outside. The intimacy that had blossomed with the old woman that day at the hairdresser was still fresh in her memory. Not that she had forgotten the ban on leaving Bonbon Palace, with the exception of attending school…but on second thoughts, the flat right across could not be considered 'outside', could it?

Thus, she did what she had never done before, daring to visit the neighbour next door. Not a sound was heard from the flat after she rang the bell. She pressed it again, this time a bit more tenaciously and was just about to give up when the door of Flat Number 10 opened.

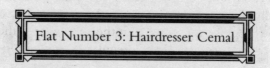

Flat Number 3: Hairdresser Cemal

Offended that his twin brother had not come back, Cemal saw off the last customer and turning over the beauty parlour to the apprentices, went out into the street feeling depressed. The night breeze felt good. He blasted through the back streets with speedy steps, as if sliding, and went right out onto the main street. After walking for about fifteen minutes in the crowd without even knowing where he was headed, he entered a street lined up with five bars, all looking exactly alike. Though not at all his habit, he felt like having a beer. Among all the bars on his way, he randomly chose one and dashed in. Inside it was crammed full. He headed directly to the table closest to the door as it was his habit to be as near to the exit as possible. He then asked for a beer and also fries from the gaunt, runty waiter with gestures that displayed not only his distaste for his job but also that his mind was hooked-up somewhere else.

As he waited to give his order, Cemal spotted at the table opposite a swarthy man with three rings in three different shades of purple under his eyes, who either could not stand still or was simply on the verge of collapsing onto the table. Still without shifting his gaze from the *rakı* in front of him, the man beckoned the waiter and whispered, his breath smelling profusely of liquor, to the latter's ear: 'Ask-him-why-he-is-back-let-us-know.' Upon seeing the confusion on the waiter's face, he impatiently clarified: 'Ask-him-why-did-he-leave-if-he-was-to-come-back-if-he-was-to-come-back-why-he-did-he-leave-if?'

By now Cemal had realized the man across was talking about him but he just could not gauge what on earth he was saying. He shrunk on his chair not knowing what to say, but thankfully the waiter sprung up by his side at precisely that moment: 'Take it easy on him, brother,' murmured the waiter in an exasperated voice. 'He's a regular customer. Just feeling down today, provokes whoever he sees, but he'll never behave shamefully.'

The beer was decent enough, the fries not at all. There were lengthy strings of mayonnaise and ketchup spurted on them. Ketchup was fine but Cemal would have none of that mayonnaise. He got angry at himself for not having warned the waiter. Fidgeting edgily he turned aside so as not to have to face the table opposite.

At the table to his right were four strapping men, one of whom had lifted up the thumb of his right hand which was bandaged in gauze with a lump of dried blood around the nail, and kept sitting like a statue. One of the others quietly murmured: 'Why don't you go home man, why are you still sitting around with a bandage and stitches?' The one next to him piped up in support: 'Anyhow, I do not have the foggiest idea why we came back here. We're probably the only ones on earth to return to the bar after a visit to the emergency room.'

'No!' thundered the big and burly man with the hooked nose, shaking his head vehemently. 'We made a bet, didn't we? Since I lost the bet, I'll face my punishment like a man. If I were scared of three stitches and one injection, I'd have to wear a skirt, isn't that so? Since we are here to drink; drink we shall! We will drink to my thumb. For if I weren't an honest man, if I hadn't kept my word, this thumb of mine would still be in one piece, isn't that so? But what did I do, I kept my word. So this knife wound is proof of my honesty, isn't it? Therefore if we drink to my thumb, we'll be drinking to honesty, isn't that so?' As the others reluctantly raised their glasses, a chill swept over the table.

If it were any other time, afraid of a row, Cemal would have left the place, but today he felt like drinking. So he stayed and continued to drink in spite of the provocations of the drunk at the table across from him, the mayonnaise on the fries and the thumb terrorizing the next table.

Unused to alcohol, his eyes turned bloodshot before he was halfway through the second beer. Fixating his glance on the stains and cigarette burns of the tablecloth, he heaved a deep sigh. Why was his twin so different from him? They did not have one single thing in common. Why were they not alike in any way? And if they were so very dissimilar, why did they still work together? By the time the third beer had vanished, he had reached the decision to part ways with Celal.

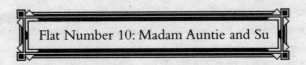

Flat Number 10: Madam Auntie and Su

When the doorbell rang, Madam Auntie was busy emptying out the bags she had brought in from the street. She stood still, completely startled. No one rang her door except Meryem who distributed bread every morning and collected the apartment maintenance fees once a month. At first she thought the bell might have been accidentally pushed downstairs, but when it rang again, this time even more tenaciously, a gnawing worry grabbed hold of her. She thrust into the bags everything she had taken out and then carried them all to the small room. Panting hard she closed shut the white door with the frosted glass separating the living room from the rest of the house and double locked it just in case. As for the key hanging on a purplish velvet ribbon, knowing too well she would lose it otherwise, she hung it around her neck. Giving the living room a last once over, she headed to the outside door feeling hesitant and anxious.

'Oh, was it you, Su?' she marvelled, relaxing visibly, as soon as she had opened the door. 'How are things my dear, are you comfortable with your hair short?'

Su, three and a half centimetres taller than Madam Auntie when in sneakers, nodded with a beaming smile. The old woman once again felt ill at ease with the exuberant joy of the child. Her discomfort gave way to considerable anxiety upon realizing the other was there to be invited in. Warily she threw a glance back at the living room. For years not a single visitor had stepped into this house. Not even her brother whom she loved so much. They would instead meet at a patisserie adorned with stained glass and famous for its age, where they would, every time without fail, have a piece of apple pie and drink two cappuccinos amidst the scent of cinnamon and whipped cream. Though still thinking of excuses that would send the child away without breaking her heart, she was drawn into the depths of the latter's large, black eyes. In spite of the cheeky smile stuck on her face, this child was extremely unhappy. She did not find it in her heart to send her away. Besides, she had taken all the necessary precautions, what harm could it cause to invite her in?

'Come, let's have coffee with milk,' she said, moving aside to let the child in.

'I don't like milk,' Su exclaimed.

'I've never met a child who liked milk,' Madam Auntie nodded. 'But since you're grown up enough to be a fifth grader, I thought you might enjoy drinking it.'

Faced with a line of reasoning she could barely object to, Su took her shoes off without a sound and unable to see a basket with disposable sanitary slippers at the entrance, realized in wonder that this was a house where one could walk in her socks.

'It smells worse here than at our house,' Su exclaimed, as soon as she entered the living room, and with an effervescent smile as if proud of making this observation, she started to scan her surroundings whilst whistling a song she heard on the minibus on the way to school every morning.

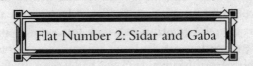

Flat Number 2: Sidar and Gaba

As he watched the items the girl took out one by one from her backpack Sidar felt a tension descend upon him: a turquoise toothbrush (so now there were two toothbrushes in the house), an unpalatable mug with popped-out eyeballs on it, some open and others shut (so now there two mugs in the house), one jojoba shampoo for frequently washed hair (so now there were two shampoos in the house), one box of tampons (there was none of these in the house), one towel (so now there were two towels in the house), a lot of books and CDs (so now there were a lot of books and CDs in the house).

This was not what he had in mind when agreeing to the girl's wish to stay here. He had said she could stay once in a while, not move in permanently. If this girl with beautifully solemn eyes and coppery hair wanted to feed Gaba with hazelnut wafers, lie down on this couch to watch the ceiling, make love to him, that was OK. He had no problem with her presence as long as there was only one Sidar, one Gaba and one girl. What disturbed him so much were these possessions of hers. The instant people infiltrated others' lives they seemed to feel obliged to bring their belongings along.

Yet, whenever Sidar rode the ochre cart of hashish or the chromatic horses of acid galloping into the uncharted maze of his brain, he would stumble at the threshold of the same old question: 'Which one?' That was the quandary he most feared when high. Failing to come up with an answer he would each time be catapulted into a bottomless torpor. If, say, there were two mugs in front of him, he could never decide which one to drink from; if there were two towels, he wouldn't know which one to wipe his face with; two books, two CD's…any option would be more than baffling. As long as there was more than one, the question of which fork or glass or plate or coffee-pot turned into a daunting enigma worthy of the ones asked in purgatory. Many a time he had been petrified with a sesame cookie in one hand and a creamy cookie in the other, only to realize he had been standing at the same spot without budging for forty minutes or so. Wrestling his way out of this tight bind, he would sink in deeper; whenever he felt inclined to choose one item, his thoughts would get stuck onto the one left behind. The objects would then, just like rowdy baby birds whose mother had still not returned, open their little mouths wide and shout in unison: 'Me! Me! Me Sidar! Please choose me!'

However, he did not want to choose. Everyone thought he had made a choice between Switzerland and Turkey in coming to live in the latter. That was not true. He had not decided on anything, he had merely arrived and maybe some day he would merely leave. Likewise, the act of suicide, which he had lately started to think about more often than ever, did not mean, as deemed by everyone, choosing death over life. Suicide was like Gaba, the one and only. He would merely commit it.

Of course, that credo was subject to scrutiny when not the why but the way of suicide was considered because in that case he would once again be confronted with the question 'Which one?' There was such an assortment of choices presenting so many different ways of committing suicide, and whenever Sidar rode the ochre cart of hashish or the chromatic horses of acid galloping into the uncharted maze of suicide, he got stuck there on the verge of the same quandary. Then the gas oven in the kitchen, the rope waiting to be hung down from the gas pipe crossing through the living room, the pills in the bottles, the razor in the bathtub and the Bosphorus Bridge with its Goliath feet would start to scream in unison: 'Me! Me! Me,

Sidar! Please choose me!'

'You cannot stay here,' he mumbled, averting his eyes away from hers.

'But I asked before. You didn't object then.'

'I know,' Sidar admitted fretfully as he spotted the spider dangling from the ceiling. 'But I've changed my mind.'

Though Cemal had intended to go home directly after the bar, either because he found it hard to walk straight or came to realize his decision to part ways with his twin meant saying farewell to their joint workplace as well, he soon found himself in front of Bonbon Palace. Trying not to touch the reeking, leaking garbage bags huddled on the sidewalk, he leaned over the pistachio green writing on the garden wall and stared at the beauty parlour with sorrowful eyes, but what he spotted there was quick to replace his sorrow with agitation. There was a candle flickering inside. He had no doubt that the apprentices had locked up the door and left hours ago. With a frown on his face he stood still, staring at the low set balcony of their flat. That must be where the thief had gained entrance.

Though he was hardly experiencing a tidal wave of courage, after guzzling three large beers, Cemal was more than ready to give any thief a black eye. Grabbing a broken hanger godknowswho had thrown in the garbage he rushed into the garden, passed by the rose acacia and managed to land on the balcony on his first try. As predicted, the door was slightly ajar. He rushed inside toward the shadow of a man standing by the candle…and instantly dropped his weapon of a broken hanger…

Meanwhile, the other, faced with such an aggressive silhouette plunging in from the balcony, had scampered to his feet, taking cover behind a hair-removal machine. Celal was hardly experiencing a tidal wave of courage. Had it been any other time, he would have been scared to death but he too had left three large, emptied beer mugs behind. Nonetheless, probably because compared to his twin, he was either less impervious to alcohol or simply less agile, even though he had indeed unravelled the identity of the encroaching silhouette at the very last moment, he could not withhold his arm quickly enough. By the time Celal's right arm had processed the 'Retreat!' command coming from the brain, it was already too late. In a flash, the hair-removal machine smashed onto Cemal's shoulder, leaving its heat control button there.

★★★

The twins were ten years old when their father had returned from Australia where he had emigrated many years previously. In united awe they had listened to the stories the man they so much admired told them. He had worked hard, made heaps of money, and had now returned to take his family back with him to that land of prosperity. Awaiting them there was a house, vivid yellow like boiled corn, with a tyre swing in the backyard. While the twins had listened to their father with bated breath, their mother had been busy packing, bidding farewell to the neighbours and doling out all their belongings, since they weren't going to take any of these things with them.

The day before their departure, while Celal and Cemal tossed and turned in their beds on the floor, their father had sneaked into their room. Patting their heads, he had taken out from his chest-pocket one photograph. There was a house in the photograph which indeed looked huge and corn yellow; and the backyard was just as he had described. There was a swing there as well and on that swing sat a plump woman with a smile blooming on her face. She had ginger hair with a strand curled, thickly braided and loosely fastened into a bun at the nape of the neck. 'What do you think of her? Beautiful, isn't she?' their father had asked. The twins had nodded shyly. She did not at all look like the women they had hitherto seen, especially not like their mother. Putting the photograph back, their father had once again patted them on their heads. 'Tomorrow, we three are gonna leave,' he had whispered. 'Let your mother stay here for the time being. Once we get to Australia and settle down there, we can come pick her up.'

Though their age was small and their admiration of their father only too deep, both boys had instantly grasped that this was a lie. When left alone in the room they had shunned any further word on this matter. Both had feigned ignorance, as if by doing so they could manage to somehow unlearn what they had learned. When they had finally fallen asleep that night, both had beckoned to the ginger-haired woman in their dreams. The following morning, however, neither could tell for sure if she had come or not.

'I was so thrilled to hear the things daddy had told us then...' Cemal murmured to his twin whilst still on his knees and searching for the heat control button.

'That vast country, that pretty woman,' Cemal droned on broodingly. 'I sold my mother in exchange for those. That's what a despicable person I am. In return for these, I peddled the woman who had given birth to me, suckled and raised me. God damn it, one can become a materialist in time, so you'd think life made a person one, but how on earth could one be a materialist when still a child, at that age?!'

The following day, once having sent their mother away on a pretext, the three of them had loaded the suitcases into the car.

'But you? You did not peddle our mother for these things!' Cemal sighed, as he watched his brother crawl under a swivel chair to dig out the heat control button. 'You didn't put your soul up for sale or your very humanity! Fuck the money, fuck the luxury, you decided, and jumped off the car. You chose to stay with our mother and you tried to persuade me too. You were running so hard behind the car as dad and I drove away from the village. That poignant scene was seared forever in my mind. You were yelling so hard: 'Stop! Stop!' You ran after us all the way to the end of the village.'

As Cemal folded a handkerchief into two, four, eight, sixteen folds, blowing his nose on the last fold, the power came back. Celal ran to the kitchen to fetch his twin a glass of water. Before handing him the glass, he put in five drops of lemon cologne.

'Thank you,' Cemal said.

'I had lost my shoe,' Celal replied.

Staring with lustreless eyes at the candle flame, which looked so rickety and flimsy now that the electricity had come, Cemal tried to make sense of what he had just heard.

'I had lost my shoe,' Celal repeated. He would rather have remained silent but his mouth talked without consulting him. How he wished he had not had that third beer. 'Just as I was getting into the car, one of my shoes fell off. That's why I got off the car, to put on my shoe. However, before I had the chance, mother showed up. As soon as father spotted her coming, he started the engine. I ran after you with one shoe on but the car careered away. I kept yelling at the top of my voice. I ran after you all the way to the end of the village.'

Celal, bruised all through his life from being the child his father had abandoned and Cemal, bruised all through his life from being the child who had abandoned his mother, stood staring at one another, half-dejected, half-confused, their respective identities turned inside out in the mirror that each provided for the other...and whatever it was that they saw there led each to believe that his situation had been graver than the other's...

'There's one more thing I need to tell you,' Celal bumbled. 'You know ma was an uneducated woman. After your departure, she fell ill with sorrow. People urged her to seek help from this famous spell-caster. She took me there with her. A young man with eyes like glass, turns out he was blind. He must have taken pity on my mother. "To this day I have never prepared a bad spell," he said, "and I never will hereafter, but this husband of yours deserves the worst so I'll make an exception and help you. Let's block their way, capsize their car, sink their ship if need be, let's make sure they never make it to Australia. Do you want me to do that? Do tell, is this what you really want?" he asked. Poor ma stood still, cried, moaned and then unable to take it any longer she said: "Yes!"

As that night it was taking Cemal longer than usual to comprehend his twin's words, he was lagging behind, his mind functioning no quicker than an icicle feigning ignorance of the sun. He would have liked to intervene and put in a few words himself but not only did he not know what to say, at that moment even the idea of moving his jaw tired him. How he wished he had not finished off that third beer...

'Poor ma, she was so exhausted she couldn't even follow what was said. So it was me who had to get the instructions on how to cast the spell. The sorcerer gave me a corn husk, filled a bottle with blessed water and wrote who knows what on a piece of paper. "Separate the corn husk into two pinches and tie them tight. Put them in the paper and roll the paper up lengthwise like a cigarette. Then burn it all up" he instructed. "Right then, you'll hear a voice. A sound will speak out of the fire. When you hear that sound, rest assured you're doing the right thing. Do not ever touch the fire. Let it burn away its course. When the flames are entirely out, sprinkle the ashes over the blessed water and then pour the water at the bottom of a red rose tree. The rest will come by itself,' he concluded."

The power went out once again. The puny flame of the candle visibly heartened, appreciating the sudden darkness.

"As soon as we reach home, get to it," said ma, "Do exactly what the sorcerer told you!" So I tied the cornhusks, making two bunches (one small, the other big), put them in the paper, wrapped it up nicely and then kindled it. You should have seen ma, her eyes were wide as saucers! God, that hope in her stare, she expected so much from me. The paper really went up in flames. I tried to convince myself, "Nothing will happen," but suddenly I heard, just like the sorcerer said I would, a scream...as if someone was crying...then another scream. I thought I heard your voice. Shaken up I took the blessed water and poured it right onto the burning fire. It went out with a hiss. I felt so relieved. Of course, I didn't tell my mother what I had done. She thought I'd poured it all out at the bottom of the red rose tree. Next we went to bed. At dawn a noise woke me up, I get out of bed and what do I see? Ma is out in the garden weeping on her knees! "Celal, what have I done? How could I have murdered my sweetheart son," she moaned, "I wish to God not a single stroke of harm happens to them on the way"."You mean both?" I asked."Yes, I mean both," she said. I noticed her hands were covered with scratches. She had uprooted the rose tree to break the spell. "Nothing bad will happen, right, Celal?" she begged. "Nothing," I consoled. "You didn't do everything you were told, right" she asked. "Right," I replied. She was so relieved. "Good for you, my smart boy," she smiled. Then hugged me with such gratitude that I understood right then. I understood she loved you more than me. The son who had left was the one she loved the most.'

Cemal shivered. He struggled to get up to close the balcony door but was so dizzy he had to squat right back down.

'From that day on Cemal, whenever someone mentions saints, sorcerers and the like, I get scared. Not that I believe it or anything. If you ask my opinion, I believe none of it. If the truth be told, after all these years, I even doubt those corn husks had really made a sound. I was so frightened I must have imagined it. However, the doubt is always with me. Were it not for that doubt my poor mother would spin in her grave. That's how I feel.'

The silence that ensued lasted two minutes. The lights came back right in the middle, leaving one minute in the darkness and the other in the light.

'So that's why you got so mad at my making fun of the saint in the garden! But I promise you, I'll never ever open my mouth again!'

Celal sighed. His twin set the gage of his temperament to either excess or dearth.

'Let's close down this parlour if you'd like. That is, if you're worried about this idea that cutting hair is against the holy saint's wishes. We can get a parlour somewhere else.'

'Oh, come on!' Celal said laughing. 'I think you are confusing me with the brush with the bone handle.'

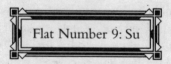

Flat Number 9: Su

'At the fatsos with the headscarves! The fatsos with the headscarves!' yelled Su, her head popping in and out of the rear window like the wound up bird of a clock. In the front seat two boys with chickpea guns in their hands were waiting, taking turns sliding into the window seat where they would shoot at the targets she pointed out.

The women with the headscarves Su had her eyes on had been caught in the middle of a two-lane road struggling to cross. They did not notice the school minibus hurtling along behind, never mind being aware of the chickpeas whizzing past them. Before the boy who missed his goal turned his seat over to his friend with a long face, Su had already designated the new target: 'At the chap with the dog! The chap with the dog!'

One of the chickpeas made it into the hood of the casually dressed man but his terrier was not as lucky. It took a couple of barks and tail-chases to figure out what was raining on it. It could only chase the minibus the length of its leash, at the end of which it stopped with a painful whine waiting for its owner to catch up. One of the chickpeas must have hit the dog in the eye for it constantly winked after them. 'Awesome!!!' exclaimed the sniper commending himself – 'awesome' being more in fashion in their circles these days than 'cool'.

The three pony-tailed girls, who always sat in front and treated the driver as their buddy of many years, goading him to play their pop cassettes over and over, turned back simultaneously to throw daggers-of-looks at the perpetrators of the incident. Su paid no attention to them. Ever since the day her hair was cropped short she had abandoned the world of girls from which she had already been banished the moment the news of her having lice had spread out and which she had had difficulty in joining in the first place. She only ever got together with the other girls before and after gym, in the changing room. At those moments Su simply pretended they did not exist. What she asked for in return was to be treated likewise, as if she did not exist. But whenever they lined up on the benches, stinking-out the squat, narrow changing room with their flowery, syrupy deodorants and putting on their pantyhose while exchanging meaningful looks, speaking in some sort of a cryptic code, they wanted to make Su feel how unpopular and unwanted she was. However, boys were different. Getting lice was deemed so ordinary in their circles it was scarcely news.

Su leaned out of the window up to her waist, tweaking her thumb at the terrier left behind, but just as she was about to draw back, she caught sight of a man a few metres ahead, with an unkempt beard and hair long unwashed, digging around in the garbage. The man was busily stuffing the sacks on his shoulders with tin cans he fished from the thrash. Now and then he scratched his head pensively as if some mysterious voice was addressing him with taxing questions from within the trash container. He had a burgundy beret and petroleum green overalls which were worn to shreds. From the rips on the overalls one could see his kneecaps covered with dirt.

'At the hobo! At the hobo!' Su shouted.

The sniper boy on duty by the window loaded the paper roll with new chickpeas and blew with all his might. Exactly at the same moment, however, the targeted vagabond stopped doing what he was doing, turned around with an animal-like intuition and, like victims smiling at their murderers before taking the bullet, opened his mouth wide and caught the chickpea in one move while it was still in the air, gulping it down without even caring to chew. Pressing his hand on his heart he subtly tilted his head forward as if to thank them in return and opened his mouth once again for the second bullet. When no chickpea was fired, he impatiently rattled his yellowed teeth. The sniper boy flinched in horror. Su stared flabbergasted at this weirdest man she had ever seen, a man who did not at all look like anyone she knew.

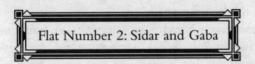

Flat Number 2: Sidar and Gaba

As soon as the girl left, banging the door behind her, Sidar felt like shit. He waited until midnight, hoping she would forgive him and return. It was only when he had to accept the fact that he was waiting to no avail, that he put the leash on Gaba and threw himself out of the house.

The Armenian Catholic Cemetery was twenty-five minutes by foot. This was the one he liked the most among all the cemeteries in Istanbul. To help Gaba pass through he pushed all the way back the humongous ornate door that did not give even the slightest hint about what a luminous space was hidden behind. Upon seeing him coming, the guard grumbled as usual. Though suspicious of Sidar's every move the first time around, he had gotten used to him over time and must have finally deemed this wiry, scruffy young guy batty but harmless; for he didn't object to his presence anymore.

When Sidar showed up on the wide stone road intersecting each and every path in the cemetery, an old man sitting alone on a bench waved at him. They had run into each other a couple of times. Though they had been exchanging greetings, they had never conversed before.

'So you've come again,' smiled the old man, patting the seat next to him. 'But you're still too young. Why the hurry?'

Sidar perched on the other end of the bench. Before responding, he inspected the old man. He must have been at least seventy-five years old, maybe even eighty. Small and round were his eyes, a deep bluish-grey.

'But I've seen lots of children's graves here,' Sidar replied obstinately.

'I didn't say you were too young to die, I said you are too young to think about death.'

Gaba's bark was heard from a distance, probably nothing to be worried about. Some stranger must be giving him something to eat. He barked like that when he was about to get a treat from a stranger. It was the 'Thank you for the *simit*, you are very kind!' bark.

'I too was thinking about death today,' muttered the man, apparently interested in a chat. 'This morning my sister called, she'd had a bad dream last night. We were children with milk bottles in our hands. Yet the milk was kind of strange; it wouldn't flow but came out in lumps. White mice the size of my little finger scurried from within. My mother grabbed our hands and took us away, but my sister went back. In spite of knowing too well that the milk was contaminated, she drank. My mother was furious at her. "Why did you do that? You sinned!" she yelled, but she couldn't bear my sister's tears and seated her on her lap to console her. "Don't you worry," she soothed her, "God will certainly forgive you."

Gaba started barking once again, probably because some stranger had attempted to pat him. Both Sidar and the old man turned around inadvertently, looking at the entrance of the cemetery though they knew they could not see him from this angle. No problem. It was probably just the 'I will let you pat me if you give me one more *simit*!' bark.

'I haven't dreamt in years, wouldn't even remember it if I did, but my sister does and her dreams always come true. She is a cultured woman. If you had just seen her as a young girl, she wasn't interested in anyone. All she thought about were books! My mother, the poor thing, was distressed; she forbid my sister to read too much for it made her nose bleed, but my sister still kept reading secretly, novels mostly…from the French originals… In my mind's eye I can still picture her bent double over a book, lost in another world. I always knew when her nose was going to start bleeding again. I could have warned her but, I don't know why, I could not even get near her while she was reading. I just watched, waiting soundlessly for that drop of blood to fall. There were many such red stains on the pages of the novels she read back then. You couldn't wipe them off or tear them out, so what could you do? They remained like that. She also had a diary, wouldn't talk to us, but she did to her diary. Then one day my sister and I returned from school to find all the books and the diary gone. "I threw them all away!" mother snapped. My sister turned white. She loved ma, she did, but I don't think she ever forgave her.'

Gaba's barks accelerated in folds, getting louder each time, he was probably upset by something. It was the 'If you are not going to give me any more *simit*s, could you please leave me alone!' bark.

'As she was so fastidious, she married very late. Her husband was an eye doctor, had an office in Sisli. They truly loved one another. Didn't have any children. Then the poor man unexpectedly died; simply crossing the street, must have lost his foresight or something, stepped on the road without even looking. The car 'hit and ran' in plain daylight. I've seen many a person's hair turning white with grief, but with my sister it was her body that shrivelled from grief. Before long she had shrunk into an elfin, doleful woman. She gave up everything, went off food. Hung her husband's pictures all around the house. Just like she used to talk to her diary as a young girl, she started to talk to those photographs. I made a grave mistake then. I thought if I removed my brother-in-law's belongings out of her sight, it would be easier for her to forget. One day, I secretly gathered the photographs, all of them, and gave them away to friends and relatives. Just as she had never forgiven mother, my sister did not forgive me either. That was when she moved to another house. You see, I had presumed it would be hard for her to live in a house surrounded by my brother-in-law's memory. To the contrary, it was hard for my sister to live there the moment those reminiscences were gone. She moved somewhere else. After all these years she still doesn't let me into her house. She didn't get re-married either. All this time she stayed single like that. Whenever we get together, we meet at a patisserie. Do you know anything about dream interpretations? My sister sure does and her dreams always come true.'

'So how did she interpret this dream?' Sidar wondered.

'She said she might die before waiting for her time to come. That's why my mother was angry at her like that.'

'You mean suicide?' Sidar exclaimed with a tinge of a thrill in his voice.

However, blinking his bluish-grey eyes the old man looked deadpan, as if never before had he thought of such a word or even heard of it.

Gaba sounded far more distraught now. He was using the, 'If you so insist on not leaving me alone, then I will leave!' bark. Sidar scurried to his feet though he had more questions to ask. At the entrance of the cemetery, he found Gaba, just as he had predicted, barking in distress in the middle of a circle of affection and attention formed by inquisitive onlookers. Before he ran to the rescue of his dog, he stopped for a second to wave to the old man, but the latter had turned to the other side still murmuring, as if he was unaware that he was now alone on the bench.

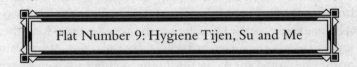

Flat Number 9: Hygiene Tijen, Su and Me

6:54 p.m.: Dangling from the armchair, her stick-thin legs covered with myriad mosquito bites each of which she had turned into an abrasion from scratching non-stop, Su thrust her hands into the pockets of her shorts and fully concentrated her gaze on the minute hand of the clock on the wall, as if by so doing she could make time run faster. Her tutor was always prompt. To this day he had never been late, not even a delay of few minutes, but such punctuality had recoil of its own. He always ended the lesson right on the dot. He had never stayed longer, not even for a few minutes. The instant he started the lesson, he placed his watch with the leather strap between the two of them on the table and though he did not keep glancing at it as a bored man would, he still jumped to his feet as soon as the hour was up.

6:57 p.m.: She sprung up with the ring of the doorbell. Three minutes early!

Hygiene Tijen was by the kitchen sink, scraping off the sediment that had collected at the bottom of the teapot. Drying on her snow-white apron her hands with fingertips creased from having stayed in hot water for hours on end, she headed to the door. Upon opening it, she inspected her daughter's tutor from head-to-toe. The man looked neat and trim as always. He submissively took off his shoes before entering and put on his beige-socked feet a pair of sanitary slippers from the basket. The mother and daughter meanwhile watched his gestures with deferential courtesy. Then all three of them moved to the living room, making squishy noises as they walked. On one end of the rectangular dining room table there was, as usual, especially prepared for the lesson ahead of time: coconut cake slices lined up on two porcelain plates with white napkins on the side, the notebook with the white lilies spread open, pencil tips carefully sharpened, the ashtray laid ready. One could smoke in this house. Neither smoke nor ash fell into the realm of Hygiene Tijen's conception of 'filth.'

'I hope it won't be impolite if we keep working inside as you lecture here?'

She always asked the same question before every lesson. I always gave the same response: 'Not at all, Mrs. Tijen. Please continue with your work.'

The new cleaning lady showed up at that instant scuffling out of the bathroom, in one hand a pail filled with soapy water and in the other hand a doormat with tassels so messed up it looked trodden on. Behind her trundled Meryem with her sharply protruding belly. She had dangled a longish, snow-white towel from one shoulder like a boxing trainer or a Turkish bath massager. Both women seemed to be waddling with the discomfort of wearing sanitary slippers.

'How come you are still working?' I asked her.

However, before she could respond, Hygiene Tijen jumped in. 'No, no, Meryem isn't working really, she stopped doing so last week, but I was in dire straits without her assistance. So this is the solution we came up with: Meryem says what needs to be done and Esma Hanim, thanks be upon her, does it.'

Upon hearing her name mentioned Esma Hanim tilted her head and gave a lackadaisical greeting, apparently not as enthusiastic as others about her share in the division of labour. Then all three women squished on their slippers back to their respective chores, leaving the tutor and student alone.

7:00 p.m.: As Su pulled her chair closer to the table, she threw a distressed glance at the wristwatch with the leather strap stretched like a barrier between them.

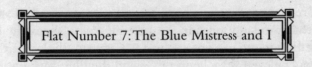

Flat Number 7: The Blue Mistress and I

Back home after the lesson, I found the Blue Mistress still there. What's more, she had put in place a number of the boxes that had been waiting to be opened since the day I moved in and had also straightened the place up. However, she told me she would soon leave to go cook for the olive oil merchant. I refrained from delving into that story – it being no news to me that things were not going well between them lately.

'Tell me,' she cooed. 'What sort of food do you want?'

'Pasta,' I grumbled. Despite her initial frown, she found the idea practical. As I boiled the pasta, she set out to prepare a tomato and thyme sauce with the limited ingredients in the house. I guess that is why she loves me. Unlike the other men in her life, I demand from her far less than what she is willing to give. In return, I receive far more than what I had demanded initially.

The doorbell rang just when we had sat down at the table. Su was such an odd little girl. With her book in her hand, there she was, telling me I had forgotten to give her homework for the weekend. The Blue Mistress invited her to the table. She did not want to come. While they talked, I chose a number of exercises way above her level. If ruining her weekend with extra homework is what she pines for, so be it.

'Well, it turns out I am not the only neighbour to have fallen for that handsome face of yours, Mister,' snorted the Blue Mistress when we were able to sit down again to eat.

'Don't talk nonsense, she's just a child.'

'So what? Can't children fall in love? I swear to God, I know I could when I was about that age. Weren't you in love with anyone as a child?'

It suddenly felt so awkward. The Blue Mistress talked about her childhood as if referring to a distant past whereas she must be at most ten to twelve years past it. Come to think of it, there was only eleven years between Su and the Blue Mistress.

'You didn't answer! Have you ever been in love as a child or not?' she insisted, apparently annoyed with my silence.

I indeed had, except that it had never been a memory worth recording. There was a flighty, freckled, loud-mouthed girl I went to school with. I recall being attracted to her. To this day I have never met someone so naturally inclined to theft. All that mattered was that an item belonged to someone else, there was nothing on earth she would not enjoy stealing: fruit from the neighbouring gardens, slippers from the thresholds of homely homes, pencils and erasers of classmates…she would embezzle them all and share her loot with me each time… Every now and then she lurched into the foul-smelling store of a hideous, glue-addicted shoe repairman we passed by on our way to school. While I chatted up the man, she would fill her pockets with handfuls of nails and soles. God knows why, we would then hammer these onto all the fences, benches, cases or doors we came across. After all we shared, however, my beloved played dirty for no good reason and ratted to my parents. My father was barely shaken upon receiving the news of his son's thefts but with my mother it was a completely different story. She blew her top, exaggerating her parental punishment out of proportion. Ten days later, however, my father died, thereby erasing off my mother's agenda the scandal of my offence forever.

'What was her name?' asked the Blue Mistress, shaking the salt-mill for the umpteenth time, as if determined to find its bottom.

Hard as I tried, I couldn't remember her name – just as I can't remember what the majority of my childhood friends

were called. I confessed to her how hard it usually was for me
to remember people's names but I did not reveal how this habit
of mine used to infuriate Ayshin. The Blue Mistress asks little
about my ex-marriage anyhow. Perhaps because she is sick of
hearing about the marriage of the olive oil merchant or
perhaps she is one of those people who are all ears when it
comes to hearing about still enduring childhoods but not
immediate pasts. I told her I was much better with nicknames
– those I don't easily forget.

'Then find me a nickname as well,' she said finally able to let
go of the salt-mill and dizzy from all that shaking.

'You already have one,' I confirmed. 'You are "The
Blue Mistress."'

She did not say anything but I could see it in her eyes all the
same. She liked the name I had given her.

***

3:33 a.m.: I woke up, she was not by my side.

I found her on the balcony. She looked pale, as if she had
woken up in the middle of a nightmare so daunting that it had
robbed her off the longing to go back to sleep. I sank into the
chair next to her and lit a cigarette. Under the coffee table in
between us, there were armies of ants circumambulating a
piece of melon that had started to rot where it had fallen. As
they toiled we sat still, watching the empty street.

'I bet that girl didn't rat on you,' she murmured
absentmindedly. 'It must have reached your mother through
another route. Why would she do it? You two were
accomplices.'

I went in and fetched two double *rakı* for us. She took hers
with a smile but only slightly sipped, evidently not a drinker.
Yet she evidently didn't want to display this, probably because
she had always run into men who drank like sponges. On
second thoughts, I decided that I was perhaps wrong about
this, after all she was not the type to fool others. Perhaps she

herself was unaware of her dislike for alcohol in the first place.

'Maybe it is just the reverse,' I said. When I finish my *rakı*, I will drink hers as well – as long as she does not smear the glass with lipstick. 'Being accomplices might connect people to one another but that union is bound to be fleeting. In reality, if you are accomplices with someone, you will try to get rid of then at the first opportunity. If you don't, they will. A wrongdoer might indeed return to the scene of crime but not to the partner in crime.'

'Oh, blessings to you, my teacher, you sure know how to talk.' She placed on the table the glass she had been fiddling with. Good, no lipstick. 'Do your students enjoy listening to you?'

'Come to a class with me one day, sit among the students and decide for yourself.'

'What if someone asks, "Who is this person?" What'll you say?'

'You'll be a student from somewhere else coming to listen to the lecture. You're so young, they'd buy it,' I muttered while caressing her face. The scar on her left cheek is not at all visible in this dim light. 'But I can, if you want, tell them instead that you're a friend of mine.'

'That would be blatant lie!' she frowned, suddenly riled. 'How could I ever be regarded as your friend? It would take them only a minute's chat with me to fathom the lie. I haven't the foggiest idea about many of the things you talk about. I didn't go to college. It's too evident that I'm not going to do so at this age.'

What age? At times I doubt if she is really aware how young she is.

'Friendship is based on compatibility,' she volleyed upon realizing I was about to object. 'One can fall in love with someone incompatible but one can't be friends with them. For one thing, when you talk the other has to get it in an instant. To do so one has to be at the same cultural level. You and I can't ever be friends. We can't be married either or be lovers. We tried to be neighbours but made a mess of that as well.'

'And why on earth can't we be lovers?'

Instead of answering my question, my little lover with no lipstick and no serenity, took a large sip from the drink I thought she had long abandoned. Her face soured right away. Why does she force herself to drink when she does not like alcohol at all?

'I think if we ever could be anything together, we'd be accomplices,' she blurted out all of a sudden, the harshness of her words incongruent with the indolence of her moves as she reached for the stale nuts to get rid of the taste in her mouth.

A white car with black windows ploughed through Cabal Street, its cassette tape turned on full blast. The Blue Mistress jerked her head over the railing and swore without any reservations whatsoever. I gently pulled her towards me, kissed her. The piercing music of the car decreased bit by bit. In that stillness, a hurried mosquito slyly made a dive, buzzing. The wind came to a standstill, filling the air with the sour garbage smell. The Blue Mistress finished the pistachios in the bowl and I the *rakı* in my glass, continuing on to hers. In the next attack of the mosquito, my applause echoed in the air. I opened my hands hoping to see it dead. They were empty.

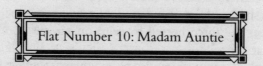

Flat Number 10: Madam Auntie

'Are you upset about something Su?'

'I'm fine,' Su grunted a jagged response, constantly squeezing the English exercise book she had rolled up.

'Why don't I make us a nice cup of coffee with milk and you go choose two coffee cups from the glass cupboard honey,' Madam Auntie said, trying not to fret over the child's bitterness. Despite having solemnly pledged to herself to send the girl away with an appropriate excuse if and when she appeared at her door again, seeing her in such a sullen state today, she had not been able to keep her word.

Su heaved a pompous sigh as she followed the old woman inside. In this warm weather coffee with milk was the last thing she wanted to drink but what difference would it make, things were 'crappy' anyway – 'crappy' being in fashion in their circles nowadays instead of 'awesome'. What difference would it make if she had a crappy coke or a crappy coffee with milk? Scratching her scrawny legs, droopily and indolently, she walked into the living room, opened the glass cupboard at the corner and peered inside in deep wonder. There were so many things in here! Lined up on the shelves were inverted porcelain cups, liquor cups, champagne flutes, crystal pitchers, embroidered frames and all kinds of tiny carved boxes the function of which she could not fathom. After a quick survey, she honed in on two amethyst cups with intertwined ivy handles. Right behind them was a round, glazed, illustrated tray: a robust man with a moustache and raven-black hat was carrying a woman down a ladder in his lap, her tulle dress flowing to her heels. The woman had put her head on the man's shoulder, dreamily gazing into the horizon, as if she were not on top of a ladder from which they could topple down any minute but on an idyllic hill with a magnificent panorama. It was as if they were fleeing the fairy tale to which they belonged. One could distinguish a few houses and behind them a forest in shades of green. Su turned the back of the tray as if hoping to see there the fate awaiting this dignified couple, but there was no other illustration at the back, only an inscription at one corner: 'Vishniakov'.

Placing the amethyst cups on the tray, she closed the cupboard door shut with her foot. Just as she was about to go back, her eyes caught a spot further down. The living room door leading to the hall was partly open and the interior...the interior looked somewhat uncanny...

Without really thinking she approached the door, opened it all the way and stood almost petrified. As if lured, she started to advance step by step down the hall of Madam Auntie's house. With every step, her uneasiness gave way to utmost incredulity.

'How much sugar would you like?' Madam Auntie called out from the kitchen but when there came no response, she turned down the heat under the milk and went back to retrieve her guest. Finding the living room empty she first suspected the child had left, but then she noticed the wide open hallway door. In escalating panic, she involuntarily brought her hand up to her neck. It was not there. Her bluish-grey eyes fretfully scanned the living room until she spotted the velvet beribboned key sitting guiltily on the coffee table at the corner. Colour drained from her face. Her heart pummelling hard, she dashed into the hall after the girl.

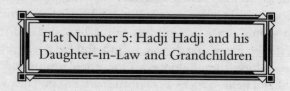

Flat Number 5: Hadji Hadji and his Daughter-in-Law and Grandchildren

'Keep walking,' the Daughter-in-Law bellowed. 'Keep walking or I'll break your legs!'

Upon hearing these words, the two children tugged along by their hands started to cry even harder. The seven and a half year old walked behind languidly, tranquilly. Though he had indeed had lots of fun today, it had been a rather awful time for his mom. Probably as a result of the other box office worker complaining, the big boss who usually showed up once in a blue moon had appeared at the movie theatre around noon. 'Do you think we run a daycare centre here?' he growled, scowling at the five and a half and six and a half year olds who were standing in the corner, mouths agape at the huge Aladdin and the big-bellied genie sitting cross-legged on the 1 x 2 metre cardboard carpet hanging from the ceiling to promote the film. Both had been crying non-stop from that moment on.

'If you could only manage for a couple of days, I'm sure I'll sure find a solution by then,' the Daughter-in-Law had pleaded crestfallen, though she knew only too well how unlikely that would be.

As they approached Bonbon Palace, the kids' crying dwindled and their bawl transformed finally into a barely audible buzz but as soon as they plunged through the door of Flat 5, like a watch with its spring loose, both ran screaming to their grandfather's lap. At that moment, Hadji Hadji was having a little snooze on the divan with one of his four books slipping off his hand. Bowled over by this unexpected deluge of love, blinking in bewilderment he struggled to get to his feet.

'Father, I'm entrusting the kids to you,' said the Daughter-in-Law, averting her eyes. 'I have to get back to work.'

Hadji Hadji pulled the heads of the little girl and the little boy into his beard. Thus encouraged, the kids started another round of crying. The Daughter-in-Law stood silently, forlornly watching this scene whilst she heard herself mumble:

'But I beg you, please have some mercy and don't poison their infantile minds with those fairy tales of yours.'

The door closed. The three young children and the old man were left alone. As the little kids, feeling drained from all that crying, sighed deeply and their grandfather collected the hair shed from his beard during that uproar, a prickly silence settled among them. They did not know what to do next. Before long, the seven and a half year old threw his big head back and smiled with a glint in his mossy green eyes. In point of fact, he too had enjoyed coming back home. Being outside had indeed been fun, but he had also felt himself as tiny as a flea and just as alien among all those people who watched his every move with pity. Unlike the outside world, here in this house he was the sole commander of his little kingdom and the only undisputed sovereign of his cocooned life.

'Come on, grandpa,' he proclaimed solemnly. 'No need to dilly-dally. You can tell us whatever story you want!'

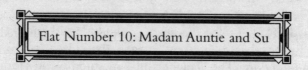

Flat Number 10: Madam Auntie and Su

'You have so much stuff in here Madam Auntie?!' exclaimed Su, bobbing her head in escalating amazement.

When the old woman had caught up with her, the child had already reached the end of the hall; reached it and seen inside the three rooms opening up to the hallway.

'It isn't all mine.'

'Really, then whose is it?'

'It belongs to different people. I'm looking after their things,' said Madam Auntie, without taking her eyes off the tray carrying the amethyst cups. Her mind was pullulated with the fear that they would break, but she was so stunned that could not make any move to snatch the boyar and his lover from the child.

Yet at this particular instant, Su was the one who was most astounded. Brought up in a house with white as the dominant colour, where everything was incessantly cleaned and polished, swept and purified, relentlessly whitened and yet never whitened enough, the child now felt as if she had been dropped into a magical garden she could not have even fathomed to exist upon earth. There was plenty of every colour, except white. The belongings, piled on top of one another, one inside the other, had seeped into each and every nook and cranny so that all three rooms were jam-packed up to the ceiling. Amid this multihued jumble it was impossible to separate the valuable from the useless. All was inextricably mixed up. With so much stuff, Su couldn't help but suspect this place was way bigger than their flat. Never mind their flat, it was much bigger than all the other flats in this apartment building, even larger than all the flats she had hitherto seen put together! In fact, it seemed that Number 10 was not a flat at all, but a convoluted contraption with heaps of different pieces and hundreds of different buttons. If even one piece pulled out, the whole structure would break down and become inoperable.

There were ballpoint pens everywhere...and burnt-out bulbs, used up batteries, torn tulles, burst balloons, expired medicine, used clothing, buttons with no two looking alike, stickers that had lost their adhesive, empty cartridges, lighters without gas, glasses with broken lenses, jar-lids of all sizes, money no longer in circulation, torn pieces of cloth, cracked trinkets, photographs turned yellow, pictures with no frames left, torn tassels, tattered wigs, keys that had lost their key chains, mugs with broken handles, baby bottles without the nipples, threadbare lampshades, worn out books, boxes of all sizes (some plastic, others wood), lustreless mother-of-pearl, cardboard, empty milk bottles, candied apple sticks, ice-cream sticks, food bowls, dolls with missing heads or limbs, umbrellas with wires sticking out, strainers turned black, doorbells that even themselves could not recall which doors they used to make ring, pantyhose with runs stopped by nail polish, wrapping paper, door knobs, broken household items, filled out notebooks, journals turned yellow, empty perfume bottles, single odd shoes, shattered remote-controls, rusty metals, stale candy, rings with missing stones, macramé flower-holders, shoe liners, rubber bands, bird cages, typewriters with missing letters, mildewed tea in tin boxes, tobacco parcels, bracelets of all colours, barrettes each more beautiful than the other, binocular lenses... As Su looked around in bewilderment, her eyes caught a large fishing net hanging over a pile of objects.

'The sea brought that,' Madame Auntie said, her voice lilting with pride.

'You said the sea brought it?'

'The sea becomes so generous when the *lodos* blows hard,

carrying piles of items by the shore. With all these the waves playing the way children do with balls, passing these items back and forth to one another, they bring these to the shore. Waves, like human beings, quickly tire of things and you know, I'm not the only one there by the shore. Many other Istanbulites are also after the items the sea conveys.'

However, Su was no longer listening to her, she was instead eyeing-up a child's hat of purple velvet. It was beautiful and looked brand new:

'Madam Auntie, where did you get this?' she asked as she thrust the tray into its owner's hands and shot off to touch the soft surface of the hat.

The old woman hesitated for a split second but what was done could not be undone. What could she now hide from her little friend who had already gone too far, and for how long?

'It was in the garbage,' she replied. 'I don't know why they threw away such a beautiful hat.'

Su caressed the hat absentmindedly. In her mind's eye, the hobo who had boldly confronted their bullets gave a dirty smile, waving a bag of chickpeas he taken out of the garbage. His yellowed teeth became all the more visible.

'What about these. Why did you take them?'

'Are they bad?' wondered the old woman, throwing a cursory glance at the empty pill bottles. 'One always needs empty bottles. It's not right to throw them away.'

Su inspected the old woman's teeth. Oddly enough, they were white and clean. Just like her mother's.

'If you like the hat, do take it. It's perfect for you.'

'Really?' Her large eyes glimmered as she eagerly reached out for the mirror she had seen among the empty tin cans piled up by the wall. As soon as she donned the purple velvet hat, she burst out laughing. It turned out to be a magnifying mirror.

'Oh, no, we forgot about the milk!' bellowed Madam Auntie at the same moment. 'Run! Run!'

With Su in front and the old woman rattling the amethyst cups behind, both raced into the kitchen. The milk in the small pot had long boiled over and spread everywhere over the oven, putting out the gas fire.

Once they had cleaned the oven and moved back to the living room, Su took another look into the still ajar hallway door, exclaiming at full blast, 'Heavens dubetsy!' – 'heavens dubetsy' being in fashion in their circles these days instead of 'crappy'. Perching on the nearest armchair, she started to swing her scrawny legs. 'This is the Castle of Garbage. If only the boys saw this, they'd be thrilled.'

'But the boys shouldn't know about this place! No one should…' the old woman stammered as she handed the child the coffee with milk. She then offered white chocolate from the crystal candy bowl on the coffee table. Su threw one into her mouth without thinking only to tense up right away. What if this chocolate had been dug out of the garbage as well? Su gaped fretfully at the old woman as if the answer was written somewhere on her forehead. Yet, before the chocolate melted in her mouth, a new question struck her mind.

'Madam Auntie,' she hooted, her voice instantly, inadvertently dwindling into a whisper. 'Is this why Bonbon Palace smells so bad?'

Flat Number 3: Hairdressers Cemal and Celal

'Hey, what's the matter with you? Did the cat get your tongue?' asked the blonde with one eye cast, there yet again to have her hair dyed, never persuaded that she need not have this done so often.

Cemal paid no heed to the woman's teasing, preferring instead to fully focus on the strand of her hair he was about to highlight. Though determined not to respond to his customers, by now the pressure of each word squelched on the tip of his tongue had so much inflated that in an urge to speak, he turned around and yelled at the pimpled apprentice for no reason. Being wound-up in front of all these women the apprentice, who was already hapless enough to have to spend this delicate pubescent stage of his life working in a woman's beauty parlour, blushed crimson. As soon as the gaze he averted from everyone accidentally met the Blue Mistress's, he blushed even more, turning a darker hue. He didn't know it, but when he flashed this particular shade of red his pimples almost disappeared.

'What's wrong with Cemal?' whispered the Blue Mistress to the manicurist next to her. She had never had a manicure before, but today was no ordinary day as, after a lengthy hiatus, she was going to meet the olive oil merchant again. He had sent a text message to her mobile phone in the afternoon saying he wanted to stop by and have a heart-to-heart. Not that the man had any special interest in manicured hands; if the truth be told, it was doubtful whether he would even be able to tell the difference, but as she sat there with one hand pleasantly numbed in a bowl of lukewarm foamy water, the Blue Mistress still believed she was doing the right thing. Why they remain oblivious to the fact that they are getting prepared for men who will remain oblivious to their preparations is a riddle germane to women.

The manicurist, now concentrating on a broken nail, answered in a hoarse whisper: 'We have no idea what's got into him. He's like a powdered keg, ready to blow his top off. He hasn't uttered a single word to the customers but keeps lashing out at us. You'd think he's a chain-smoker who quit cold this morning. That touchy! It's as if he's got PMS.'

Cemal frowned at the manicurist and the Blue Mistress giggling between them. Afraid of another rebuke the pimpled apprentice held out four aluminium folios at once. 'Sonny, why don't you hand them out one at a time?' growled the other with the thrill of having found another excuse to scold the hapless apprentice. It was precisely then that a hand tapped on his shoulder.

'Could you come to the kitchen for a moment?' said Celal, careful not to draw attention to himself or his brother.

There they stood in the kitchen, with the persistently, passionately boiling *samovar* in between them. Celal stared with compassion at the man who today looked more like himself than his twin, solemn and almost stock-still inside his sage green shirt.

'I surrender,' Celal said with a weary smile. 'For God's sake, please just go back to being your old self. Just be like you used to be. I had no idea how unbearable you'd become when solemn.'

Before the other found a chance to bear a grudge, Celal put his hand on his shoulder, giving an avuncular squeeze. 'Frankly brother, when you don't chat and make these women cackle, the beauty parlour becomes dull.'

In a few minutes, the twins drew open the curtain separating the tiny kitchen from the parlour. All heads popping-out of leopard patterned smocks turned toward them. Celal gingerly pushed his brother to step forward as if encouraging an actor afraid to get on stage. Then, with a smile, he winked at the apprentice without the pimples: 'Sonny, make some nice foamy coffee for us all so that we can slurp away at it whilst gazing at the holy saint.'

His edginess thawing visibly upon hearing these words, Cemal at long last gave the smile he had been withholding since early morning.

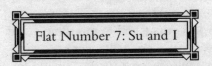

Flat Number 7: Su and I

At first I thought the kid was lying. Children make things up. I checked my watch. It had been fifteen minutes since the end of the lesson. We had been whispering since then. Just as I was about to leave, she said, 'Sir, I need to tell you something.' Hygiene Tijen, Meryem and Esma Hanim were all in the next room busily putting up the curtains they had just washed. From the way they were talking, one could tell that Esma Hanim was up somewhere high, probably on top of the ladder, and Hygiene Tijen was holding her steady from down below. Meryem seemed to be the one giving out instructions. As for us, we talked in wary whispers so as not to be heard.

'I swear to God I'm telling the truth,' Su groaned, miffed at my lack of faith.

I feigned being convinced but this time it was her turn to doubt. She wanted me to give my word that I would never ever let slip the secret she had entrusted me with. My word must not have been enough for she then made me repeatedly swear an oath – first on my honour and after that, one by one and name by name, on all my loved ones. Just so that the angst in her big black eyes would abate, I obeyed her every demand. Yet it was as if, far from comforting her, each of my promises rendered her even more anxious. At one point, she went inside swishing around on her slippers and came back carrying a miniature Qur'an with an emerald green cover, the type that people carry in their wallets and handbags. Just so she could be soothed, I swore with the Qur'an in my palm. When I finished,

389

realizing there was nothing else left to do except trust me, she breathed out a final sigh. Demanding as she is, how could I become annoyed by her demands? Love makes all and sundry miserable, even a child.

'Come on, let's put an end to this topic,' I said. 'Don't worry. My lips are sealed. I won't tell anyone.'

Seeing her smile cheered me up. 'If I do tell your secret to anyone, let God turn me into an ass!'

'Not an ass, not an ass!' she objected in a voice that sounded like a chirp.

'What should I be then?'

By now she had shrugged off all her anxieties and regained that galling glee of hers. She walked around me talking pedantically, listing all the repulsive creatures she knew, in order to find the worst beast ever on the face of the earth. Owls were macabre but not sufficiently wretched; rats were dirty but not gross enough. Cockroaches were nauseating, spiders bloodcurdling, alligators chilling, jellyfish odious, scorpions poisonous, wasps dangerous. Pigs scrabbled in dirt, vultures fed on carrion, bears could devour their own offspring, bats sucked blood. Sea urchins pricked, frogs gave us warts, centipedes snuck into our ears. The worm that emerged from the soil after a rain, the caterpillar that writhed in lettuce, the grasshopper gobbling up the field, the lizard running away leaving behind its tail, the fly not giving anyone peace, the mosquito sucking blood…all had an unpleasant side to them but none were malicious enough. Even the leech, which looked more disgusting than all of them put together, could be of use to humans and was thus disqualified. What she searched for was something much worse than all of these creatures: something that was of no use either to itself or to others, something incompatible with any kind of benevolence, whose existence was apparently without any real purpose and one comparatively worse than all those absolutely useless but just as harmless creatures God had created with leftover clay. Such was the sort of creature she needed to scare me with turning into if I did not hold my oath one day.

'If you're searching for the worst creature, you should pay attention to the eyes. Those whose eyes you can look into are usually not as bad as those whose eyes you can't see.'

This she liked so much that she instantly ripped out a page from her lily adorned notebook and started making a list of creatures whose eyes could not be seen. So seriously she took the task that it wasn't possible to change the topic or to get up and leave. While she tried to pick up a punishment among an assortment of punishments for my potential betrayal, I tried to help her as best as I could.

'Let me be a rattle snake,' I hissed, squeezing my tongue in between my teeth.

'Nooooo!'

'Let me be a piranha,' I rattled, opening my mouth wide.

'Come on, noooo!'

'I can't get you to like anything,' I pretended to be disgruntled.

I guess until that moment, I was having fun, but all of a sudden an abstruse distress descended upon me. I put on my watch. This preposterous game had gone on too long and I don't know why but it had started to get on my nerves. Just as I was thinking about leaving, 'I found it, I found it,' she cackled her voice lilting with delight. 'There was no need to search after all!'

'You're now going to repeat after me, ok?' she asked, so easily and swiftly shifting from the formal speech form we normally used to a far more casual one. I nodded meekly. She stood across from me, staring at me directly in the eye.

'I'm a big man.'

'I'm a big man.'

'But if I tell our secret to anyone else...'

'But if I tell our secret to anyone else...' I said, as I narrowed my eyes and added a furtive tinge to my voice. Yet she no longer smiled. In the darkness of her eyes, two slender, pitch black water snakes slithered in silvery sparkles.

'May God turn me into a louse! The biggest louse ever!' Su hollered, pompously stressing each word.

'May God turn me into a louse!' I hollered, pompously stressing each word. 'The biggest louse ever!'

I jumped to my feet, assuming as fearsome an expression as possible, crossing my eyes, pushing my front teeth onto my lower lip like a vampire, jutting my jaw forward, making my hair stand up, my forehead all wrinkled, opening my nostrils wide and moving my eyebrows up and down. I had never attempted to imitate a louse before. I'd never realized how tough it could be! I did not have the foggiest idea what the faces of lice looked like. In point of fact, I could not even tell whether lice had faces or not. One of the few things I knew about lice was that they could be identified from afar, only from afar, as no one could tell what they looked like up close. Another thing: I also knew lice were petite enough not to be seen by the naked eye and evil enough not to display their eyes.

Mulling it over together we came up with further assumptions. Perhaps what rendered a louse so base and bad was its unique ability to become one with its victim. As such, a louse was not some sort of a foe lying in ambush outside, waiting for an occasion to assail, but rather an affliction that gnaws surreptitiously from within. The mosquito sucks our blood as well, for instance, but it leaves its victim alone once it finishes its job and has gotten what it hankered after. A mosquito, even at the instant it finds our vein, continues to be a part of the outside, never a part of us. So apparent is this detachment that even when we squish a mosquito that has just stung us, we are disgusted by the blood in our palms as if it was not ours but the mosquito's. Nevertheless when it comes to lice exactly the reverse is true. The louse belongs not to the exterior but the interior, distinctively to us in person.

To picture it, I too tore a page from the lily-bedecked notebook. Since we could not figure out whether a louse had a face and, if it indeed had one, what it would look like, and since our only hint was that it stood out as the worst of the worse, we could capture its monstrosity by borrowing a bit from each bad creature on earth and then bestowing upon it the imaginary body we had thus formulated. When I was done, what emerged was a real freak. Since it had borrowed each part of its body from a different creature, it resembled many life forms but did not look like any particular one of them. The eyes, one borrowed from a frog and the other an owl, appeared so strange together that it was as if it had been hit on the head with a sledgehammer. Below the page, I wrote, 'Dazed Drunk Louse' in small letters.

Su started to giggle as soon as she saw the picture. 'Excellent! That's exactly it. If you don't keep your mouth shut, God will turn you into Dazed Drunk Louse!' I tried to act as if I was scared but could not help laughing midway. She tried to act as if she was offended but could not help laughing midway.

Then abruptly, apprehensively, she stopped talking as if scolded by an invisible authority in the room. The vulnerability of someone who had just realized they had revealed things that could never be taken back cast a shadow over her juvenile face. It was only then that I had a sneaking suspicion that what she had told me could actually be true.

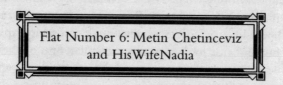

Flat Number 6: Metin Chetinceviz and HisWifeNadia

'I told you not to give up hope in God, Loretta. My daughter, you should be grateful now that you have recovered your memory. You so much deserve to be happy,' cooed the nurse to the woman who was about to be discharged.

'It's so strange,' the other one smiled, opening wide the green eyes which she had made more dramatic with loads of even greener eye shadow. 'What I most desired thus far was to remember my past, but now I want to escape from it. I'm going to start a new life nurse, and will never leave you from now on.'

'See? Loretta will never leave us from now on,' snorted HisWifeNadia to the bug struggling in the empty jelly jar she kept rotating in her palms. 'Unlike you, *Blatella Germanica,* you were going to abandon us, weren't you?'

Toward the end of last the century, on a dreary, hazy day in the middle of a dirty, muddy street, a scientist excitedly reported witnessing the en masse migration of a cockroach breed named *Blatella Germanica.* Of the migrating flock almost all were female and when Dr. Howard encountered them, they were in the process of leaving the restaurant they used to reside in, getting ready to cross the street. The migration of the bugs took approximately three hours, at which point they reached the place they would hereafter dwell in. When Dr. Howard started to question why these cockroaches had left the restaurant in the first place, he could not come up with a satisfactory answer. As much as one could observe, nothing extraordinary had happened at the restaurant on that day; neither large-scale cleaning nor fumigating. There remained only one other factor that might have triggered the migration: overcrowding! For these female bugs to risk abandoning both their males and domicile even though no catastrophe had fallen upon them, it must have been crammed pretty tight back at that restaurant. Since hundreds had taken to the streets, there must be thousands left behind.

HisWifeNadia pensively pouted at the jar. How could so many *Blatella Germanica* – notorious for their deep dislike of daylight – keep appearing in the middle of the day at different corners of the house and particularly in the wardrobe where she kept her potato lamps? More significantly, did this obscured migration of flocks of cockroaches up and down the apartment building mean there could be hundreds or perhaps even thousands more someplace nearby?

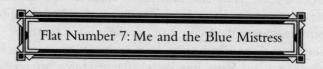

Flat Number 7: Me and the Blue Mistress

As I was heating up the leftover pasta from the day before, the doorbell rang piercingly and persistently. I opened the door. I had never seen her like this.

'I sure deserved this,' she moaned. Swollen bags as red as raw meat had gathered under her eyes; the gleam of her young face had vanished along with the brilliance of her eyes and the lustre of her skin. The sides of her nose were so irritated from the constant wiping that they were peeling off. This was a strange face and since the Blue Mistress existed and subsisted with and within her face, she too was a strange woman now. Still waiting for the pasta to heat up, I held out my *rakı* to her. She refused to sip from my drink but waited patiently for me to swig half a glass before starting to speak.

'He was going to come tonight,' she sighed, 'having sent me a message on the mobile phone. I made puréed eggplants. I was actually going to prepare chicken with ground walnuts but didn't feel like it this time. I guess I was a bit offended. You know he hadn't stopped by for ten days. That's why I prepared the puréed eggplants. He likes that dish too, but not as much as the chicken with ground walnuts. All day long, I grilled eggplants.'

Stern as I stared at her, she did not even notice how uninterested I was in all these details. Hurrying full blast, as if someone might any minute declare her time was up, she sliced to shreds dozens of details each more meaningless than the one before and piled them all up in front of me. I did not intervene anymore.

'He's had a heart attack. Can you imagine? He had a heart attack on the way here,' she cried out when she had finally finished with the dinner details. 'They called from the hospital. I guess since mine was the last number on his mobile phone, they thought I was his wife or family.'

'I'm sorry...'

As soon as she heard me, she started to choke and sob as if I had disclosed a long awaited decision in the negative. Perhaps she doubted the sincerity behind my words. Not that she would be wrong. The olive oil merchant, whom I had not met face to face and whom I passed judgement upon though I had seen him twice at most and only from a distance, was no more than a typecast for me: a hairy, greasy pitiable excuse of a rival with his belly hanging over his pants. I was sorry for my little lover more than him...and also somewhat surprised. Up until now I had not considered the possibility that she could have been so attached to that coarse figure of a man. That she loved to rat on him, did not object to and even enjoyed hearing me insulting him, was no indication that she was not attached to the man. Indeed she was more committed to him than I had ever suspected. I raked my fingers through her hair. Yet she harshly pushed away my hand.

'You don't understand,' she snorted her disapproval. 'It's my fault. If the poor thing can't make it through to the morning, it's all because of me.' She swallowed stiffly, as if trying to get rid of an acidic taste in her mouth. 'I paid a visit to the saint.'

'What did you do? What did you do?'

'Well, you can't actually call it paying a visit. Meryem put the idea into my head. There were a few bottles of banana liquor left in the house. I gave them to her a few days ago. I don't drink the liquor and she likes them a lot. We were talking about whether it would be harmful to the baby and that kind of chit-chat. Thank goodness this time around her pregnancy is not as difficult. Meryem told me she lost three male babies before Muhammet, two were stillborn, one died when six months old. So when Muhammet was born, she let his hair grow long like a girl. The kid went around like a girl until he started school, in order to trick *Azrael*.'

I am curious, do women have special machinery or something chemical in their brains that prevents them from expressing themselves straight out. So many details, so many introductory statements, so many stories whirling circles within circles that never get to the point… I refreshed my *rakı* but found no soda left on the empty shelves of my huge refrigerator. I needed to go out and get some.

'Anyway, the kid survived but he was then constantly beaten-up at school. Yet, Meryem said recently he had changed so much. That fainthearted boy was replaced by someone utterly different and is no longer beaten up by his friends. It's like a miracle.'

I wondered whether the Islamist grocer across the street had closed yet. Though he did not sell gin, he carried tonic. Though he did not sell liquor, he stocked chocolate with liquor. In a similar vein, he does not sell *rakı* but indeed sells soda to mix with *rakı*.

'We were talking about how it could be possible for this child to change so drastically. Meryem then confided to me that she had made a vow to the saint. 'Which saint?' I asked. 'Don't ask!' she replied puzzlingly. 'If you have a long awaiting wish, you too should go for it. If it ever comes true, only then will I tell you which saint I visited.' So she asked me for a clean scarf. I wrote my wish inside, then folded it up like a *Hıdrellez* request and gave it to her.'

I gave up. By the time this story was over, the Islamist grocer would have long closed the store and gone home. Given my preferences, I decided to make do with water.

'She said, 'If your wish comes true, so much the better. It would be my gift to you. You gave me so many banana liquors. If it doesn't come true, no one will know. All we would have done is try.' That's what she said. Well, maybe that's not exactly what she said but it was something like that. I can't remember right now.'

The *rakı* tasted awful! That damn drink is no good with water.

'So I folded it like a *Hıdrellez* letter, as she'd instructed me. 'Let me be freed of this state!' I wrote. Or perhaps I wrote, 'Let me be freed of this man!'... If I could only remember! Everything got mixed up. What did I write? God, what did the saint understand? The man is dying there because of me.'

What I had just heard was so enormously, astoundingly and fantastically ridiculous. I could not even consider it likely that she could really have believed this claptrap. Even if she did, I couldn't place much significance on the pain she would suffer because of it. After all, that is how things are. In order for us to truly share a person's pain, they first have to share the same reality with us. When we calm down a child who is crying because a part of her rickety toy is broken; when we swear to the anorexic who looks skeletal but still imagines herself obese that she really is not a fatso; when we put up with the absurd talk of our best buddy, mad at life having been cheated on by a worthless woman he's only been with for a total of two weeks; when we strive to distract until the arrival of his psychiatrist the mentally ill man who suspects his soul has been stolen by a pigeon and thereby chases all the pigeons out in the square to search inside the beaks of each and every one; in all of these cases we stand by these people but look at their pain from way yonder. The child shedding tears for such a simple thing, the anorexic who camps so far away from reality, the miserable buddy who cannot see it is not worth getting upset by such a worthless woman, the nut incapable of comprehending that the poor pigeons flock around real concrete for wheat kernels instead of intangible elusive souls; all might plausibly expect from us some degree of attention and compassion, soothing or solidarity. They'll most likely get it too. We could indeed fulfill the role of comforter without much hesitation. Upon seeing how they talk nonsense because of their suffering and how they suffer because of their nonsensical talk, the chances are we might even feel emotionally close to them deep down...but that is the very limit. They might require and possibly receive our kindheartedness at one of those moments but they cannot convince us to enter their reality. We can pity or even love them, provided they do not expect us to sincerely share in their suffering.

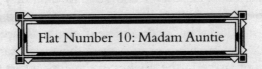

At room temperature of 27° C and a humidity rate of 65%, the early stages of a housefly's lifecycle involve one to two days as eggs, eight to ten days as larvae and nine to ten days as pupa. In laboratory research conducted under the same conditions, it has been observed that 50% of the male flies die within the first fourteen days and 50% of the female flies die within the first twenty-four days.

At a room temperature of 27° C and a humidity rate of 36–40%, cockroaches prove to be far more resistant than flies. Under such circumstances, they can survive without any food intake for twenty days. With only water, they can stay alive for thirty-five days. The eggs laid under the same temperature and humidity levels hatch between twenty-seven to thirty days. The hatched offspring change skin between five and ten times to become adults. Adults can live for approximately six to twelve months. Then they too die. They rot and decompose, break apart and scatter, are no longer themselves and are muddled up into different things.

Just like flies and cockroaches, food too has a lifecycle. In a cool and dry place, pasteurized milk stays fresh for one year, *halva* with pistachios, two years, diet biscuit with cinnamon, two years, granulated coffee, two years, raspberry chewing gum, ten to twelve months, chocolate with rice crackers, one year, a can of tuna, four years, a can of coke, six months and corn nut with cheese flavour, six months. If left in a refrigerator sliced whiting stays fresh for one and a half weeks, yoghurt drink for seven days, mozzarella one and a half months, packaged chicken twelve to fourteen days. At the end of this period, these things also start to die. They rot and decompose, break apart and scatter, are no longer themselves and get muddled up with different things. Once tea or tobacco, wheat or cheese expires, these things start to produce lice, bugs or larvae in the cavities of the cups where they are kept. Clothes engender moths, furniture becomes infested with worms and grain gets raided by beetles. Cockroaches too arrive at such places. Cockroaches are everywhere anyhow.

Just like flies and cockroaches and food, objects also have a lifecycle. On average, overalls worn as a baby last one to two months, a battery powered train acquired as a child lasts one hour and one year, diaries kept at puberty thirty to sixty days, the sweater given as a gift by a relative with no fashion taste ten seconds, the pipe bought with the desire to stop smoking only to discover afterward how difficult it is to clean, two to six puffs, a printer cartridge fifteen days and three months, a train ticket one to twenty hours, the gaudy ornament lovingly acquired when drunk only to seem not that nice when sober, one long night. Then they too die. They die and are thrown away, either to one side or to the garbage.

From the moment they wake up till they go to bed the denizens of Istanbul pass their days incessantly, unconsciously throwing things away. When calculated in terms of weeks, months, and years, a considerable garbage heap accumulates behind each and every person and just like flies and cockroaches and food and objects, humans too have an expiration date. The average life expectancy is sixty five years for males and seventy years for females. Then the inevitable end comes and they too die. They rot and decompose, break apart and scatter, are no longer themselves and get muddled up with different things.

***

When, after losing her husband in an accident twenty-five years ago, Madam Auntie had moved alone into Flat Number 10 of Bonbon Palace, she had encountered there objects belonging to the former residents: a hundred and eighty-one ownerless and out-of-date objects. Even though the letter from the building's new owner in France had openly stated that she could dispense with these objects in any manner she chose, she hadn't felt like throwing away even a single one of them. When she read the letter from Pavel Antipovíc's daughter in France, she had not been infuriated. Yet there were times in the past she had been infuriated at the ease with which people dispensed with the objects of others. Yes, she had been infuriated before…and even before… When she had been a young woman, her mother had thrown away her novels and diaries and years later, when she had suddenly lost her husband, her brother had dispersed all photographs she had of him to friends and relatives. Perhaps she had not been able to reclaim her belongings in the past, but from now on she was going to look after the belongings of others as a steadfast safe-keeper.

To acquire items so as to use them for awhile and then throw them in the garbage, is a habit germane to those who believe themselves to be in possession of these items. Yet objects have no possessors. If anything they have their stories, and at times it is these stories that have possession of the people who have meddled with them…

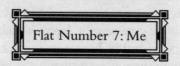

Flat Number 7: Me

Following the lecture, Ethel came to pick me up in a honey-coloured Cherokee. We left my car at the faculty parking lot and continued on our way in this new toy of hers. She did not seem in the mood for chatting at first but then, as we got stuck in the traffic jam her tongue loosened. I would have rather she had just paid attention to the traffic. Her driving gets worse by the day. As she started to chatter about the last phase they had reached in the university project, I noticed she had lost her initial enthusiasm. Either this business is going totally down the tubes or Ethel has decided to part ways with it. I refrained from asking which. She will eventually, if not today, tomorrow, report to me everything anyhow.

'Hey, tell me, how are things going at the apartment building of the wacky?' was the first thing she said when, after struggling in traffic for fifty minutes, we had finally reached our reserved table at the restaurant; just as I wanted, all the way down, by the window... I chose to turn my back and Ethel her face to other diners. She apparently wants to keep an eye on other people. What do I care?

'Don't ask! Bugs all over the place.'

'So bugs too are coming for entertainment. What a blessed bastard you are! You've ended up dwelling in a most hilarious place. Rather than an apartment building it resembles an insane asylum.'

'I know it's hard for you but try not to exaggerate,' I groaned. 'God knows, the apartment building I formerly lived

404

in was probably no different, but back then I didn't have a clue. The only difference now is that I'm not indifferent to the neighbours at Bonbon Palace.'

'Oh, yeah, I can see that. You're particularly interested in one among those,' she snorted as she placed the first cigarette of the night onto her jasmine-wood cigarette holder and sent in my direction three smoke rings, one after the other.

I pretended not to have heard that last comment, having no intentions of quarrelling with her tonight, but my deafness seemed to provoke her even more.

'You can't make it with that woman, sugar-plum. You know why? Not because of a moral reason or anything, but simply because of keeping up images! At present there are no problems. You stay indoors, screw as you like, all is fine and dandy, but what will happen afterwards? Could you go out into the public with her? Could you take the arm of your twenty-two year old high school dropout, deeply religious but just as immoral and decisively-indecisive lover, to promenade and hang around together? Do you really believe an academic with such a clear-cut intellect can ever make it with that walking confusion of an ignorant petite missie?'

I could not come back with a response. Instead I laughed away whatever she said. Before long, she got fed up with pestering me. Neither of us were in good spirits. As we waited for the mixed fruit plate, we made guesses about the people at adjacent tables, thus keeping the damage we could have inflicted on each other to a minimum, but it turned out Ethel had saved her real surprise to the end.

'Listen sugar-plum, I didn't want to be the one to tell you this, but, maybe it's better that you hear it from me. Who else but me do you have to pour out your poison? Anyway, let's save the conjectural comments till the end. First the actual data! Here's the astounding news: Ayshin is getting married, oops, re-married!'

Timing was the gravest error the moon-faced albino waiter committed when at that instant he reached out to change my plate. Not that I am one of those people who constantly cause trouble at restaurants, shouting reprimands left and right, but I do hate to have my plate changed without my asking for it. Waiters generally do not want to even consider this as a possibility but there are people in this city who relish the pleasure of munching on their leftovers. I cannot stand seeing the remains of my food being instantly removed as if it were something disgraceful. If it were up to me, I would not part with my plate until the very moment I leave the table. I could mix the remnants of the cold appetizers with the hot ones and keep nibbling for a whole night. Not only do I not feel the slightest discomfort at having the fruit slices smeared with the oil, sauce, salt and spice of the hot appetizers, I sometimes sit down and make sweet and sour compositions with these. If I like this final fusion, I eat it: if I do not, I ruin it. Ethel knows this habit of mine. She does not meddle. The waiters do not know it. They meddle.

'Please excuse him. It's just that he's going through a tough phase, just got divorced from his wife,' croaked Ethel to the waiter now standing beside me with a scratched white plate utterly unable to comprehend why he had been snapped at. The man intuited the mockery in these words and curled his pale lips into a smile, but at the same moment he must have felt the need to be cautious just in case, for he suppressed his lip movement, thereby lingering behind me with a face like a mask; one half smiling, the other half sad.

'Please, go ahead, you can change my plate. I'm perfectly normal,' Ethel smirked. The waiter, defeated by this proposal to share a confidence, grinned with her while removing the dirty plate in front of her.

'If you ask me, the guy is a total pushover,' Ethel said shrugging, when we were once again left alone. It took me an additional minute to fathom it was not the waiter she was talking about but Ayshin's husband-to-be. 'He's a well-intentioned pushover – meek and almost gullible – but a pushover nonetheless. Docile, compliant, and of course, domesticated. His limits are only too evident, corners on each side. Whichever way he faces you run into a wall. In order to find just a spark of vigour in the guy, you have to dig at least seven layers deep down into his past. I wonder if he ever experienced any exuberance, probably once in his childhood. Even then, don't expect much, only a few drops. Now you'll be curious about his appearance!' she conjectured, holding my hand. 'Let me put it this way: next to you, he would look like a senile badger.'

So that's it. Ayshin is going to get married to a senile badger. I place a slice of melon onto the corner of my plate where a thick garlic and walnut sauce had spread out.

'The buck-toothed one, was that a badger or a mole?' Ethel mumbled as she removed her hand, leaving on my wrist traces of her nails painted a glittery indigo. 'Anyway sugar-plum, one thing I know for sure is this guy is really, really ugly. Basically, I'd say, Ayshin is using the trial and error technique. Once bitten, twice shy, she shuns handsome young academics.'

When we left, I sat next to her with more confidence, knowing that compared to when she is sober, she drives more carefully when drunk. She brought me all the way to Bonbon Palace without any trouble. Then she took off in the gloomy street radiating a corona of honey in the dark.

★★★

Once on the third floor, I stopped to eavesdrop at the door of the flat across from me. No sound came from within. Though I had not been planning to see her tonight, I rang the doorbell without really thinking. She had forbidden me to come unannounced but I could violate the ban that night. The olive oil merchant would not probably spend the night in his mistress's bed right after a heart attack.

Soft, almost fluffy footsteps approached. The golden light seeping through the peephole darkened. We stayed just like that on either side of the door for a long minute. The door opened with an annoying tardiness. Her chestnut eyes looked at me with no radiance, love or feeling. Without uttering a single word, good or bad, she turned her back and staggered into the living room dragging her feet. I did not care. However weird her movements were, my drunkenness was just as good. I parked myself on the couch, turned on the TV. We started to watch without a sound. A singer of classical music, having smeared gold glitter on all parts of her body under her transparent, stone studded, lilac costume, was telling the microphone what she had been through. She had broken her leg during a skiing trip, but because she could not bear to cancel the concert tickets and upset her dear fans, she had made the heroic decision to appear on stage in crutches. Standing next to her was her physician, who occasionally intervened to answer the questions the journalists spurted backstage.

'Dead,' croaked the Blue Mistress.

I looked at her face in perplexity, unable to figure out who on earth she was talking about. My eyes slid of their own accord in the direction of the television screen. The singer looked alive but perhaps paler now. She blew a kiss toward the camera. I turned off the TV. Not knowing what to say, I sat next to the Blue Mistress. I held her hand. She did not hold my hand. She went to sleep. So calm… Too calm…

I sat alone in the living room trying to collect my thoughts. I hadn't realized how much I had drunk tonight. A bulky lethargy swathed my movements. I could not think fast, act agile. Not only did I not know how to comfort my little lover, I did not feel a wee bit of sadness. The only thing I wanted to do was to go home and pass out.

Still however, I headed not towards the door, but to her bedroom. In the darkness, I laid next to her, pricking my ears up to all sounds to try and work out whether she was asleep or not. She was awake. 'He couldn't get over the attack,' she whispered. 'He died at three in the morning.' I touched her cheeks: dry. She was not crying. I snuck closer to her. She neither pushed me away nor responded to my touch. She kept lying down like an empty sack. The bed was warm. We embraced. I fell asleep.

I woke up during the night burning up with thirst. Glugging down all the water in the glass on the table, I shuffled to the bathroom. As I peed, I gazed groggily at the perfumed soaps in a glass stilt, the papaya shampoos lined up at the corner of the sink, the delicate perfume bottles shining in front of the mirror, the turquoise bath sponges, body lotions and minutely detailed middle-aged supplies. I flushed the toilet. Amidst all these knick-knacks I caught sight of two razors. One had fallen on the ground and the other in the sink.

This was enough to sober me up. I dashed to the bedroom. I turned the light on, drew the bedspread away from her. As she tried to sit up from her sleep, I pulled up her aquamarine nightgown extending down to her knees. There was nothing on her left leg, nothing new, but the top part of her right leg was wrapped up with a towel covered with wide, brick red stains. This loose wrap was so bulgy I could not understand how I had previously failed to notice it. As I hurried to untie the thin, long towel, she simply, patiently waited without resistance.

Five scarlet cuts emerged from under the towel, each one almost the length of a hand span. Three of them did not seem that deep. It was as if they were opened accidentally or reluctantly, as if they were the rehearsal for the other two. For those were awful. I ran back to the bathroom. Unable to find anything useful in the cupboards, I scampered to my house. As I ran from one end of Bonbon Palace to the other with hydrogen peroxide and cotton balls, the entire effect of all the alcohol I had consumed tonight evaporated.

She watched me mutely, as I cleaned and wrapped up her wounds. Then, thanking me, half-bashful, half-glum, she pulled over her the aquamarine nightgown that had somehow not been stained during this period of time, and once again curled up as round as a ball. I turned off the light. I waited for her to cry, blab, snuggle, seek shelter. In the dark, when she curled up into herself leaving me alone by her side, I had to admit to myself that I did not know her at all. It is such an inexcusable gullibility to think that by cracking open the vaginas of women we make love to we can see through their body and, upon entering them, reach into their depths...

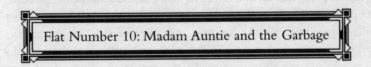

The first garbage trucks and garbage company in Istanbul started work in 1868. Before them, the same job was incumbent upon the Guild of Seekers working under the control of the Litter Superintendent. Just like today's garbage men, the seekers of old times were in charge of getting rid – even if only partially – of what the inhabitants of Istanbul wanted to get rid of entirely, eternally. However, when the issue came to how they did so, there was a grinding difference between the contemporary garbage men and their predecessors. The foremost purpose of the Guild of Seekers in gathering what was to be thrown away was to find among the gathered what should be saved from being thrown away. Before they discarded the waste, muck and debris they had collected into dumps, they would carry it all to the seashore in their haversacks and there they would sort, rinse and rummage through this pile over and over. There were times when they encountered copper plates, steel rods, nails that could be re-used, clothes not yet threadbare, non-oxidized silver or gifts that had been unappreciated. If lucky enough, they could even hit upon lost jewellery.

The Guild of Seekers visited the sites of fire frequently. Whenever a house turned into ashes in Istanbul, the city of fires, they carried away the wreckage. Just like from the garbage, from the ashes too, they collected items. The seekers would gather to sift through. Yet the garbage men collected to throw away. For the city to modernize the order of things had to be capsized. Once what was thrown away on all sides was gathered in one place by the seashore, now what was gathered on all sides was thrown away in one place by the Garbage Hills.

As for Madam Auntie, being a seeker she didn't belong to this age. Just like the bygone members of the Guild, she too was rummaging around in the garbage for objects that should not have been thrown away. To this day she had never failed to find them.

In spite of sleeping only in dribs and drabs, I woke up early this morning. As I tucked the hair stuck on her sweaty forehead behind her ear, the Blue Mistress stirred slightly. I let her sleep. Lighting a cigarette I headed to the kitchen. She had crammed the refrigerator with food, as usual. All of the things the olive merchant would have liked. In our happier days with Ayshin, I had become used to getting up late during the weekends to have lengthy, lazy breakfasts. Now she is probably breaking that old badger in to her own rhythm. If the man is as Ethel describes, I have to meet him. Not that I expect to change anything, but I still want him to see me. I could trigger the fuse of the inferiority complex in him. I may even succeed in embedding in his mind the tiniest louse of suspicion. Let him then struggle with sifting through the sourness of the possibility that the woman he is about to marry might go back to her old husband one day.

I must have awakened the Blue Mistress with my clatter. As she stood by the kitchen door wrapped up in her speckled shawl, she looked much better than the night before even though her face was still pale and her eyes miserably baggy.

'I hope you are not blaming yourself anymore,' I said, as I filled up her teacup.

She does…and I blame her too… I blame her and everyone who acts as if they are the god of their squat universe. There is no way I can comprehend those who first pray with all their heart that harm be given to someone they cannot reach otherwise and then, when fortuitously their wishes happen to come true, simply breakdown in guilt and shame. I cannot stand those who, on the one side, delegate all the problems they cannot handle and don't even lift a finger to resolve, to some otherworldliness purportedly purified of all evil and, on the other side, yearn for receiving a slice of otherworldly evil to purify their most mundane problems. It enrages me to see what people are capable of doing to themselves when they fail to distinguish their limits. Not because they overestimate themselves way too much but because they underestimate evil way too much. The world is full of people who watch from afar for a chance to hurt someone and, when by chance that happens, do not hold Fortuna responsible but the thoughts and wishes that had once crossed their minds. I did not want the Blue Mistress to join their ranks. I did not want to lose her in this way and instead hoped to spare this lovely naïve creature who believed that this God of hers who created the universe by pronouncing 'BE!' could likewise destroy with the pronouncement of 'DIE!'★ So I decided to explain what I had done.

'Will you please get this saint's tale out of your mind? There's no truth to it,' I said, as I slid onto her plate half of the best omelet I had made in a long while. 'The holy saint Meryem talked to you about most likely emerged from the writing on the garden wall but it was I who wrote that.'

If I could only have grasped what she was thinking right at that instant. If I could only be sure that I was doing the right thing by disclosing this.

'Look, I'm sorry about the olive oil merchant – and don't get mad at me for referring to him as the 'olive oil merchant'. I hope you're aware of the fact that even if there were a saint lying under the garden wall with his bones crumbled to dust, the outcome would not have been any different. Sim-ply-be-ca-use-my-litt-le-one-your-guy-pass-ed-a-way-not-be-ca-

★According to the Muslim faith, in order to create the universe Allah uttered 'BE!'

414

use-you-wan-ted-to-get-rid-of-him-but-be-ca-use-he-had-a-
he-art-at-tack.'

There it was again. Her looks became cast in shadow. Once
again in my life, I witnessed that dusky phase wherein I started
to awaken hatred in a woman whose loving eyes I had been
accustomed to.

'Basically my sweet, if you are going to blame yourself for
every calamity and keep slicing up your body, there is no way
I can stop you, but if you intend to give this habit up, I'll do
everything to help. Now, if you'll see me not as your enemy
but as your friend, let's sit down together and talk about what's
going to happen from now on. After all your life won't be like
it used to be. But maybe, why not, it can be more beautiful.'

'Why did you lie?' she maundered.

'If you mean the saint business, I don't consider myself as
having lied. The only thing I wanted was to get the apartment
building rid of this awful smell. I just wanted to make those
who dump their garbage here feel uncomfortable. It didn't
even cross my mind that anyone would take that silly writing
seriously.'

Her face clouded up, as she once again got immersed in a
thorny silence. I made a last effort to win her heart.

'The truth is, if the smell had indeed been coming from the
outside, my writing might have helped to overcome this
problem but we'd been suspecting the source of the smell to
be in the wrong place all this time. It turns out the smell was
coming from the inside, from within Bonbon Palace.'

It worked. Now she was looking at me with less hatred and
more interest. I shovelled the breakfast plate toward her. Seeing
her take the fork into her hand I felt a childish joy. She was
going to taste the omelet I had made. She was going to make
love to me again.

'I'm announcing our Garbage Commander. Hold onto your
seat!' I rasped. The thrill dribbling from my voice disturbed me
for a fleeting moment but I did not mind. 'Flat Number 10!
Our respected neighbour, the widow.'

'You mean Madam Auntie?' whispered the Blue Mistress. 'No way, I won't believe that. You must be mistaken. She wouldn't do such a thing!'

'She has indeed, my beauty. She's filled her house with garbage all the way up.'

'How do you know?' she asked, narrowing her chestnut eyes.

'Forget about where I've found out about it. I'm telling the truth. God knows that's the reason for all those bugs infesting your house.' Oddly enough, I had not thought about this link previously, but all of a sudden all the bits and pieces of events interconnected in my mind.

'I don't believe you. I won't believe you any more,' she said, putting down her fork.

'Oh really?' I repined, feeling no need to hide my loss of composure. 'What if I prove it, my sweet?'

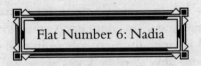

'Let's throw a big party, nurse. Let's invite everyone, even our enemies!' hollered Loretta, as she slid at the clinic door away from the arms of the faithful elderly woman crying tears of joy. Standing by her was the husband–physician who had been struggling for so long to treat her, so that she could remember being married to him. Before they got into the car that was waiting for them, they turned around and waved simultaneously to the continuously crying wet nurse and the continuously smiling clinic personnel.

HisWifeNadia turned off the TV. Then, inspecting the contents of the smelly, amber suitcase for the last time, pulled the zipper shut. The shadow puppets looked at her offended from the corner in which they had been thrown. She could easily have picked up another suitcase, but for some reason unknown to her, she wanted to take this one in particular. HisWifeNadia was leaving. The State of Dormancy had ended.

Just like bugs, humans too, have an ecological potency, that is, an endurance limit. When and where they run into negative circumstances, they react by limiting their life functions. Their bodily mechanisms thus function less or perhaps differently and, thanks to this ability, they adjust their metabolisms to the new conditions they are subjected to. Within the circle of life, such a state of consecutive dormancy could emerge at any time, at any phase, and could be repeated many times over. Certain types of bugs, for instance, survive through winter by going through different stages of larvae as an egg. They minimize their material change by either stopping or slowing down their transformation until the cold weather has passed. Nevertheless, there is a limit to this stationary phase whereupon it has to cease. If the inappropriateness of the surrounding circumstances continues way too long, irreparable damage could be done to the metabolisms of the bugs.

In order to be able to really know what we already know, every now and then we insist on waiting for a sign, if not a messenger, but who says the messenger has to be in a certain form and of a certain proportion? What matters eventually is not the guise of the messenger but our very ability to decipher the message. As Nadia Onissimovna pouted at the bugs infesting the cupboard where she kept her potato lamps, she had abruptly been swept by the thought that this 'His Wife Nadia' state of her life had been a state of consecutive dormancy. All though this period she had limited her life functions, dropped down below her capacity and frozen her transformation, and if she did not get out of this shallow stage as soon as possible, irreparable damage would be done to her personality.

She was going back to the Ukraine. Taking with her the *Blatella Germanica* that had come all the way to her feet to give her the message, to remind her that she was something else in addition to and beyond being baffled and lonesome, a bewildered soul searching for difference within sameness, a foreigner out of synch with the city she lived in, a spouse openly cheated on, a housewife incompetent in making *ashure* savoury enough, a victim of the domestic violence of a wine imbiber even the grapes of Leon the Sage could not satiate, glum enough to expect help from her monotonous correspondence with a religiously strict aunt who heard god's voice in the bubbling of soup cauldrons, a dispirited person whose every day was just like the previous one and blind enough to expect enlightenment from potato lamps... In addition and beyond all of these things, the bug had helped her remember, she was a scientist who loved the world of bugs way more than that of humans.

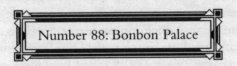

Number 88: Bonbon Palace

On Wednesday May 1st 2002, at 12:20 p.m., a white van – in need of a wash and decorated with the picture of a huge rat with needle-sharp teeth on one side, a hairy humongous spider on the other and signs of various sizes all over it – stopped in front of Bonbon Palace. The ginger haired, funny-faced, flap-eared driver who did not at all look his age was named Injustice Pureturk. He had been fumigating bugs for thirty-three years and had never hated his job as much as he did today. As he parked close to the sidewalk, he suspiciously eyed the gathering at the entrance of the apartment building. He checked the address his chatterbox of a secretary had handed him in the morning: 'Cabal Street, Number 88 (Bonbon Palace).' The chatterbox secretary had also put down a small note below: 'The apartment building with a rose acacia tree in the garden.' As Injustice Pureturk wiped off the sweat beads covering his forehead, he inspected the tree in the garden with pinkish flowers on some branches and purplish ones on others. This must be, he thought, what they called a rose acacia.

Still, since he did not trust his secretary, whom he planned to replace as soon as possible, he wanted to see personally what was written on the door with his near-sighted eyes. He could easily have asked the people gathered in front of the apartment building but having become so terribly, immovably used to taking care of his own business and as he never trusted others, he left the van askew in the middle of the street and jumped down. As soon as he had taken a step, however, the small girl among the three children standing within the crowd screamed in horror: 'The genie is here! Grandpaaa, grandpa, look, the genie is here!' The older man with the round, greying beard, wide forehead and a skull cap on his head whose trousers the kid tugged, turned and eyed with a displeased look first the van, then the van driver. He must not have liked what he had seen, for his face turned even more sour as he drew all three children toward himself.

Trying not to be offended, Injustice Pureturk plunged into the crowd with determined steps. He shoved the people aside, got near the apartment block and succeeded in reading the sign, relieved to see he had arrived at the right address. After removing a business card squeezed in between the lined up buzzers and putting his own in its stead, he jumped back onto his driver's seat and put his van in reverse. Just then a female head popped in.

'You came with only one van? It won't be enough,' hooted a cross-eyed blond woman with a plastic bib with leopard patterns tied to her neck. 'They had said they were going to send two trucks. Even two trucks could barely pick up all this garbage.'

As Injustice Pureturk tried to decipher what the hell this woman was talking about, and manoeuvre his van amongst the trucks plunging into the street from two opposite ends on the other side, he lost his control over the wheel, crushing the garbage pile by the garden wall.

***

That day, other than the van driven by Injustice Pureturk, two other trucks turned up in front of Bonbon Palace as well as the car of a private television channel. They left Bonbon Palace at the end of the day, the trucks jammed with garbage and the vehicle of the television channel with all the shots it required. Rather than the neighbours who were eager to be interviewed, the anchorman had wanted to interview the woman living in the garbage house, but once her apartment had been emptied out and fumigated she had sealed the door of Flat Number 10, refusing to open it to anyone.

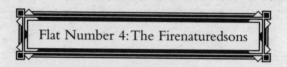

Flat Number 4: The Firenaturedsons

Zelish Firenaturedsons panted as she closed herself up in her room and hurled her little suitcase onto her bed. As she tried to regain her balance by holding onto the side of the bed, she waited for her heartbeat to return to normal. She had chosen the wrong day to run away from home. As soon as she had stepped out to the street, she had found herself in the middle of an insane mayhem with two bright red trucks approaching from either direction. It was unbearably red out there in the outside world. Amongst all the colours, the streets of Istanbul were closest to red.

'Why am I so disconsolate? I should have known I'll never be able to get out of this house.'

She picked up the mirror. The rash had covered up her entire face. The rash too was red as hell. She cried, first noiselessly and then howling increasingly. All of a sudden she heard a chirpy sound. Someone was answering her from inside. Though her head still swam and her sight fading out from seeing too much red, she followed the sound with wobbly steps. The canary in its cage by the window in the living room was merrily chirping.

'Why are you so joyful? You'll never be able to leave this house either.'

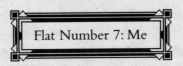

Flat Number 7: Me

No matter how hard I try not to, I recurrently recall everything we talked about that day. As to what happened afterward, I'd rather entirely erase it from my memory or at least only rarely, vaguely remember. However, Su's curse seems to be working. Even if my body didn't, my memory did turn into a louse. Like a fleshy louse wedged tightly onto my head, my memory has become menacing, procreating every passing day. In my mind's eye I see my memory wandering around my head, sometimes on top of it, inside it at other times, making squeaky sounds as it lays its invisibly small, innumerably many, white eggs all around. Out of these eggs thousands of damned and unabashed hungry mouths come out, feeding on me, in spite of me. In tandem with their number, their appetite also escalates. Voraciously they bite through my flesh, numbing my head from pain as if thousands of pins have been stuck on it. I do not mention this to anyone. As I can no longer stand the person I am when with others, I try to stay alone as much as possible and seek out the answers to the same unanswerable questions.

If I had not written that nonsensical writing on the garden wall and had not babbled away, if I had used the intellect which I prided myself on so much and so unreservedly to fathom the consequences of my act, to foresee the damage I was about to cause to another person, would all this still have happened? If I had never moved into Bonbon Palace and had not mixed with these people or learned their secrets, if I had succeeded for once in my life in being someone other than my typical self, would this tale still wind through the same routes toward the same ill-fated end? I can think of two different answers. One belongs to my mentality and the other to my heart. My mind says: 'Don't worry, sooner or later this catastrophe would have occurred anyhow. You are not as significant as you think or as malicious as you fear. What difference does it make whether this tragedy happened because of you or for another reason, as long as the end result is the same? If it makes you feel better, call it 'Fortuna'. In any case, what else but Fortuna can account for the fact that every secret eventually ends up in the hands of the one who will divulge it?'

I console myself. I need to believe in the righteousness of my mind. 'The issue is neither this incessant failing nor that flawed willpower of yours. Whether you like it or not, you are not the one making the impossible possible.' There is an offensive consolation in what my mind claims. 'The human being is so vulnerable and primordial. It is coincidences rather than the consequences he causes that make an imprint on his life. Given that humankind is so weak, to what extent could you be blamed for what you did?' The more I am degraded, the more I get acquitted.

My heart instantly protests. 'Even if there is a Fortuna, weren't you the one who deemed its whorishness doubtful? Are we to own up to all victories but blame adversities on the vileness of an uncanny feminine power? Wasn't the individual supposed to admit right out that he himself is the maker of his own fate rather than attributing the course of events to hollow superstitions?' There is an honouring indictment in what my heart claims. 'The human being is so complex and capable. What we consider to be chance only marks the results we personally cause. Given that humankind is so capable to what extent could you be absolved for what you did?' The more I am elevated, the more I get besmirched.

I do not drink more than before, but these days, I do sleep more than I used to. As my anguish swells, I seek refuge in sleep to then wake up even more anguished. It does not matter anymore if I leave or stay. However far I move out, never will I be able to step outside the range of the stink emitting from Flat Number 10. At my every awakening, the smell has become even more sour.

No smell in life, even that of garbage could be as venomous as this one.

Occasionally I overhear the neighbours. They are planning to break down her door. I do not want to be here when they break into Flat Number 10.

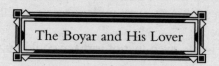

The Boyar and His Lover

The boyar and his lover on the wooden ladder leaning against the wall fretfully snuggled closer. The house smelt of death. They no longer dared to breathe. Averting their eyes from one another, they stared at the half-emerald, half-obscure forest extending languorously yonder.

When the door was broken, men with masks fully clad in white dashed inside. They placed the stinking corpse on a stretcher and carried it away. The old widow's corpse was so light, so petite...the residue of a body that had refused for days to eat—to drink—to take its pills... Madam Auntie had not been half as resistant to thirst and hunger as cockroaches.

As soon as the men departed, the flat was fumigated once again. The insecticide spray drizzled on the eggs of the bugs, as well as on the one hundred and eighty-one objects from the past, but fortuitously the boyar and his lover managed to escape at the last minute. They went down the ladder, ploughed into the woods and walked out of the round, glazed, delicate tray of Vishniakov.

A shadowy forest, half-emerald, half-obscure remained behind on the tray. The forest smelt of neither death nor garbage, but solely of cinnamon and cream.

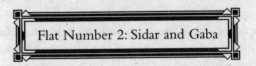

Flat Number 2: Sidar and Gaba

Back in his house, Sidar threw himself on the couch, gasping hard. He had been brooding on suicide for so long, but that old widow who in all likelihood had never contemplated it as much, perhaps not even considered it until the last moment, had committed it much faster. When he got up, he wrote on small pieces of paper the nine factors he had deduced that day and stuck them on whatever empty spot could be found on the ceiling:

1 Just like civilizations, suicides too, have an East and a West.

2 The progressive mentality focused on rendering life meaningful through reason and reason alone, and expecting each day to be more advanced than the preceding one, feels the need to weigh suicide meticulously, reasoning it soundly. People of this mentality, regardless of where they happen to be living, commit suicide in the West.

3 The suicides of those in their early-to-middle, middle and late-to-middle ages usually fall within this category.

4 Since the close relatives of those who commit suicide in the West cannot find comfort until they

427

get a satisfactory answer to the question, "Why?"
they follow the same line of reasoning to make an
analysis of cause and consequence.

5   There are also those who commit suicide at the least
     expected moment, the very last minute, without
     having organized the details. Such people, regardless
     of where they happen to be living, commit suicide
     in the realm of the East.

6   When children and the elderly commit suicide they
     do it in the East.

7   There is nothing as mind-boggling as the suicides of
     the elderly who-were-so-close-to-death-anyhow and
     children who-were-yet-so-far-away-from-death.

8   The suicides in the East, unlike the ones in the West,
     are in essence a mystery, or *'esrar'* as the Istanbulites say.

9   *Esrar* should not be given an explanation.

Flat Number 7: Me

At the beginning I used to draw circles around Bonbon Palace, brief walks that did not end up anywhere. Step by step the circles started to widen. Over time I started to veer, sometimes on foot, sometimes by car, into the far-flung neighbourhoods of Istanbul. It was the writings on the walls on the streets I was after.

When Ethel told me she wanted to keep me company on these urban trips, I did not object. While I took notes on the writings, she filmed them one by one with her digital camera. With the honey Cherokee, we snaked the rugged streets of destitute quarters, steered through the middle-income vicinities flickering with the ambition of opportunities long lost, toured around mansions, derelict grasslands, sanctums and dens. At squares, courtyards, construction sites, squat houses, places of worship: far and wide the writings were everywhere. Most had been written on the walls with paint but there were also some written with chalk, pencil, coal and brick on doors, cardboard and assorted signs. Just like garbage, the writings about garbage had also been scattered everywhere in the city.

At the places we went, we were immediately noticed. Children followed us curiously. Women suspiciously spied on our every move from behind the lattice tulle of windows. The most inquisitive among the artisans surrounded us each time and showered us with questions. When forced to offer a plausible explanation, we told them it was our school project to gather the 'Garbage Writings' of Istanbul. Despite the absurdity, it made sense to them. It did not at all stick out that both Ethel and I were too old to be students. In their eyes somehow school was deemed untouchable – a place where every absurdity was considered permissible.

Finding the people who had written these things proved to be more arduous than finding the writings themselves. We had to accept the fact that nearly all the writings were anonymous, but I did once manage to find out the perpetrator behind the writing on the wall of a dilapidated, soot grey edifice. 'Don't make me swer, I'll say bad things to garbage trowers. He who trows plaster here, come and get it, don't trow agen and make me swer.'

The children of the street knew the man who had written it. Though nobody knew his name, they knew his profession. He was a gatekeeper at one of the universities who had resided there with his bedridden wife and mother-in-law until last spring. While the adjacent construction continued, he was so infuriated at the construction workers dumping plaster in front of his house that he had gone out and written that. The man had passed away in the fall, the construction had ended right afterwards, but the writing on the wall had stayed all this time.

'Can't you dress more modestly seeing as we create a centre of attention wherever we go anyhow?' I grumbled at Ethel after we left the neighbourhood of the gatekeeper.

'Don't pick on me. Our subject matter is not my clothing but your guilty conscience,' she snapped as she changed gears. 'This mess we are in is your "PAGHHC", not mine.' She pushed on the gas pedal though the road was getting rougher, narrower ahead. 'We hit the road for the "Project to Acquit the Gentleman's Heedlessly Hardened Conscience"! All your life you saw yourself as different from, if not superior to everyone around you, but the moment you realize you've messed up the whole lot, you need to prove to yourself that, after all, you are like everyone else! Only that conviction can ease your guilt. You seem to hope that the more we go around collecting garbage writing, the more uncontestable your innocence will be. "God what have I done! On me resides, if not the blood, the curse of an old woman. I am paying heavily for treating people lightly. At long last I saw the devil and with my very own eyes. I indeed saw him but believed in you, my God. I'm just like everyone else. Look, your other subjects too have written on the walls of Istanbul. Thus what I had done in the past was way too ordinary. Accordingly, I wasn't as extraordinary a man as I thought I was. Thank God for my ordinariness! If you do love them, you can forgive me as well…You will forgive me God, won't you?" Pull yourself together sugar-plum! You won't get anywhere with such futile hopes. Don't you see the irony in your efforts to purify yourself via garbage?'

★★★

After a while, we began to classify the writings into groups. Ethel would transfer the pictures she took to her computer the same day, filing them separately, scrupulously. The most packed category comprised those writings with a slur or smear in them. "He who dumps garbage here is an ass," was undoubtedly the most popular one. In Galata, on a wall at the Old Bank Street rested: "HE WHO DUMPS GARBAGE HERE IS SON OF A *****!" The rest of the sentence was scrawled out. In Fatih, just at the corner of Usturumcu Street, both fronts of a house with its plaster falling apart were entirely filled up with garbage writings, as if inscribed by someone punished by the teacher who had to write the same thing over a hundred times: "SHE WHO DUMPS GARBAGE IS A WHORE." Again in the same neighbourhood, in the Broken Water Pump Street it read: "HE WHO DUMPS GARBAGE HERE IS AN ASS WHO IS ALSO THE SON OF AN ASS." Though swearwords were widespread, the variety was rather limited. In Dolapdere, on the wooden sign tied onto a mulberry tree with a string was written: "IF THE PERSON WHO DUMPS GARBAGE HERE IS A WOMAN, SHE IS

A WHORE, IF A MAN, HE IS A PIMP." A few steps down the street, another bit of writing caught the eye, this time in front of a house: "THOSE WHO THROW GARBAGE HERE DESERVE ALL SORTS OF SWEARWORDS." In Örnektepe, on top of a wall that was falling to pieces, there was loads of writing in black and white. Each bit of writing seemed to have been produced on top of an earlier one, augmenting the bedlam. One among them, written in indigo, looked pretty new: "HE WHO DUMPS GARBAGE HERE IS A SON OF A BITCH: ONE WHO IS A HUMAN BEING WILL UNDERSTAND WHAT I MEAN." The most vulgar in the swearword file was some writing in Dolapdere: "HE WHO THROWS GARBAGE HERE, FUCK HIS MOTHER, WIFE, SISTER, HIS PAST, HIS FUTURE, HIS WHOLE FAMILY."

Second in popularity were the ones based on human-animal distinctions. In Galata, at Display Window Street a sign said: "IF YOU ARE A HUMAN BEING YOU WON'T DUMP GARBAGE, IF YOU ARE A BEAR, YOU SURE WILL." In the Little Ditch Street on the side-wall of a bank was written in coal: "HE WHO IS FAR FROM BEING A HUMAN WILL DUMP GARBAGE HERE". In Dolapdere, at the entrance to an apartment building was written with chalk: "HUMANLIKE HUMANS DO NOT DUMP GARBAGE." Similar writings had covered both walls of the ancient Assyrian church: "DON'T DUMP GARBAGE, BE A HUMAN", "THE ONE WHO DUMPS GARBAGE HERE IS AS BASE AS GARBAGE ITSELF...'

In the third category, were those writings we gathered which tried to promote consciousness of citizenship. In Kustepe, for instance, it was written: "HE WITH A HABIT OF POLLUTING THE ENVIRONMENT HAS A HEAD BUT NOT A BRAIN." Again in the same neighbourhood, on a tin sign hammered on an intersection, was the sentence: "LET US NOT LEAVE GARBAGE HERE, LET US NOT DISRESPECT THE ENVIRONMENT." Unlike most of the other garbage writings, this one was neatly written. In Balat, around the old well in the middle of the bazaar, one read: "THE ONE WHO DUMPS GARBAGE HAS NO HONOUR. THIS PLACE BELONGS TO ALL OF US"; in Örnektepe, on the wall of a house that looked ready to collapse at the slightest earthquake, was written: "THE ONE WHO DUMPS GARBAGE HERE WOULD HAVE DONE INJUSTICE TO HIS NEIGHBOURS." The visitors of the Greek Patriarchate in Fener were welcomed from afar by the sign: "HE WHO DUMPS GARBAGE HERE WILL GROW TO BE A MOST DESPICABLE PERSON."

Quite a number of these writings were left incomplete. Some looked worn out over time, others as if incomplete from the start. "THE ONE WHO DUMPS…" was written at all kinds of corners in Istanbul, with the rest of the sentence not following. In Harbiye at Papa Roncalli Street, across the walls of the elementary school, letters had dropped off the writing: "THE ONE WH DMPS GARBAGE HRE WILL BECOM AN AS."

Then there were also many bits of writing that gave outright threats. Among them, the one most often repeated was: "HE WHO DUMPS GARBAGE HERE WILL GET INTO BIG TROUBLE." In Fatih, the historic fountain next to the Three Heads Mosque, was filled with garbage writings loaded with threats: "DO NOT DUMP GARBAGE HERE/OR ELSE YOU WILL BE DUMPED WITH TROUBLE." Yet the worst among those containing threats and curses was the one written on a piece of cardboard with a felt-tip pen hanging on the wall of a busy street in the same neighbourhood: "MAY THE CHILD OF HE WHO THROWS GARBAGE HERE BREATHE HIS LAST."

In addition to the insulting, there were also many that were way too polite: 'WILL YOU PLEASE DO NOT DUMP GARBAGE,' or 'IT IS KINDLY REQUESTED THAT YOU DO NOT DUMP GARBAGE AT THIS SPOT.' In the entrance of the Kaptanpasa, an elementary school, there were two signs back to back, one written for the students inside and the other addressing the passers-by outside: "PLEASE DO NOT THROW GARBAGE INTO OUR SCHOOL GARDEN FROM THE OUTSIDE." There was a similar sign on the wooden boards surrounding the construction at the entrance to Asmalımescit, this time half-Turkish, half-English: "DUMPING GARBAGE IS STRICTLY PROHIBITED, PLEASE!" Once again, at Good Fortune Street: "WHOEVER LOVES GOD SHOULD NOT DUMP GARBAGE HERE IT IS KINDLY REQUESTED."

Among the garbage writings, 'prohibited' was the most frequent word. On the walls surrounding the Wallachian Palace, engraved with big letters, was: "IT IS VERY PROHIBITED TO THROW GARBAGE." Likewise, on the side wall of a famous tailor in Harbiye, the writing was short and to the point: "GARBAGE HERE FORBIDDEN." The word 'absolutely' was just as widespread. On the humongous wall of the SSK Okmeydanı Education Hospital Polyclinics, highly visible from down the street was: "DUMPING GARBAGE IS ABSOLUTELY PROHIBITED!" and a few steps away from it: "TO DUMP GARBAGE DEBRIS FORBIDDEN UNCONDITIONALLY."

There was almost never a name given under any of the writing. They remained absolutely anonymous. Still, now and then we bumped into some exceptions. In those situations where the need to invest the writings with some sort of authority was crystal clear, the name of the head of the neighbourhood was encountered the most. On the Mesnevihane Street it was written: "IT IS REQUESTED THAT NO GARBAGE BE DUMPED, OTHERWISE A FINE WILL BE APPLIED!/THE NEIGHBOURHOOD HEAD." Municipalities also got involved in the business: "THE MUNICIPALITY WILL UNDERTAKE PENALTY PROCEDURES CONCERNING THOSE DUMPING GARBAGE HERE." Sometimes the inhabitants of the neighbourhood owned up to the writing, as seen in Zeyrek:

"MAY GOD BRING MISFORTUNE ON THOSE WHO PARK OR DUMP THEIR GARBAGE HERE/NEIGHBOURHOOD RESIDENTS."

Writings concerning religion and faith came next. Around the remains of the palace rebuilt by the Moldavian Prince Dmitri Cantemir during 1688-1710, it was written: "FOR ALLAH'S SAKE DO NOT THROW GARBAGE HERE." Like the Private Fener Greek High School, the surroundings of various mosques too were filled with similar writings. At Kagıthane Smoky Street was a computer print-out: "THOSE WHO HAVE RELIGION AND FAITH WILL KNOW BETTER THAN THROWING GARBAGE HERE," and a hundred metres down: "MAY THOSE WHO DUMP GARBAGE BE ETERNALLY PARALYZED." On one of the side streets opening up to the Kadıköy Square was: "GOD WILL POUR CALAMITY ON THOSE WHO DUMP THEIR GARBAGE HERE." In Fatih, at a garden wall swathed with political campaign posters it said: "PLEASE DO REFRAIN FROM THROWING GARBAGE HERE. THEY CURSE YOU." In the same borough, an old cemetery squeezed between two apartment buildings had also had its share of garbage writings. The front of an apartment building facing the cemetery was painted from one end to the other in capital letters: "FOR ALLAH'S SAKE DO NOT DUMP GARBAGE." Then in Cihangir, on a historic, dry fountain we chanced upon some writing, looking awesomely familiar: "THERE LIES A SACRED SAINT AT THIS SPOT. DO NOT DUMP GARBAGE."

The smell of Istanbul reached the writings everywhere: at an unexpected arc, on a secluded hill where genies congregated, in an ancient cistern, on the long lost remnants of a mansion; in dead end streets, flea markets and bazaars; on the façades of stylish apartment buildings, dingy headquarters or hospitals with an appearance so awful it made you sick; in cold looking schools and at shrines the names of which were not even included in God's maps...in each and every spot where the aged and the recent intertwined there was garbage writing scattered all around…

It did not take Ethel long to get bored. Before I knew it, she drifted away from both the garbage project and me. In her warehouse of lovers wherein each lover remained as just another unfinished project, I too became an unfinished project.

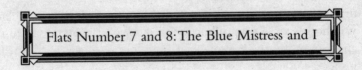

Flats Number 7 and 8: The Blue Mistress and I

'What are you going to do with so many photographs,' frowned the Blue Mistress, discontentedly scanning my flat, which increasingly resembled a depot more than a house. 'What purpose will they serve?'

'I do not accumulate them to serve a purpose.'

'Why on earth are you doing this?' she insisted.

I do not have the impression of doing anything. I guess in the last analysis, all my actions are determined more by not doing than by my doing; lack of action rather than action. I cannot help searching: when I search, I find, what I find I collect, what I collect I accumulate and what I accumulate I cannot bear to throw away.

'What is going to happen next?' asked the Blue Mistress adamantly.

NEXT...

'WHAT IS GOING TO HAPPEN NEXT?' asked my cellmate adamantly.

'There is no next. The guy just accumulates garbage writings that will never be of any use to him.'

'Nonsense!' said my cellmate. I wasn't offended. After all, that is the coarsest way ever invented of saying 'You have a fanciful mind!' and he might be right. Whenever I get anxious and mess up what I have to say, am scared of people's stares and pretend not to be so, introduce myself to strangers and feign ignorance about how estranged I am from myself, feel hurt by the past and find it hard to admit the future won't be any better or fail to come to terms with either where or who I am; at any one of these all too frequently recurring moments, I know I don't make much sense, but nonsense is just as far removed from deception as truth. Deception turns truth inside out. As for nonsense, it solders deception and truth to each other so much so as to make them indistinguishable. Though this might seem complicated, it's actually very simple. So simple that it can be expressed by a single line.

———————

Truth is a horizontal line. Be it a hotel corridor, hospital ward, rehabilitation centre or train compartment; all are horizontal. In such places, all your neighbours are lined up next to you on a horizontal plane, for a fleeting moment. You cannot grow roots at these places. Horizontality is the haven of evanescence. I too have been living on a horizontal line for sixty-six days – in the seventh of the ten cells lined up next to each other here.

Lies are a vertical line. An apartment building, for instance, erected with flats on top of one another with two layers of cemeteries underneath and seven planes of skies above. Here you can spread roots and grow branches as you please. Verticality is the shelter of permanence, a tribute to immortality.

Bonbon Palace is an apartment building constructed on an area of cemeteries. A vertical line that ascends floor by floor. It is my lie. For I am narrating these stories not from a flat there, but from the prison.

When on the 1st of May a group of revolutionaries impatiently decided to break through the police barricade, I was among them. When we were all detained and thrust in a police bus, I chanced to sit beside a ginger-haired, flap-eared, funny-faced man who did not at all show his age. I am grateful to him as that day on that bus, seeing the fear in his widely opened eyes enabled me to forget my own. While we were taken to the police headquarters, he kept whining, whimpering and wailing that he had no interest in politics, that all he did in life was to fumigate bugs. That man was telling the truth. He was indeed a bug fumigator and had probably never hated his job as much as he had done then. His name was not Injustice; that I made up myself. The name is not entirely bogus, however, for he looked like someone who had seen plenty of injustice in life; besides, his surname is true. He was released the same day anyhow. They released him, but arrested me.

Ever since I came here, I have not spent a single day without thinking of Injustice Pureturk. It's all because of these bugs. I happen to be a radical with a deep fear of insects. Unfortunately there are too many of them here, especially cockroaches. I hear them in the toilets, air vents and even the dents and crevices in the walls. They keep scurrying around and encouraged by darkness, incessantly multiply...but I can assure you that the louse is the very worst...

No doubt, in order to observe all of these creatures better, you should come visit me and spend some time here. If you have no time, however, you ought to be content with my version of the story. Yet I too, ultimately speak only in my own voice. Not that I'll foist my own views onto what transpires but I might, here and there, solder the horizontal line of truth to the vertical line of deception in order to escape the wearisome humdrum reality of where I am anchored right now. After all, I am bored stiff here. If someone brought me the good news that my life would be less dreary tomorrow, I might feel less bored today. Yet I know only too well that tomorrow will be just the same and so will the succeeding days. Nevertheless, I should not give you the impression with my fondness of circles that it is only my life that persistently repeats itself. In the final instance, the vertical is just as faithful to its recurrence as the horizontal. Contrary to what many presume, that which is called 'Eternal Recurrence' is germane less to circles than to lines and linear arrangements.

I cooked up this story basically to overcome my bug phobia. Dreaming of a surreptitiously garbage-collecting old widow in some vertical world helped me to survive better the horizontal line here of cells next to one another. Still, I cannot be regarded as having entirely lied. If anything, I can be accused of merging the truth with lies. Of returning to the beginning rather than reaching a decisive end.

As for me, I will not be staying in this prison too long. The sentence they deemed fit for me is one year and two months. Sixty-six days of that sentence are already over. Of these sixty-six days, I passed the first week by getting used to my place and fearing the bugs, and passed the rest trying to forget my fear by way of making up the story you read. Now that the circle of the greyish tin lid of garbage has stopped turning, I frankly do not know how I am going to spend the remaining three hundred and sixty days here.

However, as soon as I am released, the very first thing I want to do is pay a visit to Injustice Pureturk. The first bug fumigator in Turkey taken into custody for being a revolutionary. Life is absurd, at its core lies nonsense, and if you ask me, Fortuna must be long fed up with tackling the possible answers to the impossible question: 'What will happen to whom when?'

GLOSSARY

Ashure	A turkish desert made of fruits, nuts and rice
Azrael	The angel of death
Baqiya hawas	A common stone inscription meaning, 'God is strength, all else is folly.'
Birhruz	A fictive character that symbolises the over-westernised dandy
Börek	A stuffed pastry or pie containing spinach or feta cheese
Bulgur	Cracked wheat
Chibouk	Cigarette holder
Cintemani	An Ottoman ornamental design
Dede	This word has two meanings in Turkish: grandfather and a senior religious person, usually in a *tarikat*
Halva	A traditional Turkish sweet made from nuts and honey
Hidrellez	Turkish festival symbolizing spring and new life, during which women write down their wishes on paper and tie them to red roses
Hizma	Decorative nose stud
Houris	The virgins in heaven

Jinni/jinn	An Islamic term meaning invisible spirit, mentioned in the Koran and believed by Muslims to inhabit the earth, influencing mankind by appearing in the form of humans or animals
Kader	Fortune
Katzenjammer	Loud noise from various sources; from the German word, meaning anxiety or jitters following intoxication
Lodos	The famous wind in Istanbul that blows in from the sea and is said to cause dizziness
Mezes	A variety of small dishes served instead of a main course
Ney	A reed flute played especially in Mawlawi music
Oleaster	One of several shrubs of the genus *Elaegnus* with yellow flowers followed by olive-like fruits containing a powery dust
Rakı	Turkish spirit of aniseed flavour
Simit	A pastry baked in the shape of a circle with a hole in the centre
Tarikat	Mystical sisterhoods/brotherhoods of Muslims that were historically separate from the mainstream
Zurna	A shrill Turkish pipe used to accompany drums